THE SPICE KING

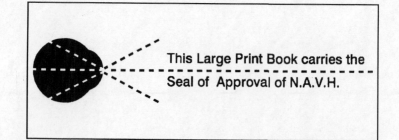

THE SPICE KING

ELIZABETH CAMDEN

THORNDIKE PRESS
A part of Gale, a Cengage Company

Farmington Hills, Mich • San Francisco • New York • Waterville, Maine
Meriden, Conn • Mason, Ohio • Chicago

LIBRARY OF CONGRESS CIP DATA ON FILE.
CATALOGUING IN PUBLICATION FOR THIS BOOK
IS AVAILABLE FROM THE LIBRARY OF CONGRESS

ISBN-13: 978-1-4328-7062-1 (hardcover alk. paper)

Published in 2019 by arrangement with Bethany House Publishers, a division of Baker Publishing Group

Printed in Mexico
1 2 3 4 5 6 7 23 22 21 20 19

THE SPICE KING

ONE

Annabelle Larkin hadn't meant to offend the world's leading spice tycoon with her bold request, yet it seemed she had. The letter he'd written in reply made that clear, but she read it a second time, searching for a shred of hope in its prickly text.

Dear Miss Larkin,

I am in receipt of your letter asking me to donate my plant collection to the Smithsonian Institution. I spent two decades searching the world to gather those rare specimens, during which I sacrificed, sweat, and nearly died. Please be assured I have a better track record of nurturing plants than the feeble assortment I've seen at the Smithsonian, most of which are dead and mounted for display. I must therefore decline your

7

offer to take the collection off my hands.

Gray Delacroix
Owner, Delacroix Global Spice

She dropped the letter onto her laboratory worktable with a sigh. Winning the donation of the Delacroixs' plant collection had always been a long shot, but desperation gave her few options.

"Dare I ask?" Mr. Bittles inquired from the opposite side of the table.

Mr. Bittles was her supervisor and had had nothing but contempt for her since the day she began working at the Smithsonian only two months earlier. Fresh from Kansas and needing a tourist's map to find the famous research museum, Annabelle didn't really belong in Washington, where she felt as green as a newly sprouted hayseed. While everyone else at the Smithsonian had studied at places like Harvard and Princeton, Annabelle's diploma came from Kansas State Agricultural College. She was not the most glittering ornament among the scientists at the Smithsonian.

"Mr. Delacroix declined our offer, but I still have hope," she said, refusing to take his blunt refusal as a personal insult. She was merely the latest in a long line of botanists who'd tried and failed to make

8

headway with Gray Delacroix.

The lab where she worked with Mr. Bittles was tiny, and she needed to nudge her way around him to reach the office typewriter. She pecked out a brisk response.

Dear Mr. Delacroix,

I meant no disrespect in my previous letter. Everyone at the Smithsonian is impressed by your remarkable collection, especially given the challenge of transporting exotic plants to America while they are still alive and fruitful. The rarity of your accomplishment is why we hope you will share the plants with world-class scientists who might build upon your success for the betterment of the nation.

Should you donate your collection to us, the Smithsonian would be prepared to name a wing in your honor.

Sincerely,
Miss Annabelle
Larkin Botanical Specialist,
The Smithsonian Institution

The promise of a wing was genuine, for the director of the Smithsonian had already authorized it, and everyone knew that Dr. Norwood would barter his own grandchildren to get his hands on Gray Delacroix's plants. Dr. Norwood's main interest was the orchids, but he'd asked her to go after the entire collection. She didn't understand his zeal, but she would do her best to get it for him.

This task was especially important, for her job here was only temporary. She'd been hired for a six-month position to preserve and catalog a large shipment of plants from Africa and Australia, but in a few months she would be out of work. Dr. Norwood had dangled the prize of a permanent position if she could persuade the famously reclusive Gray Delacroix to donate his extraordinary plant collection.

As she set her letter to him in the outgoing mailbox, she silently prayed for success. It was an honor to work at the Smithsonian with scientists who sought to explore and understand the world around them, and she desperately needed to keep this position. Even if it meant cooperating with people like Mr. Bittles. Her supervisor didn't like any woman unless she was bringing him coffee or ironing his shirts. He'd been appalled when Dr. Norwood appointed her to be his assistant, but Annabelle was merely happy to have the job.

"Come, get back to work," Mr. Bittles

ordered, setting a new crate from Australia before her. The box was filled with grasses, moss, and seedpods, and it was her job to catalog them for posterity. Each plant would be dried and preserved on a sheet of parchment, its seeds packaged in an accompanying envelope, and then stored in oversized metal filing drawers. She liked to imagine that hundreds of years from now, scientists would consult these specimens, fascinated by this glimpse into the botanical treasures of the past.

"Why do you suppose Dr. Norwood is so anxious to get inside the Delacroix collection?" she asked.

"It's all about the vanilla orchid," Mr. Bittles replied. "He doesn't give a fig about the other plants, only that original vanilla orchid. I don't think it even exists anymore."

Annabelle had already heard about Dr. Norwood's quest to hunt down the progenitor of the modern vanilla orchid. The Spaniards came upon it when they encountered the Aztecs in the sixteenth century. They smuggled it into monasteries and overseas to the eastern spice islands, where over the centuries it had been crossbred with other varieties of vanilla and was now believed to have been hybridized out of existence. No one had seen a living example of

11

the original vanilla orchid in over a hundred years.

Despite herself, Annabelle was intrigued. "Do you think Mr. Delacroix has one?"

"Dr. Norwood does. Gray Delacroix collects all types of vanilla orchids, but he keeps them under lock and key, which is stoking Dr. Norwood's curiosity. You may as well give up. I think that original orchid went extinct long ago. No more dawdling. Get that crate unpacked."

Annabelle nodded and reached for another cluster of grass from Australia. Most of the grasses she cataloged looked similar to what they had in America, but tiny differences in a plant's biology could alter its flavor, fragrance, or hardiness. Indeed, those tiny differences were causing her family's wheat farm to fail after years of drought. Her parents had gone into debt to buy her train ticket to Washington, and she couldn't afford to lose this job.

Which was why she waited with pained anticipation for Mr. Delacroix's response to her second letter. It arrived the following morning, and Mr. Bittles snatched it out of the delivery boy's hand before she could intercept it.

"That's my letter," she gasped, trying to grab it from Mr. Bittles as he dangled it well above her head. Sometimes it was horrible being short. She made a leap for it, and Mr. Bittles stifled a giggle as he continued waving it just beyond her reach.

"But it's addressed to the Botanical Department, of which I am the supervisor," he said, yanking the single page from the envelope. Frustration nearly choked her as his eyes traveled along the lines of the letter. He shook his head in mock despair. "Such a pity," he murmured.

"What does it say?"

A smile hovered over his face as he read the letter aloud. " 'Dear Miss Larkin. Under no circumstances will I grant you access to my plant collection. Stop asking. Sincerely, Gray Delacroix.' " He didn't hide his gloat as he gave her the letter.

She turned away to read it, praying Mr. Bittles was only being cruel, but it was exactly as he had said. She masked her discouragement as she tucked the letter into her satchel, for she wasn't ready to give up yet.

"I'm going downstairs to tell Dr. Norwood of this latest development," she said. "It's time to shift strategy."

"Best of luck," Mr. Bittles said with a sarcastic wink.

That wink renewed her determination as

she headed to the director's office. Mr. Bittles had been rude and bad-tempered from the very beginning, but bad tempers didn't frighten her. She had come of age on the plains of Kansas, where she'd battled ice storms, wind storms, crippling droughts, and plagues of locusts that literally darkened the wide prairie skies. There weren't many things she feared, but losing her job at the Smithsonian was one of them.

Dr. Norwood's office was a reflection of his obsession with orchids. Rows of the exotic flowers lined the windowsill, and their sweet, spicy scent perfumed the air. Maps on the wall documented orchid fields around the world, and fossilized blossoms filled a bookshelf.

Wiry, balding, and bespectacled, Dr. Norwood was pruning a vibrant *Cephalanthera* orchid when she entered. He didn't even look up from his work as she summarized Mr. Delacroix's latest rejection, but he paid fierce attention when she proposed a different approach.

"I have a feeling that as a man of business, Mr. Delacroix will respect forthright dealing," she said. "Perhaps if we directly ask for access only to that single vanilla orchid, he would be more forthcoming."

Dr. Norwood shook his head. "Vanilla is

14

one of the most valuable commodities in the world, and Delacroix only wants that orchid for its monetary value. His father was different. His father could be reasoned with, but ever since the old man died, Gray Delacroix holds the keys to the kingdom. He has no respect for scientific marvels, only monetary profit."

Between the two, Annabelle had more sympathy for monetary profit, but maybe that was her practical farming heritage coming to the fore. Nevertheless, she would do whatever was necessary to please Dr. Norwood.

"Sir, I am painfully aware that the clock is ticking on my temporary appointment. If you want that orchid, I *will* figure out a way to get it. All I need is your permission to approach Mr. Delacroix directly. Face to face. I think I can reason with him."

Dr. Norwood set down the pruning shears and looked her in the eyes. "When your college professor recommended you for this position, he claimed you were one of the sunniest, most optimistic people he'd ever met."

"I am," she admitted with a pleased smile.

"That's the kind of person who drives Gray Delacroix insane," Dr. Norwood said. "He is all business and has no patience, no manners, and is immune to female charm."

Which was why Annabelle planned a different strategy. Mr. Delacroix might be rude, but everything she knew about him indicated he had a deep and abiding passion for the plant world, and on that level, they could connect. His travels spanned the globe, and wherever he went, he collected a seed, a bulb, a cutting, or a root. She admired a man like that.

"If you want that orchid, I'll get a cutting," she told Dr. Norwood confidently. "And Mr. Delacroix will be smiling as he hands it over to me." She outlined her unconventional plan that would only cost a blow to her pride if it didn't work.

Dr. Norwood seemed intrigued. "I suspect he'll laugh you out of his office. It's likely to be a complete failure."

"The Smithsonian has had years of failure," she said. "Nothing else has worked. You might as well let me try."

Dr. Norwood picked up his pruning shears, trying not to laugh. "You are likely to fall flat on your face, but I wish you luck."

Two

Two days later, Annabelle took a series of streetcars to the nearby town of Alexandria, where the Delacroix family had lived for generations. Instead of asking favors, Annabelle had come prepared to offer Mr. Delacroix something first. She'd brought a charming gift to honor his fascination with spices and plants, and new plant specimens to demonstrate how the Smithsonian could help his business if he would cooperate with them. The oversized portfolio made walking ungainly, but the gift she carried was neatly rolled up beneath her arm.

She'd first spotted the whimsical map in a curio shop shortly after arriving in Washington. Printed on soft leather, it looked like a Renaissance map that could have been carried by an old-world conquistador. Compact illustrations covered the fanciful image, like a treasure chest on the Malabar coast brimming with peppercorns and a Spanish galleon near the port of Genoa carrying ginger and nutmeg. A dragon frolicked in the treacherous waters along Cape Horn. The useless map was a charming celebration of the flavors of the world, and maybe it would help get her foot in the door. It was a spice map for a spice king!

The oversized portfolio was cumbersome after she disembarked from the streetcar in Alexandria, a port town starkly different from the classical splendor of Washington. Alexandria had a quaint charm, with worn brick sidewalks carrying an echo of its colonial past. Linden trees shaded the narrow streets where townhouses abutted coffee shops and lawyer's offices, and the Potomac River could be glimpsed in the distance.

By the time she reached the street where Gray Delacroix lived, the shops and townhouses seemed grander, but most impressive were the ladies who strolled through the shopping district. Did women really dress like that on an ordinary Thursday afternoon? They wore elegant ensembles of wraps, sashes, and scarves. Annabelle wore a practical cotton dress of maroon gingham with sensible buttons down the front. While the other ladies had their upswept hair styled with jeweled clips, Annabelle's dark hair was worn in a simple braid down the center of her back.

A drizzle of rain caused her to quicken her steps, the bulky portfolio banging against her hip. The cobblestone street eventually came to the three-story townhouse belonging to the Delacroix family. Glossy black railings led up a flight of steps to a home that looked like it had been there for centuries. Probably because it had. When Mr. Delacroix's forefathers built their shipping empire in Virginia, Annabelle's ancestors had been pulling potatoes out of the rocky soil in Ireland.

She hurried up the short flight of steps to knock on the front door. The black man who answered looked about her age but was a lot taller.

"Mr. Delacroix is not seeing visitors," he responded to her request to visit.

"Can I make an appointment to see him later today?"

"Unlikely." The answer was blunt but not rude, which gave her courage.

"Mr. Delacroix and I have been engaged in business correspondence, and I believe it will go better if we meet in person rather than continue through letters."

The drizzle intensified, bringing a spattering of fat raindrops. There was no overhang protecting the front stoop, and this spice map wouldn't stand up to a soaking.

"Might I come inside until the rain lets up? I have a valuable artifact to show Mr. Delacroix." Or rather, a cheap curio map, but the sight of it caused the young man to beckon her inside.

It wasn't the sort of place she expected an international shipping magnate to live. The spare front hall, low ceilings, and plain colonial furnishings seemed homespun and comforting. The center hallway stretched all the way to the back of the house, where an open door led to a small garden behind the house.

"You can wait in the parlor until the rain lets up, but then you'll have to be on your way. Mr. Delacroix is in no condition to receive visitors."

If he was ill, she shouldn't take her dismissal personally. And the young man seemed nice.

She stuck out her hand. "Hello. I'm Annabelle Larkin. And you are?"

He must have been surprised, because he stared at her outstretched hand for a moment before offering his own. "I'm Otis. Otis LaRue."

She returned the handshake with vigor and a healthy smile, for this man was her first hurdle in getting to Mr. Delacroix. "Nice to meet you, Otis. Is there a towel I could borrow to dry the artifact? It's very rare."

Otis nodded. "Have a seat in the parlor, and I'll fetch a cloth so you can dry the . . . the artifact," he said with a curious glance at both the rolled map and the bulky portfolio.

"I'd be grateful," she said. She walked into the front room, where nautical maps and a shiny brass captain's wheel decorated the walls. Old floorboards creaked as she moved farther inside. Well-made but simple colonial furniture sat in groupings before a brick fireplace.

Otis returned, standing before her with a cloth at the ready. "Ma'am?"

She wasn't accustomed to being waited on, and it took a moment to realize he was prepared to help dry the map.

"Yes, here. Thank you." She unrolled the map to blot the back, but Otis flipped it over to study the front.

"What a fantastic map," he said with a laugh. "I've never seen anything like it."

"Isn't it delightful? I saw it and immediately thought of Mr. Delacroix."

Otis nodded. "I agree. On a good day, I think he might like it very much."

"Otis!" a voice roared from somewhere deep in the house.

"One moment, sir," the young man called down the hall, then handed the map back to her. "Wait here. I'll be back in a minute." He dashed down the hall with admirable agility.

Why did women have to be burdened by so many skirts and layers? On the farm she usually wore her father's old denim pants to scramble up into haylofts or tend the goats, but that probably wouldn't go over well in Washington.

Muffled voices leaked out from a closed door at the end of a hall, and a few moments later, Otis returned with his hand outstretched.

"Mr. Delacroix overheard our conversation. He wants to see the map."

Annabelle tightened her grip on it. If Mr. Delacroix wanted to see the map, he could meet her like any other civilized person. "Oh dear . . . it is a very valuable map. I hate to let it go. Perhaps I can make an appointment to come back and show it to him at a more convenient time?"

Given the uneasy look on Otis's face, it didn't feel right to paint him into such an awkward position, but she needed to meet Mr. Delacroix in person.

"Otis, send her back here," the grumpy voice hollered.

Hope welled inside her, and she followed Otis down the hallway. More antiques hung on the wall, where dour-looking people in white wigs frowned from old family portraits. She was shown through a door into a book-lined study. When she got a look at the man behind the desk, she gasped.

The surly expression on his face darkened. "Don't worry. I'm not contagious," he said.

But he looked horrible! He wasn't even dressed properly, wearing only a loosely tied dressing robe. He had bloodshot eyes and unkempt black hair, but most appalling was his skin. He was sickly white and soaking wet, with trails of perspiration rolling down his face and dampening his robe. His untidy appearance didn't stop him from rudely looking her up and down.

"You're short," he said.

She straightened. Her height was always the first thing people noticed about her, but rarely were they so rude as to comment on it. "And you are very ill."

"But not contagious," he said bluntly. "And I want to see this valuable map. Where is it?"

Maybe he wasn't contagious, but there was something seriously wrong with him.

23

She took a single step forward and extended the rolled map, then retreated the instant he snatched it.

While he unfurled the map across his desk, she took a deeper look at him, for he was a handsome man despite the sickly pallor, with finely molded features and deep-set eyes. But most fascinating to her was his jaw. It was strong and chiseled, the kind of jaw that spoke of strength and looked like it was accustomed to carrying the weight of responsibility. She loved the way he rubbed it as he scrutinized the map, and his gaze morphed from skeptical to curious to interested.

To her amazement, a slow smile crept across his face. A raspy, weak laugh started, but it was only a single breath, as though he didn't have the strength to finish it off.

"I love it," he said. He put on a pair of spectacles and leaned closer to the map. "Ha! They've got the cloves wrong in Malabar. They ship them dried, not green." He leaned back in his chair, drumming his fingers on the desk. "So you're the tedious Miss Larkin from the Smithsonian."

"I am Miss Larkin from the Smithsonian." It was hard not to smile, for it was obvious he was testing her, but he had no idea who he was up against.

24

"And you come bearing gifts. Hoping to soften me up."

"Is it working?"

"Not yet. I'm curious, though. My last letter to you was final, and you have zero chance of changing my mind, so why are you here?" He spoke with no sign of hostility, only genuine curiosity. It made her believe there was hope.

"You wouldn't respect me if I gave up too easily."

"What makes you think I respect you at all?" A challenging glint lurked in his dark eyes, and it was oddly intriguing. How could a man be so rude and yet appealing at the same time?

She rose to the test. "As a human being, I am worthy of respect by default. And as one botanist to another, I think you and I should cooperate."

"I'm not a botanist. I'm a businessman."

"I won't hold it against you, Mr. Delacroix. Especially if you don't hold my association with the Smithsonian against me."

He took off his spectacles, then mopped his face with a handkerchief before looking at her through bloodshot eyes. "The Smithsonian has been trying for years to get their hands on my vanilla orchid, but this is the first time they've sent a woman to try for it.

I've actually got it quite well guarded, and I'm protective of my plants, so I'm afraid your visit here is going to be fruitless."

So he knew the value of what he had. "Can you tell me how you managed to keep it alive during transportation?"

"No."

"Perhaps you could tell me how you are caring for it. As a tropical vine, Virginia must be a challenging environment for it."

He shrugged and remained silent.

"Come, Mr. Delacroix," she said. "Science shouldn't be performed in a vacuum. Why can't we pool our resources and expertise?"

"Because I don't trust the government," he stated flatly. "I know exactly what you would do if I gave you a cutting from my orchid."

"And what is that?"

"You would slice pieces off to study under a microscope. You'd press the rest of it, glue it onto parchment, and store it away in one of your attics. Am I right?"

Actually, they stored their specimens in metal drawers, but mostly he was right. If the sample was large enough, they might try to reproduce it and establish another vine. But why did he have to be so intrinsically hostile to the entire principle of scientific study?

"The Smithsonian is curious about all forms of plants, which are constantly evolving. Yes, of course we need to collect and preserve samples."

He nodded to the sunflower brooch pinned to her collar. It was the only jewelry she wore, a reminder of Kansas. "Is that what you specialize in? Sunflowers?"

"My specialty is cereal grasses. All kinds of wheat, barley, and in a pinch, I know a little about millet. I wear the sunflower because it's impossible not to smile when you see a sunflower." The corners of his mouth twitched, and she pounced. "See? Even you can't do it. Just thinking about a field of sunflowers is making you smile. Go ahead, admit it."

For the first time she saw a genuine smile from him, along with another weak laugh as he conceded defeat. He gestured for her to take a seat in the chair opposite his desk, and she sensed she had successfully cleared her first hurdle. She sat, then lifted the portfolio onto her lap.

"If you won't show me your orchid, may I show you some newly arrived specimens of vanilla orchids from the African coast?"

It was the right thing to say. He straightened, his entire attention swiveling to her portfolio. "Is that what's in your bag?"

"Yes. Eight newly arrived species of vanilla orchids."

It was as if a bolt of electricity shot through him. His nonchalant air vanished, and he pushed her cheap map aside and cleared the surface of his desk. When he stood to reach for the portfolio, he lurched as though about to keel over. She instinctively rushed to his side, propping him up. His skin was scorching!

"Can I get you something? A glass of water? Or call for someone?"

He shook his head but lowered himself back into his chair, as though winded by that momentary burst of energy. "I'm fine. I should know better than to stand so quickly. No more delays. Let's see what you've got."

His complexion was even paler than before. He said he wasn't contagious, but his fever was shockingly high, and she couldn't risk getting ill. She noticed a large bottle of quinine on the corner of the desk.

"Malaria?" she guessed.

He gave a brusque nod. "And I assure you it isn't contagious."

She understood. Too many of the scientists the Smithsonian sent to the tropics eventually contracted malaria, and it was a wretched, debilitating condition that could haunt a person with periodic bouts for the rest of their life. Quinine was the only known remedy, but all it did was treat the symptoms, it could not cure it.

It was hard to imagine a man this sick would want to see botanical specimens, but he took a magnifying glass from his drawer and waited as she opened the portfolio. After unbuckling the straps of the deep interior pocket, she lifted out the first of several specimens. The plants had been meticulously pressed, then secured with tiny strips of gummed linen to the parchment.

He used his magnifying glass to scrutinize the leaves and stem. "What's in the envelope?" he asked, nodding to the packet taped to the bottom of the page.

She opened the flap to extract a pod and dozens of tiny seeds, laying them on the white parchment for closer examination. He denied being a botanist, but the fierce way he studied the seeds could have fooled her.

When he spoke, he said the last thing she expected.

"You have no idea how badly I want to taste those seeds."

"You can't!" she gasped.

"Why not?"

"They are valuable scientific specimens," she sputtered.

"Bah! They're useless to mankind unless we know how they taste. There are over a hundred varieties of vanilla orchids. How can I know if this one is worth cultivating without a taste?"

She swept the seeds into her palm and carefully replaced them in the envelope. She risked a glance at him and was once again caught off guard by the humor glinting in his eyes.

She stilled. "Were you joking?"

"Were you trying to pass off a cheap reproduction as a valuable map?"

She sent him a helpless smile. "I needed to get my foot in the door."

"And you succeeded. Let's see the rest of what you've got. I promise not to wolf down any of your valuable samples. Besides, as a botanist, you ought to know that vanilla seeds aren't all that special. Most of the flavor is in the skin of the pod, and even then, it's not fully developed until it has been processed."

They spent the next hour studying the eight specimens she'd brought. The world of orchids was a mystery to her, and she listened in fascination as he explained how he cultivated thousands of vanilla orchid vines in the steeply sloped hills of Madagascar. Vanilla orchids were fussy plants that required hand pollination and bloomed for only a single day each year. That day could make or break a harvest. The vanilla orchid would have been driven to extinction but for the farmers and spice traders who rescued it.

The way he spoke with such passion about vanilla was appealing. He probably knew as much as any of their botanists, most of whom worked only in a laboratory. She gazed around his library, the shelves brimming with books and heavy scientific binders.

"Where did you study?" she asked.

"I never went to college, if that's what you're asking. I studied in the belly of a ship. Tromping through jungles and deserts. Talking to people. Trial and error. I envy you, Miss Larkin."

She couldn't imagine someone like him envying four years at the Kansas State Agricultural College, but there was no doubting his sincerity, for the longing on his face was profound.

She could have stayed all afternoon, learning about his tropical fields, but she had responsibilities in town. Elaine was depending on her.

"I should go," she said.

"Do you have to?"

Her gaze locked with his. Despite his haggard appearance and illness, it seemed he genuinely wanted her to stay. She wished she could, but Elaine was waiting.

"I have responsibilities," she said, standing to slide the specimen pages back into the portfolio. "I hope you will keep the map."

He rolled it up and pushed it toward her. "It's yours."

"Oh, please keep it. I can't imagine anyone who would appreciate the world of the spice trade as much as you. Even if the mapmaker got his cloves wrong."

He stood more carefully this time, bracing a hand on the desk as he slowly pushed to his feet. "I don't like to be indebted. I've enjoyed your visit, but you must understand that I am violently opposed to sharing anything with the Smithsonian. It will never happen, so I'd feel better if you took your map back."

She leaned over to pick up her portfolio. She'd lingered far too long as it was, but she wasn't going to leave with that map. It had cracked open the door to his world, and she *wanted* him to feel indebted, even if only for a foolish trinket.

"It's yours," she said simply. "Do with it as you like."

32

She felt his gaze on her back as she walked down the hallway and out the door. Her heart pounded the entire way, partly from her minor victory, but mostly from something else she was afraid to name.

Annabelle silently urged the streetcar to move faster as it traveled down Second Street toward the Library of Congress, where her sister volunteered five days a week. It was this chance for Elaine to do productive work that had brought them both from the heartland of Kansas all the way to the nation's capital. Only two months earlier, neither of them had traveled more than fifty miles from the farm where they'd been born.

Now they had ventured across the country, found and leased their own apartment, learned to use the streetcar system, and were embarking on a new way of life. Annabelle prayed it would be the answer for Elaine. If this didn't work, she wasn't sure what else could be done to save her adored older sister.

Annabelle bit her lip as the streetcar made yet another stop at East Capitol Street. So many people getting on and off! She was already forty minutes late picking up Elaine, and she silently urged the two jabbering businessmen to hurry up and disembark.

At last the streetcar was on its way, and Annabelle grabbed the hold bar as she moved to the front so she could be first off at the next stop. Elaine must be out of her mind with worry by now. So far their system had worked quite well, for the Smithsonian was only a few blocks from the Library of Congress. Annabelle escorted Elaine to work each morning and picked her up at the end of the day, but the trip to Alexandria had taken longer than expected.

A gust of relief escaped her when she saw Elaine waiting safely at the bench on the corner of Second and Independence Avenue. The streetcar door opened, and Annabelle was the first person off.

"I'm here, Elaine," she called out the moment her feet touched the ground.

Elaine swiveled her head, her blue eyes staring sightlessly past Annabelle. "Oh, thank heavens," she said on a shaky breath.

Forty minutes might not seem like a lot to a sighted person, but the city was a new and terrifying environment for Elaine. Instead of birdsong and wind rustling through wheat fields, the busy street corner had honking horns, rattling streetcars, and hucksters shouting their wares. Any move from the safety of the bench might send

Elaine straight into the path of a streetcar or over the edge of the curb.

Annabelle joined her sister on the bench, taking her hand. "Were you all right?"

"Of course I was," Elaine said. "One of the security guards walked me here at five o'clock. What time is it now?"

Annabelle glanced at her pocket watch. "Twenty minutes to six. Alexandria didn't look that far away on the map. I'm so sorry."

"Well . . . it's all right," Elaine said after a pause. "At least I had a productive morning."

"Tell me about it," Annabelle coaxed. They still had a few minutes before the Green Line streetcar arrived, and she hoped conversation would divert Elaine's thoughts from the frightening forty minutes she'd spent alone on a street corner.

"The Library of Congress bought a new brailler," she reported. "The machine seems like a regular typewriter, but the keys are different. I've asked to be trained on how to use it. Then I can communicate on my own instead of asking you to write everything out for me."

Annabelle's smile was pained. She liked reading and writing for Elaine. It was little enough she could do to make up for the catastrophe that had befallen her sister. "I don't mind," she said.

"No, no," Elaine insisted, a little of her old gumption coming to the fore. "I refuse to be any more of a burden than necessary. The more I can learn, the better off we'll both be. But please . . ." She swallowed hard, and when she spoke again, her voice was barely a whisper. "Please don't ever leave me alone on a horrible bench like this again. You can't imagine how awful it was."

It was true, and another wave of guilt raced through Annabelle. "I'm so sorry," she said again. If she lived to be a hundred, she could never apologize enough, for Elaine's blindness was her fault.

Elaine squeezed Annabelle's hand. "Don't feel bad," she said. "Even though I'm blind, I can tell there is regret all over your face. I'm fine," she added in a reassuring voice. "It will only take me a little longer to get familiar with these loud city streets, and soon I'll be using the streetcars without any help." She flashed a smile. "I can do anything. *Anything*, Annabelle."

But Elaine sounded like she was trying to convince herself as much as Annabelle.

THREE

The Leander Regatta was one of the premier social events of the season, which was why Gray felt distinctly out of place as he strolled along the boardwalk with his sister on his arm. The Delacroix family had helped found the yachting club generations earlier, but Gray had always been too busy resurrecting the family fortune to frolic in pointless boat races.

A wooden promenade lined the Potomac River and led to the clubhouse. Hundreds had turned out to watch the annual regatta beneath the cloudless blue sky. Flags snapped in the breeze, and the air was alive with laughter and music. The young men competing in the races wore ridiculous striped blazers in their team's colors, while women sported wide-brimmed bonnets that were literal works of art.

Gray's brother and sister adored the annual regatta, and since he had recovered

37

from his bout with malaria, he had no excuse to avoid it. Besides, he desperately needed the opportunity to start guiding Caroline and Luke toward a more responsible life. The twins were the product of his father's second marriage, and they'd been so young when Gray's responsibilities took him abroad that it seemed each time he returned to America, they were an inch taller and a mile more reckless. He'd recently caught Caroline smoking cigarettes on the roof of their house with some of her disreputable city friends, and last week he'd had to bail Luke out of jail for drunkenness.

The hardest thing when he first went overseas was leaving Caroline and Luke behind, for during their early years, it was as though they were his own children. He was twelve when the twins were born, and he guided their first steps, bandaged their skinned knees, and taught them to read. He loved them down to the marrow of his bones, but they had both grown wild, and he didn't know what to do about them. At twenty-eight, it seemed the only thing Luke truly loved was boat racing, so Gray would dutifully watch his brother compete in this afternoon's double-scull races.

"Oh, look, there is the Secretary of the

Treasury and his wife," Caroline said as she nodded toward an older couple holding court near the refreshment stand. "Would you like me to introduce you?"

Gray looked at his pocket watch. "Luke's race begins in five minutes."

"Bah!" Caroline said. "No one is here to watch the races. This is an opportunity to see and be seen." She smiled at each couple they passed on the promenade.

The society pages had dubbed Caroline "the Contessa" for the way she effortlessly captured the attention of a crowd. She was the cream of high society: beautiful, flirtatious, and wickedly charming. She was also completely useless. If the world needed a tea party, Caroline would outshine every hostess on the Eastern Seaboard. For anything else, she knew how to summon her maid.

Caroline steered him toward the group of fashionable people near the refreshment stand, but an old acquaintance intercepted them.

"Mr. Delacroix, I'm sorry to hear of your father's passing," the middle-aged gentleman said. "Nicholas Delacroix was truly one of our finest."

"He was indeed," Gray said. "Thank you for your kind words."

His father had died six months ago, but the pain was still raw. Gray had been in Ceylon when news of his father's stroke reached him. He took the fastest steamship home but still arrived the day after Nicholas breathed his last. On that day Gray lost his mentor, his business partner, and the best man he'd ever known.

Few people could understand their bond. Gray's mother had died when he was an infant, so Nicholas was the only parent he'd ever known. Most of Gray's adult life had been spent abroad, but even so, he and his father jointly built a global spice empire and resurrected the family fortune that had been demolished during the Civil War.

Gray was only a child at the end of the war, but he remembered what it was to be hungry, frightened, and burned out of his home. His father hadn't been too proud to roll up his sleeves and tackle manual labor, and Gray had worked right alongside him. It took years of backbreaking exertion and clever business investments, but by the time his father remarried, their family's coffers were healthy once again. Luke and Caroline never wanted for anything, and his father had been glad of that, but Gray wasn't so sure. There was honor in a hard day of labor. While Nicholas thought the sun, the moon, and the stars revolved around his adored daughter, Gray couldn't respect Caroline's undiluted frivolity. But he and his father were in full agreement about Luke, in whom they were both deeply disappointed.

Gray dragged his thoughts back to the present, trying to ignore the gnawing ache in his chest. He was lonely. He missed his father and never felt at home in Alexandria. He was an outsider here, and mingling with these people was awkward, but he'd get through it, since his sister had asked it of him.

Caroline flirted effortlessly with an admiral home on leave. With her golden blond hair and bright personality, she sparkled brighter than a diamond. She glided with ease through fashionable society, which was especially impressive since his stepmother had died when Caroline was still young. It was as though Caroline had been imbued at birth with an innate ability to shine in the very best of settings.

"Shall we go watch the first of the races?" the admiral asked. "I gather your brother is competing."

"Must we?" Caroline asked. "I'd rather discuss the navy's white dress uniforms. I wish you'd let your officers wear them more

41

often. It would delight every lady in the city."

Gray eventually nudged Caroline toward the bleachers. The race started a mile downriver, and two-man teams would row their narrow boats until they crossed the finish line here at the bleachers. Luke was rowing with a friend from the Naval Academy. Gray would have thought Luke would be embarrassed to maintain a friendship with Philip Ransom, who'd graduated at the top of his class seven years ago. Luke, on the other hand, had been kicked out of the Naval Academy a semester shy of graduation and never did earn a college degree. But the two men remained friends and crewed a shell each year at the annual regatta. Gray could only hope some of Philip's sober good sense would eventually wear off on Luke.

The two men raced in Nicholas Delacroix's prized racing shell, a memento from his father's racing days at Harvard. After the war, his father never rowed again, but he'd lovingly waxed and maintained the racing boat for his sons to use someday. Gray never saw the point in recreational games, but it seemed to be the only thing at which Luke excelled.

"Here they come!" Caroline said, shooting to her feet and gazing through her miniature binoculars.

Luke and Philip were half a length ahead of their nearest competition. Both men used their whole bodies as they pulled their oars in a smooth, synchronized motion, their shell slicing through the water as the crowd cheered.

Luke's face was tight with concentration as he rowed to a first-place finish. Both men released their oars and raised tired arms in victory. Gray couldn't contain his pleased smile. Whatever else Luke's failings — and there were many — his brother trained hard, and his victory was well earned.

"Let's go congratulate them," Caroline urged, squeezing Gray's arm so hard it hurt.

They wended their way through the bleachers to the staging area where the shells were pulled ashore and the age-old traditions following a race were in full swing. Men from the losing teams stripped off their shirts and surrendered them to the victors. Luke and Philip grinned as they scooped up the sweaty shirts and draped them across their shoulders, proudly wearing their foul-smelling trophies.

"Don't come any closer," Caroline laughed in mock horror.

Luke grinned and spread his arms wide. "Darling sister, come give me a hug," he roared as he chased Caroline. She didn't have much choice as he dragged her into a sweaty embrace. She squealed in horrified delight until she managed to twist away.

Gray offered a gentlemanly handshake. "Congratulations, Luke. And to you, Philip."

Both men nodded respectfully, but the hooting and jesting immediately surged back to life as the last-place team finally dragged their shell to dry land. The hazing was merciless as Luke lunged forward to claim their shirts. One of the rowers shook a bottle of champagne to spray over the others and then passed it around for the men to drink straight from the bottle.

"Let's step back a bit," Gray muttered to Caroline, but the hilarity of the athletes continued unabated.

Tradition dictated that the victorious crew be carried to the clubhouse for a well-deserved celebration. Luke and Philip were hoisted overhead by bare-chested rowers. The rowdy men were already exhausted from the race as they trudged higher up the bank with Luke and Philip held high. Luke made it worse by grabbing a few sweaty shirts and whirling them around. One of the men stumbled, dumping Luke on the ground and onto their father's shell.

Gray winced, but Luke grinned as he sprang back onto his feet. "No harm done!" he assured the men, but Gray frowned at the shell.

"You've just cracked the hull," he said grimly.

Some of the rowers looked remorseful, but Luke shrugged it off. "Don't worry, it can be fixed."

"That was Dad's favorite boat," Gray said in a warning tone. Didn't Luke have respect for anything or anyone? Their father had treasured that boat as a memento of a world they'd lost during the war, but Luke had already moved on to the clubhouse, leaving the cracked shell on the riverbank.

Gray squatted down to assess the damage. Could it be made watertight again? A trained craftsman could probably repair it, but it would cost money, and Gray intended to deduct it from Luke's allowance.

It wasn't the money that bothered him, it was the pain of seeing his father's boat so thoughtlessly treated. The others streamed toward the clubhouse, leaving him alone. He didn't want to leave this boat broken and abandoned on shore, so he summoned a pair of attendants to stow it in the boathouse. Gray watched as they lifted the shell and secured it on a storage rack.

Don't worry, Dad. I'll get it fixed.

But it was Luke his father would want him to fix, not the boat.

Luke missed dinner that night, but Gray left a message with the butler to notify him the moment Luke arrived back at the townhouse. It was time to demand his little brother start pulling his own weight in the family business. It was after nine o'clock when their butler, Mr. Holder, knocked on the study door.

"Your brother has returned, sir."

Gray nodded. "Send him in, please."

He braced himself for a difficult meeting, but Luke was smiling as he sauntered in, wolfing down a handful of strawberries. A swath of dark hair partially obstructed his eyes, and he flashed his unmistakable grin. Luke had relied on a bottomless well of daredevil charm his entire life, but Gray was immune to it, especially when Luke began juggling the berries.

"Are you drunk?" Gray asked.

"Not drunk, just happy," Luke said as he flung himself into the chair opposite the desk and draped a leg over the arm. "You should try it sometime."

"And why should I be happy?"

"Because the century is young and so are

46

we. Because it was a crystal-clear day spent with good friends and healthy sport. And most importantly, because I found a shipwright who can fix Dad's boat. I've bartered the use of my horse for a couple of weeks to pay for it."

That was a surprise, and a welcome one. "I didn't think you could make arrangements so quickly," Gray admitted.

Luke shrugged. "I can do anything. You know that."

"Is the deal with the shipwright why you missed dinner?"

"Philip and I went out to celebrate with the other teams. There is a magician in town who twisted his own head off in front of the crowd. I don't know how he did it. Mirrors? I'm stumped. You should have been there."

Gray didn't bother to acknowledge that. "Luke, it's time you took a more active role in the family business."

"Not that again."

"Yes, that again. You've done a decent job managing the factory since Dad died, but now that I'm back, I'll take over management of the factory and the warehouse. I need someone to go overseas and work with our suppliers."

Luke looked appalled. "So I can contract malaria and dysentery like you?"

"If need be. I want you to go to Cuba. I'm expanding our Caribbean spices, and we need more suppliers."

Luke straightened in his chair. "Look, I can't be you, Gray. I'm not cut out for business. We all know what happened the first time Dad tried to get me on board."

"That's in the past. You can't let one bad experience taint you for life. It's time to start doing your fair share. You're earning more from the company than Otis, and that's not fair."

"Otis again," Luke muttered with a roll of his eyes.

"Yes, Otis," Gray asserted. "Dad and I have always depended on Otis, and he's never let us down."

Otis entered their household as a twelve-year-old orphan his father had found in New Orleans, the son of a formerly enslaved woman who worked as a cook for Dominican friars. After his mother died, the Dominicans still provided Otis with an excellent education. He was fluent in Spanish and French, and their father had hired him on the spot. Over the years, Otis had learned Morse code to handle communication between Nicholas and Gray as he traveled. Otis was paid a respectable wage and was fiercely loyal to Delacroix Global Spice. As

48

their chief assistant, Otis knew everything about their business dealings and was one of the few people Gray trusted without reserve.

"You inherited a third of the company, while Otis is merely paid a salary," Gray said. "That's not fair, but it was Dad's company, and he made the call. I'm in charge now, and you need to work at least as hard as Otis."

For the first time, Luke showed a hint of excitement. "I know that. And look, I've already got a plan. I've written a couple of articles for *The Modern Century*. I think I can make a go of it as a journalist."

But Luke hadn't been able to make a go of college, and over the years he'd dipped his toe into one pond after another, always flitting away when he got bored. Luke was fiercely intelligent, if he could only funnel that drive into something besides dangerous, risky, and self-destructive behavior.

"Go to Cuba and finalize some contracts for new spice fields. I know you've already been there. Caroline says you started importing cigars while I was gone."

A reckless smile lit Luke's face. *"Amoroso Rosa,"* he said. "The best cigars are from Cuba, and I turned a pretty penny on those deals. I've got more lined up."

"Good. Then go back to Cuba and finalize some spice contracts while you're down there."

"No deal." Luke shook his head. "Look, I can't talk about it, but I'm in the middle of something big. Something important. And I'd be a disaster in business; you know what happened last time."

The catastrophe that happened four years ago wasn't Luke's fault, but it still seemed to haunt him. "You need to put that in your past." Gray softened his voice. "Don't let it cripple you. There is a saying in Japan for people who get knocked off course: If you fall seven times; stand up eight. That's what I need you to do."

Luke shot to his feet. "Forget it, Gray. We're rich enough. We don't need to move into Caribbean spices or peppers or anything else you've got up your sleeve. Why can't you just be happy? Why do you have to keep pushing and striving and draining all the joy out of life?"

He stormed out of the study, slamming the door hard enough for the spice map to drop off its hook.

Gray sighed as he stood and wandered over to the map. That woman from the Smithsonian had more self-directed drive in her little finger than Luke had in his entire body. What was her name?

Annabelle Larkin.

Such a prim name for a woman whose entire persona crackled with determination. When his letters bluntly refused her access to his plant collection, she had shown up in person to make her case. That took grit, and he respected her for it.

Yet even with her he hadn't yielded an inch. Luke had a point. They *were* rich enough, but where business was concerned, it wasn't in Gray's nature to do anything but plow forward with all engines stoked on high. He never yielded. Never softened. He knocked competitors out of the way in a relentless quest to be the first, the fastest, the biggest, and the best.

He hung the map back on its hook, smiling a little at the whimsical figures harvesting cloves and nutmeg. His days of exploring the world for more spice fields was at an end. Now that Dad was gone, someone needed to be in Virginia to helm the business.

Besides, he was tired. He wanted a family of his own. He didn't feel comfortable in Virginia any more than he belonged in Africa or Asia or the Caribbean, but he had just turned forty and wanted to settle down.

His analytical mind clicked into gear. He'd

never considered a serious courtship before because his life was spent overseas, but if Virginia was going to be his permanent home, that needed to change, and he immediately thought of Annabelle. He had been attracted to her from the moment she walked into his office with that charmingly ridiculous map. Her smile could light up an entire room with fresh-spun wholesomeness. Her curiosity about his vanilla plants wasn't feigned any more than his interest in her world of farming in Kansas. She'd been smart and funny and curious.

And yet he'd pushed her away because he was determined not to budge, especially where business was concerned. It was simply the way he had operated all his adult life. But like any good businessman, he could adjust his sails and shift course to get what he wanted.

First he had to make amends for his blunt treatment of her requests. It wouldn't be hard, for he already knew exactly what she wanted: access to his greenhouses. The greenhouses were two hours away by boat, but he instinctively knew she'd agree to come, and that brought a smile to his face.

He wouldn't hand her the keys to his kingdom; he wasn't *that* irrational. But he could crack open the door and see what happened. Frankly, he was eager to see where this might lead.

FOUR

A newly delivered crate of moss and lichen samples from Australia awaited Annabelle at the Smithsonian, along with the surprise of a letter from Gray Delacroix. She yanked the letter from its envelope, and her jaw dropped as she read his stunning offer. Unlike countless botanists before her, he had invited her to explore his botanical collections. And contrary to popular belief, he had not one but *four* greenhouses hidden away at his remote property in Fairfax County. One held tropical plants, one herbs and spices, a third tailored to simulate a desert environment, and an entire greenhouse with nothing but orchids. Orchids! Those secretive greenhouses contained the living samples Gray Delacroix had collected during two decades of traveling the world, and he had invited her to see them all this weekend.

His letter went on to explain that week-ends were the only time he was free of "infernal business meetings" to show her the greenhouses properly. Given the distance to travel, he recommended she stay at the farmhouse located on the property so she could use the entire weekend to explore.

She wanted to see that rare collection so badly her teeth ached, but how could she leave Elaine? Her sister panicked at being left alone for an hour, let alone an entire weekend. And Elaine would never agree to come, for as the letter explained, getting to the greenhouses would involve river travel, and Elaine was terrified of water. She had never learned to swim, which had always made her leery of water, but last winter she'd gotten lost while fetching wood for the stove. Her markers were buried in snow, and she wandered onto the frozen pond, falling through the ice and nearly drowning. She'd been terrified of water ever since.

Which meant Annabelle would go on her own, and Elaine would have to stay by herself for the weekend.

Annabelle braced for the difficult conversation as she prepared dinner in their tiny two-room apartment that evening. She cooked beef in a skillet while Elaine cleaned strawberries at the washstand and talked about her volunteer work at the library's reading room for the blind. Her first student was a young soldier who had been blinded in the Spanish-American War.

"Harry came back again today, but only because his wife dragged him in," Elaine said. "He's memorized the braille cells, but his wife says he refuses to practice at home. All he does in the evenings is shuffle playing cards. Martha says he does it for hours and hours, and the sound of those shuffling cards is like acid to her. She hears it in her dreams."

Annabelle said nothing as she nudged the beef around the skillet along with some carrots and onions. It was common for depression to cripple a person suddenly afflicted with blindness. It had happened to Elaine. Their entire family had watched a beautiful, curious young woman sink into despondency after illness struck her blind three years earlier.

Annabelle quickly seasoned the food with salt and pepper, spooned it onto plates, and joined Elaine at the dining table. Before she was even finished saying the blessing, a crash sounded from the alley outside, and Elaine startled, covering her head with her hands. Annabelle darted to the window where a squealing horse mingled with the shouts from some men in the street below.

56

"No need to worry," she said. "There's an overturned cart in the alley. Potatoes scattered everywhere."

The racket wasn't going to end anytime soon, so Annabelle closed the window. It was warm in the apartment, but the commotion outside was needlessly stressful for Elaine.

Annabelle leaned her forehead against the glass and framed her words carefully. "I've been offered an interesting opportunity," she began. "The Smithsonian has long wanted to get a peek inside a rather unique collection of greenhouses. The owner is notoriously private and has always refused . . . but he's going to open it up to me this weekend."

Elaine set her fork down. "Where is it?"

"It's around thirty miles from here. It's in a very rural area, and I was told I'll need to get there by river. I could leave Saturday morning and be back by nightfall on Sunday."

Elaine's hand clenched around the fork, and her entire body tensed. "I can't get on a boat. You know I can't."

"You can stay here. I'll only be gone two days."

"I can't be alone that long. *I can't.*"

"You won't be entirely alone. You've met

57

Mr. and Mrs. Hillenbrand across the hall. They're here if you need help."

Elaine shook her head, tight little movements like a bumblebee trapped in a jar. "I know I ask a lot of you, but you can't leave me alone. You can't."

"It's summer, so there won't be any need for a flame. I'll lay in food that won't need heating. You can bring home braille books from the library. You'll be all right."

Her sister's entire body started to shake, and her breath came short and fast as panic descended. "You can't go."

"I'm doing this for *us*. If I can get cuttings of a particular orchid, the director has promised to find me a permanent position. In the long run it will be for the best."

Elaine clenched her eyes shut and clamped her jaw, but a long keening scream leaked out anyway. Annabelle reached out to grab Elaine's hands, for these attacks of panic were terrifying to both of them, with the panting, dizziness, and trembling. Once begun, an overwhelming sense of dread could overcome Elaine for hours.

"You can't know," Elaine wailed. "You can't know what it's like to hear a board creak and not know what's going on. Don't talk about 'the long run,' because it's all I can do to get through today. 'The long run' terrifies me because I'll be old and gray but I'll still be blind!"

She sobbed, rocking back and forth and accidentally knocking over the water pitcher. It smashed on the floor with a loud crash, which frightened Elaine all over again. She flinched, covering her head and shaking as the panic took root.

"It's all right," Annabelle said. "It's only a broken pitcher, it's all right."

But it wasn't, and Elaine struggled to breathe through the endless sobs. Then came a pounding on their front door.

"Miss Larkin? What's going on in there?" The door handle wiggled, but it was locked.

Annabelle raced to the door and cracked it open to see old Mr. Hillenbrand looking in with concern.

"It's okay. We're fine," she lied before closing the door and returning to Elaine, stepping around the broken shards of the pitcher.

Elaine's breathing was still ragged but had begun to slow. These attacks of crushing panic were rare now, and moving to Washington had sparked a glimmer of hope that Elaine could find a meaningful outlet for her intelligence, but it was still a struggle. Every day was still a struggle, and the spells of panic could descend without warning.

"Please don't go," Elaine said. "Some other job opportunity will come up. It doesn't have to be at the Smithsonian."

"Of course." Work as a botanist suited Annabelle perfectly, but she could find some other job if need be. Sacrifices were going to have to be made, for sometimes there weren't many choices in life. After all, Elaine would never have chosen to be blind, so they had to find a way to make the best of it.

"Stay where you are while I clean up the glass," Annabelle said.

She swept the broken shards into a mound while Elaine sat weak and despondent. "I'm such a useless person," she whispered. "I don't know why I'm still alive."

Annabelle took a steadying breath. "You're still alive because as hard as it is, you are further along than that soldier who won't do anything but shuffle cards all night. He needs you. His wife needs you. You're still alive because God has plans for you, even if we don't understand what they are yet."

It was impossible for mere mortals to understand the tapestry of blessings and tragedies God wove into their lives, but there had to be a meaning in it somewhere, and it was her duty to help Elaine find it.

"God led us here," Annabelle whispered.

"He planted a hope in your heart that was strong enough to send us a thousand miles across the country. There is a reason, and we'll keep going until we find it. We can't falter now."

The prospect of Mr. Bittles gloating at her failure was palpable, and that night Annabelle lay sleepless in the bed she shared with Elaine, staring at the ceiling of the darkened apartment. At times like this, it was hard to remember how happy they'd once been. If their father had ever wanted sons instead of daughters, he never gave a hint of it as he taught his daughters the art of farming on the Kansas plains. For Annabelle, the most beautiful sight on earth was endless fields of golden wheat as thunderheads gathered above in an awesome display of God's grandeur. But the rains didn't always come, and years of drought had put their farm on the verge of failure.

Roy Larkin had risked everything to send both his daughters to college. Elaine was two years older, but they left for the Kansas State Agricultural College the same year so they could share expenses. Their father mortgaged a hundred acres to pay for it, even though their penny-pinching mother disapproved. After college, Elaine returned to the farm while Annabelle stayed to work in a laboratory that was developing new strains of drought-resistant wheat. She even sent some to her father to test on patches of their farm, but so far they'd had only middling success.

Then Annabelle got clobbered with a case of the flu so bad that the doctor feared for her life. Elaine came to nurse her but ultimately caught the terrible illness too. It hadn't been the flu but a dangerous case of viral meningitis. They both survived, but Elaine's vision started failing almost immediately, and within a month she was blind.

Robbed of her eyesight and ability to make any useful contribution at the farm, Elaine sank into crippling depression. Over time she learned to read braille to occupy her mind, but braille books were shockingly expensive and hard to find. It was their father's insatiable quest to find more braille books that led to the discovery that the Library of Congress had an educational program for the blind.

The entire focus of Elaine's world shifted toward a new and exciting possibility in Washington. The chance to volunteer at the world's grandest library was a shining talisman in Elaine's dark world, and Annabelle agreed to take her to Washington. One of the professors she worked for at the college knew Dr. Norwood, and a temporary position was found for Annabelle at the Smithsonian. It was rare for a woman to land a professional position, so she was especially grateful for the six-month appointment.

But unless she could find a permanent income, they could not afford to stay. There was no possibility of help from home. She had to find a way to make it work on her own.

Elaine rolled over on the mattress beside her. "I think you should go see the greenhouses," she said in a soft whisper.

Annabelle shot bolt upright. It was so unexpected that she couldn't be certain she'd heard right. "You want me to go?"

Elaine sighed. "I don't *want* you to go, but you should. And I need to learn how to be on my own for a while."

It was obviously true, but what a blessing that Elaine had arrived at the conclusion without Annabelle having to press it.

"We'll give the Hillenbrands a key so they can get in if there is an emergency," Annabelle said.

Elaine nodded, but it was clear she was terrified. Annabelle couldn't begin to imagine the fear her sister was willing to endure, and it intensified her determination to succeed.

FIVE

Annabelle arrived at the boat depot at the appointed time despite hauling an oversized portfolio, an overnight bag, and a heavy box of equipment. Heavy in her skirt pocket was the horseshoe Elaine had given her for luck. So far that horseshoe had brought them both safely here from Kansas, and Annabelle prayed it would continue to serve them well.

Mr. Delacroix's letter had instructed her to go to boat slip twelve at the Potomac River dock, where someone named Luke would take her by sailboat to the rural Delacroix property. Her boots clicked on dry wooden planking, and the slosh of water on the pilings smelled musty and strange. So many people! Sailors lugged heavy packs, and travelers carried small cases. Huge mechanical cranes lowered cargo onto ships. She paused to watch and nearly jumped out of her skin when a sea gull swooped and hovered over her handbag, apparently sensing the warm muffin she'd been too nervous to eat for breakfast.

No one was waiting for her at the designated boat slip. She set the heavy equipment box on the dock with a *thud,* wondering what on earth she was to do now.

"Miss Larkin?"

She startled, for the voice came from under the dock. She hunkered down to look beneath the planks and spotted a handsome man sprawled in a boat tied to the pilings. The dock was so high above the water that she hadn't noticed him down there.

"Are you Luke?"

He sprang to his feet and seemed limber as a monkey as he climbed a rope ladder to the dock. "I'm Luke," he confirmed with a grin. "Rumor has it my brother has opened his greenhouses to you. I'm not quite sure I believe it, because Gray guards them like he's got the Holy Grail inside. He doesn't even let *me* in."

"Really?"

"Really," he said in a wry tone. "Only he and the groundskeeper have keys. He seems to believe the populace is drooling with eagerness to get inside his precious greenhouses."

She cocked a brow at him. "I'm prepared

to travel quite a distance for it."

"Then you and Gray can wallow in your botanical paradise," he said with a grin. "Come on, let's climb aboard so we can be on our way."

"Am I supposed to get down into that boat the same way you got up here?"

Luke seemed surprised. "My brother told me you were brave, that you had spunk. Not the sort to quake in fear at a five-foot rope ladder."

She laughed and gamely collected her skirts, turned around, and lowered herself down the ladder and onto the wobbling boat. She managed to get on board without embarrassing herself, even though transferring her bags and the equipment box was awkward.

"What am I supposed to do?" she asked once she was seated on a wooden bench opposite Luke.

He grabbed a rope and began hoisting a sail. The canvas billowed out, and the boat started moving with surprising speed. "You sit there like Cleopatra while I sail us to Windover Landing."

As the dock slid into the distance, Luke explained how Windover Landing had once been a grand plantation estate owned by the Delacroix family for generations. "The house burned down during the war, but we still owned the land, so that's where my father built the greenhouses and went back into business."

As they moved farther into the center of the river, the sailboat picked up speed and listed to one side. Annabelle clenched the portfolio, for it contained rare specimens of vanilla orchids that had been collected by explorers all over the world.

"You're not going to tip us over, are you?"

Luke laughed. "You're not doing a very good Cleopatra imitation. If I'm making you nervous, you need to order me to sheet out and slow down. Then look me in the eye and call me a peasant in a withering voice."

If there was a peasant in this boat, it was her. But it didn't take her long to relax, because Luke immediately slowed the boat and seemed perfectly capable as he guided it down the river. The city was soon behind them, and within an hour, the river took them into a rural, marshy landscape where the air still carried a faint salty tang.

"What are those grasses growing along the bank?" she asked.

"Cordgrass," Luke replied. "Depending on the season, the water can get a little salty, and cordgrass can stand up to it."

How different from Kansas it was here.

Great blue herons glided above the river, and long-legged birds poked through the marsh. Luke expertly handled the rigging as he steered the boat up a narrow tributary to take them inland. He kept her entertained with stories about how planters had been using these waterways for generations.

"My father had a whole fleet of ships for exporting cotton and tobacco," he said. "That all ended when the government seized our ships during the war."

She trailed her fingertips along the surface of the water, enjoying its coolness as she listened. She had been under the impression that Gray Delacroix sailed his own cargo all over the world.

"But you have ships again?" she asked.

"Just one, but it's huge," Luke said. "The *Pelican* is a merchant steamship that brings in spices from Africa and the Far East, and we have a packing factory in Alexandria where we bottle them up and sell them. Gray uses the greenhouses for researching the plants he finds overseas, seeing if he can someday turn a profit from them. Look over there — that's Windover Landing."

A cluster of buildings nestled alongside the river. Luke explained that the plantation house had been completely destroyed during the war, but his father eventually built the modest farmhouse where the grounds-keeper lived. There was a barn, storage sheds, and a farmhouse with a welcoming front porch, but her eye instinctively traveled to the four greenhouses huddled against a tree line in the distance.

"Welcome to Windover Landing," Luke said as he turned the sailboat toward a dock. His arms pumped as he tugged on ropes and sails. It felt odd not to help, but she was completely out of her element and would probably capsize them if she tried.

Ten minutes later, they had disembarked and were headed toward the farmhouse. A side door opened, and Gray Delacroix came striding down the path toward them. How different he seemed from the last time she saw him in the throes of a fever. Today he looked vibrant and healthy in plain black trousers and an open-throated white shirt. His confident stride made him seem eager to see her, and it was flattering.

"The journey was uneventful?" he asked politely.

"I took care of her as though she were the queen of the Nile," Luke said. "She was a complete failure at the haughty-command stuff, but she likes ugly marsh grass as much as you."

A hint of humor lit Gray's dark eyes. "You

70

like ugly marsh grass?"

"If a plant is useful, I am intrigued," she admitted.

"Me too." His eyes warmed, and his smile made the cleft of his chin look strong and appealing. A breeze ruffled his hair, and she fought the temptation to smooth it back from his face, but she loved the way he smiled down at her.

Gray broke the gaze first, gesturing to Luke. "Let me help carry those things." Luke passed the box to Gray, and he grunted at its weight. "What have you got in here? Boulders?" he asked as he hefted the ungainly box.

"Close," she admitted. "It's a microtome."

The warmth vanished from his face, and he set the box on the ground with a *thump.* "And what do you intend to do with that?"

The misgiving in his voice was apparent, for there was only one use for a microtome. The heavy brass machine cut paper-thin samples from plant material for study under a microscope. It was an essential tool for any botanist hoping to understand the cellular structure of a plant.

"It's a very useful tool for the study of plant biology," she stated needlessly.

"I invited you here to *look* at my plants. Not dissect them."

71

Before she could reply, Luke flashed a smile. "Brace yourself, Miss Larkin. Here comes the battering ram of my brother's unstoppable charm. Can't she at least have a few minutes before we break out the fire and brimstone?"

Gray ignored his brother and looked her directly in the eye. "I want it understood that I'm not giving anything to the Smithsonian. Not plants, not bulbs, not even cuttings. Are we clear?"

It was easy to take a cutting from a plant without hurting it, but he seemed unusually possessive of his plants. Nevertheless, it was his greenhouse and his rules.

"I shall take nothing unless you personally authorize it," she said.

His face gentled. "Good. Luke can take your overnight bag inside while I show you the first of the greenhouses. Unless you would like a break first? I can arrange for lunch or something to drink if you'd like."

She shook her head. "I don't want to waste a single minute."

He gave her a gentlemanly nod and extended his arm to her. His old-fashioned formality was so much more potent than the charm poured on by his younger brother. It made her feel ladylike, and it was a nice sensation.

Their shoes crunched along a gravel pathway as they rounded the bend toward the greenhouses. Birds chattered in nearby trees, and a squirrel darted across the path. The green scent of wild grass was like a balm to her spirit. She'd missed the countryside.

A huge flat slab of foundation stones looked starkly out of place in the rural splendor. When Gray noticed where she was looking, the corners of his mouth turned down.

"That's the remnants of the house where I was born," he said. "It was burned by the Yankees in 1864. I keep the foundation as a reminder."

The house must have been a mansion, for its foundation was enormous. It surely had excellent access to the river and was probably one of those grand plantation estates she'd seen pictures of in magazines.

Gray went on to explain that the Jenkins family lived in the farmhouse. The married couple maintained the grounds, but Gray visited a couple of days per month because he enjoyed tending the plants himself. "Sinking my hands into the soil is a balm to the spirit," he said, and she completely agreed.

They rounded a bend, and she got her

first close-up view of the greenhouses. They were huge, each of them larger than the farmhouse where she'd lived most of her life. Keys jangled as Gray unlocked the door to the first greenhouse, and she stepped inside.

It was Eden. Moss and jasmine perfumed the air, and a fountain splashed in the center of the structure. Tables overflowed with potted herbs, climbing roses, and lush vines. Towering palms were tucked into the corners, along with lemon, lime, and fig trees. Heavy fruit she didn't recognize hung from the tree beside her.

"What is this?" she asked, cupping a smooth green fruit slightly larger than a baseball.

"A mango," he said. "Native to India."

"And this?" What a treasure trove he had, a literal feast for the eyes.

"Papaya. Native to Mexico."

"Oh yes. Yes, yes, yes! I've heard of papaya. The Department of Agriculture is trying to import them. A whole team of scientists are seeing if they can be cultivated in California, but I've never seen one before."

She must have said something wrong, for he crossed his arms, and that dark, suspicious look was on his face again. This was ridiculous. They were two people with a common interest, so why did he get so moody all the time? She would confront it with a chiding sense of humor, which was always more effective than scolding.

She pretended to shiver. "That scowl just caused the temperature in here to drop ten degrees. Please tell me what I've done."

He gave a nervous laugh and turned away. Was he actually blushing? She couldn't read him as he gestured to a cluster of chairs near the fountain.

"Have a seat," he said, not unkindly. "Let's talk."

She joined him, still fascinated by the bounty of ferns, bamboo, and bromeliads. It was such an earthly paradise in here, but she turned her attention to the darkly attractive man opposite her.

"Look," he began tersely. "The only people I mistrust more than the Smithsonian is the Department of Agriculture."

"But why?" she sputtered. "That's like resenting yeoman farmers and the salt of the earth."

"They give their information away for free," he said, as though it were a crime. "They use taxpayer money to send scientists all over the world, hunting plants and seeds, then help farmers profit from it. How am I supposed to compete with that?"

75

It was hard to form a coherent sentence when she was so flabbergasted. "You don't have to. The information they are compiling is for the good of everyone."

"And yet I'm investing a fortune in it. All I want is to be left alone to cultivate plants, strike deals, and turn a profit. But the government taxes me left, right, and center, using my money to compile research they give away to others. You aren't the first government official to try to steal what I've accomplished."

"We're not stealing anything. We're learning from each other."

"Knowledge is the most valuable commodity on the face of the earth, and I won't let the government take it for free."

"We can both benefit from sharing information. It isn't stealing."

He snorted. "I know you want to see a particular vanilla orchid. In fact, I'll bet you were sent here specifically for that purpose."

It was true, but how could she admit that? All she or the Smithsonian wanted was the answer to a scientific mystery. They didn't intend to steal anything from him.

"We have no plan to capitalize on your orchid. Dr. Norwood might build an altar to it and brag to all his orchid-loving friends, but we're in the business of science, not sales."

His face gentled. "Miss Larkin, you are so naïve," he said softly. "You've got this irresistible, sunshiny quality that both fascinates and frustrates me. I don't know what is in the water out there in Kansas, but you seem as innocent and trusting as a lone sunflower standing in a field, doomed to be pummeled to the ground in the first windstorm."

"And you're the complete opposite," she said. "Like you were raised on a diet of skepticism and mistrust."

His laughter began deep in his chest. "There's probably some truth in that." He shifted in his chair and pointed outside toward a small outbuilding a few acres away. "You see that shed?"

She nodded. With peeling paint and a sagging roof, the shed seemed out of place among the other well-tended buildings on the property.

"My father and I lived in that shed for three years after the war. The government burned our house, gutted the estate, seized our ships, and levied outrageous taxes on us. So, yes, to use your phrase, I have been raised on a diet of mistrust. It happened right over there in that dilapidated shed."

He didn't sound bitter. He sounded like

he was trying to persuade her to his point of view, which would never happen. She was a patriotic American who was proud of the work the government did, and Gray was wasting time.

Her eyes traveled to the papaya tree a few yards away. "What does a papaya taste like?" she asked, and the corners of his eyes crinkled.

"Trying to divert the conversation?"

"Yes."

"Fair enough."

His smile returned as he plucked a papaya, then used a pocketknife to expertly peel and seed the fruit. The vibrant orange flesh looked so tender it made her mouth water. She leaned forward to enjoy the heady fragrance, and he passed her a wedge.

The fruit was mushy and mild and odd. She scrambled for something nice to say, but it turned out there was no need. Gray seemed to be reading her mind.

"The taste doesn't live up to the color, does it?"

He promised that she'd like kiwi fruit better, and she did. After the kiwi, he shared a mango and an avocado with her. She'd heard of these fruits but never seen them before and was completely entranced. She fingered petals, sniffed blossoms, and tested the soil.

But when she asked to see the orchids, he smoothly diverted the conversation by showing her an African cherry orange and explaining how it differed from those grown in Florida. He explained the hot water piping system used to keep the tropical greenhouse warm and humid, and how he had transported the various plants during his long ocean voyages.

It felt like paradise, but she needed to search for Dr. Norwood's orchid. "Can we see the orchid greenhouse?" she asked again late in the afternoon.

He glanced at his pocket watch. "It's time to change for dinner."

She helplessly looked down at her red gingham dress. "This is all I've got."

"Perfectly fine," he assured her. "I won't change either. I'm just warning you, because for all his rowdy behavior, Luke is a sharp dresser and likely to be in black coat and tie. He enjoys the trappings of high society." He stood and held out his arm. "Let's head back to the farmhouse, where you can freshen up. We can discuss the orchid at dinner."

"I'm looking forward to it," she said, determined not to be discouraged by his suddenly somber mood.

Six

Gray leaned closer to the mirror as he dragged the straight-edged razor along his jawline. Shaving before dinner was a rarity for him, but he wanted to look respectable tonight. He had asked Mrs. Jenkins to pull out all the stops with the evening meal, using a variety of exotic spices he had traveled the world to collect. Normally they weren't so formal out at the farmhouse, but he wanted this night to be special.

Why was he so fascinated with Annabelle Larkin? This sort of attraction was out of character for him, and he couldn't pinpoint how she'd captured his interest with such ease. Maybe because she understood his work so well?

Gray snorted and almost cut himself. She didn't understand him; they were polar opposites. He saw plants as a commodity upon which he'd built an empire and resurrected a family fortune. She liked plants because . . . well, simply because she was one of those curious people who liked every-thing. Her naiveté was appalling. Fresh off the farm and with the wide-eyed innocence to prove it. He had no intention of letting her take so much as a leaf off his property.

At least not yet.

A knock on the door broke his concentra-tion. He swiped the remaining soap from his face and answered it. Luke stepped inside, already dressed for dinner in a formal coat and starched collar.

"I wanted to pass on some family news," he said casually.

Gray stiffened. This sort of statement was usually prelude to something bad. "What's going on?" he asked tightly.

"Your baby sister has gotten herself a job," Luke said.

It was hard to believe. If Caroline had run off with a foreign aristocrat or squandered a fortune to buy the Hope Diamond, he could believe it. But found a job?

"What sort of job?" he asked skeptically.

"Brace yourself. She will be working at the White House as social secretary for the first lady."

"What in the world is a social secretary?"

Luke sauntered toward the bedroom window, casually propping a shoulder

81

against the molding. "Apparently Mrs. McKinley is a notorious recluse. She doesn't like mingling with the public, is homesick for Ohio, and needs someone to help her navigate the DC social whirl. Caroline will be good at that."

Gray tossed down the towel and reached for a shirt, jerking it on with stiff motions. "I don't like President McKinley," he said tersely. "She shouldn't have anything to do with him or his administration."

"Is that the best you can say? All these years you've been nagging us to lead responsible lives, and now Caroline has a plum position, one of the best in the city. Do you need to immediately lunge for the fly in the ointment to criticize her?"

"You consider the Spanish-American War a fly in the ointment? Thousands of Americans died. Our government barged into places we have no business being."

"Oh, that's rich," Luke said sarcastically. "You criticize the president for conquering Cuba, but you want me to go down there to capitalize on the results of the war."

It was a ridiculous accusation, and Gray wasn't about to accept it. "I do business with nations all over the world by setting up mutually beneficial trade alliances. I don't sign contracts while pointing a gun at anyone. The United States shouldn't be in the business of collecting colonies, and that's precisely what President McKinley has done."

Luke rolled his eyes. "We both know Caroline doesn't have a political bone in her body. She's helping an awkward woman host a few tea parties. Let her do it. Tell her you're proud of her."

Was it possible to be proud of his sister for working for a presidential administration he instinctively mistrusted? But Luke was right. He'd always wanted Caroline to funnel her talents toward something beyond the latest hairstyle or ball gown, but that didn't mean he was overjoyed by this latest development.

"She's twenty-eight years old," he conceded. "She's chosen her own course, however distasteful, but I suppose she shall perform it well." Caroline had earned her reputation by flying high in the social whirl and always knowing the perfect quip.

Luke pushed away from the wall, disapproval rampant on his face. "You've made it very apparent that we are both crushing disappointments in your eyes, but try to summon up a little more enthusiasm the next time you see Caroline. She deserves better than what you think of her."

The door closed behind him with a gentle click.

Annabelle was determined to spend dinner picking Gray's mind for insight into the rare orchid. At the very least, if she could confirm Gray had one, perhaps it would please Dr. Norwood. But her intention to focus on the orchid flew out the window the moment she entered the farmhouse dining room.

"What am I smelling?" she asked. She'd begun noticing the heavenly aromas while resting in the upstairs guest room, but they got stronger as she descended the staircase.

Gray smiled as he led her toward the table. The dining room was a cozy mix of comfortable farmhouse furniture set alongside elegant candelabras, china, and silver laid on a lace tablecloth. "The housekeeper has prepared a lamb roast seasoned with a dry rub of smoked Hungarian paprika, a little dried coriander, some ground sumac and cumin, and a dash of curry powder."

Most of those spices were new to her, but if they tasted as good as they smelled, this dinner was going to be unforgettable. "In my world, seasoning means salt and pepper," she admitted.

Gray's face lit with amusement, but before

he could respond, his younger brother came bounding down the staircase. As Gray had predicted, Luke was indeed wearing a formal coat with a snowy white dress shirt and tie. It made his daredevil recklessness even more handsome as he flashed her a smile.

"Welcome to Delacroix dining," Luke said as he grabbed her shoulders and pressed a quick kiss to each cheek. "Gray rarely invites guests unless he intends to pull out all the stops. It's a subtle sales pitch to promote our spices to every person who crosses the threshold."

"I'm already sold," she said.

"Is it true the only seasonings you use are salt and pepper?" Gray asked as he held out a chair for her.

And he called her naïve! They lived in the same country, yet he had no idea how people in the Great Plains lived.

"The nearest general store to our farm is an hour by wagon," she said as she draped a napkin across her lap. "It sells everything from plowshares to horse feed to bolts of cloth. Their seasonings are limited to vinegar, salt, and pepper. For such a worldly man, you don't seem to know much about life in the United States," she teased. "The *real* United States, not a fancy east coast

85

city that has papayas from Mexico and vanilla from Madagascar."

Dinner was superb, with herbed potatoes, asparagus with fresh ginger, and wonderfully seasoned lamb. Every bite was an explosion of flavor. The evening finished with the most divine vanilla tart she'd ever tasted. Everything served had a complex, multi-dimensional flavor that would have been fit for a king, and she told him so. It would be foolish to deny the value of what he bottled and sold.

Gray sent a triumphant look Luke's way. "See? Delacroix Global Spice has a long way to go in extending our reach right here in America. More than half of the population still lives in rural communities, and there's no reason we can't ship our spices to them."

"Aren't you the one who warned me not to talk business at dinner?" Luke asked. "That we were to act like gracious hosts?"

Gray sent her an apologetic glance. "Guilty. It appears I've spent too many years with my head buried in shipping invoices and contracts."

"We could talk about orchids," she broached. "I'm still eager for a chance to see your orchid house."

Luke shuddered. "It's humid in there, and

all those plants look alike."

"But one of them is extraordinary," Annabelle told him. "Have you seen it? The original vanilla orchid?"

"What makes that one special?"

She explained the historical mystery behind the orchid that hadn't been seen in over a hundred years. "Botanists and orchid hunters have been looking for decades but can't find it. Rumor claims that your brother has one, which would make it the only known survivor anywhere in the world."

Luke leaned forward, his voice intrigued. "Do you mean my brother has some rare plant in that greenhouse and has yet to capitalize on it?"

"This has nothing to do with money," she rushed to assure Gray, who remained annoyingly impassive. "It's a scientific mystery we are dying to solve. We'd like to see what the original vanilla orchid was like before it was hybridized overseas."

Gray said nothing, and the silence began to stretch. Only the sound of a grandfather clock ticking somewhere down the hall broke the quiet. She held her breath, for if she could find that orchid, a permanent job at the Smithsonian was waiting for her.

"I know you are loyal to the Smithsonian," Gray finally said. "I know you consider them peaceable, harmless scientists. They aren't. They have an agenda."

"Yes!" she said passionately. "Their agenda is to unlock the mysteries of the world around us. There's no profit motive involved, just the insatiable, unquenchable need to know. Curiosity is what makes us different from the animals. It's what makes us strive to discover new things or come up with remarkable products like the spices and herbs that came out of your kitchen tonight. If you have that orchid in your greenhouse, it might be another piece of the grand, worldwide puzzle botanists are trying to piece together."

He scrutinized her for so long it became uncomfortable. Candlelight flickered on the planes of his face, and it was impossible to read him. "All right," he finally said. "Tomorrow morning I'll show you everything I have."

Relief flooded through her.

At the end of the meal, Annabelle wanted to thank the cook, for everything had been marvelous. The kitchen was modest, with copper pots and pans hanging from the ceiling alongside bundles of dried herbs.

The housekeeper took her compliment in stride, nodding to a row of spices stored on a shelf above the counter. "It all comes from

88

proper seasoning," she said simply.

Gray gestured Annabelle over to the shelf containing dozens of identical bottles, all sporting the Delacroix label. In short order, he collected six bottles and set them on the counter.

"Take these home with you," he said. "Aside from the cayenne, they are easy to use and won't ruin your meal. Be brave."

The bottles contained cardamom, cumin, sumac, paprika, turmeric, and cayenne pepper. She picked up a glass bottle that easily sat in the palm of her hand. "How much does a jar like this cost?"

"Fifty cents," he said. "I still need to get the price lower and figure out a distribution system to get them affordably shipped all over the country. Soon even Kansas won't be safe from properly seasoned food."

She loved his dry sense of humor, but before she could reply, he opened a cabinet and retrieved a different sort of bottle. It was tiny and dark. He unscrewed the cap and extended it to her.

"Your collection would not be complete without this," he said. "Smell."

She took a whiff and almost fainted with pleasure. "Vanilla?"

"Yes."

"But it's liquid!"

"Yes," he said again. "We've been working on it for a decade. Vanilla extract is a challenging process, but it stays fresh longer than the ground seeds."

It was late, but when Gray escorted her to the base of the stairs, Annabelle didn't want the evening to end. Darkness had fallen, allowing the kerosene lanterns to provide soft illumination in the hallway.

Gray paused, as though hesitant to speak. "That bottle of vanilla is for you alone," he said. "No handing it over to the Smithsonian or the Department of Agriculture."

She'd heard that vanilla extract was appallingly expensive, but something about his stern tone indicated his concern had nothing to do with its cost. "Is there something unique about this particular bottle of vanilla?"

"Yes," he said simply. "It's the real thing. I'm in a race against chemists who are working toward creating an imitation vanilla extract by distilling wood-tar creosote along with a little clove oil and chemicals."

"Yuck," she instinctively said.

"My thoughts exactly," he replied. "The quest to develop real vanilla extract is the holy grail for spice manufacturers. The chemists can make a fake version cheaper than anything I can produce, but mine tastes better."

She held the bottle aloft. "Is this what made the vanilla tart taste so good tonight?"

His eyes warmed. "It is. My father and I worked for years on a cold-pressed solution for vanilla extract. It's the best in the world." He reached out to fold her hand around the bottle of vanilla, triggering an involuntary thrill, for it felt wonderfully tender and intimate. "This is for you alone," he repeated, his voice a rough whisper in the darkness. "Do what you wish with the spices, but don't share the vanilla extract."

"Why are you giving it to me?" she asked, her hand still encased in his. For all his vaunted sense of privacy, he'd been consistently generous with her.

"Because I like you," he said simply.

Only four words, yet they had the power to make her heart skip a beat and brighten her entire world. Silence stretched between them, but it didn't feel uncomfortable. Crickets sounded in the distance, and the house made settling noises as the night cooled. She could stand here and stare up into his darkly handsome face all evening as this strange magnetism hummed between them.

"I'll see you tomorrow morning," Gray finally said, promise in his voice as he

91

stepped back a few paces.

His words echoed in her mind as she headed upstairs. The first thing she saw in the guest room was Elaine's horseshoe, gleaming on the bed in the dim light. Her giddy euphoria popped like a soap bubble. Elaine's work at the library had been a shining beacon of hope, but unless Annabelle could please Dr. Norwood with that orchid, they could both find themselves on a train back to Kansas.

She ended the evening on her knees, giving thanks for getting her this far, but praying for guidance. Gray had promised to show her the orchid house tomorrow, but she'd heard the hint of caution in his tone. He'd been attentive and charming all day, but if he had that orchid, he was going to guard it.

SEVEN

Annabelle tried not to get her hopes up as Gray walked her toward the orchid greenhouse the following morning. *This was it.* She had one more day to find that orchid, and she wouldn't let Gray distract her with spices or papayas like he had yesterday.

She studied Gray's hands as he unlocked the door. Why would he have this greenhouse under lock and key unless he had something valuable inside? Her anticipation climbed higher as she stepped inside and into the warm, humid air. Gravel crunched beneath her feet as he led down the center aisle toward the back of the building.

"The vanilla orchids are along the southern wall. I imagine this is the one that triggered Dr. Norwood's interest," he said, pointing to a climbing vanilla vine that grew on a trellis propped in the corner. The stems grew in a jointed, zigzag pattern, and long green pods dangled from the stems. It was an extraordinary vine, at least thirty feet long, but she instantly recognized the waxy yellow leaves.

"It's a *Vanilla pompona*," she said, unable to mask the crushing disappointment in her tone.

"It was given to me by a monk in Mexico. They've been cultivating them in their monastery garden for centuries," he said gently. "It's rare, but not the extraordinary plant you're looking for."

The sympathy in his eyes made her feel even worse, but she couldn't give up yet. "Why does Dr. Norwood think you have it?"

"Because the monks never let outsiders into their garden, and people wonder why. I only got in because my great-uncle was once a monk there, so they trusted me. Someone must have seen me leaving the monastery with the orchid and jumped to conclusions."

Her shoulders sagged. She walked down the row of vanilla orchids, all slightly different in their nodes, root structure, and blooms. She'd wanted this too desperately to give up the search, but she recognized them all. She plopped down onto a potting bench, staring blankly at the tables brimming with orchids. All beautiful; none of them unique.

"Do you know if the progenitor of the vanilla orchid still exists?" she asked, holding her breath.

"If it does, I've never caught wind of it. I've been looking too." His voice was kind, face tender with sympathy.

An overwhelming, strangling sense of failure crept closer. The prospect of loading Elaine onto a train back to Kansas was unbearable.

She refused to fail. God hadn't guided her and Elaine halfway across the country to let her quit so soon. She would think of something else to please Dr. Norwood. Gray Delacroix's collection rivaled anything in the United States, and she was the first outsider he'd allowed inside his greenhouse.

She straightened her shoulders. "Show me the rest of your plants."

Over the next few hours, they explored his remaining greenhouses. She loved the way he spoke so confidently about the rare plants he had collected from all over the world. With competent hands, he clipped specimens and showed her the unique scents, textures, and techniques for cultivation. He had a dozen saffron crocuses. While showing her the task of delicately gathering the stamens, he spoke of a tense, four-month negotiation with Arab traders in

Morocco to buy their saffron crop.

"Weren't you afraid?" she asked.

She expected a quick denial but didn't get one. He set the plate of saffron threads down and pondered the question. "Those years were mostly an adventure," he finally said. "They were hard, but my biggest fear was letting my father down. We gambled everything on those overseas ventures to resurrect our fortune, and he depended on what I could deliver. When malaria clobbered me, I swallowed quinine, took an ice-water bath, and got on with business. They were hard years, but not bad ones."

The more she learned about Gray, the more she stood in awe of him. She was terrified of failing both her parents and Elaine. She needed something to balance the scales.

"Everyone is afraid of something. Go ahead, confess. What are you afraid of?"

He grimaced in good-natured embarrassment. "I'm afraid of raccoons."

"Raccoons?" she asked in astonishment.

"Can't stand them," he admitted. "After our house burned down, my father and I lived in that shed." He gestured to the dilapidated shed with peeling paint. "Raccoons loved it," he continued. "They'd drop onto it from the tree branches overhead. The first night we slept in there, I woke in

96

the middle of the night when the entire shed started shaking. Endless thumping and scratching. I was only five and completely terrified. I thought the Yankees were back and pounding on the roof to drive us out."

He set the crocuses back on the ledge where they'd get the most sunlight. "Our townhouse in Alexandria was occupied by the Yankees for three years after the war, so that shed was the only roof we had left. On most nights the raccoons came sniffing around, making a racket. I've hated them ever since, and I hate that shed. It's got a dirt floor and stinks inside, but I keep it as a reminder. The lessons I learned as a child shouldn't be forgotten."

Annabelle stared at the dilapidated shed and the old foundation of the burned-down plantation house. Gray was wrong. Some things *should* be forgotten, or the scars would eventually warp a person. Had that already happened to Gray? She had no experience with his sort of deep, ingrained bitterness. He was a brilliant man who succeeded in everything he touched, but a part of her feared those blessings were taken for granted, and lurking beneath the surface of his success was a dangerous acrimony that could ruin him.

After lunch they returned to the orchid house, where Annabelle hoped she could find something else to make her indispensable to Dr. Norwood. She lingered all afternoon, listening to Gray as he recounted the story behind each orchid he'd collected.

One caught her eye. It was smaller than most, its petals a conglomeration of green and purple stripes. It almost looked gaudy, and it was tucked in a corner behind a screen of other orchids. She'd never seen anything like it in Dr. Norwood's collection, and its coloring was so odd that she was determined to get a cutting from it, but Gray wasn't going to make it easy. He freely showed her all the orchids in the greenhouse except that one.

It was nearing time for her to return home, and the housekeeper brought a large pitcher of lemonade to the table in the center of the orchid house. Annabelle joined Gray, listening to the splash of the fountain and breathing in the heady fragrance.

"Yesterday I promised not to take anything from your greenhouse unless you personally authorized it."

His expression became guarded. "What is

it you want?"

"A cutting."

"From?"

She stood and walked directly to the green and purple orchid, lifting it from its sheltered position. The petals of the fragile blossom trembled as she carried it to the table and set it down. She sat opposite Gray and waited.

He folded his arms and looked at her with challenge in his eyes. "You have good taste. That's the only orchid of its kind in the United States."

"The color has faded since you brought it here." It was a wild guess, but she must be right, for he looked both surprised and impressed. She pressed her case. "If you let me take a cutting, we can study it. We can figure out exactly what it needs to thrive."

Gray leaned forward until his smiling face was only inches from hers. She felt entirely captured by his dark, delighted gaze and held her breath, eager to hear what he said next.

"Miss Larkin," he murmured, "I already know exactly what it needs."

"You do?"

"A light mix of iron and phosphorus, and two hours more daylight than the state of Virginia can provide. I won't let you take a cutting." He straightened and slid the plant across the table toward her. "Take the whole thing."

She sucked in a quick breath. "You're giving it to me?"

"I'm giving it to you so that you may turn it over to the director of the Smithsonian. I know he's a lunatic when it comes to orchids. Perhaps this will buffer his disappointment at not getting the vanilla orchid."

Her heart filled. Knowing how possessive he was of his orchids made the gift especially meaningful.

She placed her hand inside his and squeezed. "Thank you."

Her gesture seemed to embarrass him, but he didn't withdraw his hand. "I'm sorry this trip wasn't what you hoped for," he said hesitantly. "But maybe it can turn into something more. I'd like to see you again, if that would be agreeable."

His old-world formality constantly thrilled her. She tried not to smile too much when she replied. "That would be agreeable."

That evening Gray took her in his family's sailboat back to the city. He even accompanied her on the streetcar to help with her ungainly bags while she carried the orchid, then escorted her all the way back to her apartment building. They stood beneath the streetlamp to say good-bye.

"Can I come back to Windover Landing sometime?" she asked boldly.

"I hope you do."

The affection burning in his gaze stayed with her long after she climbed into bed that evening. Her trip had been a failure, but she still felt euphoric.

Annabelle didn't understand the magnitude of the gift Gray had given her until she saw Dr. Norwood's reaction to the orchid. He gasped and clutched his chest, almost as though having a heart attack.

"A *Paphiopedilum callosum*," he managed to choke out. "I've only seen them in paintings. Wait until the gentlemen at the Orchid Society get a look at this." He shooed her from his office. "Go, go. I must propagate this beauty immediately. And tell my secretary to cancel the rest of my appointments for the day."

He hovered over the plant with a magnifying glass, his hands trembling in excitement. Would this be enough for him to offer her a permanent position? The craving to ask clawed at her, but before she could speak, Dr. Norwood surprised her.

He looked up with a calculating expression on his face. "Don't go yet," he said as he straightened to his full height.

"Yes?"

He set down his magnifying glass. "You've done very well, Miss Larkin," he said. "We may have more uses for you yet. I will be in touch soon."

"Thank you, sir."

What was she to make of that odd comment? It seemed . . . well, *sinister* wasn't the right word. Scheming? Calculating?

Whatever it was, she suspected it involved more than orchids, and it worried her.

EIGHT

Gray stared at the paperwork lying on the desk before him. The contract for the sale of the *Pelican* was only three pages long, but signing it would change the direction of his life forever. Owning a steamship had been his father's dream, never Gray's. As soon as the sale was concluded, it would mark the end of his travels and the beginning of a new life in Virginia.

He glanced at the clock. The bank wanted the paperwork completed today, but he needed to review it again before signing, and Annabelle Larkin was due to visit within the hour.

It had been two weeks since their courtship began, and she was never far from his mind. Five days a week, he escorted her to lunch at the small café in the basement of the Smithsonian. Even with the crowds of tourists, the noise, and the mundane food,

103

that hour had become the highlight of his day.

Each day his fascination with Annabelle grew. He learned of her blind sister and how Annabelle had left a respectable job at a college in Kansas to accompany Elaine here. Family meant everything to her, as it did to Gray. The true test of loyalty lay in hard times and sacrifices, and in coming to Washington, Annabelle had proven herself a woman of steadfast honor.

Today was a Saturday, so Annabelle was visiting him at the townhouse, where he'd treat her to a spicy fruit punch he'd become enamored of while living in Ceylon. He looked forward to the chance to court her in blessed quiet, something that was in short supply at the Smithsonian.

Except he'd forgotten to put the punch on ice. Muttering a curse, he shot out of his study and headed toward the icehouse tucked into the alley behind his house.

"Otis, come help me chip some ice!" he hollered through the still-open door. It would be a race to cool the punch before Annabelle's arrival, but he wanted every-thing to be perfect. Someone like Luke could charm the birds out of a tree, but it had never been easy for Gray. Frankly, he didn't know *how* to flirt with a woman. He knew business, negotiation, and accomplishments. For the first time in his life, he envied Luke's breezy charm.

"Someone just knocked on the door," Otis said as he ambled toward the icehouse.

Annabelle was earlier than expected, but Gray could trust Otis to get everything prepared.

"I'll get it," he said as he tossed the ice pick to the younger man.

He dragged his hands through his hair and straightened his collar as he bounded down the center hallway to the door. He nearly yanked it off its hinges in his excitement.

"Who are you?" he asked in confusion. A middle-aged man and woman stood on the front stoop with a trunk at their feet.

"I'm Monsieur Chastain," the man said in a thick French accent. "My wife and I are delivering Miss Delacroix's new wardrobe. It is *magnifique*," he purred. "Your sister is a true artisan. Her taste is exquisite. She shall illuminate all of Washington society."

The Frenchman kept rambling, but Gray's eyes grew wide as he eyed the trunks and boxes mounded on his front stoop. There were more in the wagon on the street. "Don't tell me the boxes in the wagon are also for my sister."

"But of course!" Monsieur Chastain said.

"Miss Caroline insisted she needed an entirely new wardrobe for her position in the White House. Such an honor! My wife and I have been sewing around the clock for two weeks."

"And how much is Miss Caroline's new wardrobe going to cost me?"

The Frenchman reached into his breast pocket and presented him with an envelope. "She has already paid a portion of the fee but assured us you would gladly pay the balance upon delivery."

Gray wasn't going to *gladly* do anything, but if Caroline had signed a contract, it needed to be honored. She wasn't home to consult, and the invoice was five pages long. Five pages! Morning gowns, evening gowns, walking suits, riding habits, and what on earth was a polonaise overskirt? The tally at the bottom nearly drove the breath from his lungs.

He strode to the kitchen, where Otis was dumping shards of ice into a bucket. "Did you know about Caroline's attempt to drive us into bankruptcy with a wardrobe fit for Marie Antoinette?"

"She mentioned that since you'd be flush with cash after selling the *Pelican,* she might buy a new dress or two."

"Or fifty," Gray muttered as he headed

back to the front room. Typical Caroline, spending money before it even hit their bank account. The sale of the steamship would take months to complete and could still fall through.

He intended to verify every piece of this delivery before he paid the invoice. The parlor was a spacious room, but it felt cramped once it was filled with trunks and hatboxes. Monsieur Chastain opened the first trunk and peeled tissue paper away from a lemony yellow gown with lace trim.

"Which one is that?" Gray asked.

"The silk bombazine walking dress," the Frenchman said, pointing to a line on the last page of the invoice.

Gray made a tiny check beside the item. "Continue," he ordered. He sat on the sofa and inspected each piece as it was lifted from the wrappings. The items were carefully draped over the sofa, the chairs, and the coat-tree until the parlor was festooned with gowns of every shade.

The worst was a box containing mounds of silken undergarments. Why did Caroline need new *underwear* for this job? He could appreciate that she needed to be finely turned out for life inside the White House, but she surely already had perfectly serviceable underwear.

"Take the underclothes back," he ordered. "I'm not paying for them."

"But Miss Caroline asked for them," the Frenchman said delicately. "They were custom-made to her specifications."

"Then she can pay for them. I'm not, so please take them away. What's in the next box?"

The husband carried the undergarments out to the wagon while the wife continued unwrapping more clothes. They hadn't even gone through half of it, but the parlor was buried in an avalanche of silk, satin, and lace. A series of wire hoops had Gray completely baffled until Madame Chastain explained it was the cage over which a bustle was to be draped.

"She's already got one, so that can go back too."

Madame Chastain was trying to explain how this year's bustle was a different shape than last season's when the doorbell rang. The husband must have gotten locked out, and Gray strode to the door with the wire bustle, prepared to order him to take this contraption back as well.

His scowl vanished as he recognized Annabelle. She glanced at the bustle, apparently as confused as he was.

"It's not mine," he said.

108

Her smile was blinding. "Good to know."

He smiled back. What was it about this woman that she could banish his black mood with only her smile? "Come in," he said. "Please overlook the infestation of clothing that has assaulted my house. My sister has expensive taste."

Annabelle stepped inside and looked at the clothes in astonishment. "I've never seen anything so lovely," she said breathlessly. "I never even knew such beautiful clothes *existed*. What kind of fabric is this?" she asked, running a finger along a mauve gown.

"Silk charmeuse," Madame Chastain said with pride. "It has fluid sophistication and a buttery texture that makes it drape beautifully."

"It *does* feel buttery!" Annabelle laughed. "Gray, come feel this."

"I'm not touching buttery fabric."

The wife gathered up a handful of the mauve fabric. "Here," she said, gently stroking Annabelle's cheek with it. "This is the only way to truly appreciate silk charmeuse. We can make such a gown for you. It will look so much nicer than this terrible —"

The Frenchwoman stumbled into mortified silence at the blunder. Annabelle's beige twill gown looked like a potato sack next to the spectacular array of gowns. A part of

109

Gray wanted to leap to her defense, but it didn't look like Annabelle was offended. If anything, she seemed amused by the Frenchwoman's slip.

"Here comes the true test of your diplomacy," Annabelle joked, her dark eyes sparkling with humor.

Madam Chastain looked mortified. "I did not mean to imply . . ." she stammered. "Your dress is fine. It is quite well made."

"It's plain," Annabelle said, then gave Madame Chastain a friendly hug. "Please don't feel bad. Not everyone should wear silk charmeuse. I choose dresses that are good for walking across town or a tromp through the woods. But you should be very proud of these beautiful gowns. What an artist you are!"

Gray watched the exchange with fascination. There wasn't an ounce of guile on Annabelle's face. She meant every word she said, and he adored her for it. This was a woman with brains and kindness and a bottomless well of humor. He wanted to court her, not haggle with Caroline's dressmakers.

"You can bring the other box back in," he said gruffly. "I'll pay for it." He didn't want to say *underwear* in front of Annabelle. It was embarrassing enough to have a sister

110

who squandered a fortune on fripperies, let alone mention such intimate items in front of Annabelle. He asked Otis to write a check for the entire invoice. Anything to get the dressmakers on their way.

Monsieur Chastain was effusive in his gratitude as he accepted the bank note. "It is an honor to dress a lady for the White House. Should Miss Caroline need any additional —"

"She won't," Gray said as he ushered the pair toward the door.

"It is still an honor that our clothes shall grace the president's home. Please convey our gratitude."

The door closed behind the dressmakers, and he was alone with Annabelle.

"Your sister visits the White House?" she asked, her eyes as disbelieving as if Caroline visited the moon.

"She works for the first lady. She is a 'social secretary,' whatever that means."

"It sounds very impressive."

"I find *your* sister more impressive," he said honestly. "Your sister has a perfect excuse for never lifting a finger, and yet she moved across the country to volunteer her time in a meaningful endeavor. I fear that Caroline cares for nothing but parties and fancy clothes. I told her about you and Elaine."

"You did?"

How could he not? He'd been preoccupied by thoughts of Annabelle from the moment she walked into his house with that ridiculous spice map, but he didn't want to speak of his frustration with the beautiful, frivolous Caroline.

"Come on back to the kitchen. I've made something for you."

His nerves started getting to him. What a stupid idea to try to impress her with a spicy fruit punch instead of the safe option of a simple cup of tea.

"It smells good in here," Annabelle said as she joined him in the kitchen.

It was a narrow room with a stove and shelving on one side and a small dining table on the other. The carafe of spice-infused citrus punch sat in the bucket of ice on the back counter. He poured her a tall glass over ice and watched carefully as she took her first sip. Her eyes widened, her brows rose. She took another sip and looked as if she wanted to levitate.

"Oh my heavens. Does your company sell this?"

"No. I never thought of such a thing." Selling small bottles of spice was easier than

112

the hassle of brewing and bottling, but it pleased him that she had capitalist tendencies hidden beneath her instinct to give things away for free. "It's an interesting idea, though. I've moved into bottling with the vanilla extract. Perhaps there is potential in spiced fruit drinks. If there's enough profit, I'll consider it."

"I think it's wonderful that your sister gets to work in the White House," Annabelle said as she settled herself at the dining table.

"*Gets* to work in the White House?" he asked skeptically.

"Yes, gets!" Her face glowed. "When I was a girl, I had a picture book about Washington and all its iconic buildings, like the Capitol and the White House. It told stories about the founding fathers and the risky years building the nation. It awakened something in me. I remember wanting to grow up and do something really great. I lived in Kansas, so I figured that meant raising a bumper crop of wheat." She dissolved into laughter, but he loved watching her unabashed optimism.

"And now?" he asked.

"Now I'm actually *here* and get to see those buildings almost every day. They're more magnificent in person than in the books. Being here makes me proud to be an

American."

She was so innocent and wonderfully naïve, but it was part of her wholesome charm. "Have you had a chance to see all the places in your picture book?"

"All except Mount Vernon."

He could remedy that. "It's not far. Mount Vernon hosts an annual celebration on the Fourth of July," he said. "There will be a brass band and fireworks in the evening. I would be happy to escort you and your sister."

"You'd do that for us?"

He'd bring her pearls from the bottom of the ocean if she wanted them. "I would be honored to spend the day with the Larkin sisters."

She stayed for hours while they finished the last of the spiced fruit punch, and it was the most delightful afternoon in his memory. Courting a woman couldn't be this easy. Could it?

He silenced the warning bell in the back of his mind, for surely Annabelle was exactly what she appeared to be. At last he felt like he was coming home to something wonderful.

NINE

Annabelle was surprised to be summoned to Dr. Norwood's office first thing on Monday morning. She hadn't spoken to him since the day she'd given him the rare orchid from Windover Landing. In failing to locate the elusive original vanilla orchid, she'd lost her best shot at securing a permanent position here, but was it possible Dr. Norwood had found another opportunity for her?

Dr. Norwood's secretary looked up from her desk when Annabelle entered the waiting room outside the director's office. "Good, you're here," Miss Abernathy said. "No need to sit down. Both generals are already here, and they want to see you at once."

Generals? Before Annabelle could process that odd remark, the secretary rapped on the closed door of Dr. Norwood's office and cracked it open.

"Miss Larkin is here, sir."

Annabelle was shown inside, bewildered to see two men in uniform rise to their feet as she entered. Dr. Norwood looked nervous as he introduced her to General Molinaro, a grim-faced man who nodded to her from a shadowy corner. The other man was General Cornell, whose grandfatherly appearance and kindly smile made it easy to overlook his intimidating title. They both looked out of place here. Military spit and polish didn't belong amidst an explosion of orchids, fossils, and books.

"Close the door, please," Dr. Norwood instructed the secretary, whose curiosity seemed boundless as she slowly closed the door, peering through the narrowing gap the entire time.

The shadowy general spoke softly. "Is your secretary an eavesdropper?"

Dr. Norwood looked insulted. "Miss Abernathy has worked for this institution for thirty-five years."

"She's also nosy, and this is a private conversation," General Molinaro said as he emerged from the shadows and crossed the room to yank open the door. "Miss Abernathy, please take your lunch break now."

"But it's nine thirty in the morning," the secretary sputtered.

"Then an early tea. Either way, please vacate the office."

Annabelle's unease grew as she watched Miss Abernathy collect a handbag, shoot the general a chilly glare, then slam the door on her way out of the reception area. General Molinaro strode out and locked the reception area door before returning to his shadowy corner in Dr. Norwood's office.

"Please, have a seat," General Cornell said kindly.

She didn't trust him. She didn't understand why she'd been summoned here, and she looked to Dr. Norwood for direction. For once the elderly man paid no attention to his orchids and only looked at her in tense expectation.

"Thank you for joining us," Dr. Norwood said after she sat in one of the old leather chairs opposite his desk. "I could not help noticing your association with Gray Delacroix has continued, even after learning he does not possess the rare vanilla orchid we hoped for."

Was that a crime? "Yes," she admitted. "We are friends."

"What sort of friends?" the shadowy general asked.

"I don't think that's any of your business." She might look and sound like a hayseed,

117

but these men had no right to probe into her private life.

General Cornell held up a hand as if to pacify her. "Forgive our bluntness," he said. "A matter of national importance has come to our attention. Before we begin the discussion, I need your assurance that this conversation will go no further than the walls of this office."

"I can't promise you anything," she said. "I don't understand what you're asking of me."

General Cornell casually lit a pipe, the sweet scent of tobacco filling the room. "Then let me explain. It has come to our attention that Gray Delacroix holds highly critical views of the American government."

That was an understatement. "He's no fan of the Department of Agriculture, that's for sure."

General Cornell drew on his pipe with a hint of amusement in his eyes. "What have the farmers and bean counters over at the ag department done to rouse his ire?"

"He believes the government is giving valuable information away for free, and he resents it. He is completely irrational about it, but it's harmless."

The shadowy general leaned forward. "What if you learned it wasn't harmless?

118

That thousands of American lives might be in danger because of Mr. Delacroix's views?"

"Because he doesn't like the Department of Agriculture?" She felt silly even saying such a thing.

General Cornell set down his pipe, and he wasn't smiling anymore. "Miss Larkin, I must ask for your complete confidentiality. What we are about to say may not leave this room, and you can be held accountable if it leaks. Especially if it leaks to Mr. Delacroix."

She stood. "Then maybe I should leave now."

Dr. Norwood moved to block the door. "Don't be hasty," he said. "We need your help. If you cooperate with the government, I am certain a permanent and well-compensated position can be found for you here in Washington. General Molinaro is correct. I am very much afraid this issue puts thousands of American lives at risk, and we need your help."

She sat back down. Were they playing a joke on her? What could a specialist in cereal grasses do to save lives? General Cornell's scrutiny made her uncomfortable, and suddenly it felt very chilly in here.

"Aside from his hostility to the Department of Agriculture, have you heard Mr. Delacroix make other statements hostile to the American government?" the general asked.

"Sometimes," she admitted. Actually, he'd said a lot. Dating all the way back to his childhood, when Union troops destroyed his ancestral home.

A quick glance was exchanged between the two generals. "Tell us more."

"Not until you tell me what's going on," she replied. "This entire conversation is alarming."

"Fair enough," General Cornell said grimly. "We have reason to believe Mr. Delacroix is tightly involved with a group of insurgents fomenting rebellion against the American occupation in Cuba. Last month a rebel leader in Havana was arrested, and his house was searched. Among the man's papers were the address of Mr. Delacroix's home in Alexandria as well as that of his business holdings in Fairfax County. The rebel leader had received payments issued from Mr. Delacroix's bank in Alexandria. All this leads us to believe he is funneling money, information, and support to the Cuban insurgency."

Her mouth dropped open. This couldn't be true. "I don't believe it," she stammered, but even as she spoke, misgivings arose. Gray had mentioned his fierce opposition to the Spanish-American War and his dislike of the president. Would it run so deep that he would actively engage with the enemy?

"Delacroix has spent too many years abroad," General Cornell continued. "He's no longer loyal to the United States. His sister has secured a position in the White House, and she may be part of the plot as well. We have been monitoring telegrams sent to his Alexandria townhouse that make it obvious he is in communication with members of the Cuban insurgency. Gray Delacroix is notoriously reclusive, but he has allowed you unprecedented access to his home. We need you to look for the names of his contacts in Cuba."

While she sat in stunned disbelief, General Cornell relayed how they'd been watching Gray and noticed his newfound relationship with Annabelle. The army had approached Dr. Norwood for his help in recruiting Annabelle to the investigation.

"If you help us, you will be rewarded," Dr. Norwood said. "Even if you are unsuccessful, we need you to scour his library and his desk for the names of the insurgents. The army has offered funding to create a permanent position for you here at the Smithsonian."

"Do you think I would spy for a *job*?" she cried out. "Why don't you just offer me thirty pieces of silver?"

General Molinaro stepped out of the shadows. "We expect you to help because you are a loyal American. We have thousands of troops stationed in Cuba, and even more in the Philippines. Momentum is gathering behind the insurgents in Cuba who agitate for the withdrawal of American troops. Malcontents like Delacroix are throwing oil on the fire."

She sat plastered in her chair, barely able to think or even breathe. Her hands felt icy, and she clenched them together to stop the shaking. "I'm a botanist," she stammered. "I specialize in wheat and barley. If necessary, I know a little about millet. I'm not a spy."

"All we need you to do is get inside his study and see if you can find the names of his contacts in Cuba," General Molinaro said.

"And what if I don't find anything?"

The two generals glanced at each other, then the grandfatherly one sent her a reassuring smile. "In that case, you will have helped clear an innocent man's name. And a permanent job at the Smithsonian will still be forthcoming, so long as you give it your best shot."

Dr. Norwood looked haggard as he leaned toward her. "My grandson is in Cuba," he said. "He is helping rebuild the water and irrigation systems that were destroyed during the war. No one wants a rebellion. Thousands of lives, both American and Cuban, will be at risk if that happens."

She turned away from the burning appeal in his eyes. She wasn't the right person for this. She didn't have the heart or cunning for this sort of work. Her gaze trailed to a framed photograph of Dr. Norwood and a young man wearing the uniform of the Army Corps of Engineers. It hurt to look at the young man's wholesome, smiling face.

Gray was an obsessively private man, but he had been open with her. It was unlikely the government could find anyone else with such access. Maybe there was an innocent explanation for all this. Gray could have been engaged in harmless business correspondence with Cuban planters who had somehow gotten mixed up in an insurgency. That didn't mean Gray had anything to do with it; she might even be able to exonerate him. She could *probably* exonerate him, for surely this was all a terrible misunderstanding.

But if Gray was guilty, he needed to be stopped.

Her entire body felt heavy as she turned her attention back to the generals. "Tell me what you need me to do."

TEN

Ever since resolving to send Luke to Cuba, Gray had been racked with a gnawing sense of doubt. Which was ridiculous. It wasn't as if he were sending Luke into the unexplored jungles of Asia or the frozen Arctic. He was sending Luke to Cuba to meet with a few planters and finally start contributing to the family coffers.

Caroline didn't try to hide her annoyance as she accompanied Gray to the port to bid Luke farewell. The early morning air was damp as they walked toward the harbor, but Caroline's tone was briskly awake.

"Luke has been doing quite well as a journalist," she said. "If you could lift your head out of the financial ledgers and read what he's published, you might actually be impressed."

"And has he been paid for any of those publications?"

"That's not how it works. He writes for

125

love, not money."

Gray held his tongue. Caroline wore one of her spectacular new gowns, a royal blue confection that looked impossible to breathe in. The yearly stipend she earned from being Mrs. McKinley's social secretary wouldn't have paid for even half the gowns she'd bought, so Caroline was in no position to lecture him about money.

"I don't want to argue about Luke," he said. "This is the last time the three of us will be together for a while. Can we please have a cup of tea without sniping at each other?"

Caroline raised a finely arched eyebrow. "That's entirely up to you. Luke and I never snipe."

The statement was unsettling, mostly because it was true. Luke and Caroline were naturally buoyant people; he was the gloomy one.

It was a windy morning, and the waves were capped with white foam as gulls wheeled in the sky. He shaded his eyes to peer across the jetty, looking for Luke. A few sailors lugged their packs, stevedores operated cranes to load cargo, and passengers mingled on the pier, waiting to board.

No sign of Luke. Gray's temper began to

heat. He'd dragged Luke out of bed an hour before sunrise and sent him ahead to register a crate of spices for export, but there were half a dozen taverns lining the docks, and if Luke had found his way into one of them —

"There he is." Caroline laughed and sprang ahead toward the jetty.

Sure enough, Luke sat on a stack of coiled rope, playing jacks with a couple of ragged children. To Gray's surprise, Philip Ransom, Luke's old college roommate from the Naval Academy, stood alongside, casually watching the game. Luke had seen Gray and Caroline approaching but did a good job of ignoring them as he tossed the ball and was uncharacteristically clumsy while scooping up jacks. Both boys leapt into the air and cheered, and Luke reached into his pocket and turned over a few bills.

"You've cleaned me out, boys," Luke said with a rueful smile before he and Philip began strolling to greet them.

"Morning, Gray," Luke said. "Can you spare a few bucks? I just lost my last five dollars to Eddie and Dan."

"You lost five dollars before eight o'clock in the morning?" Gray couldn't mask the displeasure from his voice.

"*Look* at them, Gray," Luke said in an

impatient voice.

Gray didn't need to look; he'd seen the bare feet and filthy clothes. Those boys should be in school or helping their parents, not loitering on a dock.

"I've got something," Caroline said as she opened her reticule.

Luke burst into laughter as he reached out to close Caroline's bag. "I've got plenty of money. I just wanted to see what Mr. Sunshine would say."

Gray's ire faded. Luke had always known how to get beneath his skin, and losing a game of jacks to a pair of waifs wasn't necessarily a bad thing.

He nodded a polite greeting to Lieutenant Ransom, then pulled Luke aside. "Let's go for a walk," he said casually. He needed to impart some important information and didn't want Caroline or Luke's old college friend in on the conversation.

Their footsteps thudded on the wharf as they walked toward the customs house.

"Luke, I want you to forget what happened four years ago. It was an unfortunate incident, but it shouldn't cripple you for the rest of your life."

"Easy for you to say."

"Perhaps, but it's also true. Neither Dad nor I blamed you for what happened with the Magruders."

Luke chewed on a toothpick as he glowered out at the horizon. "I really hate Clyde Magruder," he said. "I heard he got his children's nanny pregnant, then accused her of theft so she would run away before his wife found out. He's a vile piece of work."

That went without saying. The Magruders were their biggest rival in the food industry and wealthy beyond all imagination. Clyde could have paid the nanny off, but a pregnant mistress could be a problem in his pending run for Congress in November. All the Magruders were mean, underhanded men of business, but Clyde plastered it over with a sheen of oily charm.

"Don't worry about Clyde Magruder," Gray said. "Just go to Cuba and get those contracts finalized."

"I *always* worry about the Magruders," Luke said tightly, but then a hint of mischief flashed across his face. He lowered his voice and spoke conspiratorially. "Look, I think I've found a way to finally get the upper hand on them."

"How about landing those Cuban contracts? That would be a start."

Luke tossed the toothpick away and straightened. "Yeah, I can do that, but I've still got a plan for the Magruders. I'll let

129

you know about it once I get back." He glanced over his shoulder at Caroline and Philip Ransom, who were tossing breadcrumbs to the ducks. "You're not off base when you say I've been a little shiftless, but you're dead wrong about Caroline. You have no idea what she's been up against inside the White House because you've never asked her about it, you just keep grousing about the president."

Gray gave a curt nod of acknowledgment as they headed back to have a farewell breakfast at one of the port taverns. Both Caroline and Luke mercilessly teased Philip over his dreary job cataloging maps in the basement of the War Department.

"The moment you send up a distress call, we shall race to the rescue," Caroline assured Philip. "You're starting to look pale. Doesn't he look pale, Luke? We must devise a way to liberate him from the dungeon."

Philip was no match for Caroline, blushing furiously at her teasing. "It's where the cartography division is. I'm destined for the life of an underground mole."

"Meanwhile I'm off to Cuba for the rum, cigars, and tropical sunsets," Luke quipped. "I think I got the better deal."

They escorted Luke to the gangway to say their final farewells. Caroline's tight corset didn't stop her from leaping into Luke's arms for an embrace. He lifted her from the ground and twirled her in a circle, then gave a back-pounding hug to his old college roommate. Gray managed a smile and held out his hand, but Luke knocked it aside and gave him a solid embrace instead. Gray returned it.

Philip needed to return to his dull job in the cartography office, but Gray and Caroline stayed to wave the ship off. Even after the steamship gave two long blasts of its horn as it pulled out of port, he and Caroline remained to watch it sail toward the horizon.

Luke's parting words lingered in Gray's mind. It was true that whenever Caroline's new job came up, he grumbled about the McKinley administration instead of inquiring about her actual work, and he needed to do better. Once the ship was out to sea, he escorted his sister back to their carriage and began driving her to the White House.

"What is on your schedule for today?" he asked as they turned onto K Street.

"A women's group from Indiana is visiting to ask the first lady to endorse a school for orphans. Then I will host a tea for them, since Mrs. McKinley isn't comfortable with such duties. After the tea, I'll open and sort through her mail. The president is very protective of his wife and asked me to screen all her mail so she sees nothing upsetting. Then she and I will visit the Naval Hospital on Ninth Street so she may welcome newly arrived servicemen from the Philippines."

Normally at this point Gray would interrupt to vent over the American invasion in the Philippines, but he bit his tongue, for visiting the hospital was admirable work.

"The seating chart for the Supreme Court dinner needs to be decided today," she continued. "We also need to finalize plans for a trip to Baltimore so the first lady may visit a lace-making factory. Given her precarious health, a trip like that requires a lot of planning."

As Caroline continued outlining her day, Gray was forced to conclude that Luke was right and he was wrong. He drew the carriage to a halt before the White House, and Caroline sprang to the ground with an abundance of energy. He tossed the reins over a hitching post so he could intercept her before she got far.

He opened his mouth to speak but was struck unexpectedly mute. He wasn't good at compliments, and where Caroline was concerned, he'd always been stingy with them.

He clasped her hands and met her eyes. "Dad would be proud of you," he managed to stammer. "I am too."

Her blue eyes grew wide, and she looked unexpectedly moved. "Thank you for that," she said. "I know your political leanings, and I know this isn't what you would have wished for me —"

"Shh," he said. "You're doing good work. And you're making your own way in life. That's all I could ever ask for."

She kissed him on the cheek, then turned to walk into the north entrance of the building. As he walked back to the carriage, he gazed at the shockingly blue sky overhead.

"Thank you," he whispered.

He had never been much of a praying man, but God had blessed him with the foundation of a strong family. Luke and Caroline were both on their way to becoming admirable, successful people, and for the first time in a decade, Gray truly believed everything was going to be all right.

ELEVEN

Annabelle wrestled with how best to approach Gray to gain access to his house, but finally she simply opened the negotiation the same way they'd first met. Through a letter.

Gray,

My work at the Smithsonian will be light for the next week until a delivery of moss from Australia arrives. While I await the moss with bated breath, I hope to take advantage of the unexpected freedom to explore your extensive library of herb and spice lore. May I visit?

Annabelle

She was at her bench in the workroom, carefully emptying the contents of a seed pod from some Australian eucalyptus, when a messenger arrived with a reply from Gray.

Annabelle,

Come to my bottling factory. I want to show you what I'm working on. Come quickly. It won't last long.

Gray

Postscript: In the interest of full disclosure, I confess an embarrassing desire simply to see you again. I miss your smile.

The sweet message pricked her conscience. Everything about her deceitful motives felt wrong, but she needed to stop thinking of this as spying. Her mission was to exonerate Gray. She didn't believe he was a traitor, but the government did.

The address of his bottling factory was at the bottom of the letter. The generals had told her that the most likely place to find evidence of espionage was in Gray's townhouse, but how could she decline this invitation? He was eager and wanted to share his work with her.

An ache twisted her abdomen, and she curled over in her chair. She drew a ragged breath and prayed for guidance. A moral person had an obligation to protect her country and thousands of people. How dare she let her growing affection for a man interfere with that? It made her ill, but she knew what she had to do.

"Mr. Delacroix wants to know if you can come now," the messenger boy said. "If you can't, I've got another letter I'm supposed to give you."

"You can't," Mr. Bittles said from across the room. "I want those seed pods cataloged by the end of the day. I'm allergic to eucalyptus oil, so I'm not touching them."

But all Annabelle could see was the edge of the second letter peeking out from the boy's coat pocket, and it was irresistible. "Let me see that other letter," she said, and the boy handed it over.

Annabelle,
Quit being such a rule follower. The Smithsonian will survive if you play hooky for an afternoon. What I have to show you will not.

Gray

Now she was dying of curiosity, and Dr. Norwood had granted her all the time she needed where Gray Delacroix was concerned. She stood and tipped the remainder of the seeds into an envelope, then returned them to the box of eucalyptus samples.

"I'm going on an errand for Dr. Nor-

136

wood," she told Mr. Bittles. "I don't know when I'll be back."

Her nerves were stretched tight the entire journey to the factory. Everything about this felt wrong. She wasn't a woman of tremendous valor or daring heroism, but she'd always tried to lead her life in a way that would honor Jesus through small acts of goodness every day. Hour by hour, brick by brick, these small choices had slowly built a life of integrity. How could she reconcile that view of her world while betraying Gray's trust?

At the end of her life, she wanted to know she had made a difference for the better, and that meant she couldn't avert her eyes while treason or sabotage found a foothold. She couldn't overlook it because of her affection for a single man. All she could do was use her best judgment and pray.

The sooner she began this awful task, the sooner she could exonerate Gray and move forward with her life.

Gray sat at his factory office desk, forehead in his hands as he tried to will the pain away. He should have known he was in trouble as soon as he awoke this morning, but he'd assumed it was a simple headache as he set off for the ten-minute carriage ride to the spice factory.

This wasn't a simple headache. This was a malaria relapse, but with luck it wouldn't be too bad for at least another day. He'd already taken a dose of quinine and a swig of iodine for good measure, so he ought to be able to get through the day.

He straightened to gaze into the factory through the window in his office door. He wanted more than to "get through the day." He wanted to show his magnificent production facility to Annabelle, possibly the only woman of his acquaintance who would appreciate the dovetailing of science, botany, and culinary usefulness. He wanted to show her their technique for creating vanilla extract, even though he knew she might take that information straight back to the Smithsonian. He didn't care. He just wanted to spend time with her and savor the way she made him feel.

He walked onto the production floor, stepping carefully so as not to awaken the pounding in his head. The scent of herbs surrounded him. Workers at the nearby tables labeled bottles of thyme and bay laurel while the drying ovens at the far end of the factory were being prepared for the next batch of cumin seeds.

"Jacob, can we get this floor swept?" he

asked one of his employees.

Jacob set down a rack of thyme bottles. "It's just herb grit, nothing dirty."

"It looks messy. We've got a visitor coming, so please sweep it up."

Jacob nodded and went for a broom. Normally they didn't sweep until the end of the day, but Annabelle should see the factory at its best.

Their facility was spotlessly clean, with dozens of tables covered by a sheet-metal alloy to ensure near-sterile conditions. The painted concrete floor was swept and mopped with a disinfecting solution daily. Huge windows let in plenty of light, which was good, because the factory floor was an entire acre, and it would be gloomy without natural light.

Jacob had just finished sweeping when a carriage arrived outside. Gray grinned and jogged toward the door. The pain that roared to life in his head forced him to slow down, but he still smiled like an idiot as he helped Annabelle alight from the carriage.

"You look spectacular," he said. The loose bun in her hair allowed tendrils to dangle and float around her face, but it was her smile — *that smile* — that captured him. It lit up her entire face, and he could have stood there and admired it all day.

"I can't wait to see your factory," she said. "This is where all the famous Delacroix spices get bottled?"

"Right here," he said, holding an arm out to lead her into the factory.

He loved the way she gaped at the stainless-steel spice mills, for they were twelve feet tall with automated grinders for pulverizing material fed in through the hopper. He stopped at each mill, letting the operator explain the unique features of the various machines they used. Some were customized for lumpy plants, while others were designed for seed. The hammer mills used rotating weights to pulverize dry spices like cinnamon, coriander, cloves, and allspice. Calibrated machines produced the exact particle size for each spice in a reliable, consistent fashion, while high-oil spices like mace and nutmeg needed to be processed by a roller mill.

Annabelle asked all the right questions, but the noise from the hammer mill was ratcheting Gray's headache up to unbearable levels. A trickle of sweat rolled down his back, and he wasn't sure if it was from the drying ovens or if his fever was on the rise. He should have doubled his dose of iodine that morning.

"Let me show you the vanilla," he said

over the din. "It's done in a separate building out back." Anything to get away from the heat and noise.

"You have a whole building just for vanilla?" she asked.

He nodded. "Vanilla is very delicate. It can't be exposed to heat once the processing begins. We just added the pods this morning, so you can catch a glimpse of this early stage."

He breathed a sigh of relief as they left the main factory and headed to the brick building behind it. This facility was the last project he and his father had completed together. It was their finest accomplishment, both a scientific and a commercial marvel. It looked like a plain brick building on the outside, but as they stepped inside, the pair of five-hundred-gallon gleaming steel vats dominated the view. There was no one inside, for once the process had begun, vanilla distillation required little attention.

He glanced at Annabelle to gauge her reaction, but her eyes were closed and she looked in ecstasy. Her hand was over her heart as she breathed deeply.

"I think I can die happy now," she said. He was used to the aroma but loved watching Annabelle experience it for the first time. The smooth, luscious scent was flowery, sweet, and a little milky. It was possibly the most universally beloved scent in the world.

"We developed a cold extraction process," he explained. "Most vanilla extract is made by heating the pods, which means it only takes four or five days. Vanilla has a complex bouquet of flavors, and heat will kill off most of them, leaving a one-dimensional taste. My cold process takes almost a month, but you can smell and taste the difference."

A small crate of vanilla beans sat on the worktable. They arrived from Madagascar in a dried state, looking brown, shriveled, and a little oily. He used a blade to slice a bean down the center, then grabbed a butter knife to scrape out the seeds.

"Give me your hand," he said, then spread the grainy paste on her fingertip.

She looked delighted as she touched, smelled, and scrutinized the oily seeds. "Can I taste it?"

"Please," he said with pride. "The grains are only a piece of the flavor. I'll show you how we prepare the mash."

He chopped the skin of the vanilla pod into one-inch sections, then added it to the paste. "We prepare several pounds of vanilla pods just like this. Scrape out the seeds, chop the skins, then add it to a screen. We use a cold infusion of water and alcohol to continually bathe the mash. That's what's going on in those tanks behind you. A pump is circulating the liquid through the mash, and over time it absorbs the flavor."

"It sounds like a coffee percolator."

He smiled. "It's exactly like a coffee percolator, but with cold water instead of hot. It would be faster if we heated the water, but it would destroy what makes our extract so fine."

"I'll bet you charge a lot for it."

"It's the best. Of course I charge a lot for it."

"Do you have this process written down anywhere?"

His headache started to pound. "No. And if I did, I wouldn't give it to you."

"You don't have to sound so gruff," she said. "I was merely curious."

Other people took shortcuts. Heating vanilla pods was one way to reduce costs, and of course, the Magruders avoided the hassle of dealing with vanilla pods altogether by using chemicals instead. Thinking about the Magruders made his head hurt even worse, and he pushed the thoughts away.

"Can I see the rest of your facility?" Annabelle asked.

It was a strange question. The vanilla distillery was the only unique operation he had. He'd wanted to show it to her as a sign of trust, but she didn't seem all that interested. Instead she was looking out the windows at the main factory and the storage sheds.

"You already saw the spice bottling. There's not much else to see."

"But there were some rooms near the front of the factory. And the sheds. What's in there?"

"Follow me." He ushered her outside and toward the first shed, hauling the sliding door open. "Wagons," he said shortly. He dragged the door shut and went to the next, opening both double doors so she could look to her heart's content, because the cold-press extraction of vanilla obviously didn't excite her. "Hardware, cleaning supplies, and a roller mill in need of repair. Come on, let's go see the rest of the main factory."

"I'm sorry. I didn't mean to offend you."

He didn't break stride. "Come along. You wanted to see everything, so I'm showing you."

He blotted his forehead with a handkerchief. It was a warm day, but this sweating had nothing to do with the weather. All the symptoms were roaring to life — the muscle aches, the violent headache, and now a ringing in his ears that made it hard to hear.

He moved quickly, striding ahead of Annabelle so he could get to his office first. She scurried behind him but couldn't keep up. The second he was in his office, he reached for the bottle of iodine and stole a quick swig, wincing at the metallic taste that scorched its way down his throat. It was so revolting it threatened to come back up, but Gray forced it down, holding his breath until the nausea passed.

The bottle was still clutched in his hand when Annabelle entered the office. He slipped the bottle into a drawer and slid it shut, wincing at the noise. She said something, but he couldn't understand.

He had to get ahold of himself. It wasn't her fault he was sick or that she wasn't impressed with a cold-extraction process for vanilla. He forced himself to be calm and turned to face her.

"I didn't hear what you said. Can you repeat it?"

"Is it the malaria?" she asked. He could barely hear her through the ringing in his ears.

He nodded. "I'm sorry. It's coming on fast."

He lowered himself into his desk chair, wondering how this day had collapsed so quickly but fairly certain it was all his fault. He gestured to the chair before his desk. "Have a seat. Please."

She looked hesitant, which was odd for the fearless Annabelle.

He managed a smile and spoke softly. "I promise not to bite your head off."

She sat, but her face was still closed and cautious.

"I first contracted malaria in Ceylon. I've always known that I would have to live with it for the rest of my life, but I can't predict when the relapses will happen. I've been trying to find a cure, or at least something to make these episodes more bearable."

He opened the drawer and took out the iodine, setting it on the desk before her. Then the bottle of quinine. Then the bottles of cinchonidine, feverfew, and valerian root. He'd tried them all but found only limited relief.

"I've been looking for a cure for years, but ever since I met you, it's gotten more important. I know I get bad-tempered. I'm sorry for how short I was with you in our first letters, and I'm sorry for today. The pain is real, and it's bad, and it's bound to come back again and again, so I apologize in advance." He was losing his energy, but he raised his eyes to her and spoke straight from the heart. "Annabelle, I'm so sorry."

Her eyes were sad as she picked up the bottle of iodine. "You actually *drink* this?" she asked in a horrified voice.

"I wouldn't recommend it," he said dryly. "It tastes awful, it gives me cramps, and the ringing in my ears is so loud I can barely hear what you're saying. But, Annabelle . . . I need to get better. I know a ship captain who drinks iodine, and he swears it helps."

"Have you ever heard a doctor say that?"

A gulp of laughter escaped, making his head hurt. "No," he admitted. "My doctor warned me against it."

"But you drink it anyway."

He sighed. Annabelle was vibrant and healthy; she probably had no idea what pain could drive a man to do. His head hurt so badly he could barely see straight, and the ringing in his ears would make it impossible to sleep tonight. "I don't think it's going to help, but I had to try. Annabelle . . . I don't want to risk losing you over this."

For some reason that seemed to upset her. "Don't kill yourself for me. I'm not worth it."

"I disagree." Their friendship had flared quickly, but maybe he needed to let her see this angry, difficult side of himself, because he wanted to be completely open and honest with her. Such a thing didn't come naturally to him, but he could learn. He wanted her too badly to fail.

"Maybe you should go home and rest," she said gently. "The factory will keep running even if you aren't here. You should be in bed."

"I couldn't get out of bed for two weeks the first time I got clobbered with malaria, but I've worked through every relapse since."

"Why?"

His answer was matter-of-fact. "Because that's what a man does. I have a business to run. I've got forty employees and a family to support."

Her eyes looked pained with sympathy as she shook her head. "You have a ridiculously successful company. The wheels will keep turning even if you aren't here for a few days. And if you go home and rest, maybe you won't feel so compelled to imbibe dangerous home remedies overheard from ship captains. Stay in bed for a few days. Relax. Read a good book."

He snorted. "The only books I read are

trade manuals and science reports."

"No novels?"

"I don't have time for fairy tales or make-believe."

"Oh, Gray." He loved the way she said his name, a combination of exasperation and fondness. "I think it's time for you to get lost in the world of Charles Dickens. Or perhaps Jane Austen. I could bring you a copy."

"I don't read girly literature." He threw it out as a deliberate provocation, just to see how she would respond. She took the bait and came alive.

"Jane Austen is a master of social satire," she said. "Her novels are a salvo against the pompous egos of her age."

"And you think I could benefit from her instruction?"

A fascinating array of emotions crossed her face. She opened and closed her mouth several times before looking at him again. A gorgeous flush bloomed across her cheeks.

"I hate to admit it," she said, "but I think Jane Austen might cast you as a hero in one of her novels, much like a Mr. Darcy or a Colonel Brandon. Jane Austen loved her serious, sober men."

He fought to keep his face immobile. "She sounds like a font of wisdom and should be

149

required reading for all our youth. Perhaps starting with my brother and sister."

Her laughter was like a pure, clear waterfall. Before long she was summarizing a novel featuring the long-suffering Colonel Brandon, who sounded like a bit of a bore to Gray, but he didn't care. He loved listening to her. He leaned back in his chair to watch her through half-closed eyes and wallowed in her soothing voice. She was better than any medicinal tonic. What was it about her that kept him so captivated? A few minutes ago he was racked with pain and surly to the world. Now he was completely pacified, total putty in her hands while she rambled about Jane Austen. The pain was still there, but he didn't mind it so much anymore.

He only minded that he hadn't been much use to her. She teetered on the edge of collapse if she couldn't secure her position at the Smithsonian, and he desperately wanted to help her.

"How is the quest for a permanent position at the Smithsonian?" he asked gently and was sorry to see her sag a little.

"Not so good. I'm still on the hunt for something to make myself indispensable."

He curled his hands around the arm of his chair, debating his options. He didn't want her to go back to Kansas. He wanted to step up his courtship of her. If all went well, he could easily provide for her and Elaine both, but it wasn't his nature to be impulsive.

He could still help her, though.

"Come to my townhouse in Alexandria," he said. "You asked about seeing my library. My father amassed an impressive collection of botanical observations gathered over forty years. You can have free rein, although I'll warn you, it is a mess. Dad crammed all his papers into boxes and binders. He was also a packrat, so there's a lot to go through."

Her eyes widened in surprise and something else. Trepidation? He smiled. His study wasn't *that* terrifying.

"You'll really let me explore your study?" she asked, and he had the strangest feeling she hoped he would say no.

"Of course. The study will be entirely yours. I won't need it, as I plan on taking your advice. Actually, taking my *doctor's* advice. Every doctor I've ever consulted has recommended the same thing."

"And what is that?"

"Bedrest. And a little quinine if I can tolerate it." He got his feet beneath him and managed to stand. "I'll ask the foreman to summon a carriage. You can come with me

151

to the townhouse today if you like, or come any time this week. I've had enough of these attacks to know I'll be laid low for around five days. You can have complete run of the rest of my house."

She walked around his desk and slipped an arm around his middle. He was capable of walking without help, but he loved that she offered it.

"I'll come home with you," she said. "I'd like to get started today."

He had the oddest feeling she was about to cry.

TWELVE

In the end, Annabelle couldn't do it. By the time the carriage arrived at Gray's townhouse, there was only an hour before she needed to escort Elaine home, and she seized on the excuse to delay the inevitable task of spying.

It meant that she arrived at the Library of Congress with plenty of time to spare, so she headed upstairs to the blind reading room, where two actors were performing a reading from a Shakespeare play. She spotted Elaine, who looked entranced while listening to the actors perform the classic banter of Benedick and Beatrice from *Much Ado About Nothing.*

Close to a hundred people, both blind and sighted, had gathered to listen to the performance. From the back of the room, Annabelle had a good view of Elaine. It had been years since she'd seen her sister look this happy. As the actors came to the end of the

153

reading, the crowd showered them with applause, and Annabelle wended her way toward Elaine, who was taken aback by the sound of her voice.

"Annabelle! I didn't expect you up here."

"My work finished early."

Elaine was strangely flustered as she adjusted the cuffs at her wrists. "Oh. Well! I'd like to introduce you to some people. This is Harry Talbot, the soldier I've told you so much about. And this . . ." She fumbled, and an older man grasped her hand. "This is Walter, his father. And Margaret and Sally, his sisters. The Talbots always come for the Tuesday readings. The actors are from the National Theatre company, so it's a real treat."

"I can see that. And it's very nice to meet you all," Annabelle said with a nod to the father.

Apparently the Talbots were a large family, for in addition to his daughters, Mr. Talbot introduced her to an assortment of cousins and uncles who'd also come to the performance.

"Are there always so many people?" Annabelle asked as she and Elaine settled onto the streetcar bench for the ride home.

"We're like a family there," Elaine said. "I thank God for the gift of being able to find meaningful work. They've asked me to take on another student, but I'll keep working with Harry, because he's made so much progress and I can't step back. Even if I weren't blind, I would want to work here."

The satisfaction in her sister's voice confirmed Annabelle's need for a solid job in Washington, for returning to the yawning emptiness of the farm was no longer a possibility for Elaine.

Annabelle's newfound resolve wavered as she mounted the steps to Gray's townhouse the following morning, dreading what she was about to do. Treason was a hanging offense. If she found evidence of it, could she turn him in?

She clutched a copy of *Sense and Sensibility* as she stood on his front stoop, waiting to be let inside. The novel was a masterpiece of family dynamics, and Gray did remind her of Colonel Brandon, a character who had fascinated her since she first read the novel years ago. Colonel Brandon could never be guilty of treason, and in her heart, she didn't believe Gray could either.

"How is Mr. Delacroix feeling today?" she asked when Mr. Holder opened the door and beckoned her inside.

"No better, but he's agreed to stay in bed

155

today. He told me you are to be granted the run of his library. I'll fetch Otis to let you in."

"You don't have a key?" she asked.

Mr. Holder delicately cleared his throat, as if somewhat embarrassed. "Mr. Delacroix is very particular about who may enter the study. Only he and Otis have a key."

For a man to be so paranoid about the security of his office did not bode well. A headache began gathering, and she just wanted this day to be over.

She managed a pleasant expression and extended the book to Mr. Holder. "Will you give this to Mr. Delacroix? I'm sure it's difficult for a man of his temperament to be confined to bed. Perhaps this will help."

"Of course, ma'am."

The butler carried the novel up the staircase, and she longed to follow and beg Gray to tell her that all this espionage suspicion was pure foolishness. Instead she had to snoop through his files in search of information that could hang him.

Two minutes later Otis arrived, his face curious as he escorted her to the library, a set of keys in his hand. "You've got to tell me how you persuaded him to give you access to his sacred space," he teased.

"A shared fascination with Tahitian orchids," she said in an off-handed voice.

The keys rattled as Otis unlocked the door and let her into the dimly lit, book-lined office. A massive desk dominated the center of the room, and three sides were lined with bookshelves and filing drawers. Maps covered one wall, and a standing globe stood in one corner.

"These three shelves document Africa," Otis said. "This entire wall is the Far East and the Spice Islands. And these are Central and South America. The filing drawers are all correspondence with American distribution companies, so I doubt you'll find much of interest there. The antique chest is mostly old family papers and letters. Probably best that you stay out of those."

"And what is that?" she asked, nodding to an apparatus the size of a shoe box on a separate table beneath the room's only window.

"That's the telegraph machine," Otis said. "The Delacroixs have always been very private about their business dealings, so I send all their messages rather than use a public line at the local post office."

"You know Morse code?" she asked.

"Learning Morse code was the first request old Mr. Delacroix ever had for me. I think it was the reason he hired me in the first place," Otis said. "I'll leave you to it. If you need help with anything, just holler."

He closed the door softly behind him. That was when Annabelle noticed her spice map hanging on the wall. Amidst the practical maps and shipping schedules, space had been cleared for her ridiculous piece of whimsy.

She ignored the ache in her chest and forced herself to walk toward the first filing cabinet. The cold metal handle triggered a swirl of nausea as she pulled the drawer open. Everything about this was wrong. She wasn't a snoop. She wasn't a spy.

But you are.

It didn't take long to figure out the filing system Gray used, and it brought an unwilling smile to her face. He organized the work by plant taxonomy, making the files nearly irresistible to her botanist's heart. Most of the information was about herbs, but he had files on orchids, cacti, and roses. Why roses? Why would a stern man like Gray Delacroix be interested in something as frivolous as roses? She desperately wanted to know. Every time she learned something new about Gray, it revived her fascination with him.

Unless he was a traitor. Hopefully she could absolve him of that charge. She closed

the file on Mexican roses to continue looking for information about Cuban revolutionaries. The faster she paged through documents, the harder she prayed she would find
nothing.

And it seemed her prayers were answered.
After three days she'd found no evidence to
implicate him in treasonous activity. Nothing! She'd gone practically cross-eyed reading shipping records, account ledgers, and
scientific reports. She'd even read the letters Gray sent home to his father. At first it
was in search of suspicious dealings, but it
was impossible to look for such evidence
without reading the personal messages as
well.

And in so doing, she fell a little in love
with him. These letters were stunning in
their beauty and the affinity between Gray
and his father. Most of it was business, but
each letter carried a few personal sentiments
as well. Many of Gray's letters included
sketches of the ports he visited, charcoal
rubbings of interesting leaves, even a few
drawings of the people he met, and he was
a surprisingly good artist.

Everything about this job was troubling,
but as she neared the end of the files, a seed
of hope took root. She stood on the edge of
being able to exonerate Gray and return to

her normal, mundane scientific job. There were still more letters in the trunk of personal family correspondence to read, but those seemed the least likely to contain anything nefarious. She'd found nothing so far, and each night she prayed nothing would emerge.

Gray finished *Sense and Sensibility* shortly after Annabelle brought it to him. He hadn't read a book for pleasure in decades, and Jane Austen's merciless social commentary was impressive. The social-climbing Mrs. Fanny Dashwood, with her sense of entitlement and ravenous greed, reminded him of the Magruders. Despite his muscle aches, despite his fever and exhaustion, he lit every lamp in his bedroom to stay awake and keep turning the pages late into the evenings.

As for Annabelle's assertion that he reminded her of Colonel Brandon, well, it was probably a compliment. The character was a little stuffy, but a man of honor on whom his entire family could depend.

But Gray worried about Annabelle. For the past two days he'd watched from his bedroom window as she came and went from his house. Her shoulders drooped, and she seemed dispirited as she headed up the walk each day.

Something was wrong. She was usually such a sunny person, but it seemed the stress of her sister's situation was wearing on her. Everything in him admired Annabelle and wanted to save her. He wanted to rush downstairs and plow through the library alongside her in search of something to please the bureaucratic paper-pushers in the government. He'd even considered sending Otis to Mexico in search of that elusive orchid the Smithsonian seemed so eager to discover. Which was ridiculous. That orchid was long extinct, and he depended on Otis for the daily operations of his business.

But the burning urgency to help Annabelle would not ease. He'd use the book she loaned him as an excuse to talk to her.

Pulling on a pair of pants made his head whirl, and he had to sit for a moment to regain his balance. He put on a necktie, combed his hair, washed his face, then grabbed the book and carefully headed down the stairs.

He moved slowly, placing his feet gently to avoid setting off a firestorm in his head. The door to the library was closed, but he knew she was inside because he'd watched her arrive only an hour earlier.

He opened the door to see her sitting on

161

the floor, an explosion of paperwork in stacks around her. It didn't make any sense. What was she doing with all those old papers? When she looked up, her face was awash with guilt.

The antique chest containing his most private letters was open. He looked at the papers before her, unable to believe his eyes. He moved closer, and there could be no doubt. She was looking through *his family's personal correspondence.*

"What are you doing with those?"

She abruptly closed the trunk and gaped at him, apparently speechless. His father had saved his letters, hundreds of them sent from the Far East, Africa, and Central America. Those letters were like peeling back the skin on his soul, and she had been reading them. It took every ounce of will-power not to snatch them from her hand.

Dizziness drove him to reach for a chair before his knees gave out. He held on to the back, bracing himself against the anger roiling inside.

"I am a private person," he ground out. "My father was as well."

"I'm sorry," she stammered.

The letter on top of the stack was from his station in Patagonia. Gray had written of the terror he'd suffered when his ship

162

rounded the infamous Cape Horn, long known as the sailor's graveyard. The letter was barely legible, written with half-frozen hands while his ship battled surging waves and dangerous winds. Over the years, he'd shared everything with his father, all his triumphs and letdowns. He'd written of his disappointment in failing to establish ties with the Dutch and his confession of the time he had been swindled of their investment in a nutmeg plantation. He wrote of the beauty of the Polynesian women as they danced. He wrote of drinking yak milk and learning the art of pollinating rare vanilla orchids by hand.

Gray closed his eyes and gathered his thoughts. Maybe there was an innocent explanation. After all, he was fascinated by the details of Annabelle's life, but even if he'd stumbled across a treasure trove of her diaries, he never would have snuck a peek. He valued privacy too much for that sort of violation.

"Why were you reading those letters?" he finally asked.

"I'm sorry," she said on a shaking breath. "That's all I can say. I know it was wrong, but I was curious, and I'm sorry."

It had the ring of truth. While a piece of him was tempted to go on one of his typical

163

rants, there would be no point in it, as she was already awash with shame. The offense was done, and there was no undoing it. He didn't want to resent her over this. He hadn't told her she couldn't explore the trunk, so he needed to let this go.

He shook with exhaustion as he lowered himself into a chair, relieved to be off his feet. "What did you think of them? Our letters?"

Her eyes widened in surprise, and after a moment the shame drained from her face as she pondered his question.

"I'm envious," she finally said. "You and your father shared a wonderful friendship. That much is obvious from every letter."

An ache bloomed in his chest as he looked at the letters, the only tangible memento of the bond he'd shared with Nicholas Delacroix. Maybe because the two of them had survived the crucible of war and then years of struggling back to stability, they were closer than a typical father and son. He was proud of what they'd built together, and those letters documented every risk, plan, triumph, and failure.

"We were very lucky."

"The world you paint in these letters is fascinating," she said. "I could never be brave enough to sail to Java or Madagascar, but I love that you did. And these letters . . . I can see how hard it was for you. The distance, the heat, the illness. But also the people, the spices, and the adventure. A piece of my heart has always longed to do something big. Epic. I love that you were brave enough to do it."

He stared at her, mesmerized. She understood. They couldn't be more different in background or temperament, but she understood what drove him out into the world and the compulsion to work. His sense of unity with her grew stronger. He had never met anyone like her, and once again his attraction to her was spiraling out of control.

This was dangerous. Why would a girl this young and naïve want a stodgy, serious man like him? He was letting his emotions run amok, when in all likelihood she was only here to find something to impress her masters at the Smithsonian.

From the moment they'd met, they'd been completely honest with each other, and he didn't want to stray from that now. No matter how mortifying, he needed to be frank with her. He wanted their friendship to be something more but feared she didn't feel the same. After decades of loneliness, a harbor was in sight, but if it was nothing more than a mirage, he needed to know.

"Annabelle, I find myself starting to care very deeply for you," he began, tension making it hard to speak in a steady voice. "I've tried to help you by opening my home and greenhouses and library to you, but perhaps that was a mistake. I'd like a proper courtship with you, but if my feelings are not reciprocated, I don't see how we can continue this rather unconventional friendship."

She blanched, her eyes widening as she sat back a few inches. Everything he'd just said was obviously offensive to her.

He looked away, unable to witness the distress on her face. "I'm sorry —"

"Don't apologize," she interrupted. "Please don't apologize."

"But I owe you one. I'm sorry to be so blunt, but this is new and untried territory for me. I am sorry I misread —"

"You didn't misread anything."

His gaze whipped back to hers. Still sitting on the floor, gazing up at him, she looked insecure and painfully young.

"I want to be here. Please don't send me away."

The note of desperation in her voice was odd. It was the voice of a woman anxious to secure her position at the Smithsonian, not a hopeful woman who returned his affection.

"Annabelle, I can still help you. If you need a steady job, I can open doors for you."

"Are you throwing me out?" The desperation was gone, and the challenge was back.

"No! I meant to say, in my hopelessly clumsy, fever-addled brain, that I care for you. I can't keep seeing you here every day if your only interest is in exotic spices or vanilla orchids. If that's the case, for my own survival . . . I must bring this to an end."

If he lived to be a thousand, there would never be a more awkward conversation than this one. He stared out the window and wished this day was already over.

"It's you, Gray. I'm interested in *you.*"

What little strength he had in his body drained away, and he sagged against the back of his chair. She put a hand on his knee, and he covered it with his own. He was too exhausted to even smile, but inside, a hundred suns were rising. He'd never thought of himself as an overly romantic man, but suddenly everything felt right. Was it possible that God had guided Annabelle all the way from a wheat field in Kansas to his front door? It felt that way.

"I'm very glad you're here," he said, wishing he was more eloquent. "I'm sorry for the circumstances of your sister's blindness, but perhaps I can help. Whatever you need from me, Annabelle, you have only to ask."

Had he been too forward? She flinched for a moment, but then the stress on her face eased. "Thank you for that," she said.

He leaned down and kissed her, and nothing had ever felt so right.

THIRTEEN

Gray sat at his townhouse office reviewing the latest papers from his lawyers about the *Pelican*. The sale of a two-million-dollar steamship was a complicated deal requiring several rounds of negotiations, but a buyer had been found and a price settled on. Now that Gray had committed to the sale, he wanted it finalized as soon as possible. The *Pelican* was the past, and he was anxious to dive with both feet into a new life here in Washington.

Hopefully with Annabelle. It had been a week since that morning in his study, and with each passing day, he grew more confident that she was the right woman for him. She made him want to be a better man. A kinder, more optimistic man who looked for the good in life instead of fixating on the bad.

He signed the contract with a flourish, authorizing the buyer's agents to begin a series of necessary inspections. Running footsteps down the hall snagged his attention, and his door banged open.

"Gray!" Caroline said as she burst into his office. "I need your help. This is a disaster."

"What's wrong?" He stood, for her honey-blond hair was sliding from her coif, and a sheen of perspiration covered her skin.

"The first lady is having one of her fits. She won't leave her bedroom. In three hours she is supposed to christen the German emperor's new yacht, and she is refusing to go."

"Why is the German emperor christening a yacht in Washington, DC?" It was a reasonable question, but it seemed to get under Caroline's skin.

"Because Kaiser Wilhelm is currying favor," she said in exasperation. "As England's navy gets stronger, Germany has been cozying up to the United States in search of an ally. An American shipyard gets a pricey commission, the kaiser gets a new yacht, and both sides were supposed to enjoy fine publicity by having the first lady smash a bottle of champagne on its hull."

He quirked a brow. So much for Caroline not having a political bone in her body. She had just articulated a crystal-clear assessment of international diplomacy.

"What's the problem?"

"The president went to Philadelphia on business and neglected to take the first lady with him. Her anxiety goes haywire when he isn't here, and she won't cooperate. The kaiser sent his cousin Prince Gustav to be his representative, and if the first lady snubs the christening, it will be a huge embarrassment. I need something to divert attention from her absence."

"I have no idea how I can help you."

"Didn't you tell me you know a blind woman who works at the Library of Congress?"

He frowned, baffled by how this could possibly relate to the kaiser's yacht. "Elaine Larkin," he confirmed. "I don't personally know her. I only know her sister."

"Perfect," Caroline said. "Prince Gustav has a sister who is blind. She is here, and the yacht is being named in her honor. Countess Frederica will christen the yacht in place of the first lady, but this is still awkward for me. I can honor her by arranging a special tour of the blind reading room at the Library of Congress. With music and canapés, and the chance to see the special collections of maps and globes for the blind. Can you fetch Miss Larkin to join in the ceremony? I'll figure out a way to parlay

171

our government's commitment to supporting the blind to flatter the prince and his family. The christening is at two o'clock at the Washington Navy Yard."

The breath left him in a rush. "I don't know Elaine Larkin. I can't promise you anything."

"Please? You were always my hero, Gray," Caroline said in a voice both flattering and sincere, and he hated how susceptible he was to it. She kissed his cheek and scurried from his study in a swirl of blue satin and expensive perfume.

It was annoying that his sister assumed he would drop everything to do her bidding, but he wouldn't mind seeing Annabelle again. Annabelle was hopelessly patriotic and would probably be dazzled by this sort of thing.

It didn't take long to hop a streetcar and arrive at the Smithsonian. He hurried through the grand entrance of the castle-like building, then vaulted up two flights of stairs and down the hallway to the workroom where Annabelle sat behind a table weighed down with plant specimens.

She looked delighted to see him, and he smiled down at her like a lovestruck idiot. He could stand there and smile all day, but the mound of odd grass before her was too distracting to pass without comment.

"Purple grass?" he asked as he closed the distance between them.

"*Pennisetum setaceum,*" she said primly. "All the way from East Africa. You should have seen it when it first arrived. The seed heads were magenta. I'm afraid they're already starting to fade."

"There's no way to save the color?" he asked.

"No, but we had an artist make a water-color when it first arrived. See? I'll attach it to the back of the specimen page along with the envelope of seeds."

It would have been fascinating to spend the afternoon rambling about the quirks of wild grasses, but he was on a mission.

"I come bearing an invitation for you and your sister," he said. "You've both been invited to the christening of Kaiser Wilhelm's new racing yacht this afternoon."

After he explained Caroline's dilemma, Annabelle was intrigued. "This might be good for Elaine," she said. "She's terrified of water, but so long as she doesn't have to actually get on the boat, she might enjoy it. Especially meeting the countess."

Soon Gray was striding toward the Library of Congress with Annabelle on his arm.

"I'd better ask her alone," she said as they

173

neared the library. "Elaine still gets nervous whenever she ventures out of known territory, so this might take a little persuasion. It's best done without an audience."

"I understand."

She disappeared through the heavy doors, and he once again thanked God to have found Annabelle and that he hadn't frightened her off with his initial boorish behavior. While cooling his heels, he strode toward the balustrade to watch tourists wander the neatly manicured grounds, especially the young couple leading a pair of children by the hand. Maybe someday soon he'd have a family of his own to escort around the city.

He glanced at his watch. Even if they left now, it would still be a tight squeeze to make it to the Navy Yard in time. He shouldn't be asking this of Annabelle or her sister, for they had no obligation to make Caroline's life easy.

As if his thoughts had summoned her, Annabelle pushed through the heavy brass door, a radiant smile on her face. One man held the door open while Annabelle left the building, and directly behind her came a willowy woman with her hand on Annabelle's shoulder as she stared sightlessly ahead of her. Elaine was beautiful. She looked a little like Annabelle, but her hair was chestnut instead of dark —

His eyes widened in surprise, for behind Elaine walked another man with his hand braced on her shoulder. And behind him was a young boy not even old enough to shave, also holding on to the shoulder of the person before him. And another. And another. A single-file line of a dozen blind people walked out of the building as they followed Annabelle straight toward him.

"They all wanted to come," Annabelle said, excitement brimming in her voice. "Will it be possible?"

"Please say yes," Elaine said. "This will be the most exciting thing that's happened in ages."

How was he going to get a dozen blind people across town in less than thirty minutes? It was too far to walk, and they couldn't all fit in a carriage.

It didn't matter. He would find a way.

He offered his hand to Elaine. "I'm Gray Delacroix," he said formally.

"Hello, Mr. Delacroix," Elaine replied, making no move to return his handshake. Annabelle reached for Elaine's hand and placed it in his, and he nearly kicked himself for his stupidity. How could he lead a dozen blind people across town if he couldn't even manage a simple introduction?

"Gray, this is my sister, Elaine," Annabelle said. "Elaine is the woman who convinced me to look beyond the horizon of our farm to see the wider world."

"Then I shall be forever grateful to you," he said, covering Elaine's hand with both of his own. "I have a feeling the world would be far blander without both Larkin sisters."

He boarded the next streetcar and, with the help of the driver, managed to clear enough space for the blind passengers. It took a while to lead them all aboard and get them settled, and the clock continued to tick, but twenty minutes later, the streetcar arrived at the Navy Yard. A spectacular yacht was moored in port, and plenty of officers from both the U.S. and German navy were on hand. A brass band played patriotic tunes, and colorful bunting draped the raised platform at the launching area. It was crowded with men in uniforms and formal attire, but it was easy to spot the prince, who wore a scarlet sash and a collection of medals on his chest.

Elaine seemed entranced by the music and liveliness in the air. Even without sight, she must be able to sense the pageantry, for her face glowed with excitement.

Gray leaned down to speak directly to her.

"I want you to know that no matter how this afternoon turns out, you are a hero."

Elaine beamed in reply, and he guided her toward Caroline, whose demeanor was gracious as she mingled among the dignitaries, but he could tell from her ramrod spine that she was terrified. When she spotted him, she sprang across the staging area and extended both hands to him.

"Thank you for coming!" Caroline gushed. "Are you Elaine?"

"I am."

"Prince Gustav has been in this country for a month, and he's said how impressed he is with what the Library of Congress has accomplished for the blind. Your appearance here will show our country in a good light. I've already arranged for a tour of the library following the ceremony."

Then Caroline noticed the line of others standing behind Elaine. "My goodness . . . there are more?"

Elaine looked a little abashed. "Everyone wanted to come. Do you mind?"

"Not at all," Caroline exclaimed. "I shall inform the prince that a blind delegation from the Library of Congress is here to support his sister. The countess is only twelve, but it would be wonderful for her to meet all of you. Let me go make arrangements."

Caroline disappeared into the crowd while Annabelle leaned close to Elaine and described the sight. "The countess is dressed like a fabulous doll. Tight corset, hair done up in ringlets, and it looks like a real fox-fur collar. Imagine that, a fur collar in June. And a real tiara!"

"Are we underdressed?" Elaine asked.

"No, no!" Annabelle assured her. They were the only ones not dripping in jewels or medals, but Annabelle knew the perfect thing to say. "You are wearing faces more radiant and excited than all these stuffy officers."

"We start in five minutes," Caroline said as she scurried back to rejoin the group. "The prince and the countess are thrilled you are here, and guess what? Prince Gustav has issued an invitation for all of you to sail on the yacht's maiden voyage immediately following the ceremony. All of you! Won't that be wonderful?"

A handful of the blind people began to laugh and applaud, but Annabelle and Elaine both looked sick.

Annabelle was glad she stood beside Elaine, who began to keel over at the invitation to sail on the yacht. Annabelle reached out to steady her. "You don't have to do it," she whispered.

"Yes, I do."

Annabelle's eyes widened. Elaine's face was sickly white, but her voice was firm.

"I want to be a part of this," she continued. "If a twelve-year-old girl can do it, I can too. I'm tired of being afraid. I'll regret it for the rest of my life if I take the coward's way out."

Annabelle's breath left her in a rush. Never had she been so proud of Elaine.

Her sister's face was a mask of trepidation as a German officer draped in medals escorted her onto the platform to meet the young countess. Gray's sister performed the introductions, and the other blind visitors were also escorted to the platform.

So much finery, so many uniforms, patriotic bunting everywhere, and smiles all around. The band played the anthems of both nations as officers carrying the national flags moved into place, but Annabelle kept twisting her fingers so hard it hurt.

"Your sister is doing fine," Gray murmured, and the warm confidence in his voice immediately soothed her.

He was a good man. Each day she became more confident of it, for she'd thoroughly searched his house and knew he wasn't guilty of treason. Tomorrow she would make her report to the two generals, and then she could wipe her hands of this entire affair and go into their courtship with an open heart.

The music ended, and the German prince stepped forward to speak from the podium. He sounded more British than German, not at all what she was expecting. She'd have to memorize every moment of this day for her parents. She was standing only twenty yards from a real prince! And Elaine stood even closer. Her parents were *never* going to believe this.

In place of the indisposed first lady, the young countess stepped forward to formally christen the yacht. She seemed awfully young for the honor, but the prince guided her into position and grinned broadly as she wielded the heavy bottle of champagne with confidence.

"In the name of Kaiser Wilhelm, I christen thee the *Countess Frederica,*" the girl shouted, then smashed the bottle against the hull.

Cheers and applause filled the air. The young countess flushed with pleasure as members of the German officer corps came to kiss her hand. The gangway leading up to the yacht was lowered, and dignitaries began boarding. The yacht rose and fell in the mild waves, causing the gangway to move as well. Elaine would never be able to handle that.

"I should go rescue my sister," Annabelle said to Gray.

"She doesn't need rescuing."

"Don't you see how unsteady that gangway is?" Panic leaked into her voice, and even from here, the anxiety on Elaine's face was plain.

A German officer offered Elaine his arm, preparing to board the yacht. Elaine stood frozen, even as the officer tried to nudge her forward.

"I'm going to her," Annabelle said. She strode forward, but Gray grabbed her forearm and hauled her back.

"Let Elaine handle this," he said.

"But she needs help —"

"Look, she's following the officer. She wants to go. Let her tackle her fears."

Elaine clutched the German officer's arm like a lifeline as they mounted the swaying gangplank. Her yelp of fright could be heard across the dock. The officer whispered encouragement as he kept guiding her forward.

"This is so hard," Annabelle moaned.

Countess Frederica looked radiant as she put her face toward the wind, but not all blind people were so fearless. Not all blind people had plunged through the ice and floundered helplessly before being rescued.

"She's doing fine," Gray assured her. "Look, they've found her a seat right next to the countess. They are surrounded by a dozen officers. Elaine is about to have the time of her life."

It was true. The terror had vanished from Elaine's face, replaced by a look of excited trepidation. The young countess babbled to her, and the other blind people were all being guided to their seats. This was probably the happiest and hardest moment of Annabelle's life.

"Thank you," she whispered to Gray. "A thousand times, thank you for bringing us here and keeping me sane."

He squeezed her hand in reply. A few moments later, the yacht slipped out of its moorings and sliced through the water. It tilted as it veered away from the dock and toward open water as the wind filled its sails. The band struck up a patriotic tune, but Annabelle could no longer see Elaine.

"She's going to be okay," Gray murmured. "*You* are going to be okay."

She squeezed his hand. For the first time in three years, she believed it.

FOURTEEN

General Molinaro sat at his imposing desk and pinned her with a critical stare as she reported on her search of Gray's study. She'd found no suspicious letters, no lists of Cuban contacts, and absolutely nothing to implicate him. Most importantly, the telegraph transmitter in his study did not match the code the generals said was being used by the spy. The telegrams the generals intercepted had not come from Gray's townhouse.

"What about his property at Windover Landing?" General Molinaro asked.

Annabelle explained that she had spent almost two complete days exploring his greenhouses and had been inside the farm-house for all her meals and to sleep. A groundskeeper and his wife lived there, and surely no person in their right mind would store incriminating documents in a house he rarely visited and where other people lived.

"When you were at Windover Landing, I expect Gray Delacroix was within a few yards of you the entire time."

"Yes, he was always there," she admitted.

"I need you to go back," General Molinaro said. "Alone. Get into the attic of that farmhouse. The storage sheds. Anyplace Delacroix didn't let you see the first time."

It was obvious she wouldn't be able to exonerate Gray's name unless she carried out the task, but she would need Gray's permission to go.

She asked him the next time he came to the Smithsonian to escort her to lunch.

"You've already seen my only rare vanilla plants. I don't want you to be disappointed," he said gently.

"Oh, but there may be other herbs and rare plants the Smithsonian doesn't have in their collection. Dr. Norwood would welcome anything I could find as an excuse to offer me a permanent position. Please, Gray."

And like magic, he conceded. He was apologetic as he explained that the backlog of work that had accumulated during his illness required him to stay in town, but that was exactly how she wanted it. Gray sent word to Lester Jenkins, the groundskeeper who lived at the farmhouse, to expect her that weekend. Mr. Jenkins would pick her up at the dock and sail her back home.

All she had to do was make a thorough search of Windover Landing, and then she could put this entire distasteful episode behind her.

Gray waited until his housekeeper had left to do her weekly shopping to invite Otis into the library. They were alone in the townhouse, but he locked the door anyway. Caution came naturally to him, even during times when secrecy wasn't important.

But today it was, as Otis had been spying for him again. The younger man sat on the opposite side of Gray's desk and leaned forward to report what he'd learned.

"The Magruders are using a recipe cooked up by a German chemist," he said in a low voice, reaching into his pocket to extract a slip of paper. "They're using wood-tar creosote from pine trees to make the extract. They cut a deal with a paper mill down in North Carolina to get the wood pulp."

Gray studied the recipe, grim satisfaction running through him at this tangible proof that the Magruders were using a wood by-product to make their imitation vanilla extract. Their product had the same look and scent of real vanilla, but the taste wasn't there yet. Clyde Magruder had an army of chemists working on the solution, and Gray planned to stop them.

"The meeting of the Food and Spice Association is next week," he said. "I'll be there to sound the alarm. The food industry needs to start policing ourselves, or the government will do it for us."

The Food and Spice Association was the most likely group to pressure the Magruders to clean up their act. Once a year, the professional association brought rival companies together to share information and advocate for conditions favorable to their industry. Gray had secured a prime spot at the podium to discuss the problem of artificial flavorings. So far, their industry had avoided government interference, but passing off wood-tar as a food product was asking for trouble.

And Gray already had enough of that without asking for more.

His gaze tracked to the spice map tacked on the wall, and a helpless smile curved his mouth. Where was Annabelle at this very moment? With all his heart, he hoped she would find something wonderful in his greenhouses in Windover Landing. It would thrill him beyond words if one of the hundreds of specimens he'd shipped home over the years proved to be of value to her.

He wished she wasn't so obsessive about pleasing the Smithsonian. She didn't need to be. If she would marry him, he could keep her and Elaine in the lap of luxury. He'd always been decisive, and after a proper courtship, he had every intention of marrying her. A proposal at this point would be premature, but that didn't mean he couldn't begin planning for it.

It was still an hour before the banks closed, and he wanted to get his mother's engagement ring out of the vault. After decades of sitting in a locked bank vault, it was time for that ring to shine on another woman's hand.

He retrieved the tiny key for the family's safe deposit box and handed it to Otis. "When you deliver the next round of *Pelican* contracts to the bank, please get my mother's engagement ring from the vault."

It was time to start planning.

FIFTEEN

Annabelle asked the housekeeper for a tour
of the farmhouse at Windover Landing. "I
didn't get a chance to see much of it the
last time I was here," she explained as she
arrived at the house.

Lester and Tabitha Jenkins lived year-
round in the farmhouse. Lester was tall and
gangly, with leathery skin and deep grooves
along the side of his mouth. He was a man
of few words, but his wife was the opposite,
a short magpie of a woman who chattered
from the moment Annabelle arrived.

"This place is so big with just me and
Lester rattling around most of the year,"
Tabitha said as she led Annabelle through
the ground floor. "Old Mr. Delacroix used
to come out a lot. Loved the plants, he did.
Don't see so much of Mr. Gray, but he usually pops in once or twice a month, mostly
because I suspect that I'm a better cook
than that woman he's got cooking for him

in town."

Tabitha rattled on, but Annabelle was all eyes as she scanned the interior. Simple white wainscoting lined all the rooms, which boasted tall ceilings and sparse furniture. The only exception was a library with an entire wall of well-thumbed books and maps. There was no desk, no filing cabinets, and no locked cupboards.

Annabelle smiled as she took a few steps into the room. "I suppose you must have plenty of time for reading during the winters."

"Neither Lester nor I are much for reading," Tabitha admitted. "I can manage a cookbook recipe, but Lester doesn't care for reading at all."

Did that mean he couldn't read? It was none of Annabelle's business, other than that perhaps a man engaged in treason might find it convenient to have servants unable to read incriminating letters.

The older woman ushered Annabelle out of the library and into the kitchen, which was lined with fine copper pots and pans dangling from a rack and bottles of Delacroix spices on the two shelves over the countertop.

"Is there anything special you'd like me to cook while you're here?" Tabitha asked. "I expect you might like a nice roasted chicken. Doesn't that sound good? Everyone loves a roasted chicken, especially with mashed potatoes. And, of course, I'll bake a pan of gingerbread. Mr. Gray loves my gingerbread, so I'll send a loaf home with you. Just you watch for how his eyes light up when he gets a peek at it."

It was impossible to get a word in edgewise, but Annabelle needed to start exploring the attic and get another look at the library. Lester sent her a sympathetic nod as he carried her overnight bag upstairs. She finally managed to extricate herself from Tabitha's chatter and settled in the library.

There were a few books about the Civil War, reference manuals about herbs and vegetables, and plenty of old issues of the *Farmer's Almanac,* but nothing relating to the Caribbean or Cuba. There also wasn't a telephone or telegraph machine, for there were no wires marring the view anywhere on this isolated estate. Windover Landing simply showed no sign of being a headquarters for espionage or treason.

The attic proved uncomfortably hot. The coating of dust on the trunks and old furniture was a good indication that this place was rarely touched, but it still needed searching if she was to fully exonerate Gray.

The trunks contained winter blankets and old tools, but no paperwork or anything else suspicious. Afterward she had a nose twitching with dust but a growing sense of hope.

That night she flopped back onto her mattress, staring at the ceiling in exhaustion. One more day. Then she could go home and blot this horrible episode from her mind. Maybe someday she could even confess everything to Gray. He would be outraged at first, but perhaps someday they might come to laugh about it.

The following morning, she explored the other bedrooms on the second floor and was able to make quick work of them. Only a few clothes hung in the wardrobe, and the drawers were mostly empty. There was nothing under the beds or hidden beneath the mattresses.

In Gray's room there was an old, ornately framed photograph on the bedside table. Gray was easy to recognize, but Luke and Caroline looked like they were only five or six years old. The older man must be their father, for he and Gray shared the same confident, chiseled jaw.

She carried the photograph to the window to study it in better light. Their father was the only person seated, and the children stood before Gray, who rested a possessive hand on each of their shoulders. Mr. Delacroix stared boldly at the camera, but Gray watched Caroline, his face glowing with pride. He had once told Annabelle he felt more like a parent than a brother to Caroline and Luke, and that was obvious in this photograph.

She gazed out the window as daydreams carried her away. Gray would be a good father. She could see that in the loving way he looked after his siblings, even though they sometimes frustrated him. He'd surely be a good husband too. Even thinking about him in such a light made her a little breathless.

From up here, the lawns looked manicured and healthy . . . all except the raccoon-infested shed where Gray had stayed with his father after the main house burned down. It was almost completely obscured by an overgrowth of shrubs, and she had entirely forgotten about it. It was the only place she hadn't inspected.

It was surely nothing, but she set the photograph down to go outside for a better look.

Up close, the shed looked even worse than from afar. She had to bat away some shrubbery to peer through the grimy window, but it was covered from the inside. There was a padlock on the door, so she couldn't get in.

Her mouth went dry. If this was a moldy old shed like Gray said, why would there be a padlock on the door? The beginning of a headache began to pound. There was surely nothing of value inside, for it truly looked like a wreck of a building, but a troubling sense of anxiety gnawed at her. A quick glimpse inside would surely put it to rest.

She found Lester repairing a fence along the back edge of the property and asked him to unlock the shed.

He straightened and wiped his brow. "I ain't got the key for that one."

"What's inside?"

"Never asked."

Her mouth went dry, and her heartbeat sped up. "Who would have a key?"

"Couldn't tell you," he said with a shrug, then returned to repairing the fence rail. It was maddening, but Lester showed no interest or curiosity about the oddity of that shed. He was entirely absorbed in getting that rail perfectly aligned back onto the fence.

Which meant that perhaps she could break into the shed without his notice.

She gathered up her skirts and strode toward the small building, eyeing the lines of the roof and composition of the windows.

From the time Annabelle was old enough to walk, she had scrambled up into haylofts and climbed on rooftops to help her father with repairs. She could get into that shed.

The padlock held firm, and the window wouldn't budge. The only other way in was a narrow transom window over the door. In hot weather, that window probably provided plenty of relief by cracking it open to let the hot air out.

Annabelle scurried to the barn for a ladder and a crowbar. Five minutes later, she'd centered the ladder beneath the transom window, hoisted herself up, and begun prying the window open.

It didn't take long, for the window opened easily. She found a foothold on the doorknob, hiked up her skirts, then got both feet through the opening. Holding on to the lip of the roof, she paused for a quick prayer.

Please, she whispered. *Please let this be nothing.*

She wiggled inside, the window frame scraping her spine as she dropped to the ground.

It took her eyes a moment to adjust to the dimness . . . but this was no ordinary shed. The hardwood floor gleamed with a coat of varnish, and a bookcase weighed down with books and binders covered one wall. This was a well-used study, cozy and fully stocked, complete with a desk, a typewriter, and shelves full of books.

It hurt to breathe. Maybe this didn't mean anything. There could be any number of reasons this shed was fully furnished and obviously well used. Maybe Lester or Tabitha had set it up as a private study. It didn't have to belong to Gray. He could still be innocent.

She wandered to the bookcase, leaning in to study the titles.

Cuba. Navy. Spanish-American War. It was hard to keep reading as the trembling took over. This still could be entirely innocent. Gray was a well-educated man who was entitled to have political opinions and read whatever he wanted, even if it was critical of the government.

It was too hard to keep standing, so she yanked the desk chair back, collapsing into it. The desk stood before her — a very nice desk with brass knobs and inlaid wood. Searching these drawers was as terrifying as opening Pandora's box, but it had to be done.

It didn't take long, for what she found in the top drawer was damning. A folded wall map of Cuba with hand-drawn notes marking the location of American army encampments. Beneath the map was a small leather-bound booklet, the kind men kept in their breast pocket. The first page listed Cuban sympathizers, most of whom had been on the list of names General Molinaro had asked her to look for. The next page listed telegraph exchange codes. More papers and documents filled the other drawers. They were in Spanish and she couldn't read them, but she would take them all. Someone in the government would know what to make of them.

It was hard to breathe in here. The walls were closing in, and she had to get out and away from this horrible desk. She dragged the chair to the transom window and shoved the papers through to the ground outside. Then she hoisted herself out the same way she'd come in, scrambling outside, where the glare of sunlight was blinding. It felt like she had aged fifty years in the space of five minutes.

She sat on the front step of the raccoon shed as her world crumbled around her.

No.

No. Gray Delacroix was not her world, and this wasn't going to destroy her life. She had been briefly infatuated with a man who had a huge, gaping flaw that could never be overlooked.

She gathered the papers and the map, then headed toward the house. Even handling these papers was revolting, but they needed to be turned over to the government. They contained a wealth of information that might save lives on both sides of this simmering rebellion.

She went straight to her bedroom to hide them in her bag. When she returned downstairs, Tabitha nodded toward a towel-wrapped pan of cooling gingerbread.

"You'll take the gingerbread to Mr. Gray?"

The warm scent of the spices made Annabelle want to weep, and she couldn't bear to be near it. She smiled sadly. "No, keep it. I won't be seeing Gray any time soon."

It was late in the afternoon when Annabelle arrived back in Washington. She dropped her luggage off at her apartment, relieved that Elaine wasn't home yet. It would be impossible to pretend nothing was wrong.

Twenty minutes later, she'd arrived at the grand building of the War Department, situated just west of the White House. Her canvas satchel weighed heavily as she carried it up the stairs leading to the building. The weight of the satchel made her entire arm and shoulder ache, even though all it contained was a single map, a slim notebook, and a few letters.

Enough to hang a man.

Enough to save countless lives on both sides of this battle.

She continued trudging up the stairs, the heat making it hard to breathe. Each step sapped her energy a little more.

"Annabelle! Annabelle Larkin, how *are* you?"

The bright voice cut through her misery. She looked up to see Caroline Delacroix descending the steps of the War Department, both hands outstretched in friendship.

Annabelle backed down a step. Aside from Gray, his sister was quite possibly the last person on earth she wanted to see. "I'm fine," she said, unable to meet Caroline's eyes. She wanted to escape, but Caroline still blocked her way.

"We should go out for tea," Caroline said brightly. "I'd invite Gray, but he's been so busy preparing for his presentation to the Food and Spice Association. La! Seems very dull to me, but Gray can be a real zealot over that sort of thing. Until that meeting is over, he will be buried like a moth hiding from the sun."

This was torture. Annabelle had always admired the gentle teasing between the Delacroix siblings, but the contents of this satchel would blow it to smithereens.

"I have some business to attend to," she said, sliding around Caroline to continue up the steps, but once again Caroline stopped her with a gentle hand on her arm.

"I saw Countess Frederica at the embassy last week, and we reminisced about the christening of the yacht. Wasn't it marvelous? If I live to be a hundred, I shall still be in your sister's debt. Please give Elaine my regards."

"I will," Annabelle said, pulling away and heading up the steps.

A few minutes later, she was escorted into General Molinaro's private office, where the cloying cigar smoke sickened her. The general gave her a polite nod and gestured to a chair. She didn't want to sit. She just wanted this over with.

"I found something of interest." She handed over the canvas bag. Touching those notebooks and letters was impossible.

As General Molinaro emptied the bag onto his desk, she stared out the window. The White House was visible from here, sitting serenely amidst the deep green leaves of summer. She was doing the right thing. Just because she hated it didn't make it wrong.

A low whistle of admiration came from General Molinaro. "You have done very well."

"What will happen to him?" Her voice sounded small and frightened in this ornate office.

"That will be for a court of law to determine," he said. She must have flinched, for he immediately softened his voice. "Miss Larkin, this is treason. There is no room for sympathy here. Sometimes life forces us into unbearably difficult choices, but that does not absolve us from stepping up to the plate to do what is right. You did that and should be proud."

"I'm not proud."

She stood and left without another word.

SIXTEEN

The annual gathering of the Food and Spice Association was always in Washington at the finest country club in town. Almost a hundred businessmen from across the country had already gathered on the terrace overlooking the manicured grounds by the time Gray arrived. Normally the men at this meeting were fierce competitors, but during the three-day conference, they sheathed their swords and worked toward resolving common problems.

And one of those problems was headed straight toward Gray. Dickie Shuster was a reporter for *The Washington Post* who pretended to cover business and politics, but what he really craved was gossip. While attending events such as these, he was always on the lookout for who drank a little too much or who cast covetous glances at another man's wife. With his striped jacket and floppy bow tie, Dickie looked like a dilettante, but it was an illusion. A few years ago, he'd caught wind of a Russian diplomat who spent too much at the horse races. While investigating the diplomat's spending, Dickie pulled on a thread that led all the way back to inflated armament sales from a German company to the Russian czar, resulting in trials for embezzlement and collusion. Gray had never underestimated Dickie Shuster since.

"Gray!" Dickie crowed as though they were old friends. They weren't. He carried a highball glass and an overly wide grin. "Can I get you a mint julep? There's nothing like a splash of Kentucky bourbon on a warm summer evening."

Gray declined. He rarely drank at business meetings, and never when reporters were present. "How's the newspaper business?" he asked cordially.

"Fruitful as always." Dickie lowered his voice and turned to face him. "What's this I hear about your brother's vendetta against the Magruders? It sounds like it's heating up again."

Given that three generations of Magruders were holding court on the other side of the terrace, Gray wasn't inclined to reply. Clyde Magruder, the heir apparent, sported a new gold walking stick but the same oily smile.

"I would never presume to speak for my brother."

"But you must admit Luke can be a wild card," Dickie pressed. "Wouldn't it be better for me to get news straight from his family instead of from rumors on the street? You know how the street can get things wrong."

"Or perhaps there's no story at all."

Dickie smiled and shrugged. "If I can't get news about Luke, how about your sister? I saw her at the White House the other day, and she looked absolutely ravishing. Mouthwatering, even."

Gray stiffened. No man wanted to hear his sister discussed in that tone, and especially not by a reporter. The further Caroline could distance herself from reporters, the better.

"I'm not about to discuss my sister," he said, looking around the gathering in search of someone else to talk to.

"Come now!" Dickie prodded. "I hear that half of Washington is at her feet, and the other half are taking bets for when the first lady will fire her."

A gruff voice sounded behind him. "It's not fair to take aim at noncombatants,

Dickie. You know that."

It was old Jedidiah Magruder, the patriarch of the clan. His face looked like it had been carved by a battle-ax, but his suit was flawlessly tailored.

Dickie made a few more halfhearted attempts to sniff out information, but when a couple of men tried walking along the edge of a fountain like a balance beam, Dickie saw more promising material and wandered away, leaving Gray standing uncomfortably beside his family's archrival.

"I haven't had a chance to extend my condolences about your father," Jedediah said. "Nicholas Delacroix was a fine man, and the industry has suffered a true loss."

"Thank you," Gray said.

"I'm glad you're back in the country so I have a chance to apologize in person for all that nonsense a few years back."

Three dead people, and Jedidiah Magruder considered it "nonsense." Gray kept his face deliberately impassive. "Yes. Go on."

"It was an anomaly," the old man said. "It's a shame that our first attempt to do business together turned sour, but accidents happen, and there may be other chances for us to cooperate."

Clyde Magruder joined his father, and

204

Gray noticed a new sapphire pinky ring to go with the gold walking stick. At fifty, Clyde had taken over primary leadership of Magruder Food a few years ago. While old Jedidiah Magruder had been a tough competitor, the son was both a nightmare and a cheat.

"Welcome back to civilization," Clyde said. "Where were you? India, I think I heard?"

"Ceylon," Gray replied, ignoring Clyde's genteel shudder. "They have an interesting blend of mustard with a natural heat I'm interested in cultivating."

"Find the right chemist, lad," the elder Magruder advised. "You can dial in as much or as little heat as you want."

Clyde smiled pleasantly. "Dad, you know the Delacroixs don't believe in science. I'm surprised they even consent to have electricity in their factory. Then again, my chemistry degree is from Princeton, so I've never been afraid of science. Remind me where you studied, Gray?"

"I didn't go to college, Clyde."

"Oh, that's right," Clyde said in mock surprise. Somehow he managed to bring up Gray's lack of a college degree in every meeting. "Science is the wave of the future. *You* might like the idea of cooking the same way Martha Washington did a hundred years ago, but please don't stand in the way of progress for the rest of us, hmmm? Your dad was a frightened possum in the face of science, but I'm expecting more from you."

Gray would put up with a lot, but not an attack on his father. He smiled as he diverted the conversation. "I understand congratulations are in order. A new child?"

Clyde stiffened at the reference to the nanny he'd impregnated then accused of theft. Jedidiah looked at his son in surprise, and Clyde gave Gray a tight smile. "You must have misheard."

Gray nodded in concession. "No doubt. Congratulations anyway."

He scanned the crowd, glancing over the people loitering nearby, waiting for their chance to mingle with the grand old man of the packaged food industry. He noted their faces, trying to memorize everyone eager to follow the Magruder lead. The products coming from the Magruder warehouse probably outsold everyone else here combined, but at the cost of cheap fillers, misbranded products, and chemical flavorings.

The food industry stood on a cusp, and it was anyone's guess where it would go in the next decade. Either the shortcuts pioneered by the Magruders would take center stage, or the Delacroixs would figure out a way to remain competitive with pure and genuine products.

He couldn't predict the outcome, but with luck, he could use this weekend conference to turn the tide in his favor.

Annabelle had been reading the newspaper for Elaine ever since the blindness struck. That once-enjoyable task had now become a daily torture as she scanned the newspaper, desperately searching for news about Gray. Had they arrested him yet? Would that sort of story even make the newspapers? The government might handle it in a secret manner, and she'd never learn anything.

Elaine was reading one of her braille books when Annabelle arrived at their apartment with the evening edition of the paper.

"Keep reading while I find some stories of interest," she said, hoping anxiety hadn't leaked into her voice. She'd never told Elaine about spying for the government. She was ashamed of Gray and ashamed of herself. To the bottom of her soul, she wished she'd never been painted into a corner and asked to spy.

Her fingers trembled as she paged through

the newspaper, praying she'd finally learn something but equally hopeful she'd see nothing.

Nothing. She drew a steadying breath. She had another day of reprieve. She flipped back to the front page and landed on an interesting story.

"All right, I've found something," she said, and Elaine put her book aside. "It says here that David Fairchild has returned from abroad with over a hundred new specimens of fruit and edible cereal grasses collected for the Department of Agriculture."

She'd heard of Mr. Fairchild, for he was the botanist who had created the plant exploration program for the Department of Agriculture. Annabelle continued reading the article, but it seemed Elaine wasn't interested, as her fingers began surreptitiously scanning the pages of her braille book.

"Is this boring for you?" Annabelle asked.

Elaine jerked her fingers off the book as though she'd been burned. "Not at all! I'm sorry. Please continue."

Annabelle lifted the newspaper again. " 'Mr. Fairchild is especially proud of his efforts to identify more productive strains of hops while visiting Bavaria,' " she read. The story was quite exciting. It went on to recount the young botanist's efforts to select Bavarian hops that could flourish in the American heartland. Some of the farmers were so possessive of their crop, they hired young men to stand guard over the fields to prevent theft.

Elaine's fingers were creeping across her book again. She wasn't paying a bit of attention!

"What are you reading?" Annabelle asked. If Elaine had something more interesting, perhaps she could read aloud.

"I don't think you'd be interested," Elaine quickly said.

"Try me."

Elaine looked a little embarrassed but finally flipped the book closed so Annabelle could see the title, which was written both in braille and print. *The Culinary History of Delicatessen Meats.*

"What made you pick that out?" Annabelle asked, genuinely curious.

Elaine shrugged. "I don't know. It just seems interesting to me."

They decided to each read quietly to themselves, although nothing Annabelle read held her attention. Her worries continually strayed back to Gray Delacroix and what he was doing at that very moment. If he hadn't been arrested yet, he was probably enjoying his last hours of freedom on this earth. It was impossible to enjoy a simple summer evening knowing that Gray's world was about to be destroyed.

SEVENTEEN

Gray was the lunchtime speaker for the final day of the conference. The past two days had been spent with invited speakers who presented innovations in commercial drying ovens, automated packaging facilities, and new bottling techniques. Most of yesterday had been consumed with discussion about how to fight pending tariffs that would make international trade more difficult. Last night Jedidiah Magruder had shared his thoughts on the potential for chemical flavorings, and he'd held the audience of almost two hundred people in the food and spice industry spellbound.

But it was fool's gold, and it was Gray's job to outmaneuver his family's chief rival.

Lunch was coming to an end, and most of the conference attendees at the banquet set down their silverware and turned their chairs toward the podium to listen. Gray gauged the audience carefully. He was a

211

newcomer and was at a disadvantage. While everyone was intrigued by the innovative techniques pioneered by the Magruders, plenty were still skeptical, and Gray needed to learn who his allies were.

He began his speech by recounting his visit to the kitchen prior to their meal today. "I watched the chef as he prepared the mustard-cream sauce for the braised chicken we all just enjoyed," he said. "Every ingredient that went into that pan was natural. Ground mustard seeds, minced garlic, and fresh cream. He chopped dill and basil that had been snipped from the garden earlier this morning. He finished the sauce with a splash of white wine."

And given the state of the plates, it looked as if the men had enjoyed their meal. Dickie Shuster from *The Washington Post* had liked it so much, he'd ordered a second plate.

Gray continued in the same confident, clear voice. "You will be glad to know that the chef didn't add any wood-tar to the recipe. No petroleum was used to thicken the sauce. There were no attempts to use sulfur to imitate the depth and heat of natural mustard."

While he still couldn't tell who his allies were in the crowd, he could spot the ones who were hostile. Men began to shift in their seats and look away from the podium. He continued without faltering.

"As advances in science allow us to find cheaper and easier alternatives, we must begin policing ourselves. If we don't clean up our act, the government will step in and do it for us. Do you want government men in your factories, rummaging through your files and purchase orders, regulating your products? Yes, it's hard to keep agricultural goods fresh while being shipped from around the world. *That* is where we should be investing our scientific research: in how to preserve our fruits, herbs, and vegetables rather than in adulterating them with chemicals."

Now he could spot his allies. They were nodding and smiling. A few were leaning over to whisper to each other.

There was a commotion in the back of the room. A woman entered. Gray's eyes widened, for it was Caroline. An usher near the door tried to offer assistance, but she ignored him as she wended through the tables toward the stage.

Something was wrong. Her face looked sick.

Gray dropped his notes and left the podium as she reached him. "What's going on?"

213

She grabbed his forearms. She was shaking. "Luke has been arrested. You need to come now."

"What? But he's in Cuba." This didn't make sense. Luke ran afoul of the authorities all the time. It was hardly something to get so agitated about. Men swiveled in their chairs to listen in, curious about the family drama unfolding in the middle of the closing luncheon. Dickie Shuster had his notebook open and his eyes pinned on them.

Caroline lowered her voice, and he could barely hear her shaking whisper. "They are accusing him of *treason.* They say it's a hanging offense."

It was a kick in the gut. Gray was up to his eyeballs in politics, but Luke never had been. There had to be some sort of mistake.

He grabbed Caroline's arm and pulled her toward the exit. "Let's go," he said grimly.

Two hundred men watched him leave the room, but he didn't spare them a backward glance.

Caroline filled him in once they were in the carriage and heading toward the center of town.

"I got a letter from Philip Ransom," she said. "He got word that Luke was arrested this morning, accused of conspiring with the Cuban insurgency."

"Luke doesn't care about politics."

Caroline looked as helpless as he felt. "I know! That's why this doesn't make any sense. Philip should know more by now."

They sprinted up the steps of the War Department building, then headed down to the basement, where Philip worked in the Nautical Map Department. The door to his office was open, and he sprang to his feet the moment he saw them. The tiny office was windowless, and the maps crowding the walls made it feel even more claustrophobic.

"Come in," Philip said darkly, then closed the door behind them.

"What in the name of all that's holy is going on?" Gray demanded, his voice echoing off the cinderblock walls.

"I got word a few hours ago," Philip said. "Someone found letters between Luke and Cuban rebels who have been trying to throw the Americans off the island. It looks pretty bad."

"I don't believe it. I sent him down there to negotiate contracts for cayenne pepper. Luke is more likely to get into trouble chasing skirts than interfering in another country's war."

Philip looked skeptical. "Have you read any of his articles?"

215

"Look, I know he's been dabbling in journalism —"

"It's a lot more than dabbling," Philip interrupted. "Have you read any of the articles he wrote for *The Modern Century?*"

Gray instinctively recoiled at the name of the radical magazine. "I don't waste time on that kind of garbage."

"I usually don't either, but I always read whatever Luke writes. It's strong. Passionate. And I'm afraid what I read in those articles makes it plain that he's far more engaged in politics than I realized. When they arrested him, they found the current location of American warships in his briefcase."

Gray collapsed into a chair, dropped his head into his hands, and stared at the floor. This was his fault. He'd always been so hard on Luke. Unforgiving. Luke knew about Gray's hostility to the American occupation, and maybe he'd started dabbling with the rebels in a stupid, misguided attempt to be heroic.

Gray couldn't even lift his head. He just stared at the cracked tile beneath his feet. "How do we get him out?"

"We don't," Philip answered. "The best we can hope for is life imprisonment."

Gray reared up in disbelief. This wasn't

possible. Not Luke, not in a cage for the rest of his life.

Tears clouded Caroline's voice. "Philip, please . . . you have to help us."

"I would give my right arm if I could, but I don't have any influence down there. I'm sorry, Gray. To the bottom of my soul, I'm sorry."

Caroline was sobbing as they left Philip's office, and it cut Gray to shreds. She probably couldn't even manage the stairs leading out of this dank basement. He pulled her into his arms.

"Cry it all out," he whispered gently. She would be mortified to be seen like this, and there was no one down here to witness her total collapse. He rocked her in his arms, the sound of her tears making him feel more helpless than ever.

But he was not without resources. He had money and ties among the Cuban planter class he could call on. He would leave for Cuba immediately in a desperate bid to untangle this quagmire.

It meant he wouldn't be able to escort Annabelle to Mount Vernon for the Fourth of July as they had planned. He'd send a note to her, promising a later date, but cringed at the prospect of telling her of this mortifying blot on his family's honor. It would be easier to simply say he was called away on business, but he wouldn't do that.

He owed her the truth. He and Annabelle had always been honest with one another, and in this darkest hour, he would not taint their relationship with a lie.

EIGHTEEN

Dearest Annabelle,

I have been called away to Cuba on
family business. My brother has entan-
gled himself in disloyal political schemes
and has been charged with treason. I
have no explanation for why Luke
walked down this path, but those are
questions for another day. The charges
are serious, and I will do my best to
mitigate the consequences.

This means I will be unable to escort
you and Elaine to Mount Vernon. It goes
without saying that I would rather be
with you, but I shall say it anyway. My
feelings for you are deep, and I fear this
blot on our family's honor may cause
you to reconsider our relationship. While
this would be understandable, I ask for
a chance to prove myself to you. I am a
loyal man, both to my family and my
country. I beg for your patience while I

work through this crisis, and I shall notify you the moment I am back in Washington.

With deepest sincerity,
Gray

Annabelle clutched the letter to her chest as relief cascaded through her. It wasn't Gray. *It wasn't Gray!* Elaine sat on the couch beside her, or else Annabelle would have leapt into the air and shrieked with joy. All she could do was stare out the apartment window, amazed that the entire course of her life had shifted during the sixty seconds it took to read this letter.

"What does your letter say?" Elaine asked, her knitting needles clicking in a predictable rhythm.

Annabelle couldn't tell her. Normally she told Elaine exactly what had arrived in the post, but when she'd spotted Gray's return address on the envelope, she had simply said it was a letter without adding details.

"Gray reports he has gone to Cuba on business," she said, her voice still trembling in relief.

"That's all?" Elaine asked. "You seem quite taken with the news of a business trip. You're breathing so fast, it sounds like you've just sprinted up five flights of stairs."

Annabelle fanned herself with the letter. She couldn't tell Elaine about the elation still ricocheting through her at the news that Gray wasn't a traitor and wasn't destined for a hangman's noose.

But his brother might be. Somehow the fact that Gray and Luke lived under the same roof was the cause of the confusion. Between the two men, it was easy to assume that Gray, with his outspoken hostility toward the government, was the disloyal one. Luke projected an air of carefree charm that was completely at odds with international intrigue.

Maybe it was deliberate. The best spies were surely the people nobody suspected.

"I'd better get dinner ready," Annabelle said.

Ever since being asked to spy on Gray, the spices he'd given her had sat gathering dust. She had been too heartsick to use them, but tonight she would experiment. Their cheap cut of mutton would be much livelier with a hefty dose of fragrant paprika. She lit the stove, then poured a little of the aromatic spice onto a plate along with flour, salt, and pepper.

It didn't take long for the elation of Gray's letter to fade as other worries crowded her mind. Gray must never learn of her role in exposing his brother. He claimed to be horrified at what Luke had done, and she believed him, but that didn't mean he would ever forgive her if he learned she was responsible for his arrest.

It was Luke who had committed the crime, not her. Maybe there was no need for her to tell Gray anything.

Her hand shook as she dragged the mutton chops through the flour and paprika. She had to calm herself. This wasn't her fault, she had done what any loyal American would do. But she still trembled as she laid the meat in the skillet. Carrying a secret like this would be hard.

But she could do it. She would bury the memory of that terrible day and move forward with her life. The past would be forgotten.

Silverware clinked as Elaine set the table. "That smells divine," she said with a sigh.

It did. Everything about Annabelle's world had become richer and more complex after Gray came into it. Wasn't it fascinating how a scant spoonful of spice could transform an entire meal with an explosion of flavor? Just like that two-paragraph letter had sent her spirit soaring. Life was going to be good. The world was a huge, wide-open space full of choices, and anything was possible.

She had found a man of valor, and he was sailing into dark waters, but she would come alongside to help him survive the ordeal.

There seemed to be no end to the good fortune raining down on Annabelle. When she arrived at the Smithsonian on Monday morning, Dr. Norwood was at her little workroom with good news.

"A position has been found for you with the Department of Agriculture," he said. "A permanent position that pays considerably more than the modest stipend I have been able to give you here. Beginning immediately, you will be working alongside Mr. Greenfield in the division of cereal grasses. Is that acceptable to you?"

She opened her mouth but was so elated it was hard to find the right words. "Yes!" she finally managed to stammer. "Yes, I'd be very happy working for Agriculture."

Ten minutes later she was walking the six blocks to her new position at the Department of Agriculture. Her spirits lifted as she admired the extraordinary experimental gardens outside the building, for they were probably the finest and most exotic in the entire country. There was talk of someday clearing all these gardens to build a large green lawn, a mall that would let people admire unobstructed views all the way from the White House to the Washington Monument. For now, the land showcased the bounty of America with manicured gardens, experimental crops, and an arboretum.

The Department of Agriculture was housed in an imposing building with two wings and a grand marble staircase leading up to the main entrance. She was met on the front terrace by the gangly, middle-aged botanist who would be her coworker in the cereal lab.

"I'm Horace Greenfield, chief botanist for cereal grasses," he said. "Get it? Greenfield? I was born with that name, and my mother always said it was destiny I would go into agriculture. We'll be sharing a laboratory, but first, a tour!" He held the door open for her.

While the outside of the Department of Agriculture projected stately grandeur, the interior took her breath away. The vestibule was decorated by a hand-painted fresco of twining, leafy-green vines that stretched up and over the coffered ceiling. Vibrant panels of American landscapes during all four seasons covered the walls. The hallways were embellished with friezes of carved birch, black walnut, and mountain ash, a celebration of the American woodlands, and Annabelle felt ridiculously proud to know she now belonged here.

The main floor was for display, but the second floor was primarily laboratories for chemists and horticulturalists. Other floors contained the agricultural library, a museum, and an office for the statisticians. The biggest surprise was in the basement, where sixty employees worked at long tables, preparing free packets of seeds for distribution to the farms and kitchen gardens of America.

"We send more than a million packets of seeds all over the United States," Horace said with pride. "Bulbs, vines, legumes, you name it. If we can wrap it in *Sphagnum* moss or put it in an envelope, we will ship it."

After touring the basement, Horace led her into a stairwell to climb to the top floor, where their laboratory was located. "Now," he said amiably, "tell me how you got this position. We only learned this morning that we were to make space for you."

She opened her mouth, but how could she say this was a payoff for betraying a friend? All she could do was scramble for the few scraps of truth that could be shared. "I've been preserving botanical samples at the Smithsonian, but Dr. Norwood thought I'd be better off here."

Horace looked confused, but only for a moment before he launched into another stream of gossip. "Fair enough! My mother always said there is a place for everyone in this world. She never met Dr. Norwood, though! I heard he spent almost a thousand dollars importing a single rare blue orchid from Bombay. Can you believe it?"

He led her inside the laboratory where she'd be working. "Good! Our supervisor isn't here." He leaned over to whisper. "Mr. Bryant is a real stick-in-the-mud. Look at the stain on this table." He gestured to a splotch in the center of the glossy black lab table where the surface had dulled. "Two years ago, I spilled a little bleach on the slate. I wiped it up immediately, but not before it left that stain. It's harmless, but Mr. Bryant points it out at every opportunity." He brightened. "Not to worry! Tell me, I've heard that funding for a new wing at the Smithsonian is being held up because a congressman suspects one of the Smithsonian explorers is tampering with his wife. Is it true?"

Annabelle blanched at the unsavory gossip. "I have no idea."

"But has there been a delay in the funding? Because if so, I'll bet it's true."

She was saved from answering by the arrival of a white-coated man who frowned beneath his walrus mustache. He had a bald head, a sober expression, and a cynical voice as he tersely introduced himself as Milton Bryant, supervisor of the cereal grain laboratory.

He shot a surly glare at Horace. "Miss Larkin isn't here to fuel the gossip mills. She is to test leavening agents on newly imported strains of wheat." He turned his eyes to her. "Has Greenfield trained you on that yet?"

She shook her head.

"Then get on it, Mr. Greenfield. And try not to spill anything else on that stain." Mr. Bryant picked up a file and left the lab.

"Didn't I warn you he was a glorious shaft of sunlight?" Horace asked.

It was probably best not to reply. "What sort of wheat are we testing?"

Horace finally got around to showing her the various tests they were conducting, mostly on durum wheat. Soon she was seated at the lab table, a beaker of grains before her. They were studying its hardiness, suitability for milling, ability to withstand drought, and cold tolerance. This was *exactly* what she'd been hoping for. It was what her father needed to know if he was going to turn his failing crops around. It was as if God Himself had guided her to this lab.

An uneasy weight settled in the pit of her stomach. She wasn't proud of how she had earned her place here. It was a wonderful lab, filled with brand-new equipment and a lovely window overlooking the experimental gardens.

But all she could see was the splotch of old stain on the slate table before her. The stain of what she'd done to Luke Delacroix would be with her forever too.

She bowed her head. Had she done the right thing? It seemed that blessings were raining down on her. The increase in her salary meant she could send money home to her parents. She would learn the latest research for developing cereal grains suitable to the American landscape. Most importantly, Elaine could stay in Washington forever.

Annabelle ought to be happy, but the moment Horace stepped outside the lab to fetch another microscope, she clasped her hands and said a prayer for Luke.

Sometimes prayers weren't answered, and it was doubtful her prayers could save Luke. Perhaps the best she could hope for was that

Gray would never discover her role in his brother's downfall.

NINETEEN

As soon as Gray arrived in Cuba, he wasted no time seeking out the commander of the American military base, where he learned that Luke was being held at a Cuban prison near the northwest tip of the island.

"He's a civilian," the general said. "It doesn't look good to detain a civilian in a military prison, so we turned him over to the Cubans to hold until the trial."

Which was bad news. A Cuban prison would probably be worse than an American one, and Gray's fears were confirmed when he met with a planter he'd done business with in the past. They sat on the verandah of Marco Salazar's plantation, ceiling fans slowly rotating overhead, while Gray accepted a thin cheroot. He'd never been much for smoking, but he knew how to mingle among different cultures, and these rituals were important. There were going to be bills to pay, favors to call in, and dicey negotiations until he could get Luke out of prison.

"Plenty of Cubans resent the American occupation," Marco said. "After the Spanish were defeated, we thought we'd finally won our independence, but when the Spanish flag was lowered, the American flag was run up the staff. It's creating a problem, my friend."

How well Gray knew it, but Marco had not stopped talking.

"Some Cubans don't see much difference between a Spanish colonial master and an American one, but I do. This island is still in ruins. Our ports, roads, and bridges were bombarded to smithereens, but the Americans promised to rebuild them. I want those roads and bridges. I want our ruined ports rebuilt and back in operation. I want this island to flourish, but if the insurgents have their way, the Americans will leave, and we'll be left with no infrastructure to restore our way of life."

Gray had seen evidence of rebuilding everywhere. The harbor was filled with ships offloading supplies. Roads were being repaired, and bridges were under construction, but Gray was still skeptical. The American government didn't waste money where they couldn't get a return, and he

231

was doubtful the president intended to graciously leave after rebuilding the island.

"And once your roads and bridges are repaired?" he asked. "What then?"

Humor lightened Marco's eyes. "*Then* we throw the Americans out. Not before." All trace of humor vanished as he set his cigar down and leaned forward, lowering his voice. "That is why your brother is in a tight spot. If the insurgents prove difficult, the Americans will pour their money into building defenses rather than the infrastructure we need. Your brother is going to face retaliation for coming down here to stir up trouble. We're tired of war. We want to live and work on this beautiful island, but hotheaded rebels are making it hard. Most of us want to cooperate with the Americans — at least for now. Let us get clean water and roads back in working order. Then we can work toward independence. Your brother will find few friends in a Cuban prison."

It was what Gray feared.

The prison was a long, one-story brick building covered by a layer of crumbling stucco. The only windows were narrow slits no wider than Gray's hand. Chickens pecked at the hardscrabble soil, and two barrels of stagnant water rested beside the open front door.

Four soldiers sat at a table outside the prison, rifles casually slung across their backs as they played cards. Two of them pushed to their feet as they saw Gray approach. He hoped at least one of them spoke English.

"I'd like to see Luke Delacroix."

The taller of the two men nodded. "He is here," he replied in good English.

"I'd like to see him."

The soldier didn't move. "He's not a popular man. How much would you like to see him?"

Gray was prepared to play the game. After passing both men a five-dollar bill, the tall soldier gestured for Gray to hold up his hands. Gray submitted to a frisking, then followed the soldier through the open front door.

No wonder they kept the door open. It was hotter inside, and the air barely moved. The soldier said something in Spanish to the warden. Luke's name was in the mix, and after a moment, the warden's eyes brightened and he stood, smiling broadly. Gray didn't understand and looked to the tall soldier for translation.

"The warden also wants to know how

233

much you would like to see Luke Delacroix."

After Gray paid off the warden, the soldier took a ring of keys and led him down a long hallway with a series of locked wooden doors on each side. Gray covered his nose against the stench with a handkerchief. The soldier stopped at one of the doors and looked through the tiny grate at the top. He pounded on the door. "Visitor," he said, and the keys jangled as the iron lock's bolt turned. Gray lowered the handkerchief. He didn't want Luke to see how appalling he found this place.

It took a while for his eyes to adjust in the dim cell. The man lying on the cot peered at him, a hand sheltering his eyes from the hallway light.

"Hello, Luke," Gray said.

Luke rolled into a sitting position. "Gray?" A world of hope was in that single word.

"Yes." Gray turned to the soldier, who told him he would have twenty minutes for a visit, then closed and locked the door behind him.

Gray had never been claustrophobic, but the sensation of being trapped was suffocating. It felt like the walls were closing in, and there wasn't much room in the cell. A cot and an overturned wooden crate serving as a bedside table took up most of the space, and a narrow window near the top of the cell was the only source of light and air.

"You probably shouldn't come any closer," Luke said. "I stink to high heaven."

Gray ignored the comment and pulled his brother into a hug.

"Please don't tell me you came all the way to Cuba for me."

"I came all the way to Cuba for you," Gray said, and Luke sighed.

"Have a seat," Luke said. "You can have your choice of the doorway end or the window end of the cot."

Gray sat, and as his eyes adjusted, he had a better view of the room. There were a couple of books on the table and a stubby candle. A chamber pot in the corner didn't do the air any favors.

"Tell me what's going on," he said simply.

Luke gave a helpless smile. "I've been charged with collaborating with the insurgency."

"Did you?" Gray held his breath, holding on to the slim hope that this was all a misunderstanding that could be solved now that he was here.

"Yes."

Gray closed his eyes as his worst fears came true. It took an effort not to lash out and yell at his brother for pure, unadulterated stupidity, but Luke was already suffering enough. He had to play this smart.

"Who can I go to on the insurgency side to intercede for you?"

That took Luke by surprise, and he looked stunned at the offer. "There isn't anyone."

"You risked your life for those people, and it's time for them to pay you back," Gray said. "They've got political capital, and so do I. We are going to use it to get you out."

Luke shook his head. "That's . . . that's exceedingly decent of you, but it's hopeless. I'm guilty. Most of the people I worked with have been arrested too."

"Everyone?"

"Pretty much. The authorities found my code book and arrested everyone in it. I am now officially a sitting duck." Luke tried to smile but couldn't quite manage it. He provided what scant details he knew about how his cover was blown. Apparently the authorities had raided the raccoon shed, where he kept most of his correspondence.

"You were running this operation out of that ratty old shed?"

Luke shrugged. "I fixed it up pretty nice, and you never came within yards of it."

"All those times you claimed to be coming to Cuba to trade in cigars and rum . . ."

"It was just a cover."

Gray didn't care what fool act Luke had done, he wanted his brother out of this prison. "Maybe I can get you into an American prison. The conditions here are unacceptable."

"It's not so bad," Luke said, even as a bead of sweat trickled down his face. "It gets cooler at night."

It *was* that bad. It was revolting and awful, and it looked like Luke had already lost weight, but the worst thing was the despair in his brother's face. The sense of helplessness was strangling, and Gray redoubled his efforts. He had negotiated contracts all over the world and knew how to cut through red tape, but this was uncharted territory. He was floundering, and he hated it.

"Tell me what to do," he implored. "Surely someone can help. Philip Ransom? A politician here in Cuba? Tell me what to do!"

Luke smiled sadly. "Gray . . . there's nothing you can do. Go home and get the upper hand on the Magruders. Sell your spices and build your magnificent empire and don't look back. Forget about me."

"That's not possible. Tell me what I can do."

Luke looked prepared to deny him again, but then he paused. A hint of mischief lurked behind his eyes, and he leaned forward. "Actually . . . maybe there is something you can do. Before I left, I was working on a plan to bring the Magruders down a notch."

"What kind of plan?"

Genuine amusement lit Luke's face as he outlined the plan. He quivered in excitement as he laid out the details, but Gray was appalled. It was typical Luke. Audacious, extravagant, and fiendishly clever.

"Almost everything was in place," Luke said. "All I need is someone to carry it out."

"Absolutely not."

Luke reared back. "Why not? It's brilliant."

"It's nothing more than a juvenile prank."

Luke shook his head. "It will peel back the veil and show the world who the Magruders really are. It will throw a little egg on Clyde Magruder's face right before his run for Congress. And lest we forget, it will be fun."

Gray folded his arms over his chest. He didn't like the Magruders any more than Luke did, but it was important to play by the rules.

Except . . . Luke hadn't really spiraled off course until four years ago when the deal with the Magruders went south. That was the incident that started Luke down this destructive path.

Someone banged on the door. "Five more minutes," a guard shouted through the grate.

Gray stood, as did Luke. "You still haven't told me how I can get you out of here. There has to be a way."

"There's not," Luke said, trying to smile but almost weeping. "Don't worry about me. Tell Caroline the same. I want her to soar and accomplish great things. I knew this was dangerous work, and I knew the price I might have to pay. I rolled the dice and lost."

The worst thing was that for the first time in his life, everything Luke said was entirely correct. That didn't make it easier as Gray bid his brother farewell, possibly for the last time on this earth.

Caroline would not accept it. The morning after his ship docked in Alexandria, Gray headed straight for the White House to see his sister. She'd just come from facilitating a luncheon with a group of congressmen's wives and still wore an elegant day dress of pink-and-black-striped taffeta.

Oddly, she wanted to meet with him outdoors. Visitors swarmed the public gardens surrounding the White House, so she guided him to a cramped area near the service entrance that was screened from public view by a boxwood hedge. This was a part of the building few people saw, and it showed the age and genteel dilapidation of the White House. The cobblestones were buckled, and the loading area seemed too small for the traffic it received.

"There is a new security team in the White House," Caroline said. "The head of security is determined to make my life miserable, so it's easier to meet out here."

Gray and Caroline sat on a low hip wall beside the open service doors where a wagon carrying crates of oranges had just arrived. The workers paid them no attention as they offloaded the produce. Gray kept his voice low as he filled Caroline in on details of his visit to Luke, but throughout it all, she kept shaking her head.

"This doesn't sound like Luke," she insisted. "We both know he's always been the first man to dive into mischief, so it's possible he's been up to no good, but I don't believe he would give up. Something doesn't smell right."

Gray understood, for he'd wanted to deny his brother's guilt all the way up until he saw the utter hopelessness on Luke's face.

An innocent man wouldn't be so resigned.

"He's admitted his guilt. We need to accept that."

She still didn't look convinced. "But how did they find him out?"

"They found his code book with the list of his contacts in Cuba. He said he kept it in the raccoon shed out at Windover Landing."

Caroline's expression was grim as she watched the deliverymen close the wagon bed and prepare to leave. The corners of her mouth turned down, and her eyes darkened. "And how did they know about the raccoon shed?"

He'd already asked himself that a dozen times and come up empty. "I don't know."

She looked sick as she turned to him. "Otis."

The possibility hit him like a slap in the face. Otis rarely went out to Windover Landing, but when Gray was overseas, he had no idea what Otis got up to. Otis knew Morse code. Otis spoke Spanish and had contacts everywhere. And as a black man, Otis had plenty of reason to resent the government.

"Could Otis and Luke have been in this together?" he asked Caroline. "If Luke is covering for him, it would explain why he

241

isn't fighting too hard."

Caroline shook her head. "I think Otis turned him in. He's the only one with the means and the motive. And he would have been well paid for that sort of information."

Gray curled over, bracing his head in his hands. Was there no one he could trust? His father had given Otis a good job and paid him well, but Gray had been out of the country for most of the last twenty years. He didn't truly know Otis.

"I'll figure this out," he said grimly. "If Otis stabbed us in the back, I'll catch him in the act."

"In the meantime, I'm not giving up on Luke," Caroline said, but this was a battle she shouldn't waste her strength on. Luke was deliberately sacrificing himself so as not to suck the rest of his family down with him.

"Luke wants the best for you," Gray said gently. "He specifically said he wants you to soar."

She kept her chin high but blinked furiously to stop the tears from falling. "I will never, *never* give up on him."

Gray reached out an arm to pull her against him. This horrific crisis had brought him and Caroline closer than they'd ever been. She no longer bucked against his rules, and he'd lost interest in trying to mold her into the sort of sober, conventional woman he thought she should be. They both had bigger problems to confront, and the stain on their family's honor was going to scorch. Gray could afford a hit to his reputation, but Caroline couldn't.

"Once news of the scandal breaks, you may not be able to keep working here." He'd never approved of Caroline getting sucked into the McKinley administration, but she loved her work and was likely to become a casualty of Luke's disgrace.

"I've already told Mrs. McKinley and the president everything," she said.

"And how did that go?" he asked, stunned that Caroline could still be employed if news had already reached the White House.

"Not well. Mrs. McKinley was so appalled that she recoiled from me as I talked. I hadn't even finished before she raced straight to the president's office to tell him everything. But, Gray . . . President McKinley was so kind. He actually tried to comfort me instead of hurling me out of the house as I feared."

"So that's it?"

She nodded. "I think so. Mrs. McKinley takes her cue from the president, and since he accepted it, she fell into lockstep behind him."

243

"A matched pair, then."

The tone of his voice must have irked Caroline, for her spine stiffened, but her voice became earnest.

"You don't understand them," she said. "Mrs. McKinley is a fragile, difficult woman, but her husband dotes on her anyway. He dances attendance on her. You ought to see how solicitous he is."

He snorted. "So are you."

"The difference is that I'm being paid, and he has to put up with her for free."

Laughter bubbled up inside, and he didn't bother to hide it. Caroline laughed too, and he pulled her into another hug. They needed this. No matter how hard these days were, and there were plenty more darkening the horizon, it was important to celebrate these small flashes of happiness.

Annabelle would be a big part of the happiness he wanted in his life. He missed her. It had been a week since he'd left for Cuba, and he was ready to pick up where he'd left off. Perhaps this weekend they could take a trip to Mount Vernon, where she'd have a chance to pay homage to the man she'd always admired. Her wholesome, unabashed joy in the commonplace things he took for granted always impressed him. Looking at the world through her eyes was teaching him to savor the bounty around him, and now more than ever, he needed her in his life.

Luke had been corrupted and Otis may have betrayed them all, but Gray could depend on Annabelle to light these dark days.

TWENTY

Annabelle had been at her new job for only a week, but she loved every moment of it. The Department of Agriculture was huge, occupying one of the largest buildings in all of Washington, DC. Each morning Annabelle climbed to the third floor, where she worked alongside Horace Greenfield to study durum wheat. Horace was a voracious gossip, gleefully spreading the latest chatter generated in Washington's tight-knit group of government employees. While she didn't mind listening to him, she never let a word about her own life slip, for doing so could make it fodder for the Washington grapevine.

In her second week, she began measuring the effect of deep freeze on the wheat. The kernels had been in cold storage of varying conditions for three months, and she studied each batch beneath the lens of a microscope, searching for frost damage.

"Visitor for you," Horace said.

She pulled back from the microscope and froze, for the last thing she expected to see was Gray Delacroix standing in the open doorway with a rumpled shirt and a two-day growth of beard shadowing his jaw. He looked exhausted, but his eyes burned with a quiet hope. He held a bouquet of daises in his hand.

"Congratulations," he said, slowly walking into the lab and handing her the flowers. She'd never been given flowers in her life, and it made her heart skip a beat.

"For what?"

He looked around the laboratory, his gaze tracking along the black slate tables and banks of steel cabinets lining the walls. "On your new job. Coming to work for the enemy, I see."

There was no heat in his words, only a gentle humor, but Horace overheard, and his eyes nearly popped from his head. The sight of a handsome, disheveled man carrying flowers in hand and his heart in his eyes would stoke Horace's gossip-hungry appetite for weeks.

"You don't mind?" she asked.

Gray tilted his head as he gazed down at her, affection blazing in his face. "I don't

247

mind," he murmured softly. "I'm proud of you."

Her heart turned over, wondering what he would say if he knew how she'd gotten this position. She glanced away, pretending to admire the flowers. What had happened to Luke wasn't her fault. She must smother these guilty feelings and look only forward, never back. She set the daisies on the lab table, covering the pale splotch where Horace once spilled bleach. There was no need for Gray ever to learn what she'd done in regard to his brother.

Given the shadows beneath his eyes and rumpled clothing, the trip to Cuba had been difficult, and she needed to hear about it, but not within earshot of the gossipy Horace Greenfield.

"Let's step outside for a few minutes," she said, and Gray nodded.

The moment they were in the stairwell, he pulled her into his arms. Before she could even gasp in surprise, his mouth closed over hers, kissing her long and deep. She returned his embrace, clinging to him and giving as much comfort as she received. Relief trickled through her. He had no suspicion of her, no inkling about her role in this. She wasn't to blame, anyway — it was Luke's doing, not hers. Gray was her future. The stars were coming into alignment, and all was right with her world.

He lifted his head. "I really missed you," he said, a world of longing in his voice.

She wanted to drown in it but managed to hold on to a slim thread of composure. "I missed you too." Somewhere on a floor below them, a door opened and footsteps echoed in the stairwell, causing her to pull back and smooth her blouse. "Let's head outside where we can talk."

He didn't argue as he followed her. It was a crystal-blue sky, and she led him past the rose garden and experimental herb station and toward the arboretum. Pathways meandered through trees and led to a koi pond in the center of the arboretum. They were in the middle of the city, but the sheltering screen of trees provided complete privacy. She settled onto a bench and he joined her, clasping her hands tightly.

It would be best to get the hard part over with. "Tell me about Luke," she said.

"He's guilty. He admitted it."

It wasn't a surprise, but it hurt to hear anyway. "Gray, I'm so sorry."

"He's a grown man, and he knew what he was wading into. I paid for a lawyer to defend him at trial, but he plans to fall on the mercy of the court. If he's lucky, he'll get a life sentence."

She tensed. "And if he's unlucky?"

"Then he hangs."

She tried not to flinch, but it was hard. As if too restless to sit, Gray stood and wandered closer to the pond, hands stuffed into his pockets as he stared into the water. His face was drawn and sober as he spoke in a low voice. "I think Otis betrayed us."

She recoiled, so stunned by the unexpected statement that it took a moment to process the words. "What do you mean?"

"Luke said that his codebook was discovered. It was hidden in the raccoon shed out at Windover Landing. Otis had a key to that shed. He had access to everything. I think he's probably the one who turned Luke in."

Her mouth went dry, and it was hard to breathe. What a fool she'd been to imagine that if she escaped Gray's detection, he wouldn't find someone else to blame.

But she couldn't let him blame Otis.

She didn't know how she was going to survive the next few minutes, for every instinct urged her to run away and never look back, but she stood on legs that felt like water to face him. There was no easy way to do this, and no point in delaying.

"It wasn't Otis," she said quietly.

He turned to gape at her. "What? How do

you know that?"

"It was me."

There was no change in his expression. Her heart pounded so hard that she heard it in her ears, and he seemed to gape at her forever. Why didn't he say something? She had to get this over with.

"I found the codebook and the maps," she said. "I'd been told someone in your house was spying, so I was on the lookout, and I immediately recognized it for what it was. American lives depended on stopping the insurgency. I didn't know what else to do."

He still hadn't moved, still stared with that blank, uncomprehending look. "Who told you someone in my house was spying?"

"Someone from the army."

The breath left him in a rush, and it looked like he was about to topple over, but he braced a hand against the trunk of a tree. He drew several breaths and gazed around in dumbfounded anguish. Finally he straightened and looked at her.

"You didn't suspect *me*, did you?"

She hadn't thought this could get any worse, but it did as heat flushed her face and Gray's mouth turned hard. His stunned look faded as he narrowed his eyes.

"How much of it was a lie?" he demanded. "When did you start coming to my house to prowl for secrets and papers? Was it from the very beginning?"

"No," she whispered.

"Then when, Annabelle?" His voice lashed out like a whip, and she flinched but didn't back away. "When did you start faking affection and holding your nose so you could poke through my study? Through my father's letters? When did your every interaction with me become nothing more than a ploy to spy on us?"

He was losing his temper, and nothing she could say would soothe him. It would only pour oil onto the fire, and he had a right to be incensed. Why did doing the right thing feel so wrong?

"I'm not going to answer that."

His gaze slid past her shoulder to where the mansard roof of the Department of Agriculture could be seen above the trees. Comprehension dawned, and bitterness twisted his face.

"You were bought," he said in a disbelieving voice. "They promised you a plum job, and you pounced on it."

It wasn't true, but he would never believe her. It didn't matter how badly she wanted a permanent position, she had done it for Dr. Norwood's grandson and the thousands of other young men stationed in Cuba.

"I did what any loyal American would have done," she said.

"And were richly rewarded for it." He walked toward her, and the icy calm in his gaze was somehow more frightening than if he yelled and screamed. There was nothing she could say that would make sense to him. "How long was it after you turned the information over that you were offered this job? An hour? A day?"

"It wasn't long, and I'm sure you know that," she said. "I didn't know what to do, and I will forever wonder if there was a better way I could have handled it. If I acted wrongly, then I can only pray that God will forgive me. I know I've hurt you, and I am so desperately sorry."

He braced his hands on his thighs, bending over almost as though he was going to be sick. She wanted to offer comfort, but he'd only fling her away.

"Well, the scales have fallen from my eyes," he finally said. He pushed himself back to his full height. His face was twisted with bitterness and his eyes accusatory. "Good-bye, Annabelle. I hope to the bottom of my soul that I never have to see you again."

The words scorched, but she deserved it.

She stood motionless by the pond as he turned his back on her and walked away.

TWENTY-ONE

If Gray stopped to think about the devastation of Annabelle's betrayal, it would sink him. Instead, his first order of business after leaving her at the koi pond was to cancel the sale of the *Pelican*. His life in America was eroding quickly, making it impossible to predict how things would unfold in the coming months. He wanted his options open, and that meant keeping his ship. Suddenly, life on the far side of the world felt irresistibly tempting.

His banker was appalled at the prospect of canceling the deal. George Wagner would earn a generous commission from the sale of the steamship, but his fees would evaporate if it was scuttled.

"It will be very difficult to cancel at this date," he stammered from behind his huge desk at the bank.

"I know it will be difficult. Can it be done?" It would surely involve some hefty penalties, but Gray was willing to pay them.

Wagner still hesitated. "This sale will make you an extremely wealthy man."

"I'm already wealthy. I want to scrap the deal. I'm rich enough."

"That may be," the banker said delicately. "I fear that is not the case for your brother. This morning I was notified of the third bad check written against your brother's account."

Gray instantly went on alert. "What are you talking about?"

"Luke Delacroix has written three bad checks in the past month. If the situation is not remedied soon, the bank may assess overdraft fees against his account."

Gray almost wanted to laugh. The world would be a brighter place if the only problem Luke had to worry about was an overdrawn account.

"How bad is the damage?" he asked.

"Three checks totaling six thousand dollars."

That was a lot richer than anticipated, but Gray would settle the debt. Where Luke squandered his money was always a mystery, for he earned a decent income from the family business but always seemed strapped for cash.

"Who needs to be paid?"

"I'm not at liberty to say," the banker replied. "We have a fiduciary responsibility to safeguard your brother's privacy."

"And yet you're asking me to cover his debts." The banker hadn't exactly stated that, but they both knew where the deep pockets were. "I'm not paying money to unknown persons. I need to know the nature of those payments."

Mr. Wagner shifted in his chair, the corners of his mouth turning down. "All I am at liberty to say is that the checks were written to private individuals in the Philadelphia area."

Gray froze. It was in Philadelphia where Luke had run into trouble four years earlier. Was he being blackmailed? It would explain his penury these last few years.

"Give me the names."

"I can't do that," the banker demurred.

"And I can't sell my ship. Cancel the sale of the *Pelican,* and good luck tracking down my brother to settle those debts. Let me know when you're ready to give me those three names, and I'll pay them off."

The glass in the door rattled as Gray slammed out of the office.

Caroline was the most likely person to know Luke's private business. Gray didn't have an appointment with her, but neither did the dozens of other people who walked up to the front door of the White House and knocked, asking for a chance to see inside. The president's home was open to visitors every day until three o'clock, and Gray funneled in with the rest of them. A uniformed butler stood at the entrance to the East Room, an oversized chamber covered in embossed paper, gilt mirrors, and richly appointed furnishings.

Gray approached a footman. "I'd like to speak with Caroline Delacroix, secretary to the first lady. I'm her brother and need to speak with her on an urgent family matter."

"Miss Delacroix is a very busy lady," the footman said. "I'm not sure Mrs. McKinley can spare her."

"Please inquire," Gray asked. He wasn't sure what had prompted this burning sense of urgency, for Luke wasn't going anywhere, but if he was being blackmailed, Gray wanted to know.

The butler disappeared down a hallway, and Gray cooled his heels alongside the rest of the tourists gawking at the life-sized oil paintings and glittering chandeliers.

Caroline scurried into the room a few minutes later, her face tense with expectation and anxiety. "Any news?"

He shook his head, hating the disappointment that darkened her face. He wanted to protect Caroline, not pour more problems on her shoulders. "I need to speak with you privately," he said.

She nodded and beckoned for him to follow her to a small waiting room near the back of the main floor. It was a windowless room but still decorated with a grandiose coffered ceiling and velvet-flocked wallpaper. Chairs lined the wall, but they didn't bother to sit. The moment Caroline closed the door, she turned to him.

"What's going on?" she asked.

"Who does Luke know in Philadelphia?"

She stilled. "Aside from the obvious? No one."

"His bank account is overdrawn from checks written to three people in Philadelphia. I'm worried he was being blackmailed. Did he confide anything to you?"

She sank into a chair as though she didn't have the strength to keep standing. "He's still sending money to the families. He's been doing it for years."

"What?" he burst out. "I paid those people off long ago. Luke *knows* that!"

"Gray, I don't think you have any idea how miserable Luke has been over what happened. It consumes him. He's never

259

stopped obsessing over it, and he's been writing checks to those people ever since it happened."

He should have known. Luke had been knocked off-kilter when his first major business deal imploded. It was an attempt to partner with the Magruders, combining the Delacroix reputation for quality with the Magruders' ability to mass-produce food. Jedidiah Magruder had suggested a plan in which their companies would cooperate to capitalize on the American obsession with coffee. He proposed a line of pricey coffee, using the Magruder packaging facilities but branded with the Delacroix name and reputation for gourmet quality. Both companies stood to gain.

Everything began well, with the Magruders investing heavily in canisters with snug-fitting lids to preserve freshness, and elegant embossed labels with custom artwork. Luke worked with their father to import coffee beans from Kenya, the best in the world. They tested the market in Philadelphia, a city famous for its coffeehouses. Luke selected the coffeehouses and chefs with connections to the best restaurants in the city. The plan was to release the gourmet coffee in the venues Luke selected, then gauge the response before distributing it to a national market.

Nothing on the canisters coming out of the Magruder production facility indicated there was anything besides top-quality ground coffee inside. What they didn't know was that Clyde Magruder had always intended to adulterate the full-bodied Kenyan coffee beans with cheap ground chicory. To mask the chicory aftertaste, he used chemical flavoring and colored the mix with indigo dye, lead chromate, and coal tar. The coffee was excellent, with a smooth flavor and enticing aroma. In hindsight, the Magruders were paying close attention to see if their cheap mixture would fool the market.

The combination proved fatal to three people within a week of the coffee going on sale. While most people could easily digest the brew, who knew why some people had sensitivities to chicory root that proved deadly? When those three individuals all suffered swelling in the throat, wheezing, and seizures, the adulterated coffee was quickly identified as the source of their illness. There was no law against what the Magruders had done. Such techniques had been used for decades, but Gray was furious. The Delacroixs had never used adulterants or chemical flavorings in any of their products, but by partnering with the Magruders, they had lost control of the production.

Luke was devastated, feeling as though he had personally administered a cup of poison to each of those three people.

Caroline continued with the story. "The daughter of one of the men is getting married next month, and Luke didn't want her to scrimp. Her father was a factory shop foreman, and times have been hard since he died."

"I gave each family twenty thousand dollars after it happened," Gray said. "That's more than the foreman would have earned in a decade."

Caroline shrugged. "You know how Luke is."

He did. Luke was generous, funny, and completely unmoored from reality. It looked like he had been single-handedly trying to keep those families afloat, even though they'd all been compensated and signed legal documents agreeing to the settlements.

"Will you make good on the checks?" Caroline asked. "I know we are under no legal obligation, but —"

"I'll pay the checks." It was the least he could do for Luke.

"And what about Otis?" she asked quietly.

Gray braced himself for another difficult

conversation. Even thinking about Annabelle made him ill, but Caroline needed to know that Otis was innocent, and the only way to do that was to reveal everything he knew.

"Otis had nothing to do with what happened to Luke." His mouth went dry and his stomach turned. "It was Annabelle."

Caroline was stunned, and he relayed the details as quickly as possible, choking back revulsion as he talked. Caroline listened in horrified sympathy, waiting patiently until he finished.

"Oh, Gray, I'm so sorry. I'm glad about Otis, but . . ." Her voice hardened as she stood and began pacing the small room like a panther, fists clenched, jaw outthrust. "If I ever see that woman again, there won't be a rock big enough for her to hide beneath. I'll pick her up and bodily fling her into the Potomac. I'll kick her back to Kansas. I'll —"

"If you see Annabelle again, you will ignore her," he instructed calmly. It was the only thing they could do. As much as he'd like to call down fire and brimstone on her head, she hadn't done anything illegal. Some people might even side with Annabelle. Neither he nor Caroline ever would. To them, she was a snake who had slid into their world, gathered information, and used it to destroy their family.

The fight went out of Caroline. Her shoulders sagged, and she closed her eyes, but only for a moment. Then her spine straightened, her chin lifted, and she returned to sit beside him. "Tell me what I can do to help."

He bit off an ironic laugh. "There's nothing you can do. I was an idiot, and now I have to live with it."

"No, you don't," Caroline said brightly. "You're ready to start a family. That's part of the reason you fell so quickly for that person from Kansas. Don't let one bad experience dissuade you. I know plenty of eligible young ladies."

Everything in him recoiled. Even thinking about starting a courtship at this point was anathema.

Caroline noticed, and sympathy tinged her gaze. "Forgive me. Perhaps it's too early, but when you're ready, I will find the perfect woman for you. If I must climb to the top of Mount Everest, I will find her and drag her to your front door."

He struggled not to laugh. "Please don't bother. This is probably something I should handle on my own."

Caroline tutted. "It has not escaped my

264

notice that you have always looked out for Luke and me. Sometimes Dad could be a little scattered, but we could always count on you to remember our birthdays and school graduations. You might be in China or Patagonia, but there would always be a note and a gift delivered on time. When I lost my first tooth and couldn't stop crying, you wrote me the kindest note. I still have it. Gray, there isn't anything in the world I won't do for you."

He had no idea those gestures had meant so much to her. It made him regret again all the years he'd spent abroad.

"Caroline, please don't worry about me."

"But I do."

Her hand covered his, and he drew comfort from her touch. His baby sister was now propping *him* up. The worst thing was that he needed it, for Caroline was all he had left of a family.

Twenty-Two

For a week Annabelle moved through life like a sleepwalker — eating, bathing, preparing dinner, but feeling strangely disconnected, as though it were someone else performing these mundane tasks. Elaine seemed unusually happy these days. Or was it merely that Annabelle was so miserable? Most evenings, while Elaine sat reading a braille book, Annabelle kept glancing at her watch, wondering if it was too early to go to bed at eight o'clock.

But one Saturday morning, as they put the breakfast dishes away, Elaine surprised her. "Is this real vanilla?" she asked.

Annabelle had been so engrossed in staring out the window that she hadn't noticed Elaine twisting the lids off each bottle of Delacroix spice that rested on the shelf in the kitchen. Elaine held the little dark bottle of vanilla extract, delighting in the delicate aroma.

"Yes."

Elaine brightened and took another whiff. "I've heard of real vanilla liquid. It's shockingly expensive. Did Mr. Delacroix give this to you?"

"Yes," Annabelle said, praying they could move away from the topic of Gray immediately.

Mercifully, Elaine was more interested in the vanilla than in Gray. She spoke about how Harry, the blind soldier she'd been helping at the Library of Congress, used to work in a grocery, and he said vanilla was the most expensive product in the whole store. There were some cheap imitations, but real vanilla cost twenty times what the fake version cost. Most people wanted the cheaper version, for surely once it was baked into a dish there would be no difference.

"Let's try it!" Elaine said.

"What do you mean?"

"Let's buy a bottle of the cheap vanilla, then bake two cakes. We already have a bottle of the expensive stuff, so let's compare! I have an entire book of recipes I checked out from the library."

It seemed there was no stopping Elaine, who eagerly began paging through the braille cookbook. She soon settled on a vanilla-spiced pear cake for her experiment, but Annabelle wanted nothing to do with it. Elaine, however, would not relent.

"I'll go to the grocer's even if you won't accompany me," Elaine said, reaching for her coin purse and preparing to leave. It would be impossible to relax knowing Elaine was out fumbling through the shop on her own.

"I'll go," Annabelle grumbled, and an hour later, they had all the ingredients necessary to begin baking.

Annabelle measured the dry ingredients, while Elaine prepared the papery thin slices of pears, chattering the entire time. When had her sister become so fascinated with cooking? She rattled on about how the French used a special blend of wheat in their world-famous crusty bread, and about how wine could be used to improve mustard recipes. Elaine had never shown much interest in cooking back in Kansas. Their mother's culinary skills had been limited to teaching them how to light a stove and use salt and pepper.

"Where did you learn all this?" Annabelle finally asked.

"At the library, of course. They have all kinds of books about cooking and culinary history."

Finally it was time to blend the vanilla

into each bowl of batter. Gray's vanilla wafted through the entire kitchen as they poured it, while the bowl with the fake vanilla seemed just as nice. They each sampled the batter.

"They taste the same," Annabelle said, and Elaine agreed. Since losing her eyesight, Elaine had developed a keener sense of taste and smell, but even she couldn't tell the difference between the two batters. It was a little disappointing.

After putting both cakes into the oven, Annabelle prepared the vanilla glazes while Elaine kept sharing food lore she'd heard or read while working at the library. It was annoying. Each time Elaine started talking about the difference between sweet and smoky paprika, or techniques for making vinegar, it made Annabelle think of Gray, and it was torture.

At last the cakes had been baked, cooled, and were ready for the coating of vanilla glaze. By now the entire apartment smelled divine. Annabelle laid a slice of each cake on a plate and served them to Elaine, giving no indication which slice had the real vanilla and which the fake.

"Can you tell the difference?" she asked.

Elaine sampled the real vanilla cake first. Her eyes closed in ecstasy, and she moaned.

"This may be the best thing I've ever tasted. Do we have enough pears for another cake? I'd like to bake another and take it to the library. This must be shared!"

Annabelle laughed. "Try the other cake." It would probably be just as good. Gray could be such a snob, with an overly refined palate only rich people could indulge. Normal, red-blooded Americans probably couldn't taste the difference.

Elaine carefully loaded a spoon with the fake vanilla cake, sniffed it, then tasted it. A look of confusion came over her. It took her a while to swallow, and a range of emotions crossed her face while she tried to render a verdict.

"It doesn't taste as sweet," she finally said. "You try it."

To Annabelle's dismay, she agreed. There was nothing *wrong* with the fake vanilla cake . . . but something about the flavor was a letdown. It didn't seem as rich. It was still good, just not heavenly.

"Let's invite the Hillenbrands over," Elaine said impulsively. "Something this good shouldn't be hoarded."

The elderly couple across the hall had always been kind to them, and this would be a delightful way to thank them. Married for fifty-five years, the Hillenbrands had worked for decades as lamplighters, walking dozens of miles each night to light the streetlights, and again in the hours before dawn to snuff them out. The physical toll showed on their rail-thin frames and worn clothing.

Laughter abounded as the Hillenbrands took the same taste challenge and concurred with their conclusion about the cakes. Old Mr. Hillenbrand even offered to go to the store to fetch more ingredients if Elaine wished to keep developing her baking skills.

"I may take you up on that!" Elaine laughed. Annabelle hadn't seen her this animated in years.

Was this the reason they had come from Kansas? So that Elaine could discover a love for baking? Or maybe it was so they could befriend this nice elderly couple. All Annabelle knew for sure was that today had been surprisingly pleasant.

Except that as they shared cake and laughter, Luke Delacroix was sweltering in prison, and she would always feel responsible for that. If she could do it all again, would she have done anything differently? Her gaze trailed outside. She would probably struggle with that question for the rest of her life.

TWENTY-THREE

After a week of haggling with bankers and brokers, the sale of the *Pelican* had been canceled, and now Gray had to scramble to rehire the crew. Many of the *Pelican*'s crew members had quit while the ship sat in port during the sale negotiation. With luck, he might be able to find some of them. Every cargo steamer had quirks, and an experienced crew was essential.

"Sign me back up," Captain Haig said with a broad smile as they met on the bridge of the *Pelican*. The weathered old sailor wore his white hair in a ponytail that reached halfway down his back, for he'd always had a ruthless disregard for convention.

The *Pelican*'s bridge had the best view of anyplace on the ship, with windows providing a panoramic view over the harbor. Most of the bridge was taken up with the navigation equipment, but a small table near the back had just enough room for Gray, Otis, and Captain Haig to talk business.

"I wasn't too keen on those new owners," Haig said. "I probably would have quit before long."

"And why is that?" Otis asked.

"They were going to use the ship for regular coal deliveries between Baltimore and Miami. I'd die of boredom on a route like that." Working for the Delacroixs meant importing spices from distant points all over the world, and a regular coal run would be painfully mundane for a man as colorful as Captain Haig.

Gray was glad to have someone he trusted at the helm. "I'll get contracts for cargo lined up within the month, and I hope you and I can set sail for Madagascar by October."

"You're coming?" Captain Haig asked in surprise.

"I'm coming." Gray didn't add any details, even though Haig looked stunned. During their last trip from the Spice Islands, he'd told the old sailor about his plans to finally settle down and start a family. Haig had an instinctive love for the sea, but Gray never did.

Haig leaned back in his chair and drew on his pipe. "That's an abrupt turnabout for a man who took his mother's wedding ring out of the family vault only a few weeks ago."

Gray shot a look at Otis, the only person who'd known about that withdrawal. Otis had the decency to look abashed and shrugged. "Haig caught me coming out of the bank and asked me why. I was happy for you."

"And blabbed."

"And I blabbed," Otis admitted.

The last thing Gray wanted to think about was Annabelle Larkin. He needed to rehire a crew, inspect the ship, and scramble to find enough cargo to make the trip to Madagascar profitable.

"Let's go down to inspect the hold," Gray said as he stood and gestured to the door. Spices didn't take up much room, so most of their freight was supplied by other firms, and he needed to be sure everything was in order.

"Everything is in good shape," Haig said, making no move to leave the bridge. "Go find us a cargo. Anything except coal destined for Miami."

"I need to inspect the hold first." On her previous homeward voyage, the *Pelican* had carried eight thousand tons of camphor wood, and that could stink up a hold. "If the hold still smells like camphor, I need to know."

Haig kept his booted feet up on the table, blocking the doorway. "I told you . . . everything is fine."

The old sailor was acting oddly. He had been ever since Gray and Otis boarded the ship for an impromptu inspection an hour earlier. Gray had worked with Captain Haig for almost twenty years, and they usually clicked along like a well-oiled machine.

Not today. Gray had to push Haig's feet off the table to unblock the door, and then he headed out with Otis close behind. He ducked to navigate the steeply pitched stairs leading down to the first of two holds. The scent of camphor was still apparent, even in the passageway outside the hold.

Captain Haig finally joined them, sliding ahead of Gray in the narrow passageway. "I'll keep airing everything out," he said in an overly bright voice, but they both knew the problem with importing food or textiles was that they could absorb the scent of camphor, so this place needed to be sanitized. Gray couldn't risk tainting the freight.

"You haven't fumigated?" Otis asked.

Haig snorted. "I was preparing the ship for coal. No one cares if coal picks up a scent."

"Get it fumigated and sanitized," Gray said as he strode toward the starboard hold to see if it smelled as strongly.

Captain Haig hurried to slide in front of him again. "I'll get this side cleaned as well. Let's head back to the boiler room. I'd like to show you how we got the feedwater system set up with new brass fittings. Those things won't ever rust —"

"I'd like to see the starboard hold," Gray said, his suspicions deepening. The doors to the hold were closed and locked, and that wasn't protocol. If Captain Haig was hiding something in there, he needed to know.

"No need, Gray. I'll get it fumigated within the next twenty-four hours."

Gray tugged on the padlock, but it was secure. "What's behind this door?" he asked quietly, sick at the thought that Captain Haig might be disloyal. There were only so many blows a man could take, and he was reaching the limit.

"Look, I'm just storing some cargo for a friend. It doesn't concern you."

"It does if it's on my ship." It was hot down here, and a sour taste filled Gray's mouth.

"I'll get it off," Haig said.

"Not before I see it with my own eyes."

If Haig was up to something illegal, he

had to be stopped. Using the *Pelican* for smuggling was anathema. Losing confidence in a man he considered a friend was even worse. Where was he going to find an experienced captain on such short notice?

Captain Haig folded his arms across his chest, a flinty look in his eyes. "I was doing a favor for your brother," he said tightly.

Gray's mind reeled. It was bad enough to use his ship for smuggling, but *spying*? Was the *Pelican* being used to transport weapons or supplies to the revolutionaries in Cuba?

"Open it," he ordered, his voice lethally calm.

Captain Haig sighed and reached for his keys. Perspiration rolled down the side of Gray's face, and he fought back waves of nausea. Even the clattering of the keys was painful as Haig jerked the lock from the door and opened the hold.

Gray stepped inside the mostly empty hold. It reeked of camphor, and his footsteps sounded unnaturally loud in the cavernous space. He raised a ship lantern, but it revealed only a dozen crates stacked against the far side of the hold. Gray grabbed a crowbar from the wall and strode to the nearest crate to pry off the lid. There could be anything in here. Guns, bullets, dynamite. Or, given Luke's propensities, maybe incendiary literature intended to stoke the rebellion more effectively than dynamite could ever do.

Nails squeaked as he pried them free, then jerked the lid off the crate to reveal dozens of mason jars filled with some sort of pale substance. The plain glass jar he lifted was cool in his palm, and there was no label to identify what was inside.

He twisted off the lid and sniffed. Applesauce? The pieces started to click into place. He looked up at Captain Haig.

"What is it?" he asked, praying his suspicion was correct.

"Applesauce," Haig replied. "Or at least what the Magruders were hoping to pass off to the world as applesauce."

Relief rushed through Gray so fast, he almost felt dizzy. It was the plan Luke had told Gray about when he visited the prison. Gray didn't want anything to do with Luke's juvenile plot to embarrass the Magruders, but Captain Haig was obviously on board with it.

"You're too old for this sort of thing," Gray said with a reluctant smile at Haig.

A gleam flashed in the captain's eyes, but in truth, Haig was the sort who never seemed to age. He was probably seventy, but his heart beat with the mischief of a daredevil. "You have to admit, it's a wickedly clever plan."

"It's a ridiculous prank."

Haig shrugged. "Maybe. My odds of pulling it off without Luke's help aren't so good. I don't have the connections he did, but you do."

Gray shook his head. "Don't try to involve me in this. I've already told Luke I won't have anything to do with it. In fact, I want this dreck off my ship. Dump it overboard."

Otis stepped forward, both palms held out in appeal. "Don't be hasty."

Gray swiveled to gape at him. "Were you involved in this too?"

"Only a little." But the look on Otis's face made Gray suspect it was a lot more.

"How little?"

"I took the applesauce to chemists for analysis," Otis said. "Luke set up the connection with the magazines up north. We planned to launch the takedown next month."

Gray braced a hand on the wall, leaning against it for support. Had all this been happening beneath his nose and he hadn't noticed? Probably because he'd been so distracted by Annabelle that he'd been useless to his business and his family. Otis could have been hosting a circus in their

279

backyard, and he would have been oblivious.

Even with Luke in prison, it looked like Otis and Captain Haig intended to carry out the ridiculous prank. Gray shouldn't have anything to do with this sort of mischief, but as he glared at the casks of adulterated applesauce, Otis continued talking.

"That 'applesauce' is mostly pumpkin flesh boiled in cider. Two sets of chemists tested it, and their results match. Cheap filler, fake dye, fake sweeteners, and a premium price. You've got to give the Magruders credit for audacity."

Gray gave the Magruders credit for a lot more than that. Their tainted food had been at the heart of Luke's crushing sense of guilt for years. Luke had always been reckless, but it wasn't until the incident with the coffee that his rowdiness spilled over into truly destructive behavior. Gray would give his right arm if he could turn back the clock and save Luke from any association with the Magruders.

In a few months Clyde Magruder would run for a seat in Congress. If he won, he could surely craft legislation that would pave the way for more adulterated food in the future. Unless he could somehow be shamed into stopping.

"Let's go to your quarters to discuss this," Gray said to Captain Haig. Everything about this rubbed him the wrong way, but he had to agree with Haig that Luke's plan was fiendishly clever.

It was a tense walk up the companionway to the captain's quarters. Like in most merchant steamers, the crew lodged on the top cargo deck near the stern. The captain's quarters were on the starboard side, and the owner's cabin was directly opposite. Gray had long since cleared his belongings from the cabin, but he couldn't resist opening the door to peek inside. It was empty.

"I planned to let the chief engineer move in," Captain Haig said.

Gray let his eyes roam the tiny room. A bed with enough space for a trunk at its foot, a desk nailed to the wall, and a porthole for a window. It wasn't much, but he'd spent the majority of the past two decades in this cabin.

"I'll be moving my things back in soon," he said, a sense of resignation weighing heavily. It wouldn't be so bad. There had been periods of genuine satisfaction when he'd lived aboard the *Pelican.*

But for now, he needed to figure out what to do with the twelve crates of imitation

281

applesauce in his hold. He was fully prepared to look the other way while Haig and Otis tried to carry out Luke's plan, but he needed to minimize the risk to his ship and his company.

The captain's cabin had enough room for a small table, and soon they were all seated. Gray listened while they filled him in on the plan. Captain Haig showed him a jar with the original label, which simply said *Applesauce* in bold letters printed over a drawing of shiny red apples. There was no list of ingredients, which meant the label was perfectly legal. Had they lied on the label and claimed the jar contained real apples, it would be a problem, but the omission of an ingredient list was permissible.

"The labels Luke designed have already been printed, so the next step is to paste them on the jars," Otis said. He continued to outline their plan for distributing the jars to a select number of food critics, laboratories, and journalists.

It didn't sound like the contents were dangerous, just unpalatable. The Magruders probably saved only a few cents per jar by using the cheaper pumpkin. That meant they were planning on producing this counterfeit food on a massive scale to realize a profit. Likely millions of jars would be sold in the coming years to unsuspecting consumers. What if one of those customers was allergic to pumpkin?

"Under no circumstances do I want those jars in grocer's stores," Gray said.

"Amen," Otis replied. "Luke's plan was to send them to people who help shape opinion, along with the real ingredient list. He knows journalists all over the country, but Haig and I don't have those connections. We need help."

Silence hung in the air. It was obvious they expected him to step up to the plate and open those doors, but everything about this plan went against the grain for him. He wasn't a rule breaker. He wasn't reckless or foolhardy.

But he knew the food business. He knew how publicity channels and distribution to grocers worked, and could help get this slop off the market.

"I can open a few doors with the press," he conceded. "I can contact the mail order catalogs like Sears and Montgomery Ward to alert them to what's in those jars and get them to pull the product."

Otis and Captain Haig both beamed, sensing his capitulation was only moments away. And it probably was. They needed him for credibility with the journalists, but it didn't have to stop there. The government could probably help, and Caroline had access to a megaphone louder than all the others combined.

He immediately rejected the idea. "I don't want Caroline involved in this," he said, for she had too much to lose.

"You sure about that?" Otis asked. "If she knew about this, she would seize the chance."

It didn't matter. Loyalty to Luke might prompt her to participate, but Caroline had a promising future, and this plan involved risk. She didn't deserve to get sucked into Luke's schemes.

"Caroline is to know nothing about this. I don't want her within a mile of it."

"And what about you?" Captain Haig asked.

At that very moment Luke was sweltering in a Cuban jail cell, unlikely to ever get out, and it had all started because of a cup of tainted coffee. Peeling the curtain back on Clyde Magruder's schemes was the best gift Gray could give to Luke.

A smile curved his mouth. Heaven help them all, he was going to do it.

Twenty-Four

Annabelle gazed in wonder at the odd wrinkly lemon that had just landed in her palm. Hundreds of people were crammed into the meeting room on the Department of Agriculture's ground floor, where strange fruits and vegetables were being passed around the audience. They were in the middle of a presentation by David Fairchild, recently returned from the Mediterranean to recount his adventures gathering nuts, fruits, and seeds that might be adapted to the American climate.

"The Corsicans call this fruit a *citron*," Mr. Fairchild said of the wrinkled lemon. "It grows on a compact shrub, and the juice is sweet with almost no acid flavor. I believe it would be suitable for adaptation in California or other warm, dry climates."

Annabelle passed the fruit to the man sitting next to her, then turned her attention back to Mr. Fairchild, but being short made it impossible to see over the people in the seats in front of her. This was likely the only chance she'd ever have to see the famed explorer in person, and she was tired of being polite. She stood, trying to be unobtrusive as she angled down the crowded aisle so she could stand in the back of the room for a better view.

When she turned to face the podium, Mr. Fairchild met her gaze across the crowded audience and gave her a little nod. She nodded back, and he continued his speech.

That was odd. A few people noticed the momentary exchange and swiveled to look at her, but she ignored them, for the exotic fruits and plant cuttings displayed on the front table were fascinating. Mr. Fairchild gestured to several bowls that brimmed with a strange seed called a pistachio, which was a member of the cashew family. The tree was native to the Middle East, and the seeds of the tree looked like little green nuts. Mr. Fairchild had enough for everyone to sample, and as he concluded his speech, he sent the bowls of pistachios down the aisles.

People clustered around the bowls, already eating and commenting on the unique flavor. Horace Greenfield had managed to get one of the bowls and would surely spare her a few. How was it that people like Horace were always in the center of things?

"Horace?" she asked. She didn't care if it was rude, she was going to get some of those pistachios. She barely came up to these peoples' shoulders, but she gamely angled through them. Horace noticed and extended the bowl to her. She would likely only get one shot, so she scooped up a hefty amount.

She sampled a single seed as she wandered toward the back of the room. Oh my, what an odd flavor. It had a soft texture, smooth and earthy. Nutty? Well, obviously, but different. She wasn't good at putting a name to flavors.

Could she smuggle a few of these to Gray? He'd probably never tasted a pistachio, and she instinctively wanted to share them with him. They were plump and rare and exotic.

The familiar dart of pain squeezed her chest, for Gray would never again take a single thing from her — not an apology, nor an explanation, and certainly not a pistachio. She had to stop thinking about him every time she saw a rare fruit or tasted a new spice.

Still, he would be fascinated by these pistachios. Maybe she could figure out a way to send them anonymously. It was such a shame he couldn't sample them. . . .

Stop! She was being ridiculous and impulsively tipped the entire handful of nuts into her mouth. Done! Now she could quit toying with the idea of sharing them with a man who hated the sight of her. She closed her eyes, concentrating on the flavor to get the full experience.

Someone tapped her on the shoulder. "Miss Larkin?"

Her eyes flew open. David Fairchild stood directly in front of her, trying not to laugh as she struggled with a huge mouthful of pistachios. She chewed and swallowed as quickly as possible.

"Hi," she said inanely. "Thanks for the pistachios."

He nodded. "Of course. Dr. Norwood told me about you. Can we step outside to talk?"

Her stomach clenched at the mention of Dr. Norwood. Nevertheless, she followed Mr. Fairchild down the hall and out to the experimental garden. His white canvas jacket hung on his frame, making him seem painfully thin. Rumor had it that he'd contracted typhoid on his first trip overseas, and given his pallor and gaunt frame, it was probably true. The Department of Agriculture had several men out in the field to gather specimens. Were they all destined to catch such diseases? Gray certainly battled his share.

She needed to *stop* thinking about Gray, even as she wondered if Mr. Fairchild might know of a better remedy for malaria than quinine. If he did, she would certainly find a way to communicate the information to Gray, but for now she focused her entire attention on the explorer. Not many people got a chance like this, and she intended to memorize every moment and not spare another thought for Gray Delacroix.

She followed Mr. Fairchild to a bench in the herb garden. He set a leather satchel on the grass and turned to her with a pleasant smile.

"I understand you are acquainted with Gray Delacroix," he began.

She shot to her feet. "No. I mean yes, but I no longer have any association with him. So if you're hoping I'll spy on him, that's not —"

"I don't need a spy," he said, looking a little appalled at her suggestion. "I just need a favor."

Oh dear, she'd just horribly offended this nice man. Confusion riddled his handsome face, and he looked pale and thin enough that a stiff wind might carry him away. She sat back down, trying to calm the beating of her heart.

"I don't think I can help you. Not if the favor has anything to do with Gray Delacroix."

Mr. Fairchild opened his satchel and retrieved a wooden case about the size of a cigar box. He opened the lid to reveal a dozen glass vials and offered her one. "These vials are filled with different strains of rice one of our agents collected in Japan. We estimate that there are thousands of varieties of rice, and perhaps a few hundred that are suitable for human consumption."

Curiosity made it impossible to resist leaning over to inspect the vials, and she immediately spotted the differences among the grains. Rice was a cereal grass, but having come from Kansas, she had no experience with it.

"I understand Delacroix is heading to Madagascar," Mr. Fairchild said.

Her head shot up. "He is?"

Disappointment crashed down on her at Mr. Fairchild's nod. It meant Gray wasn't going to stay in America after all. His dream of settling down and starting a family was being abandoned if he planned to head to the other side of the world. How long would it take to sail to Madagascar and back? Months? Years? She was only certain that she must have wounded him more than she knew for him to take such drastic action. It was hard to breathe at the news.

"Madagascar has a unique environment," Mr. Fairchild continued. "Its isolation from the rest of Africa means they have plants and animal species that are found nowhere else on earth. Rice is a mainstay of their diet. I suspect that the uniqueness of the island has caused the rice to grow and adapt in unique ways. I want to know more."

Heaven help her, she knew what he was about to ask. Approaching Gray for a favor was unthinkable, but how could she turn down a request from the world's leading plant explorer? There wasn't a lot of money for plant exploration, and Gray could help them. All he had to do was collect some rice and put it in a test tube.

"He's already going to be there," Mr. Fairchild said. "I understand that he's not an enthusiastic supporter of the Department of Agriculture, but if you have a special friendship . . ." From his bag he pulled a set of empty test tubes, offering them to her.

She didn't want to touch them. "How did you know that? That he's going to Madagascar?"

"He's seeking cargo for his ship. Flyers are posted all over the port."

"We don't have a special friendship," Annabelle said. "I may be the last person on earth who could persuade him to collect those samples."

If Mr. Fairchild was disappointed, he did not show it. He merely set the wooden box of empty vials on her lap and refused to take them back.

"Huge swaths of our country are lying fallow because they aren't suitable for wheat or corn," he said. "Rice may be the answer. Rice is nutritious and easy to store and can feed millions of people. Whatever personal tiff you have with Delacroix pales in comparison to that."

It was true. Somehow Annabelle was going to have to find the gumption to track Gray down and get him to agree.

TWENTY-FIVE

At the rate they were moving, Gray figured he and Otis would conclude their clandestine task by midnight. They worked quietly in the townhouse kitchen after Mr. and Mrs. Holder had gone to bed, for he didn't want any witnesses.

He still couldn't help smiling as he pasted another label onto a jar of the Magruders' "applesauce." They had over a thousand jars to label, and it was slow going. Otis reported it had taken him and Luke two full days to steam the original labels from the glass jars, but Luke's arrest had prevented them from moving on to the next step of relabeling.

Luke had designed the comical label using his own artwork. A full-color drawing showed a large pumpkin with the top cut off. A pair of happy mice perched on the pumpkin's open rim and gleefully poured chemicals from test tubes into it. The name on the label was "Magruder Mash That

Tastes Like Applesauce."

Most damning was the list of ingredients printed on the back of the label: *Pumpkin stewed in cider vinegar, sugar beet glucose, chrome yellow dye made with pure lead nitrate and potassium chromate, and a hint of formaldehyde to keep food eternally fresh. Product is guaranteed to contain no apples!*

More happy mice applauded the last line. The plan was to deliver the jars to Boston, a city ideally placed to reach the publishing, culinary, and academic heart of America.

A knock on the front door interrupted their work. Gray froze, his glance darting around at the hundreds of jars.

"You expecting anybody?" Otis asked.

Gray shook his head, for it was past ten o'clock.

"I'll dart upstairs and peek out the window to see who it is," Otis said.

Gray reached for a sheet to drape over the stacks of labels and bowls of paste, but there was no way to cover the crates of bogus applesauce. Whoever was at the front door continued their incessant pounding, probably assuming the entire household was abed and needed awakening.

"It's your sister," Otis called in a harsh whisper from upstairs. "What do you want to do?"

294

Gray cursed under his breath. At all costs, he didn't want Caroline within a square mile of this brazen caper, because, quite frankly, she would love it and want to dive in. He tugged the door to the kitchen closed, wishing it had a lock, for Caroline usually helped herself to a cup of tea whenever she visited.

"I've got it covered," he called up to Otis. "Make yourself scarce until I can get rid of her."

He knew it wouldn't be easy the moment he opened the door. Caroline looked typically chic in a glamorous tailored suit, but her eyes were snapping mad.

"Why haven't you sold the *Pelican*?" she demanded.

He plastered a mild expression on his face and stood in the doorway. "That's all? No good evening or inquiry about my health? Just rude demands?"

She shoved past him as she pushed inside. "I got a note from our banker just before dinner that said he can't pay my bills because the anticipated infusion of cash hasn't arrived in my account. Why not?"

Gray folded his arms over his chest, wondering what other bills Caroline had run up since her gross over-expenditure on clothing. "However did you manage to restrain yourself during the hours since dinner?"

"I've been busy with the first lady," she snapped. "What's going on, Gray? Why haven't you sold that ship?"

"Because Dad entrusted it and all its dealings to me, and I've decided not to sell. We're keeping it."

That took her aback, but only for a moment. A range of emotions crossed her face, but finally she smiled. "Good! I rather like the *Pelican* and was sorry to lose it. Let's have a cup of tea, and you can tell me everything."

She sashayed toward the kitchen, but he slid in front of her, bracing an arm on the frame of the door to block it.

"Kitchen is closed. Mrs. Holder gave it a good scouring earlier." After which he and Otis had destroyed the place with sloppy bowls of paste and a thousand jars of mash.

Caroline pulled an amused face as she swiped at his shirt. "What is this?" She rubbed the sticky substance between her fingers. "Gray! Have you been rummaging through the trash? You're a mess."

"Yes. I'm a mess. Go home and see if the White House kitchens can produce a cup of tea for you."

She pinched his cheek. "They don't have

my big brother there to comfort me! Come, I need to complain about the new head of security. He's making my life miserable."

She tried to twist the knob, but he clamped his hand over hers, stopping her. Her humor vanished as she met his gaze.

"What's going on in there?" she asked.

"Nothing of interest."

"Does it have to do with the *Pelican*?"

He nodded. "Otis and I are preparing the cargo. Nothing to concern you. It won't earn much of a return."

She jerked her hand away. "Do you think that's why I came over tonight? That I'm angry about the money?"

His gaze darted down her ensemble, a canary yellow satin suit liberally embellished with seed pearls. He didn't want to reopen their argument about her wardrobe, and wouldn't have if she hadn't barged into his house, griping about not receiving her share of the ship money.

"Custom wardrobes are expensive," he said simply.

"So are attorneys and private investigators!"

He nearly choked. "Why do you need an attorney or private investigator?"

Caroline looked at him in exasperation. His heart split wide open, for he immediately put the pieces together.

"Caroline, he's guilty," he said as gently as possible.

She shook her head. "I don't believe it. I'll never believe it, and since you've given up on him, it's up to *me* to get Luke out. Yes, I've hired an investigator who plans to leave for Cuba this week. He needs to be paid."

He wished Caroline would accept the inevitable, but perhaps the best course of action would be to let her see it through.

"How much do you need?"

She named the figure, and he nodded. "I'll have Otis write the check."

The tension drained from her face. He'd write a thousand checks if it could buy her peace of mind, but it was probably only delaying the inevitable. Now he could understand why his father was always putty in Caroline's hands. To the outside world she looked like a Gainsborough portrait, a perfect image of feminine charm, but it was merely a veneer over an inner core of strength and loyalty. Leaving her behind would be his biggest regret in setting off to sea again.

Without warning she twisted the knob and opened the kitchen door.

"What on earth?" she asked, staring at the chaos scattered throughout the kitchen in amazement. It might bring her a small bit of comfort to know that, if nothing else, he was delivering on Luke's only request. Caroline stepped forward and picked up a label. "This looks like Luke's artwork."

"Yes." When he explained what they had planned, he couldn't tell if she was going to laugh or cry. She gazed with admiration and affection at the label in her hand.

"Ah, Luke . . ." she murmured, a world of longing in those two words.

As hard as it had been for Gray, surely the kinship between twins made Luke's dilemma even harder for Caroline. There would be no putting the genie back in the bottle this time, and he gave in to the inevitable.

"Join us," he said, and Caroline needed no further urging.

Otis came back down, and Caroline peeled off her elaborate jacket and shrugged into one of Gray's white shirts to protect her blouse. He made a pot of tea, and the three of them developed a system for labeling the jars.

Caroline was soon strategizing ways that Luke's scheme could generate even bigger waves. "The scuttlebutt is that the Magruders just landed a huge contract to sell canned food to the military. If any of this slop is being sold to the army, I'm sure the War Department will want to know."

Gray was instantly alert. "Can you get a copy of the contract?"

"Of course. The army is required to disclose large expenditures with a private company."

Gray smiled, for Luke's plan was gaining momentum by the hour. He outlined Luke's strategy to contact newspapers and restaurant critics, anyone with influence in the food trade. They wanted to drum up as much news as possible.

Caroline smoothed a freshly gummed label over a jar. "I think you're missing a big piece of the equation," she said. "Women do most of the shopping in this country, and you need to reach out to them directly. *Good Housekeeping* has been writing about adulterated food for years."

That wasn't at all the sort of publication he had in mind, but he supposed it couldn't hurt. "I'll send them a jar."

"You need to do more than that," Caroline said. "The magazine is already working with the Department of Agriculture to spread the word about dangerous food additives. They are your natural ally."

"I have no interest in partnering with the Department of Agriculture," he said shortly.

zero. None. Ever. Annabelle had betrayed him for a job at that department, and the whole purpose of publicizing the Magruders' malfeasance through the press was to avoid government interference.

"Gray, the Department of Agriculture is already ten steps ahead of you in trying to sound the alarm about adulterated food. Why don't you cooperate with them? This is for Luke, and you need to swallow your distaste for that person from Kansas if it means helping this plan succeed."

"Forget it, Caroline."

If *Good Housekeeping* was walking in lockstep behind the bureaucrats in the government, he intended to keep his distance. He would carry out Luke's mission by meeting with scientists, businessmen, and newspaper reporters. Those were the men who shaped opinion in this country. Caroline might know Washington politics, but he knew business, and he didn't need her help in this matter.

Annabelle's odds of getting Gray to accept the rice-collecting assignment were slim, but there would be no shame if she failed to recruit him to a noble cause. The only shame would be if she didn't try.

Just as Mr. Fairchild had said, the mercantile warehouses in Alexandria were blanketed with announcements about the availability of cargo space on the *Pelican*, complete with a list of the ports the ship would stop at on the journey to Madagascar. The notices directed interested merchants to the customs house at the Port of Alexandria.

Annabelle set off for the customs house, clutching the wooden box of two dozen glass vials. This might be a fool's errand, but she had to try. If nothing else, she wanted to see Gray again. Any ocean voyage was dangerous, and his health had already taken a beating from tropical diseases. She didn't want the koi pond to be the last time they saw each other on this earth.

The clerk at the customs house was brusque as he informed her where Gray could be found. "The *Pelican* is in the first berth on the third quay, right behind the shipment of dunnage. Watch out for the bollard lines."

He shoved back from the counter and disappeared into a storage room while she tried to process the terms he'd just flung at her. She might be a hayseed from Kansas, but she could still read, and the ships all had names on their side. She'd find it.

If she wasn't so anxious, she'd enjoy watching the cranes lifting cargo onto the various ships harbored in port. Men with leathery skin gave her curious glances as she walked along the wind-battered dock, carrying the box of vials carefully before her. Hopefully these vials would someday return to America filled with rare strains of African rice, but only if Gray was willing to cooperate.

She walked for several blocks along the docks before she spotted the *Pelican,* a handsome ship with a black steel hull and a glossy red stripe running along the top deck. She was completely ignorant of ships, but surely that was a smokestack on the top, and a large room near the front had wrap-around windows on all sides — was that where the captain steered the ship?

Unlike ships on the neighboring dock, there didn't seem to be much activity on the *Pelican.* Could the harbormaster have been mistaken about Gray being aboard? Aside from two men swabbing the decks, the ship looked abandoned.

"Why are you here, Annabelle?"

The voice came from directly behind her, startling her so badly that she almost dropped the box of glass vials, but Gray helped save it just before it hit the ground.

He returned it to her hastily, as though it burned his skin.

She recovered her composure quickly. "Hello, Gray. I never did get a chance to admire your ship. It certainly is impressive."

"What are you doing here?" he asked again. There was no hint of softening in his iron-hard face, but she didn't let it discourage her. She'd known this wasn't going to be easy.

"I met David Fairchild a few days ago. Did you know he was back in the States?"

Gray folded his arms across his chest and glowered at her.

"Because I think you and he have a lot in common. He's also very curious about all manner of useful plants and has amassed quite a collection. He brought back pistachios. Have you ever tried one?"

"You have sixty seconds to tell me what you've come for, and then I'm throwing you off this dock. Your clock just started."

She lifted her chin. "*Can* you throw me off this dock? Or is it like a public sidewalk where anyone has the right to stand? I came here prepared to be humble and obsequious, but you're making it hard, Gray."

A bit of humor flashed in his face, but it vanished quickly. "Why are you here, Annabelle?" he asked again. Wind ruffled his hair, and she longed to reach up and stroke it back from his face.

She turned the box and unlatched the lid to display the empty glass vials. "These are for rice samples," she said. "Rumor has it you're heading to Madagascar, and we expect they grow some unique rice cultivars. If you could collect some grains —"

"No."

"Because I have a feeling you'll be collecting some for your own research, so it shouldn't be any bother to —"

"Come on, Annabelle!" he snapped, both hands on his hips as he moved in closer to glower down at her. "You didn't really expect me to agree, did you?"

"No, but I had to try."

He looked flabbergasted as he held his arms out wide. "Why?"

"Because I'm loyal!" she burst out. "I know you hate me for what I did, but there can never be any undoing it. So now I'm trying to help the government improve the lives of farmers all over this country, and that's noble work."

"A good little foot soldier," he said bitterly.

"Yes, I am," she retorted. "I've learned that a person has to fight for what they value in life. Being here isn't easy for me, but I'm fighting for the farmers. I also felt compelled to fight for the security of this country, even though I wish I didn't have to. I will forever regret that I was forced into that corner . . . but I don't regret the choice I made."

"It's not that simple, Annabelle."

She'd had enough. "Yes, it really *is* that simple. I had plenty of choices, but none of them were good."

This was the wrong path to go down. She drew a calming breath and gazed at the massive ships preparing to transport American goods to all corners of the world. An American flag at the front of the port snapped and waved in the breeze. It stirred a bone-deep sense of allegiance in her, but not for Gray. That didn't mean he was a bad man, or that he lacked a core of integrity. Gray had the ability to help farmers and people all over this country have more productive crops and better nutrition if only he could overcome his instinctive suspicion toward the government.

"Whenever I've been offered a chance to do something meaningful, I seize it with both hands," she said in a calmer voice. "I can't sail to the other side of the world, but you can. In collecting those samples, you could help farmers find a crop that might someday feed millions. You don't know what it's like to be surrounded on all sides by crops that are failing and dying, but I do, and it's horrible. Rice might be the answer for some American farmers, but only if we find the right strain."

She held out the box, mortified at how her hands trembled. This was so important. He had a right to be angry, but he could still choose to do something selfless and good despite his resentment of her.

Take it, please, she silently implored. *Choose hope and forgiveness over anger.*

"Go home, Annabelle."

He spoke without heat, and somehow that made his rejection feel even more final. He turned away from her and strode toward the ship without a backward glance.

TWENTY-SIX

Annabelle took the case of empty rice vials back to the lab the next morning. It needed to be returned to David Fairchild so he could find someone else for the task. It was awful to have failed, but at least she'd tried. She'd given it her very best, and that was all God could ask of her.

But then . . . *had* she truly given it her best? A stronger woman wouldn't have lost her temper. A wiser one might never have betrayed Gray's trust in the first place. But surely God didn't judge her by counting her weaknesses and failures, but rather by her honest effort to live in a manner that would make Jesus proud. She had prayed, wept, and struggled over her choices, but she still wasn't proud of her actions, so how could Jesus be?

The demoralizing thoughts hammered her as she climbed the steps toward the third-floor laboratory and almost bumped into her supervisor.

"You have a visitor," Mr. Bryant said curtly. "I told her your workday begins in ten minutes, but she won't leave. I trust you will conclude your business quickly."

"Of course," she replied.

Who could be visiting her? It couldn't be Elaine, because she'd just dropped her sister off at the Library. She turned into the lab, a curious smile on her face, ready to — —

She froze. Caroline Delacroix sat in Annabelle's chair, glaring at her with a coldness that practically leapt across the lab to slap her in the face. Every instinct urged Annabelle to turn and run, but Horace Greenfield was watching. Besides, she'd faced down far bigger challenges than Caroline Delacroix.

"Hello, Caroline," she said, ignoring the hostility in the air as she set the box of collection vials on the lab table. "What can I do for you?"

Caroline's hard eyes glittered as she stood and closed the distance between them. "You owe me something," she said in a deadly calm voice.

No doubt, but this wasn't a conversation to have in front of the biggest chatterbox in all of Washington. "Let's go downstairs to discuss it," Annabelle said.

Caroline gave a regal nod and followed

her downstairs to the cafeteria, still empty at this time of morning. The lights weren't even on, and only a little weak sunlight filtered in through the single window. Dozens of empty chairs and tables were available, but this didn't seem like a social call.

Caroline got straight to the point. "My brother is rotting in prison because of you," she spat. "Even though he's trapped in a dank, miserable cell, he has asked for only one thing of his family, and I'm going to make it happen even if it kills me. Sadly, I need your help."

Annabelle listened in baffled amazement as Caroline described Luke's plan to distribute counterfeit applesauce to scientists and newspaper reporters. In so doing, they would shine a spotlight on Magruder Food's penchant for adulterating their products. The editor of *Good Housekeeping,* Mrs. Eleanor Sharpe, put a great deal of stock into the work being done by the Department of Agriculture, and Caroline wanted to capitalize on it.

"I know all about *Good Housekeeping,*" Annabelle said. The magazine had already begun an informal partnership with the Department of Agriculture to bring attention to the problem of tainted foods.

Caroline's demeanor remained glacially

cold as she continued. "Gray is under the mistaken impression that it is *men* who will sound the alarm about the Magruders' foul tactics. I disagree. I think we need the Mrs. Sharpes of the world. And the homemakers and the mothers." Her nose wrinkled. "Even the farmer's daughter from Kansas. Mrs. Sharpe is also from Kansas. Between that and your connection to the Department of Agriculture, you can get your foot in the door at *Good Housekeeping.*"

If she could do something to help Gray, she wouldn't hesitate. "How can I help?"

"Gray is sailing the *Pelican* to Boston, where he will launch the attack," Caroline said. "I want you to be on that ship."

Annabelle recoiled at the suggestion. "You want me to drop everything and run to Boston?" she asked in amazement.

"My work for the first lady means I am not at liberty to go. That leaves you."

"No." It was unthinkable. She had a life here, a job, Elaine. . . .

"You owe us," Caroline said, her voice as hard as iron. "Gray can't make an impression on *Good Housekeeping* the way you can. He's fighting with one arm tied behind his back if all he does is appeal to political journalists. We need Mrs. Sharpe, and he doesn't know how to talk to her. *Good*

Housekeeping is the most prominent ladies' magazine in the country, and it's the logical place to launch this war."

"This isn't my battle," Annabelle said. "I can't go."

Caroline moved in closer. "Gray says you're patriotic. Clyde Magruder is running for Congress, where he will clear the path for chemically treated foods and devious business practices in the legislative infra-structure of this country. You can help stop him."

"Gray will throw me off his ship."

"He'll *want* to, but he's also a logical man who has the ability to see reason. He needs your help to make Luke's plan succeed."

The only thing Annabelle truly wanted from Gray was his forgiveness. He'd already rejected her words of apology, but what if she *showed* him her desire to make amends?

Caroline outlined a plan to smuggle her aboard the *Pelican* and then get her to *Good Housekeeping* in nearby Springfield, Massachusetts, while Gray and Otis worked in Boston.

As Annabelle thought about it, more possibilities came to the fore. She could take the empty rice vials and persuade Otis to collect the samples in Madagascar. More importantly, she could serve as a neutral party in bringing the issue of the tainted applesauce to *Good Housekeeping*'s attention. As the owner of a rival company, Gray could never appear disinterested, but she could.

And although she didn't want to admit it, a tiny part of her hoped the enforced proximity over the next week might give the wounds between her and Gray a chance to heal.

"When do I leave?" she asked.

It was barely light at six o'clock in the morning when Annabelle followed Caroline to the *Pelican.* The ship would sail on the noon tide, but now was the best time to slip aboard without notice. Longshoremen scrambled to fuel the ship, and Annabelle watched the process in fascination. A conveyor belt with metal buckets, much like those used for lifting grain into silos, carried crates of coal up toward an opening on the side of the *Pelican.* She'd never put much thought into how a ship was fueled, but it was fun to watch.

"Keep moving," Caroline said impatiently, prodding Annabelle up the gangway leading into the ship.

It was dim inside and a little claustrophobic. Annabelle couldn't see much beyond

313

the skinny hallway that looked identical in both directions. The ceiling was so low that she could touch it if she stood on tiptoe, and she was short! Now that she was actually on board, doubts began to creep in, but she didn't let them take root. Gray already despised her, so the only thing she stood to lose was a little dignity if the plan failed, and she could handle that.

"This way," Caroline whispered, leading her down the passageway. Their footsteps seemed painfully loud in the metal hallway until they finally arrived at a wide doorway that opened into a huge, cavernous space. "This is one of the cargo holds," Caroline explained. "It won't be used for this trip, so it will be a safe place to hide until the ship is far out at sea."

Annabelle peered inside. It could be a ballroom, if ballrooms had steel girders, a dank smell, and barely any light. Stacks of pallets and big wooden casks clustered in one corner, and her breathing sounded unnaturally loud in the metal room.

"Wait until dinnertime to come out," Caroline advised. "It will be too late to turn back, and Gray will have to live with what we've done. A word of warning." She pointed a finger in Annabelle's face. "You are to keep your hands off my brother.

Don't get any ideas."

That pointed finger rankled. "What if he doesn't want to keep his hands off me?" Annabelle challenged.

"He will," Caroline snapped. "You are anathema to him. He is a man of sound logic and reason, and he will accept your help in Boston, but other than that, you are to keep your distance." She glanced around the cavernous interior one final time. "Make yourself at home," she said before whirling around to leave.

The sound of the door closing echoed in the horribly empty hold.

As awful as Caroline could be, her absence was even worse. Caroline was confident and knowledgeable about this ship, while Annabelle was a country mouse who'd never been to sea.

She walked to the far side of the hold to sit down and lean against a barrel to wait. A *thump* startled her, but she smiled in relief at the sight of a snowy white cat that had pounced onto a pallet to look at her curiously.

"Hello, sweetie pie," she whispered, holding out her fingers and letting the cat sniff her. A moment later the cat jumped onto her lap, and its weight was comforting as she listened to more loads of coal being dumped into the boiler room somewhere above her.

As the hours passed, more voices and footsteps could be heard boarding the ship. The noises seemed magnified in this steel monstrosity — slamming, thumping, and banging. Why did everything have to be made of metal? The rattling of chains and shouts of men were interspersed with hissing noises and what sounded like pressure valves releasing.

A bubble of nervous laughter arose. This was something of an adventure! She stroked the cat, wishing she could be up on deck to see all the excitement, but she'd have to be patient.

She nibbled on a stick of salami she'd brought, sharing bits with the cat as preparations continued above. She nearly jumped out of her skin at the mighty *boom* of a foghorn. So loud! Two long blasts sounded, and a moment later a dip and a lift of the ship signaled they were leaving port. They were moving! Oh, how she wished she could be up above to see, but just knowing this huge ship was actually on the move was one of the most oddly thrilling experiences of her life.

She settled against the wall, hauling the cat back onto her lap. "Just a few more hours, Sweetie Pie."

The wait was going to be long and boring, and at the end of it, she'd have to test the limits of Gray's temper. For all her earlier bravado, weathering the storm ahead was going to take nerves of steel.

Twenty-Seven

By five o'clock, Annabelle was tired and sore from huddling in the cargo hold, but it was time to brave Gray's wrath and let him know she was aboard the ship. Her legs felt weak as wet straw as she pushed to her feet.

"Come on, Sweetie Pie," she urged the cat, scooping it up into her arms. It would be comforting to have something to cling to as she faced Gray.

She peeked out into the hallway, which was empty and lit by strange lamps anchored high on the walls every few yards. The noises of the ship were different now, like a low, rumbling hum. Thank heavens those awful clanking chains weren't rattling anymore. She'd probably hear that sound in her sleep for weeks.

Caroline had told her to climb the stairs until she reached the top deck, then head toward the front of the ship, where she'd encounter either Gray or a man named

Captain Haig. She found the compartment with the staircase inside, but it was so steep, it was almost like climbing a ladder. Holding the cat was awkward as she climbed, and it twisted out of her arms to scamper away. She missed its comforting weight.

All too soon she arrived at the top deck. The door leading out was surprisingly heavy, but she got it open and poked her head out. Wind hit her in the face, and the glare of sunlight on the ocean made her squint. They were far out to sea — much too far to turn back now.

There was no one on deck, so she headed toward the bow while the powerful winds buffeted her hair and skirts. A covered room was near the front of the ship. A wheelhouse? A bridge? She didn't know anything about ships, but a man was inside. It was probably Captain Haig, for he looked exactly like Caroline had described, with long white hair tied back to reveal a leathery face.

Annabelle tapped on the glass, and the old man glanced over, his eyes growing wide. In two steps he jerked the door open.

"Who are you?" he demanded.

"I'm Annabelle Larkin, and I need to speak with Gray Delacroix. Can you call for him?"

"Well, Annabelle Larkin, I'd like to know

what you're doing on my ship." There was no mercy in his eyes, but she couldn't afford to be timid.

"It's actually Gray Delacroix's ship, right? I came aboard on business, and it's probably time to discuss it with him." She gave him a tentative smile despite the nerves shaking her entire body. The next ten minutes were going to be thoroughly awful, but she needed to confront it head on. "Can you send for him?" she prompted when the old man continued to do nothing but glare at her.

Captain Haig finally tugged on a cord near a control panel, and a young sailor appeared moments later. "Go get Delacroix," he bit out. "Tell him we have a stowaway."

The young sailor disappeared down the hatch, but the old one went back to staring stonily into the distance.

"Thank you," she said.

Captain Haig didn't say anything, just kept staring straight ahead as though he hadn't heard her. She refused to let his rude behavior unnerve her. She deserved every bit of it, and things were only going to get worse soon.

The thud of footsteps heralded Gray's arrival. He appeared on the opposite side of the bridge, his brows narrowed in concern and the white cat draped over one of his arms.

"What's going on?" Gray asked the captain, who sent a pointed glance her way.

Gray's face darkened like a thundercloud when he saw her, and he dropped the cat, which ran for cover. She wished she could do the same, but she squared her shoulders and met his gaze.

"This is a little awkward —"

"This is an outrage!" he roared, stepping forward to tower above her. "What are you doing on this ship?"

"Caroline sent me."

It was the only thing she needed to say. Gray's eyes morphed from shock to disbelief to anger. He turned away and let out a stream of curse words. She'd never even heard some of them but figured they were pretty bad.

"She thought you should change your mind about teaming up with *Good Housekeeping,*" she said, "and that I'd have a better shot at persuading the editor to your cause. I know you're angry. You have every right to be."

"Thanks, Annabelle, that's very generous of you." Emotions continued flashing across his face as he struggled to control himself. Finally he turned to Captain Haig. "Turn

321

this ship around. I'm not sailing with her."

"You can't!" she gasped.

To her relief, Captain Haig seemed to agree with her. "It will cost a fortune in fuel to go back," he said. "The port charges will be even worse. Add in the time to refuel, and we'll be two days behind schedule."

If possible, Gray got even angrier as he paced in the tight confines of the wheelhouse. "Then we'll stop in Philadelphia and put her ashore there. I don't care how much it costs, I want her off this ship."

This was a development she hadn't considered, and it terrified her. She didn't have enough money to make her way home from Philadelphia. But Gray was a logical man, if he could just simmer down.

"Gray, you need to care more about your cause than your hatred for me. I can help you. I can deliver on Luke's idea —"

"If you're smart, you'll stop saying my brother's name."

He was right. Saying the name Luke was like waving a red cape before a bull. Time to shift tactics. "Caroline told me about Clyde Magruder. How he's going to run for Congress and just keep getting richer as he pumps out more adulterated food. If we can get *Good Housekeeping* on our side, it might take some of the wind out of his sails."

News of her presence must have spread, for other members of the crew started gathering outside the wheelhouse, peering through the windows in curiosity. She was glad to see Otis, for he was the only semi-friendly face among the dozen sailors gaping at her.

She ignored the others and turned to Gray, flinching at the seething anger on his face. It hurt. How stupid she'd been to imagine this trip might be a chance to win his forgiveness. He didn't even look like the same man who'd once gazed at her with such tender affection.

Her lower lip began wobbling furiously, and she prayed she wouldn't be reduced to tears before all these people. If possible, Gray's face turned even harder, but he reached into his pocket and thrust a hand-kerchief at her.

"Oh, for pity's sake, don't cry," he groused. "It's bad enough having a woman on board, but I won't subject my crew to sniveling." He turned to look at the half dozen sailors who gawked at the exchange. "You can all go below," he ordered.

She was sorry to see them leave. They were a buffer between her and Gray's smoldering anger, but maybe it was a blessing. She intended to keep pressing for the chance to go to Boston, and it was unlikely Gray would cave before an audience. While the other men filed down the hatch, she scooped up the cat that had crept toward her feet, holding it against her chest for comfort.

"Put the cat down," Gray ordered, still staring stonily into the distance. "You're making it nervous."

More likely she was making him nervous, but she complied. She watched him carefully as emotions continued to play across his face. She dared not say a word. It was time to let Gray process what had happened and arrive at his own conclusions.

Finally he spoke, his voice devoid of emotion. "Haig, have someone escort her down to the starboard crew quarters. She can sleep there. It's empty."

Captain Haig looked over in surprise. "Gray, those berths are just hammocks. We could offer her —"

"A hammock is perfectly fine for a stowaway," Gray said. There was no softening in his face, but at least he turned to look at her. "I'll take you to Boston, but I expect you to help with meals while you're on board. First thing tomorrow morning, you are to be in the galley, helping the cook prepare breakfast. I won't tolerate a lay-about."

That was the end of the conversation, as he slammed the door on his way out of the wheelhouse, but relief gusted through her.

Captain Haig summoned Otis to show her to the empty crew quarters, and she happily settled for a hammock. The room had a dozen hammocks and cargo nets strung from the ceiling where sailors stowed their belongings. It smelled like damp rope, salt, and metal in here. The ropes squeaked as she cautiously sat on the hammock nearest the porthole. Lying down was awkward. The hammock swung at a terrifying angle as she cautiously lay back, but the wobbling finally slowed, and she was able to breathe again.

It was hard to sleep when the hammock swayed each time she tried to shift. The darkness was almost complete, and it was scary down here. This must be what Elaine felt like in her dark, isolated world.

Annabelle drew a calming breath. The Hillenbrands had agreed to check on Elaine until Annabelle returned from Boston, but she still worried. Her sister had come a long way in the past few months, but this week on her own would still be difficult for Elaine.

It was time to make the best of things. Elaine would be fine. Perhaps God had sent this challenge to them both as a means of forcing them to face down their fears. The next few days would be a test, and Annabelle would rise to the occasion even if it terrified her.

TWENTY-EIGHT

Gray awoke bleary-eyed and annoyed the following morning, but also a tiny bit intrigued. Just knowing that Annabelle was aboard his ship alternately thrilled and infuriated him.

They sailed with a skeleton crew, and he was tempted to order her confined to her quarters for the duration of the voyage. It would be easier to concentrate if he didn't have to look at her, but he couldn't do it. Annabelle didn't belong trapped below-decks, and he'd simply have to deal with her.

The scent of bacon and eggs drew him down the narrow corridor to the mess hall, a skinny room adjacent to the kitchen with long tables and benches, all securely anchored to the floor.

Annabelle sat with Otis, enjoying a cup of coffee and cuddling the cat. Stowaways shouldn't look that cozy.

327

"You're spoiling my cat," Gray groused as he headed to the sideboard for a plate of eggs.

"Sweetie Pie is yours?" Annabelle asked.

"Tiger is a first-rate mouser. There's nothing sweet about her. She's also a working cat, so feeding her bacon is killing her instinct and interfering with her duties."

"Does your ship have mice?" Her tone was appalled. *Of course* his ship had mice; all ships had mice.

"Maybe the steamships sailing through Kansas wheat fields don't have rodents, but all ocean-going vessels do," he said curtly.

Annabelle obligingly set down the cat but turned her attention back to him. "Tell me more about the fake applesauce. Caroline tried to explain, but I can't understand how someone can disguise pumpkins as applesauce. They taste completely different."

"With enough sweeteners and chemicals, the Magruders managed to pull it off. My job is to stop them."

"Have you tasted it?"

"I don't willingly poison myself," he said dryly.

"I want to try it," she said, a hint of excitement in her face.

He was mildly appalled but curious to see if she had the nerve to actually go through with it. He wasn't the only one. Otis had already vaulted off the bench.

"I'll go down to the hold and get a jar," Otis said and headed out the door before Gray could stop him.

It left him uncomfortably alone with Annabelle, and he didn't know what to say to her. It had been a month since that horrible afternoon by the koi pond. Was he supposed to keep being rude to her? Ignore her? Both seemed petty, but he couldn't forgive her either.

"How did you sleep?" he finally asked once the silence became unbearable.

"The hammock was . . . well, a little terrifying at first. But I loved it. It felt scary and safe at the same time. Is that possible?"

"I suppose." He shrugged, but it was maybe the most accurate description of a hammock he'd ever heard.

The silence started to stretch again, but mercifully Otis returned, along with other members of the crew eager to witness the opening of the Magruder applesauce. Otis set the jar in front of Annabelle.

"What do you think of the label?" Gray asked, watching closely.

This was their first test. He needed to see how people responded to the presentation Luke had designed. She seemed amused by the drawing on the front, looking both charmed and a little appalled by the happy mice frolicking around the pumpkin. Then she turned the jar around, and her eyes widened as she read the list of ingredients on the back.

"Formaldehyde?" she asked.

"Do you still want to try it? No one will blame you if you don't."

"I *must* know what it tastes like," she said, twisting the lid, which made a satisfying pop as she lifted it off. At least the Magruders properly sealed their jars. She held the contents to her nose. "It smells like apples," she said as she passed the jar to others.

Gray was curious too and waited for the jar to come to him. The glass was cool in his hand as he held it to his face. The contents both looked and smelled like applesauce, probably because the pumpkin had been stewed in apple cider. He poured some into a bowl, then passed it to Annabelle along with a spoon. He sank onto the bench opposite her, watching carefully as she first sniffed the concoction, then poked it with the spoon.

She took a tiny taste, her eyes widening in surprise. She held it in her mouth for a moment before swallowing.

"It's good," she said.

Captain Haig looked taken aback. "Are you sure? You read the ingredients. You know what's in that slop."

Annabelle took another bite, a bigger one this time. "It's quite good. Very sweet, and the consistency is exactly like applesauce."

"All the more reason to get it off the market," Gray said. "The Magruders set low prices, and if it still tastes good, people will buy it up and never realize the chemical cocktail they are ingesting."

"I'll need some jars to take to *Good House-keeping,*" she said. "They have an experimental kitchen where they test products for food purity."

"What's an experimental kitchen?" He'd never heard the term, and it piqued his interest.

Annabelle brightened. "It's a new initiative at the magazine. *Good Housekeeping's* editor was at the Department of Agriculture just last month to explain how it's going to work."

He listened in amazement to the plans for the magazine to start testing products for purity and efficacy. The editor believed that much of the nation's food, toiletries, and other household products were either fraudulent or dangerous, and intended to use the magazine to get the message out.

While Gray didn't like the prospect of the government nosing into private business, a magazine was a different story. If they reviewed a product, like a book or a theater review, it seemed perfectly fair.

"I like this idea of having a magazine conduct impartial tests," he admitted. "Perhaps a visit to *Good Housekeeping* would be worth the trip." Springfield was three hours west of Boston, but Caroline was right. He couldn't afford to ignore this potential alliance.

Annabelle folded her hands on the table and looked delightfully smug. "You're going to need me to open the door for you at *Good Housekeeping*."

"And why is that?" he asked, immediately suspicious. Over the past few minutes he'd forgotten how angry he was with her, but he was on guard again.

"You and the Magruders are business rivals, and the magazine editor may suspect you have an ax to grind. They're more likely to be favorably disposed to me because I work for the Department of Agriculture. *Good Housekeeping* has been working hand in hand with the department in the interest of protecting consumers. I think you should let me take the lead."

She was right. As much as he wanted to

pull into the nearest port and dump her ashore, Annabelle had a better chance of getting through to the editors of the magazine than he did, and *Good Housekeeping*'s rigorous, impartial testing in their experimental kitchen would be a godsend. Hadn't he been looking for a means to police the food industry without government interference?

But it would mean working alongside Annabelle. Every moment would stir painful memories, but he'd endure it for Luke.

Gray didn't need Annabelle's help for the first two days in Boston. He let her cool her heels in port while he worked alone, meeting with newspaper editors and presenting them with two jars: one with the original label the Magruders had already released into the market, and the other branded with Luke's label accurately reflecting its contents. The hope was to spark public reviews and commentary in the press. A few people had been appalled, but most were either amused or indifferent. Some even wanted to taste the product, and since it tasted perfectly fine, they weren't prepared to condemn the Magruders. Indeed, one editor went so far as to say the Magruders should be congratulated for developing a tasty and inexpensive alternative to real applesauce. Gray angrily replied that he knew of a wedding in Philadelphia the man might like to attend.

The real prize, the magazine with the largest national circulation and their most likely ally, was *Good Housekeeping.* This was where he'd need Annabelle, but he dreaded the prospect of being alone with her for the three-hour trip to Springfield, and he turned to Captain Haig for help.

"I'm not going to be your chaperone!" Haig groused, making Gray wish his employees didn't feel quite so free to vent their opinions. They'd been holed up in the ship's mess hall since dinner more than an hour ago, and Haig had put a healthy dent in a bottle of brandy while Gray nursed willow bark tea.

Gray pasted a pleasant expression on his face and tried again. "I need you to accompany me and Annabelle to Springfield. It is a three-hour train ride, and I refuse to be alone with her."

"And that doesn't say 'chaperone' to you? Duenna? Matronly protector? Gray! The woman is barely five feet tall and is as terrifying as a chipmunk."

She terrified *him.* "I refuse to be alone with her, and Otis will be delivering samples to the newspapers and culinary critics. That leaves you."

Captain Haig grumbled something inaudible beneath his breath, and Gray sighed as a familiar ache bloomed in his chest.

"I know I'm being irrational," he admitted. "Yes, I need you to be my chaperone. Annabelle gets to me, and I can't afford it. You have no idea how badly I want Luke's plan to succeed. It was the only thing he asked of me, and I intend to deliver."

"I'll go," Haig finally said. "It might be amusing to watch you suffer."

There was no doubt Gray *would* suffer at the enforced proximity with Annabelle. The only real question was if he'd be able to keep his smoldering resentment of her alive.

Annabelle found the train ride to Springfield a challenge. She'd repeatedly tried to initiate polite conversation with Gray, who answered her in terse, one-word responses. They rode in a private compartment with two benches facing each other, and Annabelle tried to put the time to good use by presenting Gray with a copy of *Good Housekeeping* she'd purchased in port.

"Perhaps you'd like to familiarize yourself with it ahead of our meeting," she said as she set the magazine on the table between them.

Gray acted like he didn't hear her as he stared out the window.

"A basic understanding of the publication is not only a sign of respect, it will allow us to tailor our presentation to the needs of the magazine editors."

Nothing. She'd spent all last night reading this magazine to glean insight into the nature of the publication. It had been a surprise. Far from the mundane cooking recipes or beauty advice she had expected, the magazine took a scientific approach to everything from cleaning hats and teething remedies for babies to proper attic ventilation. Gray didn't know the first thing about the most influential ladies' magazine in the country, and they were about to meet with the editors.

"Is it all going to be up to me?" she asked. "To be the only one informed? Captain Haig, perhaps you would like to have a peek at the magazine. There is an entire article on cures for a sour disposition. You might find it helpful. I've only had to tolerate Mr. Delacroix for three days, but I gather your voyage to Madagascar will take considerably longer."

At last she'd gotten Gray's attention, and

he swiveled his gaze to her. "I wonder if they have an article on how to pry a knife from the center of your own back. I've still got one buried pretty deeply."

He did, but she had already apologized for it. She was doing her best to carry out Luke's wild-eyed scheme, and if Gray would cooperate with her, they stood a much better chance.

She pretended to take his request seriously, flipping to the table of contents and skimming the entries. "Nope, nothing on back wounds, but here's an article on working toward a common goal, and another on making the best of a bad situation. Oh, look! An article on the wisdom of preparing for an important meeting by educating yourself about the people you are about to meet and the magazine they sell."

Gray's eyes glittered as he stared at her, but not with anger. It was more like . . . triumph? His voice was silky as he responded. "I wonder if that magazine might possibly contain an article on the care of mosquito bites, an organizational system for household bills, a recipe for fried gumbo, and an editorial on the legal documents every household should possess."

Heat flushed her cheeks as she stared at the table of contents. He'd just listed the articles in the magazine by order of appearance. "You've already read it?"

"I bought a copy the first morning we were in port."

Annabelle closed the magazine to cover her embarrassment. "Well, then! What shall we talk about?" They still had two hours until Springfield.

"Maybe we can talk about how much fun it is to be a chaperone," Captain Haig said.

Annabelle had no idea what he meant, but Gray looked like he wanted to laugh.

Was a bit of the ice starting to thaw? She hoped so, for she missed his laugh.

TWENTY-NINE

Gray had met with tribal leaders, government bureaucrats, and hard-nosed businessmen from all over the world, but he was uncomfortable as he braced to meet Eleanor Sharpe and Horatio Feldman, editors of the nation's foremost ladies' magazine. This was uncharted territory for him, and he was reluctantly grateful for Annabelle's help navigating it.

It was a drizzly day as they arrived in Springfield, then hired a cab to drive them to the offices of the magazine. He shared an umbrella with Annabelle, wishing this meeting was already over. *Good Housekeeping* was located in a perfectly ordinary building, four stories of buff-colored stone with uniform windows on each floor. Despite the building's pedestrian exterior, the inside was something else entirely. The windows had draperies, the office walls boasted wainscoting, and each room had at least one potted plant in a brass container.

"Welcome, welcome!" a matronly woman gushed as she swept into the foyer wearing a heavily ruffled gown, smelling of lilacs, and looking like the personification of everyone's favorite grandmother. "I'm Eleanor Sharpe, content editor for the magazine. I'm afraid Mr. Feldman is still with the accountants, but all to the good! We can get to know each other before discussing tedious business."

Annabelle stepped forward. "Annabelle Larkin from the Department of Agriculture. Thank you so much for using your publication to help spread the word about nutrition and the value of proper housekeeping."

Mrs. Sharpe pressed a hand to her ample bosom. "Miss Larkin! How wonderful to see a lady working in a professional position. We need all the allies we can get in our campaign against dishonest and adulterated food." She turned her attention to Gray, a single eyebrow raised a little skeptically. "And you are?"

"Gray Delacroix, from Delacroix Global Spice," he said. "Thank you for seeing us."

Mrs. Sharpe's smile chilled. "You are to be congratulated on the quality of your spices. All your products are marvelous, your political views much less so. We eagerly await your change of heart regarding food purity laws."

It appeared Mrs. Sharpe was a grandmother with fangs.

Before he could reply, Annabelle stepped to his side and took his hand in hers. He instinctively tried to withdraw it, but she squeezed harder.

"I've told him the same thing over and over," Annabelle said in an amused tone. "I think at last he is beginning to see the light. That's why he agreed to come with me today. Isn't that right . . . darling?"

He stiffened at the endearment, but Annabelle's instinct was a good one. His political views put him at a disadvantage with Mrs. Sharpe, but Annabelle was off to a flying start. If it killed him, he would get on Mrs. Sharpe's good side, for this woman could use her magazine to launch a salvo directly at the Magruders and any other company that misbranded their food.

"Miss Larkin has been a good influence on me," he said, patting Annabelle's hand. "I'm eager to hear more of what *Good Housekeeping* has to say on food purity laws."

The matronly woman brightened. "Excellent! But first let's get acquainted. I've asked the secretary to set up tea for us in the

341

conference room before we get down to business."

It was unlike any conference room he'd ever seen. It was huge, with a full kitchen installed along one side of the room. In addition to a typical stove, icebox, and sink, the counters held scales, test tubes, thermometers, and chemistry manuals. A long table dominated the other side of the room, covered with a lace cloth. With bone china plates and an assortment of delicacies, the "tea" looked like it had come from Buckingham Palace. Petite sandwiches, tarts, and scones were arranged with artistic flare.

As soon as they were seated, Mrs. Sharpe did the honors, pouring from a porcelain teapot into cups with elaborate grace.

"I must apologize for the honey," Mrs. Sharpe said as she passed a tray holding cream, sugar, and a pot of honey. "While most of the delicacies here come from the surrounding area, I'm afraid the local honey harvest was poor this year. We had to import it from Ohio, and it lacks the geographic integrity of local honey."

Annabelle seemed baffled by this statement. "The honey looks perfectly fine."

"Annabelle," Gray tutted. "How often have we discussed the importance of geographic integrity in honey?" Annabelle might know her durum wheat, but he was the one who knew high-end dining and was ready to flatter Mrs. Sharpe's zeal for entertaining. "I always love sampling local honey, whether it is from tupelo trees in Florida or clover blossoms in the Midwest. I'll never forget the honey gathered from orange blossoms along the Mediterranean coasts. It was like sunlight spun with sugar."

"Yes!" Mrs. Sharpe declared. "The terroir of a product is so rarely appreciated. You have a true connoisseur's palate."

"Terr-what?" Annabelle asked.

"Terroir," he said. "Tare-*WAHR*," he repeated at her blank look, savoring the heft and roll of the French word. "It's how the unique elements in soil and climate affect the flavor of an agricultural product. It's why the grapes from the south of France produce the finest wine in the world. It is why olives from the hills of Tuscany are so pure, they made emperors fight to keep them. Why an oyster harvested in the Hudson River will taste different than one from the Chesapeake Bay."

"And why the wheat from Kansas is the best in the world," Annabelle said bluntly.

"Precisely!" Mrs. Sharpe said. "My goodness, aren't the two of you a pair! At first blush it seems you don't like each other, but heavens . . . I think you're actually playing games with each other. Am I right?"

"Indeed you are!" he said heartily, for under no circumstances would the animosity between him and Annabelle interfere with his mission today. "I began courting Miss Larkin shortly after our first meeting. It has been a courtship filled with twists and surprises. Constantly peppered with spice."

"No more ups and downs than in any other loving relationship," Annabelle said. "He's only banished me from his sight once!"

"Twice, counting the incident on the *Pelican,* darling."

She smiled tightly. "How could I forget when you keep reminding me?"

Mrs. Sharpe watched the interplay in fascination, then gave a playful swat to his arm. "I can't imagine a gentleman not being able to spot this treasure from the Department of Agriculture."

He slanted Annabelle a knowing look. "I confess that I've tried to wiggle off the hook a time or two. . . ."

"I always reel him back in," Annabelle told Mrs. Sharpe with a confidential wink.

"You just keep reeling," Mrs. Sharpe said. "And give him a firm talking-to about those food purity laws. We need men from the food industry on our side." She sent him a sugary smile with only a hint of barbed wire. "And trust me, once I've got them on board, there will be no wriggling off the hook, sir."

His eyes widened. Mrs. Sharpe was a combination of Fannie Farmer and General Sherman. Anyone who underestimated her was likely to have his head handed to him on a Wedgwood china plate.

The door opened and Mr. Feldman joined them. A scarecrow-thin man wearing a dark suit, Horatio Feldman could not be more different than the matronly Mrs. Sharpe.

"I've got ten minutes to hear about this counterfeit applesauce," he announced, plunking a stack of paperwork on the table and making the teacups rattle. "Let's get down to business. Where's the applesauce?"

The atmosphere pivoted, and Gray pivoted along with it. He set a jar with an original label from the Magruder factory on the table. With its colorful label featuring shiny red apples in a basket, it looked perfectly harmless.

"We have had scientists examine the contents, and they concluded it is a cheap mixture of stewed pumpkin and chemicals that simulate apples."

Horatio Feldman twisted the lid off and

spooned some into a bowl. "Mrs. Sharpe?" he asked.

"I'll wait for our own tests," she said with a slight wrinkle in her nose.

"A wise decision," Gray said, passing her the list of ingredients. "As you can see from the test we commissioned, this is not an appealing concoction. In fact, it's outright fraud to pass off a vegetable as apples."

"A vegetable?" Mr. Feldman asked. "I thought pumpkins are considered a fruit."

"They are," Annabelle said, turning a smug look on Gray. "A fruit is a seed-bearing structure that develops from the ovary of a flowering plant. Vegetables are other edible parts of a plant, such as the leaves, roots, or stems. Everyone knows pumpkins are a fruit."

He stiffened. He hadn't gone to college and couldn't spout off formal definitions, but before he could say something to redeem himself, Mrs. Sharpe came to his rescue.

"Not precisely," she corrected Annabelle. "In culinary terms, only sweet items are deemed fruits. Savory edibles such as tomatoes and pumpkins are fruits by the botanical definition, but the culinary definition considers them vegetables, my dear."

Gray shot to his feet and kissed the back

of Mrs. Sharpe's hand. "That was exactly what I was about to say. Thank you for not forcing me to correct my beloved Miss Larkin."

"Because you hate doing that," Annabelle said.

Mr. Feldman continued in a businesslike tone. "You claim that millions of these jars might be circulated. Will they all be consumed as straight applesauce, or can applesauce be used in cooking?"

Annabelle was ready with the answer. "Applesauce is often used as a sweetening element in baked goods and sauces. Young mothers routinely use it as baby food."

"Baby food!" Mr. Feldman shouted, rising to his feet. He grabbed the list of ingredients, his face flushing red. He was so angry he stammered. "They intend to feed babies potassium chromate and formaldehyde? That's an abomination. To think of a child who has known nothing but mother's milk to have his first bite of real food be laced with formaldehyde. Science has run amok! We can't wait for the law to catch up with it. We must act now. This shall not stand."

Every instinct urged Gray to stand up and cheer, but he forced himself to remain seated. The war was tilting in his favor, and he must do nothing to interfere.

Annabelle was not so restrained. "Exactly!" she said. "If we can stop one young mother from giving her baby this tainted food, I will consider it worthwhile. Can you help us?"

Mr. Feldman sat back down and folded his arms across his chest. "The better question would be, can *you* help *us*? The Department of Agriculture has spent years advocating for purity laws but has never accomplished anything. Why is it left to a ladies' magazine to lead the charge?"

Annabelle turned to him. "Gray, darling? Perhaps you'd like to answer that."

He was outnumbered here. These people might think having government inspectors prowling through factories was a better alternative than self-policing, but he wasn't here to fight that battle today. Passing the laws Mr. Feldman alluded to could take decades, and he wanted the Magruders' applesauce yanked off the shelves today.

"The government can never hire enough inspectors to stamp out food adulteration in the thousands of factories throughout the land," he said. "But your magazine can shame producers into policing themselves. People will fight to earn your magazine's approval, and they'll cringe at the negative

348

exposure if they try to pass off adulterated food as the real thing. The power of the pen is more powerful than any legislation that is currently snarled up in Washington."

"Good point," Mr. Feldman said bluntly. "Let's get down to work. I want this applesauce to serve as a case study of the abuses in the industry."

Mr. Feldman's ten minutes stretched into an hour as he outlined his recommendations to knock the momentum out from under the Magruders' applesauce. Public awareness among consumers was only one facet of the puzzle. The bigger prize would be to stop the distributors from carrying the product. The Sears Roebuck catalog was sensitive to negative press and would likely stop carrying products believed to be tainted. Grocery stores on the local level would be a harder challenge because the industry was so decentralized, but Mr. Feldman recommended using the power of the trade associations to get the word out.

"Do you have that sort of pull?" Gray asked.

Mr. Feldman snorted. "We buy ink by the barrel. Of course we have that sort of pull! And I won't stop until this country is blanketed with the information. I don't care if a new mother lives in Boston or Des

Moines or Timbuktu. No infant shall be spoon-fed a concoction of pumpkin laced with formaldehyde if I can stop it."

Mrs. Sharpe held up the latest issue of *Good Housekeeping.* "This is our rallying cry," she said. "Never underestimate the American woman when the health and well-being of her family are at stake. We shall fight it in the press, the grocery stores, and in our kitchens." Then she turned her steely glare on Gray. "And we will fight it in the halls of Congress. Mark my words, Mr. Delacroix. Passing those laws will be a challenge, but we'll get there eventually."

She slapped the magazine down on the table, drew a calming breath, and then adopted a pleasant smile. "Now. Let me wrap up the watercress sandwiches for your train ride back to Boston. Mr. Feldman, shall we also send them home with the apricot tart? I think we shall! I'll have the secretary wrap it so it will travel well."

Mrs. Sharpe led them down the hallway toward the front of the building, stopping briefly to make arrangements for a hansom cab. It was hard for Gray to contain his sense of triumph as they walked down the hall. Annabelle instinctively reached for his hand, and he grabbed it, squeezing tight. They'd done it. They had *done it.* Mrs.

Sharpe noticed their clasped hands, but he couldn't have let Annabelle go right now if his life depended on it.

When they reached the foyer of the building, Mrs. Sharpe leaned over to speak in a stage whisper into Annabelle's ear. "I shall expect a wedding invitation in the near future!" she said with a large wink at Gray.

Anabelle choked on her breath, but Gray smiled. "Mrs. Sharpe obviously has crystal clear vision," he said with a wink of his own.

As they headed out the door, he carried the box of sandwiches in one arm and clasped Annabelle's hand in the other. The weather was wet and miserable, but the second they stepped onto the portico, Annabelle could no longer contain herself. With a shriek of happiness, she leapt into his arms for a hug. He almost dropped the box but returned her embrace as laughter bubbled up from deep inside. Rain drizzled down on them, but he didn't care. For the first time since he'd embarked on this audacious quest, it looked like they would actually succeed.

"Look, there's Captain Haig!" Annabelle said.

Sure enough, Haig huddled beneath the awning of the pharmacy across the street. He cupped his hands around his mouth and called out to them. "How did it go?"

Gray didn't even have time to open his umbrella before Annabelle started dashing across the street. He followed, splashing through rain puddles, to tell Haig everything. It couldn't have gone better if he'd written the script himself.

"It was perfect," Annabelle gushed as they reached the pharmacy. The dash through the rain had left water dripping from her hair into her eyes. Gray passed her his handkerchief, and she took it, flashing him a brilliant smile as she dried her face.

"She's right," he told Captain Haig. "The editors are complete opposites, but they were both appalled by the applesauce and will help spread the word. Annabelle, you were pitch-perfect."

"Tell me!" Haig ordered, and Annabelle obliged. Gray watched her face as she spoke, her eyes sparkling with excitement. She embodied laughter and optimism and steadfast determination. Being with her felt like wind in his sails, filling him with buoyant optimism. He couldn't even concentrate on what she was saying to Haig; all he could see was the joy in her eyes as water dripped off her hair. She glowed with happiness.

But sobering thoughts intruded. What was Luke doing at this exact moment? Was he

352

hungry? Sick? If he caught some tropical disease, would they let him see a doctor? While Gray and Annabelle dined on watercress sandwiches and apricot tart, Luke sweltered in a prison cell.

For a few hours this morning, he had forgotten Annabelle's betrayal, but he remembered now, and the pain was raw and real. Annabelle kept chattering, still bubbling with excitement as his gaze tracked to the rain spattering in the street. Soon they would be on the train to Boston, and then they'd board the *Pelican* for the two-day journey to Washington. He would be trapped with this radiant person who reminded him of everything good in the world.

He couldn't do it. Annabelle and her luminous optimism was out of his reach now. The moment he tried to join in her happiness, his mind would inevitably stray back to Luke and her role in his downfall. Luke had earned his place in that prison, and Gray couldn't let it darken the rest of his life. Somehow he would forge ahead to build a future with a good woman beside him, but that woman could never be Annabelle. Her bright exuberance would be a constant reminder. He needed to put her behind him and try to move forward. This afternoon's triumph would forever mark the end of this bittersweet chapter in his life.

A pair of horses pulling a hansom cab clopped toward them, and he raised his umbrella to draw the cabbie's attention. Annabelle and Captain Haig kept up their lively stream of conversation as they boarded, but all Gray could concentrate on was how to say good-bye to her forever.

Annabelle was still floating on air as the carriage delivered them to the Springfield train station. Captain Haig peppered her with questions the entire ride, and she joyously answered them. Gray had retreated back into silence but she wasn't dismayed, for this afternoon had been a breakthrough. She and Gray had worked and laughed together. She couldn't expect him to leap back into the whole-hearted relationship they'd had earlier, but they were moving in the right direction.

Ahead of her was another voyage on the *Pelican,* and they could begin repairing the rift between them. Her hope inched even higher as Gray helped her alight from the carriage, looking so deeply into her eyes that she felt as though he was trying to memorize them. He opened the umbrella over them both as he guided her toward the train station. When the wind picked up, he angled the umbrella to shield her, and she was almost sorry when they arrived at the overhang before the station.

He collapsed the umbrella and held the door for her and Captain Haig. "Wait here," he said as they stepped into the small lobby of the train station. "I'll get our tickets."

The interior of the station was charming, with wooden floors, coffered ceilings, and plenty of seating. The train to Boston didn't leave for an hour, so she found a table in the station's café, ordered a pot of tea, then offered Captain Haig some of the delicate watercress sandwiches. He devoured them all before Gray returned.

He handed a ticket to Captain Haig, then turned to her, his face somber. "Annabelle, will you come with me?"

She tried not to worry as she followed him to the opposite side of the station, where potted ferns created an alcove of privacy. Gray's expression was serious but not angry. Moving forward wasn't going to be easy, but they were on their way.

He turned toward her as soon as they were both behind the ferns, but didn't meet her gaze. It looked like he struggled to find words as he clenched the tickets in his hand. She wanted to tell him not to be so nervous,

355

but patience was probably best right now.

"Annabelle, I can't see you anymore," he said, still staring at the ground. He opened his wallet and extracted a few bills, holding them out along with a single ticket. "This ticket will take you straight to Washington. I'm afraid it won't be possible to take you back on the *Pelican*."

Her jaw dropped open. "What are you talking about? I'm not going with you?"

He finally met her eyes, and they were full of regret. "This is my fault," he said. "I don't . . . I can't . . ." He tried a few more times but kept struggling to form the words.

Then the rumble of an incoming train interrupted him. Brakes squealed, steam hissed, gears clicked. He clenched his jaw and waited until the roar of the engines quieted.

"I'm never going to be able to forget what happened," he said in a voice aching with tenderness. She wished he were angry, because it would have been easier to stand up to anger. This pained, regretful side of Gray was excruciating. "Please understand," he continued. "I don't think you did the wrong thing where Luke is concerned. If I were in your shoes, I might have done the same. But when I look at you, I still think of my brother, and I don't think that will ever change."

What could she say to that? She simply stood frozen and stared at him while her heart split into pieces.

"Take the ticket, Annabelle."

She couldn't. Taking it would mean things were really over. She forced herself to meet his gaze. "I'm not ready to walk away."

Gray glanced out the window at the stationmaster, who strode down the platform, unlocking doors as passengers disembarked. "That's your train," he said. "It's heading first to New York City, then down the coast until it reaches Washington. It's an overnight trip, so I've purchased a sleeping-car ticket as well."

Boarding this train would mean giving up on something wonderful, but perhaps that decision had been made the moment she agreed to spy. She ought to have been prepared to live with that decision, but it still felt wrong.

"Please take the ticket," he prompted. "It's best that we end things now."

She nodded and took the small slip of paper, her dreams collapsing around her.

"You'll need to eat," he said, pushing a few more bills at her. She took them too.

"I'm sorry about everything," she whispered, unable to look at him for fear of

357

embarrassing herself. "Truly sorry, to the bottom of my soul."

"I am too," he said, his voice rough with emotion.

She nodded and headed outside to board the train.

THIRTY

Annabelle was tired, grubby, and heartsick when she arrived in Washington the following day. It was seven o'clock in the evening by the time she got back to her apartment, and she wondered if Elaine had anything prepared for dinner or if she should use the last of Gray's money to buy something from a street vendor. But she wasn't hungry, so she dragged herself up the two flights of stairs to their apartment. She'd go back down if Elaine wanted something to eat, but for now Annabelle needed to gather the remnants of her energy to pretend all was well for her sister. Was it only a week ago that she'd left for Boston? It felt like another lifetime. One in which she'd fallen in love with Gray Delacroix all over again and had the broken heart to prove it.

The key clicked in the lock as she opened the door. "Elaine?"

Her voice echoed in the darkened apartment. The sky was still light, so she crossed to the window to open the blinds. There was no one home.

There was no one home! It was seven o'clock, and Elaine should have been home from the library more than an hour ago. Annabelle's mouth went dry and her heart started thudding. She was at a loss for what to do.

Check across the hall. The Hillenbrands had been kind to them, and maybe Elaine was spending the evening in their apartment. In three bounding steps, Annabelle was at her neighbors' door, pounding and praying they were home.

"My goodness, what is the matter, child?" Mrs. Hillenbrand asked when she opened the door.

"Have you seen my sister? She isn't home."

"No, she's been staying with the Talbots."

Annabelle rocked back on her heels. "Who are the Talbots?"

"Someone she met at the library. A soldier she's been helping. When they learned she would be on her own for a few days, they opened their home to her. Frank and I would have welcomed her, but she seemed keen on staying with the Talbots."

Now Annabelle remembered meeting the

360

Talbot family at the Library of Congress. Harry, the blind soldier, and his sisters and father. Thankfully, Elaine had given Mrs. Hillenbrand the address.

It took a while for Annabelle's heart to find its normal rhythm again, but she headed back outside and toward the streetcar stop. It didn't matter how tired she was, it would be impossible to sleep until she was assured that Elaine was all right. How well did she know these Talbot people, anyway?

Their address was unfamiliar to Annabelle, and she asked the streetcar conductor for advice. "Can you tell me which stop to get off for this address?" she asked, and he nodded.

The streetcar traveled quite a distance. The sun was beginning to set, so it was hard to see clearly, but the buildings around them now had actual lawns in front. The townhouses, although built side by side, were at least four stories tall and oozed elegance. The only thing Annabelle knew about the Talbots was that Harry used to work for a grocer, so they weren't wealthy people, but the stop where she was told to exit seemed to be a very nice neighborhood.

The streetcar conductor gestured down the lane. "Your address is about six blocks down that-a-way," he said.

It was an awfully fancy area, especially when she saw placards on some of the lawns. That building was the Belgian Embassy? Others were the Russian and the French Delegations. She walked past the embassies and soon moved into a retail area. Most of the shops were for jewelry, antiques, and imported fabrics, but at last she arrived at the door matching the address in her hand. *Talbot's Fine Food & Delicatessen* was stenciled in gold lettering across the top of the bow-fronted window. The display featured an assortment of imported cheeses, exotic blends of tea, and chocolates in hand-painted boxes. Her heart squeezed at the lavish presentation of Delacroix spices artfully arranged in an open treasure chest.

The shop was closed, the door locked. She stepped back a few paces and craned her neck to peer into the upper two floors above the shop. It looked like they were apartments, for the windows were open and framed with draperies. Laughter and piano music leaked out from the upper floor.

If she could hear them, they could surely hear her. She cupped her hands around her mouth and shouted, "Mr. Talbot?"

The laughter continued unabated, and she tried three times before a laughing young lady stuck her head out the window.

"We're closed," she called down, her face still flushed with laughter.

"I'm looking for my sister. Is Elaine Larkin there?"

"You must be Annabelle," the lady said, then turned around. "Elaine, your sister made it in time for your party!"

Party? Oh good heavens, she'd forgotten her sister's birthday!

A moment later Elaine herself was at the window. "Annabelle! Come upstairs for some cake. We've got plenty."

The sense of relief was so strong, Annabelle plopped down on the curb to sit. It had been a long few days that careened from angst to joy to heartbreak, and throughout it all she'd been worried about Elaine, but it was all right now.

"Stay right there," the other woman called to her. "We'll send someone down to let you in."

Two minutes later, she found herself welcomed into the third-floor apartment, where at least a dozen people had gathered for the party. There was nice furniture, fancy carpets, and a piano where a young man picked out some tunes. A feast had been set out on the dining table, but most impressive were the people. They welcomed

Annabelle into their fold like a long-lost friend simply because she was Elaine's sister. Annabelle recognized the elder Mr. Talbot from the one time she met him at the library. His silvery hair was neatly groomed, and he leaned against the far wall of the apartment, looking slim and elegant in a formal shirt and vest.

Someone thrust a plate of birthday cake into her hands and gestured for her to sit at the table. She was about to take her first bite of cake when a teenaged boy snatched it away. "Everyone here must sing for their supper. We even made Elaine sing, and she's the birthday girl. Now it's your turn."

The request stunned her into silence, but Elaine rushed to her rescue. "Singing was never Annabelle's strong suit."

Howls of protest greeted Elaine's comment, but these people couldn't know what they were asking. Annabelle wasn't even permitted to sing in church because the gales of children's laughter distracted the congregation.

The young man at the piano twisted in his seat to face her. He wore shaded glasses, and Annabelle recognized Harry, the blind soldier Elaine had been working with.

"Only people who sing are allowed to have cake," Harry said. "It's the rules."

The cake looked delicious, but these people truly didn't understand. "I can make grown men faint at the sound of my singing. The glasses will crack; the cake will turn rancid."

"Now we *must* hear it," Harry exclaimed, and everyone else in the apartment joined in an anticipatory drumbeat.

Even Elaine looked ready to concede. "We're all friends here. Go ahead and sing."

"A slice of gourmet birthday cake is on the line," the elder Mr. Talbot coaxed.

Annabelle wanted that cake, and these people did seem friendly. If nothing else, she had learned to be brave over the past few years.

"Don't say I didn't warn you," she cautioned, then launched into a rendition of "My Wild Irish Rose." She tried to hold the tune, but within moments the melody got away from her as she warbled off key. She completely missed the high notes, and everything was going spectacularly, horribly wrong, but her audience appreciated the effort and began cheering her on. She raced toward the end of the song before completely losing her composure and collapsing into laughter.

She earned a standing ovation for her efforts, along with hollers of praise and requests for more. Annabelle laughed so hard her sides hurt, and Elaine wiped tears of laughter from her face.

"Well done," Mr. Talbot said, presenting her with the slice of cake. She was so busy talking and laughing with the others that it was almost an hour before she finished it. Elaine formally introduced her to the blind soldier and his wife, Martha. Harry pecked out a few tunes on the piano, but Annabelle steadfastly refused to sing again.

"The paint will peel from the walls," she said, and a couple of the others playfully agreed.

Mr. Talbot eventually pulled Annabelle aside. "Your sister has done a world of good for my son," he said. "He still has a long way to go, but she pulled him out of the depths of despair, and for the first time, I am beginning to have hope for him."

This had been a good evening. Even though Annabelle's heart had been broken all over again and her sister would be blind forever, there was good in life everywhere.

God was sending her a message. The world was a good place. She needed to look for it, even when life was full of pain. Her spirit was bruised and sore, but only hours after the worst heartbreak of her life, she had found joy as a dozen complete strangers welcomed her with open arms. God had never promised them a life free of sorrow, only the tools to hold and keep them through stormy days.

"Thank you," she whispered in a quiet prayer.

THIRTY-ONE

It had been six weeks since Annabelle's fateful trip to *Good Housekeeping,* and the issue with their exposé on counterfeit food was due to be released today. Annabelle knew this because Mrs. Sharpe had written her a delightful note of thanks for bringing the applesauce to her attention, and told her to be on the lookout for a "satisfying article" beginning on page nine of the September issue.

Annabelle eyed the clock over the laboratory door, biting her lip. There were still fifteen minutes until five o'clock, when she could dash to the nearest stationer's shop to grab the new issue. Adulterated food was Gray's cause, not hers, but she still cared. It mattered. She was proud that she had helped expose tainted and misbranded food.

She went back to focusing the microscope on the samples of durum wheat she was studying. This plant had been grown under drought conditions, and yet the size of the wheat kernels seemed to be as plump as those grown with normal rainfall. Would this strain of wheat finally prove to be the answer for her parents' farm?

Guilt gnawed at her. Her parents lived a threadbare existence in Kansas, but her father had fought her penny-pinching mother so that Annabelle could go to college. So far it hadn't paid off, but if this batch of wheat looked promising, perhaps the government would let her parents serve as a test farm.

She glanced at the clock again. Twelve more minutes.

"The clock goes faster if you don't keep watching it." Mr. Bryant didn't even look up from his desk as he made the comment.

Annabelle nodded. "I'll get back to work," she said, leaning over the wheat kernels.

"Do you suppose they'll mention your name in the article?" Horace asked.

"I certainly hope not!"

Horace and Mr. Bryant knew about the pending article. They'd been fully supportive of Annabelle's participation in recruiting *Good Housekeeping* to help sound the alarm about food adulteration, but that didn't mean she wanted any personal attention.

"Why not?" Horace pressed. "How often do government bureaucrats get a chance to shine in the spotlight?"

"If a spotlight ever shines my way, I'll run for cover."

"Not me," Horace said. "Did you read about the daughter of the Attorney General? I heard she *paid* to have a rumor started that she is being courted by the Russian ambassador. It's all part of a ploy to launch her stage career. You see? There's no such thing as bad gossip."

Their supervisor's dry voice cut through Horace's delight. "Mr. Greenfield, the government is not paying you to gossip about the Attorney General's daughter."

"Pity." Horace sighed and turned his attention back to his microscope.

Annabelle glanced at the clock. Ten more minutes.

"Take off early," Mr. Bryant said.

She sucked in a quick breath. "Really?" It was so unlike the staid Mr. Bryant, but he actually managed to crack a bit of a smile.

"You're completely useless to us while your mind is on that article. Go out and get your magazine."

"Thank you!" she said as she dashed out the door.

Her footsteps echoed in the cavernous

stairwell as she bounded downstairs, then hiked up her skirts to run toward the nearest newsstand at the corner of Independence and Twelfth Street. A stitch pinched her side, and she had to wiggle through a row of other people lined up at the kiosk. Sometimes she really hated being short.

"Do you have the new *Good Housekeeping*?" she shouted.

The vendor nodded and passed her the issue. She gave him a dollar and didn't even wait for the change as she headed a few paces away, flipping to page nine. Her breath caught as she saw the headline.

Nation's Largest Food Producer Dishing Up Dishonest Food

This was it! A full three pages long too! She skimmed the article, her eyes moving faster than her brain could read, but all the right words were here. Mrs. Sharpe had indeed sent up a clarion battle cry.

Annabelle was still walking on air as she headed to the Library of Congress to pick up Elaine, who was already waiting for her at the streetcar stop.

"It's out!" Annabelle said as she joined Elaine on the bench.

"Is it good?" Elaine didn't need to ask

what Annabelle was talking about, for she'd been waiting almost a week for this issue to hit the streets.

"It's beyond good. It's perfect!"

She read the article aloud to Elaine. Everything was here, from the scientific test run in *Good Housekeeping's* own laboratory on the "applesauce" that contained no apples, to the lack of listed ingredients and the inclusion of chemicals not yet proven safe for human consumption. They even included a laudatory mention of the Department of Agriculture and their nascent efforts to ensure a pure food supply. Better still, the article never once mentioned her or Gray's name, which was all to the good, for they were both private people, and this matter was too important for either of them to claim credit.

She would send a copy of this to her parents. On that frigid day when her parents had waved good-bye to them from a train station in the middle of Kansas, none of them could have imagined such important work, and it made her sit a little taller. Was this what pride felt like? She'd played only a tiny part in this accomplishment, but it suddenly felt like she could conquer the world.

Had Gray seen it yet?

Her smile dimmed, but only a little. She

hadn't seen Gray since that day in the Springfield train station, but she thought of him daily.

Today was a good day for both of them, even if they couldn't share it together. Days this perfect didn't come along very often, and she would choose to celebrate the joy rather than dwell on the sad. The world was a huge, wide-open landscape bursting with opportunity, and it was up to her to choose how she would live in it. God had blessed her with a sound mind and the freedom to make choices in life. It was a blessing she must not squander.

Annabelle still nursed a quiet sense of elation the following morning as she headed to work. Was it just her imagination, or were the flowers in the experimental garden a little more fragrant this morning? She was finding a sense of purpose in the world, and it felt good.

She rolled the issue of *Good Housekeeping* in her hands as she mounted the steps to the lab. How could she ensure that higher-ups in the department saw it? Horace Greenfield and Mr. Bryant certainly knew, but she couldn't expect anyone outside their lab to be aware of her role in this. She didn't want to boast, but this was a significant accomplishment and perfectly aligned with one of the department's major initiatives.

She was still debating how best to alert others in the department when she arrived in the lab. Good heavens, so many people crammed into their tiny workspace!

"There's the famous Miss Larkin!" Horace said.

"Miss Prim and Practical," Mr. Bryant added. In the six weeks she'd worked here, he'd barely smiled, but now it looked as if he was battling a laughing fit.

"What's going on?" she asked. She needn't have worried about getting attention for the magazine article, for she spotted at least three copies of *Good Housekeeping* floating around, and this male-dominated department certainly didn't make a habit of reading ladies' magazines.

"You didn't tell us you were going to be featured in the magazine," Mr. Bryant said.

"I'm not." She had read the article several times last night, and there was not a single mention of her or Gray's name. Exactly how they wanted it.

"And yet you are half of a thoroughly modern couple!" Horace chortled, handing her one of the magazines opened to an article near the back.

Her mouth went dry, and her heart skipped a beat. She hadn't read anything else in the issue, and her hand shook as she took the magazine from Horace.

A Thoroughly Modern Couple
By Mrs. Eleanor Sharpe

On a perfectly ordinary day in August, a most unusual couple paid a visit to the testing kitchen at *Good Housekeeping.* As our nation embarks on a new century, we expect to see new types of romantic pairings. One couple that personifies these changing times is Miss Annabelle Larkin and Mr. Gray Delacroix.

Readers of this magazine will already know the Delacroix name, as it is proudly affixed to the finest jarred spices in the world. Readers may not be familiar with the man at the helm of the company, an experienced traveler who personally visits his spice fields around the world but still has time to supervise a modern spice production facility in Virginia. He combines culinary excellence with the roving spirit of a renaissance man.

And what sort of woman has captured the heart of this international business magnate? She is a homegrown woman from the American heartland, raised on a wheat farm and educated at Kansas State Agricultural College, a school with a long and admirable record in granting women the same educational opportunities as men. Miss Larkin is the epitome of everything Prim and Practical. She perfectly offsets the roving, romantic adventurer of Mr. Delacroix.

Miss Larkin and Mr. Delacroix each have vivid personalities and are not afraid to flaunt them. They are a perfect combination, like oil and vinegar. Unpalatable on their own, but delightful when sampled together.

The story rambled on, but she couldn't read any more. She lowered the magazine and wished the floor would open and swallow her whole. Everyone in the room watched and waited for her reaction. She forced her embarrassment down and put on a serene expression.

"Mrs. Sharpe certainly has a colorful writing style," she said.

Horace pulled up alongside her. "Oil and vinegar? How long have you been seeing Mr. Delacroix?"

"I'm *not* seeing him." And Gray was going to be furious about this.

"That's not what Mrs. Sharpe implies," Horace pointed out. "You wouldn't want to let down the American readers. Come, you visited their office weeks ago. We need an update on how oil and vinegar are getting along these days."

"You're not going to get one," she said as she headed toward her station at the far end of the lab. The wheat seeds she'd left half analyzed yesterday still sat in their beakers, waiting to be sorted and measured. "I'd like to get back to work."

Two more men entered the lab, and oh good heavens, one of them was Mr. Cabrera, the commissioner of agriculture. She didn't recognize the other, but he wore a bow tie and looked very official. He carried an issue of *Good Housekeeping.*

"Where's the lady of the hour?" the second man boomed. A silly question, since she was the only woman in the lab.

"That's me, sir." And to think, only a few minutes ago she was worried about how she could ensure the magazine article got attention outside of her immediate lab.

Heat flushed her face, and the man introduced himself as Harvey Wiley, in charge of the bureau of chemistry for the department. That was the office in charge of investigating food purity, and to her relief, Mr. Wiley had the magazine open to the important article on page nine.

"Well done!" he said, giving her a bone-crushing handshake. "It's been hard for us to get attention in the popular press. No one gets excited over agriculture, but you figured out a way to get *Good Housekeeping*'s attention, and that will go far in advancing our mission to ensure a pure food supply."

The commissioner nodded and smiled.

The muscles in Annabelle's neck began to ease. How gratifying that these two highly placed men understood what was important. She felt even better when the commissioner suggested she start attending some of the department's meetings on developing pure food and drug proposals.

"I'd be honored," she stammered.

Mr. Wiley glanced over at her supervisor. "Well, Bryant? Can my committee steal this young lady for a few hours each week?"

Mr. Bryant agreed, and Mr. Wiley walked Annabelle down the hall to show her the office where the chemists met. He gave her the date of their next meeting and a typed agenda of issues to be discussed. How wonderful that Mr. Wiley only discussed the article that would have a lasting impact on the nation's health and not sensational stories about people's personal lives.

Just before she left, Mr. Wiley leaned down. "Tell me, are you the oil or the vinegar?"

She put on a brave face. "I'm afraid I'm the laughingstock in this story."

It was going to be a long time before she lived down Mrs. Sharpe's article.

THIRTY-TWO

Gray carried a heavy suitcase down the steps of his Alexandria townhouse to wait for Mr. Holder, who had gone to fetch the carriage from the public stable a block away. This morning he would take the train to Baltimore, then catch the afternoon passenger ship to Cuba. For weeks he had been dreaming about presenting the issue of *Good Housekeeping* to Luke in person. There wasn't much he could do to brighten his brother's life, but this article would help. Luke deserved to know of the success of his applesauce plan.

After setting down his bag, Gray looked down the street for a sign of Mr. Holder and the carriage. Instead he spotted Caroline disembarking from the Red Line streetcar and heading his way with fire in her step. In her hand she carried a copy of *Good Housekeeping,* and Gray braced himself for a confrontation.

Caroline didn't slow her steps until she stood less than a yard away. "A thoroughly modern couple?" she said as she whapped the magazine against his chest. He adroitly caught it.

"Good morning, Caroline. It's nice to see you."

"There's nothing good about this morning. I just read an article that implied my brother is in the throes of enchantment with a scheming and traitorous woman. How could you!"

A pair of ladies taking their morning stroll stopped to peer at them, and he forced his voice to remain calm. "Do you believe everything you read?"

Caroline planted both fists on her hips while she took several calming breaths. "All I need is for you to assure me that not a word of that story is true."

Mrs. Sharpe had gotten a lot wrong, but she had seen and understood more than he cared to admit. He *was* still a little enthralled with Annabelle. Not that it would ever come to anything, but it was still there.

"I can't do that."

She flinched, apparently expecting an immediate denial he had no intention of delivering. An odd series of emotions played across her face. Surprise, anger, and . . . fear.

"Gray, the two of us haven't always seen eye to eye, but I would step in front of a bullet for you. She wouldn't. She proved that on the day she walked into the War Department and turned over information that sent a cannon blast into the heart of our family."

He didn't want to hear it, but there was truth in what Caroline said. He didn't doubt for a second that she'd take a bullet for him, as he would for her. He didn't have much of a family left. In fact, Caroline was the beginning and the end of it.

Mr. Holder and the carriage rounded the street corner and would be here in less than a minute, but Gray needed to make peace with Caroline before he left.

He held up the magazine. "I'm sailing for Cuba to deliver this to Luke. The first article will send him over the moon. I don't think he gives a flying fig about the other, which is mostly there to sell magazines. There's no future between me and Annabelle."

It hurt even to say the words, but the relief on Caroline's face was palpable. Mr. Holder was waiting for him, but Gray pulled her into a hug and squeezed. It didn't seem so long ago that he could pick her up and set her on his shoulders. Now she was a woman, and during this catastrophic situation with Luke, he had a new appreciation for Caroline's strength and unswerving loyalty.

He must never do anything to endanger that.

September in Cuba wasn't much cooler than it had been in July, but even those few degrees made a difference as Gray strode toward the prison where Luke was being held. Had it only been two months since he'd been here? It seemed like the entire world had been upended, yet Luke hadn't moved more than a few inches within his six-by-ten-foot cell.

Gray carried the issue of *Good Housekeeping* rolled in his hand. In his satchel he had more newspapers and pamphlets that covered the adulterated applesauce, but it was *Good Housekeeping* that had proven to be the loudest megaphone. Its huge circulation and incriminating headline were proof that Luke's audacious plan had worked.

At least this time Gray knew what to expect as he moved through the layer of guards and locked doors in the stifling prison. He paid extra to meet Luke in the prison yard. Anything to get Luke out of that matchbox of a cell for a few minutes. The prison yard was surrounded on all four sides by barracks, but it was open to the sky, and that would be a blessing for someone who rarely saw it.

Gray waited at a rustic wooden table. He'd been warned that Luke would be shackled as a condition of using the prison yard, and the sound of rattling chains was harrowing as the door opened and a guard led Luke into the yard.

Luke's beard was new, and his black hair was long enough to tie back with a leather cord. Gray ignored the smell as he pulled his brother into a hug. With his wrists shackled, Luke couldn't return it, but Gray still held on for a moment before stepping back.

"You look like a pirate," he said.

"I'd rather drink my water than shave with it."

"Probably wise."

The beard disguised how gaunt Luke had become, but Gray had felt every one of his ribs during their brief hug. It hurt to see, but Luke still flashed a warm smile as he sat down on the bench.

Gray handed him the issue of *Good Housekeeping,* open to the inflammatory article about the Magruders. Luke hunkered over it, his eyes moving quickly across the page as he devoured every word.

"The Magruders are on the defensive," Gray said once Luke finished reading. "Plenty of newspapers picked up on this story and are expressing outrage. A couple of them have undertaken their own test of Magruder products. Their 'pure' maple syrup has been found to be chemically flavored corn syrup. Same with their honey. The issue is snowballing, and the Magruders are backpedaling like mad. Every time Clyde makes a campaign speech, people ask him about it."

"Do you think he can still get elected?"

Gray shrugged. "Impossible to say. He's a glib speaker, and a lot of powerful interests are still behind him."

Luke flipped back to the beginning of the article to read it again, a distinct look of satisfaction on his pirate's face. In the endless days and months ahead, sheer boredom would no doubt drive him to devour every word of the magazine over and over, and Gray shifted uneasily on the bench.

"There's another article in there," he said reluctantly. "You can ignore it. The writer completely misinterpreted what she saw."

Luke glanced up, questions in his eyes. It was better to answer them directly than let

Luke's imagination run wild.

"It's on page thirty-two."

Luke flipped to the drippy article that implied Gray was over the moon for Annabelle Larkin. It had been six weeks since he returned to Washington, and they hadn't exchanged a single word. But that didn't mean he hadn't seen her.

Twice he had deliberately loitered outside the Library of Congress, where she came each day to escort her sister home. He'd told himself it was because he was meeting Caroline and already in that part of town, but it wasn't true. He just wanted to see Annabelle. He couldn't explain why. She never noticed him sitting on the park bench across the street, and he fully intended to quit doing it but hadn't quite yet.

"You're still seeing Annabelle Larkin?" Luke asked after finishing the article.

"No. She was there and she helped, but we have both moved on. My relationship with her is completely over."

"Really? Caroline and I both thought she was the only person who could put up with your grayer-than-Gray personality and still be in a good mood."

Should he tell Luke? He didn't want to badmouth Annabelle, but Luke deserved to know.

386

"Annabelle is the one who turned you in. She was out at Windover Landing and found what was inside the raccoon shed."

Luke's eyes widened, first in amazement, then relief. "I was afraid it might have been Otis."

"No fear of that," Gray said. "In any event, I won't be seeing Annabelle anymore. It's over."

Luke braced his elbows on the table, rubbing his jaw and looking troubled. "Caroline wrote to say that you canceled the sale of the *Pelican.* That you're going overseas again."

That was the plan, but as the scorching pain of Annabelle's betrayal eased, the urge to run had faded. Gray was tired of life at sea. He was ready to settle down, and if it couldn't be with Annabelle, he would find someone else.

"I'm keeping the ship," he said. "Otis will be heading out in my place. He's ready for a new challenge, and he gets along well with Captain Haig. I trust them both."

"Good!" Luke said. "Caroline is worried sick about you heading out again. She'll never admit it, but I think she's in over her head at the White House, and it would be good if you were nearby."

"What makes you say that?"

"Just reading between the lines of her letters," Luke said casually, but then he sobered and leaned forward, an earnest expression on his face. "Look, thanks for what you did, hauling that applesauce project across the finish line. Don't lose momentum now. The Magruders are on the ropes and might be forced to clean up their act, but I suspect they'll subcontract with other suppliers. Keep your eye on them."

He rattled off half a dozen tricks the Magruders might use and techniques to sniff them out. He was cold and clinical as he outlined strategy and provided contacts to help get the upper hand.

"Do everything quietly," Luke urged. "No matter what happens, keep your fingerprints off it. If the Delacroix name gets mixed up in this, it will look like a business rivalry, and it isn't. This is a crusade for fair play and the health of every person in America who opens a jar of food or buys a pound of coffee."

"I hear you." Maybe for the first time in his life, Gray fully heard what Luke was telling him. Gray had always belittled Luke's activities, but beneath the surface of the bon vivant, it seemed Luke operated with careful, methodical planning and cunning intelligence. How could Gray have underestimated his little brother all these years?

Luke had turned his face to the sun, a slight smile hovering on his mouth as a hint of a breeze softened the prison yard. He gazed at the wispy clouds overhead as though they were the most beautiful works of art in creation.

"How often do they let you out?" Gray asked, dreading the answer.

The way Luke gazed at the sky with that blissful expression didn't waver. "Not much," he answered, as though he didn't have a care in the world.

In their two hours this afternoon, they had talked about Caroline, the *Pelican,* and strategy against the Magruders. The one thing Luke consistently avoided was anything to do with his legal status. Every time Gray asked, Luke diverted the topic. When Gray asked about getting him transferred to an American prison, he said not to bother. He refused to comment on the pending charges or even if there had been a date set for the trial. In exasperation, Gray gave up and asked the broadest question he could think of.

"Tell me what I can do to make this better."

Luke tilted his head as he thought for a minute. No matter what he asked, Gray would deliver. Money to bribe the guards? Political favors called in? A prison escape? Gray would do his best, but when Luke finally answered, it wasn't anywhere close to what he'd been thinking.

"There are three families in Philadelphia. You know who they are. Keep an eye on them for me, will you?"

Gray swallowed back his frustration. Those families had already been richly compensated, and no amount of money would ever ease Luke's conscience, but it was the only thing Luke asked of him, and he would do it.

"Of course."

Gray stayed as long as the guards permitted, but eventually they showed up to lead Luke back to his cell. With his wrists shackled, his brother couldn't scoop up the newspapers and magazines, so Gray gathered them together and placed them atop Luke's outstretched arms. The issue of *Good Housekeeping* was on top of the stack.

Luke glanced at it. "Don't be too hard on Annabelle," he said just before being led down the hall. "I'm guilty as sin, and this wasn't her fault or anyone else's."

As he watched the door slam behind Luke, Gray couldn't be so sure. Annabelle may have turned him in, but who had failed Luke in the years leading up to his arrest?

THIRTY-THREE

Annabelle's first test in her new position supporting the food purity initiative came exactly one week after the *Good Housekeeping* article was released. She was measuring soil samples when the department's secretary entered the lab to tell her that a journalist from *The Washington Post* wanted to speak with her.

"Does he really want to speak with *me*?" she asked the secretary. "Surely there is someone more senior than me to represent the department."

The secretary shook her head. "That's what I told him, but he says he wants more details on Magruder's applesauce. I suppose you're the right person to talk to about that."

Annabelle looked at Mr. Bryant, who had worked at Agriculture for more than thirty years. "Should I go?"

Mr. Bryant nodded. "It is a challenge to

get the popular press to cover anything from the Department of Agriculture, so jump on this opportunity. I'm sure you will comport yourself professionally."

Annabelle tugged off her apron, wishing she had worn something nicer than the plain cotton dress she always donned when working with soil. She raced to the sink to scrub her hands but still felt uneasy talking to a reporter.

Dickie Shuster from *The Washington Post* was nothing like what she expected a journalist to look like. He wore a shockingly bright green bow tie embroidered with tiny ladybugs and knotted in generous loops of fabric that dangled down his chest. His flamboyant attire made him seem younger than he was, but on closer study, a spray of lines fanned from his eyes, and his hairline receded so far back that he would soon be considered bald. Nevertheless, the delightful floppy tie put her at ease.

They met in the cafeteria on the ground floor of the Department of Agriculture. There weren't many people there at this time of day, and Dickie, as he insisted she call him, managed to snag an entire custard tart for them to share.

"The chef in the kitchen here is beyond compare," he said as he cut a large wedge for her and slid it across the table. "Don't hold back. Anything that doesn't get eaten is coming straight home with me."

"I gather you saw the *Good Housekeeping* article," she said, too anxious to eat.

He nodded. "The Delacroix family has been trying to take down the Magruders for ages, but you are brand-new in town. I'm curious how you became involved in this matter."

How did he know she was new in town? She wasn't comfortable answering personal questions and immediately retreated behind her official position. "It's hard to work here and not be aware of the issue. The Department of Agriculture has been trying to pass food purity laws for years."

"Decades, actually," the reporter corrected her. He took another bite of custard, chewing thoughtfully as he framed his next question. "Now, let's move on to the subject of Luke Delacroix. He's had it in for the Magruders — what did I say wrong? You just flinched."

"I didn't flinch."

"You most certainly did. The moment I mentioned Luke Delacroix. Why?"

She didn't have to answer these questions. If *The Washington Post* wished to discuss food purity or the Magruders' applesauce, she would be happy to do so, but she had absolutely nothing to say about any of the Delacroixs.

"I barely know Luke Delacroix."

"Do you know where he is? He's usually such a man about town, but lately he seems to have vanished." He scrutinized her like a cat stalking prey. He knew something.

Her mouth went dry, and the sight of the sickeningly sweet custard tart made her feel ill. She pushed the plate back a few inches and stood. "My job is to analyze durum wheat kernels. Most people think it's boring work, but my parents live on a struggling farm, so for me it's vitally important. I don't mean to be rude, but this conversation is pointless, and I need to return to my job."

She felt the reporter's stare boring into her back as she left the cafeteria. She'd bet her bottom dollar he didn't care a fig about fake applesauce. He was after something, and it had nothing to do with food purity.

Should she tell Gray about it? The reporter's line of questioning didn't sit well with her, but Gray might misunderstand. He'd been clear in his desire to keep his distance from her. She decided to let it be. Gray was an intelligent man and far more sophisticated than she was about dealing with the press. If Dickie Shuster came after him, he would know how to handle it.

But a part of her feared there was more trouble coming where Luke was concerned.

Gray vowed that today would be the first day of his new life. It didn't matter that he was skeptical down to the marrow of his bones. It didn't matter that half his heart was still back in Cuba with Luke, and the other half mourned Annabelle's loss with an ache that might never fully heal. If he was to make a life in America, it was time to settle down and get married.

Caroline swore she had found the perfect woman to help him "move ahead with his life." Samantha Riley was the thirty-year-old widow of a senator from North Dakota. Her husband had died almost two years ago, but having sampled the comforts of Washington, she had no desire to return to the barren flatlands of her native state. Which meant Samantha was as eager to get married and settle down as he was. She was intelligent, attractive, and a skilled hostess.

"And you're so painfully bad at that," Caroline had told him the previous day when she'd nudged him into this dinner invitation. "You need someone who can pull you out of your shell."

Maybe she was right. He hadn't looked at

396

another woman since Annabelle and was never comfortable mingling in society. The only reason he'd met Annabelle to begin with was because she had barged into his office in search of him. It still hurt to remember the day she had brought him that charming spice map, but he couldn't let the catastrophic end of their relationship warp him for the rest of his life.

Which was why he'd invited Caroline and Mrs. Riley to his favorite restaurant in Alexandria. Only yards from the harbor, it boasted an exceptional variety of fresh seafood dishes. While it didn't have crystal chandeliers or a connoisseur's wine cellar like the finer restaurants of Washington, he liked it here. The food was good, the atmosphere relaxed, and the picture window overlooking the harbor was spectacular.

Mrs. Riley seemed a little less than thrilled with the dining. She poked skeptically at her parmesan-crusted cod served over a bed of sautéed spinach and artichokes. "What a shame when cod is overcooked. It turns rubbery so quickly." She went on to recount the time she had served pan-seared cod for a crowd of one hundred during election night. "The chef must always begin the sear with the skin-side down, then a quick finish on the other side with a splash of lemon. It will be perfect."

Only a few months ago, Gray would have agreed with her. The cod *was* a little over-cooked, but Mrs. Riley's critical eye was a disappointment after Annabelle's fresh enthusiasm for everything around her. Perhaps it would just take time to become comfortable with Mrs. Riley. She had high standards, but he did as well. He'd sunk a fortune into developing cold-press brewing for vanilla extract because of the slight difference in the flavor profile. He ought to appreciate Samantha Riley's insistence on fine food.

He flagged down a waiter, gesturing him in close to speak quietly. "Let's exchange the cod for three plates of lobster salad," he whispered. He'd dined here enough to know that their lobster salad, with plenty of feta cheese and a rich oregano dressing, was always exceptional. He tried to be discreet, but Mrs. Riley noticed.

"My mother always said any establishment should be given two chances to make a good first impression, because none of us are perfect," she said.

He raised a glass to her. "Here's to your mother," he said. "She sounds like a font of wisdom."

"Ha! Maybe when she wasn't tippling in

the hayloft. Mother could outdrink a crew of sailors any day of the week."

He met Caroline's gaze with a quirk of his brow. Samantha Riley's fussy palate wasn't a problem, but jesting over the failings of her own mother before a virtual stranger was.

It turned out the lobster salad wasn't to her taste either.

"Kalamata olives completely overwhelm the flavor of the lobster," she said as she used her fork to delicately separate the olives and bits of bacon from the rest of the salad. "Lobster is such a delicate meat. It can't be dumped in with this avalanche of flavors." She shook her head in disappointment.

It was time to see if there was some way to salvage this disastrous dinner.

"Mrs. Riley, is there anything I can do to make this evening more pleasant for you? It appears I have failed on all fronts." He had to hold back a smile as he spoke. He wasn't angry with her, and he truly wanted to know.

She froze, her fork halfway to her mouth with a lump of lobster. After a moment, she set it down and had the decency to blush. "Forgive me. I thought a man of your sophisticated palate would be looking for a lady who shared it."

She seemed horribly embarrassed, and he did his best to set her at ease. "I spent most of the last twenty years on a ship, eating canned food and hardtack. If a meal is hot and fresh, I'm usually over the moon."

She returned his laugh. "And I actually love bacon," she said, stirring the pile of bacon back into the lobster salad. She dropped the pretension and ate with gusto.

Maybe they could work something out after all.

Ever since their experiment with the vanilla pear cake, Elaine had become obsessed with cooking. She checked out braille books from the library on all aspects of the culinary arts and regularly presented Annabelle with recipes she wanted to try.

Today's recipe was a rhubarb chutney. It wasn't the sort of dish Annabelle imagined she would enjoy, but Elaine was adamant.

"I've heard that the combination of sweet and sour fruitiness is the perfect combination to accompany a nice sharp cheese. Perhaps a cheddar or an aged gouda."

Annabelle didn't know what to make of such extravagant food combinations, but these experiments in their kitchen always cheered Elaine, so Annabelle dutifully bought the rhubarb, red wine vinegar, onions, and dried cherries to prepare the dish. It filled the kitchen with an odd scent as Elaine stirred the mix over a low heat.

Annabelle worked on mincing the onions while, on the other side of the kitchen, Elaine kept sniffling. Which was odd, because Annabelle was the one cutting onions.

"Are you all right?" she asked.

Elaine's back was to her, but the sniffling continued, and Elaine shook her head.

Annabelle dropped the knife and went to her sister's side. "What's wrong?" she asked, for Elaine was tense and her breathing ragged.

Oh no. These fits of panic were rare now, and Annabelle couldn't imagine what had triggered it, but she moved the pot to the back of the stove and put a reassuring arm around Elaine.

"Come, sit down," she urged. "Tell me what's wrong."

Elaine fanned her face with her hands, struggling to breathe normally. "I don't know how to tell you," she finally said.

"Tell me what?"

At least Elaine seemed to be getting her composure back as she beat back the panic. She dried her eyes with her cuff and took a calming breath.

"You have been so good, bringing me all the way across the country so I could work at the library. I don't ever want you to doubt how grateful I am. The library was a miracle for me." Elaine's breathing became ragged again and her face tortured.

"Don't panic," Annabelle urged. "Just keep breathing and tell me what's bothering you. It will be all right."

"I'm going to quit working at the library. I plan to tell them tomorrow."

Annabelle was baffled. Both of their lives had been upended so Elaine could find meaning and hope for the future by helping at the blind reading room, and now she'd decided to quit?

"But why?" Annabelle asked, completely flabbergasted.

"Because I'm going to work in the Talbots' grocery store."

The Talbots? They were nice people, and the birthday party last month had been filled with laughter and good food and bad singing. But no matter how nice, work in a grocery was a comedown after the Library of Congress. They could have stayed in Kansas if all Elaine wanted to do was work in a grocery.

"Will they pay you?"

Elaine was a little taken aback by the

question. "I don't think so. I never really thought about it. Actually, I'm going to marry Mr. Talbot. The owner."

Annabelle rocked back in her chair, her mind reeling. She remembered Mr. Talbot — a gentlemanly figure who stayed in the background most of the evening, leaning against the wall and watching the younger people celebrate. She had never once sensed a hint of attraction between her sister and the much older Mr. Talbot. She said as much to Elaine.

"Really?" Elaine asked, seeming genuinely confused. "I can't stop smiling whenever he is near."

It had certainly been true the night of the birthday party. Elaine had been glowing with happiness, but Annabelle had attributed it to the unexpected treat of a birthday party. Probably because she'd been wallowing too deeply in Gray's rejection to sense anything beyond her own despondency.

"How long have you been engaged?"

"A month. Every day he comes to the library to bring us lunch. He's been so kind, and I love him very much."

"Why didn't you tell me?"

Elaine shifted on her chair, and apprehension fell across her features again. "I didn't know how," she said. "You've done so much for me, all so I could work at the Library of Congress. Now I'm leaving, but if we hadn't moved here, I would never have met Walter. I know I should have told you, but after all the sacrifices you made on my behalf, I just didn't know how."

The news felt like a weight on Annabelle's chest, making it hard to draw a deep breath. She plastered a fake smile on her face. Elaine claimed she could hear a smile in a voice, and Annabelle was determined to seem happy.

"Congratulations," she said. "When is the wedding?"

"Two weeks. Walter is fifty-two and isn't getting any younger, so we don't want a long engagement."

The plan was for Elaine to learn how to help in the grocery store, and then she would move into the Talbot family home above the store after the wedding. They wanted to have a child as soon as possible, and then Elaine would stay home with the baby.

Annabelle ought to be overjoyed, not low and gloomy. But this was such a dreary little apartment, and after Elaine left, it would be lonely. Should she even stay in Washington? Elaine wouldn't need her anymore, and her parents desperately needed help on the farm.

The only thing that Annabelle knew for sure was that after Elaine married, life would never be the same again.

Annabelle's parents arrived in Washington the following week. The intention was for Maude and Roy Larkin to meet Walter, help with the wedding preparations, and then enjoy a once-in-a-lifetime visit in the nation's capital.

It didn't work out that way. Their mother was critical from the moment Walter welcomed them at the train station. As he helped stow their luggage above the rented carriage, Maude pulled Annabelle and Elaine aside.

"His hair is entirely silver!" Maude whispered harshly.

"He told me he went prematurely gray while he was in his thirties," Elaine defended in a low voice.

"And how many decades ago was that?"

It was a pointless question, for her parents already knew that at fifty-two, Walter was twenty-three years older than Elaine. Of course, Walter's biggest crime was his intention to marry Elaine, ensuring that Maude's eldest daughter would never return to Kansas.

Maude and Roy would be staying in their tiny apartment for the duration of the visit, and it was going to be a tight fit. As soon as they settled their luggage at the apartment, Walter drove them all to his neighborhood so they could tour his grocery store.

"I'm already learning how to pickle all kinds of salads and vegetables," Elaine said as they entered the shop.

With its gleaming wood floors, colorful displays, and huge variety of delicacies, Annabelle thought her parents would be pleased with the shop and Walter's ability to support Elaine, but her mother continued to find fault.

"Four dollars for mustard," Maude said, aghast, as she held an elegant glass jar.

Walter was polite. "It is imported from France and made with fermented cranberry wine. There's nothing else quite like it. I'd be happy to serve some at a meal while you are visiting."

"I wouldn't ask that of you," Maude said, setting the jar back on the shelf. In Kansas they ground their own mustard seeds with a little vinegar and called it a day. The luxury in Walter's store was an affront to Maude's thrifty soul.

Their father didn't care about mustard prices. He was too fascinated with the spigot on the delicatessen sink and how it could supply water even though there was no well behind the shop. The concept of a municipal water system was a new and marvelous thing for Roy. Long after Maude had her fill of the shop, Roy asked Walter all kinds of questions about the plumbing, the cash register, and how the electric lamps worked.

Their father was endlessly curious about the city, wanting to know how the streetcars stayed balanced on the sunken tracks and who paid for the streetlamps. That evening Annabelle warned her parents that they would need to lower the shades on the bedroom window or else the streetlamps would keep them awake.

"They leave them on all night?" Maude asked. There was no need for window shades at their farmhouse, where only owls and raccoons roamed the night.

"All night," Annabelle confirmed. "It's for safety."

"Good heavens," Maude exclaimed. "If I'd known it was this unsafe in the city, I would never have consented for my girls to come."

Maude had resisted their move to Washington from the moment Elaine raised the possibility. Maude and Elaine had always been unusually close, but after Elaine lost her sight, Maude had continually hovered within a few feet of her daughter. The moment Elaine rose from a chair, Maude would be at her side to walk her across the room, pour her a glass of water, or cut her meat. She didn't believe Elaine could function without her and threw out one excuse after another to stop her beloved oldest daughter from leaving. She usually cited the cost, for there was never enough money on the farm.

Roy had sold the milking goats to raise money, then bought two train tickets without consulting Maude. Once the tickets were purchased, Maude could find no more excuses for standing in Elaine's way, but the night before they left, Anabelle heard her mother quietly weeping on the back porch. She'd never heard her mother cry before that night, and it was upsetting.

In her heart, Maude believed their sojourn to Washington would fail and it was only a matter of time before Elaine would return to Kansas. Walter had ruined that, and Maude could find nothing about Washington that pleased her.

Just before they all turned in for the evening, Roy beckoned Annabelle over to show her an article in the newspaper. "It says here there's a skeleton of a mastodon in the Smithsonian. What's a mastodon?"

She searched for the words. "It's like an elephant, but bigger."

Roy gazed into space. "I can't even imagine such a thing. Is it interesting?"

Her heart turned over. How much her parents had sacrificed to send her and Elaine here. In the past six months, she'd started to take these marvels for granted, but Roy certainly didn't. As soon as the wedding was over, she'd be sure her parents saw the mastodon and anything else they wanted to experience in this wonderful city.

She could only hope that by then, she would have shaken off this despondent sense of feeling like a flightless bird at the same time Elaine had found her wings.

THIRTY-FOUR

Gray rarely took the time to read *The Washington Post* first thing in the morning. Early morning hours were his most productive time, so he couldn't explain his compulsion to sit in his parlor and open the newspaper. The story that jumped out at him was a two-page spread.

Family of Saboteurs, Socialites, and Spies

The article was a kick in the gut. He battled a tightness in his chest as he read the article, a direct assault on his motives for undermining the misbranded Magruder applesauce. It painted the applesauce story as a carefully orchestrated takedown of his business rival, using the auspices of *Good Housekeeping* to carry out a personal vendetta.

Fury made it hard to see straight. He had

to set the newspaper down and draw a few breaths while his vision cleared. He'd never trusted Dickie Shuster. The man would stab his mother in the back if it would make for a juicy story.

Gray forced his ire down as he picked up the newspaper to keep reading, but it only got worse as Dickie turned his attention to Caroline and Luke.

Luke Delacroix is currently incarcerated in a Cuban jail, awaiting trial for espionage and consorting with the enemy. While there have always been traitors skulking in our nation, rarely do those villains have siblings who work within arm's length of the American president. Caroline Delacroix is the personal secretary to our country's first lady, meaning she spends most of her time inside the White House, possibly wielding undue influence over the infirm Mrs. McKinley.

He didn't care about the rehashing of his feud with the Magruders, but something needed to be done to quell the damage to Caroline, and it needed to be done fast. This was the first time news of Luke's arrest had reached the general public, and it was going to devastate Caroline. They'd always known

411

that sooner or later this story might leak, but he'd hoped for more time.

Less than an hour later, Gray was at the White House, sitting in the garden behind the house while Caroline read the article, her face white and lips tense. She didn't deserve to be punished for Luke's actions.

Gray scanned the White House grounds while she read. It was quiet back here, with a wall of hedges creating a private garden oasis behind the house. The only other person was a gardener slowly clipping lilies and carnations. It didn't seem right to employ a man that old to work in the heat of the outdoors, but the staff at the White House tended to stay for decades.

Caroline closed the newspaper. Even before it landed on her lap, she was straightening her slim shoulders and lifting her chin.

"He misspelled the name of Luke's prison," she said calmly.

"Yes, but he got the rest of the details correct, and this is going to hurt. I need to know how badly you want to keep your job at the White House. That will influence my next move."

"I want to stay." Her answer was unequivocal, but it complicated things.

"You said the president already knows about the charges against Luke."

"He does. I told him right after Luke's arrest, and he refused to take my resignation because the first lady needs me."

Thank heavens for Ida McKinley and her notoriously volatile moods. "But now the situation is public, so it will be harder for him to keep supporting you. You need to distance yourself from Luke."

"What do you mean?"

"Issue a statement. Denounce his actions and say you want nothing to do with him."

Fire flashed in Caroline's eyes. She leaned forward and spoke in a lethal whisper. "I will *never* denounce my brother."

"He's guilty. He flat-out told me so."

"And you believed him?"

How could he not? If there was the slightest chance to make a case for reasonable doubt, Gray would spend a fortune to get Luke free, but there wasn't. Then again, Caroline knew Luke better than anyone on the planet. From infancy, the twins had shared an uncanny bond that few could penetrate.

"What do you know?" he asked quietly. "Do you have any additional information?"

She shook her head. "I don't know anything beyond what you've told me, but I *do* know Luke, and I think there's more to this story. I'm not ready to give up on him. I

413

will never —"

"What are you doing out here?" The voice cut across the garden like a whip, and a man in a tailored suit strode toward them. "You're forbidden to have unauthorized visitors in the private section of the residence."

Caroline stood. "My brother is no threat to the White House."

The man with a military bearing and flinty eyes swiveled his attention toward Gray. "From the 'family of saboteurs and spies'? Then you're especially unwelcome."

Caroline put on a tight smile and an artificially bright voice. "Gray, I'd like to introduce you to Nathaniel Trask, the security agent who goes out of his way to make himself disagreeable."

Her insult didn't cause even a flicker of change in the agent's expression as he looked coolly at Gray. "I'd prefer not to have you bodily removed, but I have already warned your sister about unauthorized visitors. Her family is especially undesirable. Where there's one traitor, more are likely flourishing nearby."

It looked like he wanted to say more, but the gardener was slowly walking toward them as he wiggled a red carnation into his jacket's buttonhole.

414

"Lay off her, Mr. Trask," the gardener said curtly as he passed them on his way into the house.

Agent Trask snapped to attention. "Yes, sir," he said promptly. "Of course, sir."

Gray's mouth dropped open. He'd heard that President McKinley wore a freshly cut red carnation in his lapel each day. His gaze trailed to Caroline. "Was that the president?"

"That was the president," she confirmed. "He cuts flowers for the first lady every morning."

The security agent relaxed a fraction as he shot a surly glare at Caroline. "One might think that should be *your* job."

"Try to stop him," Caroline said. "I'd enjoy watching that. Just try, I dare you." Her taunting look made Gray suspect she was enjoying the interaction.

"The president may think you are indispensable, but I don't," Agent Trask said. "Sooner or later you're going to place a foot wrong, and when that happens, I'll be there to haul you out the door."

The agent left, Caroline watching him the whole time. "Isn't he delightful?"

"But he's right," Gray said reluctantly. "Any association you have with me or Luke can only harm you."

415

"I suppose you're both my cross to bear," she teased.

She said it affectionately, but he feared she was correct, and that hurt more than anything.

Ever since Dickie Shuster's visit, Annabelle scanned the newspaper each morning, curious about what he had up his sleeve, but the article was so much worse than she could have imagined. Dickie Shuster had no interest in food purity. He was only interested in writing a salacious exposé of the entire Delacroix family.

It was no surprise when she arrived at the laboratory to see Horace poring over the disgraceful article and not a single test tube or seed sample brought out of storage for testing.

"Have you seen this?" he asked with excitement.

"I've seen it," she replied, heading straight toward her collection of lab notebooks.

"Absolutely appalling," he said in a voice dripping with delight. "And there is more to come. Did you see that this is only the first article in a series?"

Annabelle dropped the lab books and darted to the newspaper. "No. Where?"

Sure enough, in small print near the bottom, it indicated that Mr. Shuster would release the second article about the Delacroix family and their crusade against the Magruders the following week.

Horace rubbed his hands so firmly his knuckles cracked. "Dickie Shuster recently came into possession of a matched pair of chestnut bays and has been driving them all over town. I happen to know those horses once belonged to Clyde Magruder, but now they are Dickie's, and that's no coincidence."

"Are you suggesting that Dickie Shuster *took a bribe?*" She was so aghast she could barely get the words out.

Horace giggled. "My dear, you are so naïve. I don't think Dickie would use the word *bribe,* since it has so many unsavory legal implications. But the Magruders know how to get things done, and the 'gift' of some fine horses certainly paid off for them. And trust me, there is more to come. *Much* more, and I think I know what it is."

She shouldn't be gossiping. Mr. Bryant had warned her time and again about squandering time with gossip, but this was important. It was still three minutes before nine o'clock, so technically she wasn't on duty yet.

She leaned closer and lowered her voice.

417

"What else do you know?"

"I know that Dickie didn't milk the treason angle about that Delacroix brother in Cuba nearly enough. A tidbit that scandalous belongs on the front page, not buried on page eight. He's holding something back, and it's big."

How much worse could it get than branding a man a traitor and a spy? But Horace always had his nose to the ground and knew Washington politics inside and out. "What are you expecting?"

"I expect that next week's installment will be a front-page story documenting the traitorous activities of a Naval Academy graduate and corruption within the War Department."

She shook her head. "Luke Delacroix never graduated from the Naval Academy."

"*Au contraire,*" Horace practically purred. "He graduated last year."

"No, he didn't," she insisted. "He got kicked out eight years ago, a semester shy of graduation." She still remembered the despair in Gray's voice as he talked about Luke — so much talent but so little discipline. And Luke's subsequent years of reckless living certainly didn't comport with the expected behavior of a Naval Academy graduate.

The smirk on Horace's face made it clear he didn't believe her, but it was almost time for their supervisor to arrive and shut down all superfluous chitchat. Horace darted to the hallway and looked both ways. Apparently Mr. Bryant wasn't yet in sight, as Horace closed the laboratory door and hurried back to the lab tables, gesturing for her to lean in close.

"You know my wife is a secretary at the War Department," he whispered. "And secretaries know everything."

A sense of dread loomed, for Horace wouldn't be gloating so much unless he had something truly scandalous to share.

"What does your wife know?" she asked.

"She knows that about a year ago, a special request was made at the Office of the Navy to award Luke Delacroix a diploma from the Naval Academy. It was all hush-hush, but officers from the academy arrived and met with the proper authorities, obtained the necessary signatures, and brought that paperwork back to Annapolis to be officially filed. My wife put the signed diploma in the mail. She saw it with her own eyes and personally addressed the envelope to Mr. Luke Delacroix. As of last year, he had the trust of high-ranking officers in the War Department. Now he is a traitor. Tell me, Annabelle from Kansas, don't you think that level of corruption is worthy of a front-page story?"

It was. And it was also something Gray needed to know right away.

THIRTY-FIVE

Annabelle dreaded going to see Gray. The last time they saw each other had been almost two months ago. That awful morning in the Springfield train station when Gray definitively stated there could be no future for them.

She asked Mr. Bryant for an extra hour at lunch to give her enough time to get to Gray's spice factory and back. She needed to get this information about Luke to Gray immediately if he was to have any prayer of somehow scuttling the second part of the article Horace predicted would come next week.

The nearest streetcar stop was half a mile from Gray's spice factory, and her tension ratcheted higher as she walked. The heady scent of spices greeted her the moment she stepped inside the factory, her gaze darting around in search of Gray. He wasn't there. Somehow, she instinctively knew she'd be able to spot him in less than a heartbeat if he was there. His office, perhaps?

She recognized the gangly man unloading dried herbs into a spice roller. It took only a second to recall his name.

"Good afternoon, Mr. Zimmer," she called out over the rumble of rotating spice drums.

He set down the basket of herbs. "You're the Smithsonian lady. Back for another tour?"

She shook her head. "I'm at the Department of Agriculture now. Is Mr. Delacroix available?" She held her breath, but thank heavens, Mr. Zimmer nodded.

"He's out back overseeing another batch of vanilla. You remember where that is?"

"I do."

She headed outside to the squat brick building behind the factory. She dreaded bringing this rumor to Gray's attention, for merely mentioning Luke's name would remind him who was responsible for his brother's imprisonment. Outside the door of the distillery, she drew a fortifying breath but then paused. Was that the sound of voices coming from inside? She knocked just to be safe.

"Come in!" Gray's voice was clearly recognizable.

She twisted the knob, entered, and immediately froze.

"Oh," Annabelle said stupidly. "I thought you would be alone."

A striking woman with jet-black hair stood close to Gray. Her smartly tailored suit with its tiny cinched-in waist made Annabelle's gingham dress feel like a potato sack. Gray and the woman were nestled between a huge tank of vanilla and the brick wall, her hand resting on his arm.

"I was just showing Mrs. Riley the cold extraction process for the vanilla," he said. "She wanted to learn more about the business. Samantha, this is Anabelle Larkin from the Department of Agriculture. What are you doing here?"

Her mouth went dry as her discomfort grew, for the woman made no move to lift her hand from Gray's sleeve. There was no wedding ring, and given her close proximity to Gray and the possessive smile floating on her mouth, Annabelle suspected Mrs. Riley had designs on Gray.

"I need to speak with you on a private matter," she said.

Gray glanced at Mrs. Riley, who didn't look quite so smug anymore, then back at Annabelle.

"You can speak freely in front of Mrs. Riley."

"It's about Luke."

If possible, the unease on his face deepened. He put an arm around Mrs. Riley's shoulders and gestured toward the door. "My apologies," he said to her. "I'll escort you back to my office, where Mr. Zimmer can bring you a cup of tea. We'll continue our tour after I've completed my business with Miss Larkin."

Annabelle raced to the window to spy on Gray as he headed back to the factory with Mrs. Riley. She didn't like the way he lowered his head as if to catch every syllable the elegant lady spoke. Not that she was jealous. It just hurt to see.

She crossed her arms and glowered at Gray's back. Of course she was jealous! Maybe it was Elaine's upcoming wedding that made Annabelle feel even more like a spinster. Or maybe it was because she feared that no other man would ever measure up to Gray. If only she'd never met those two generals. If only she'd never been forced to choose between loyalty to her country and loyalty to Gray. Knowing she'd made the right choice didn't soothe the drumbeat of regret.

After a few moments Gray rejoined her in

the distillery, his face drawn and sober. "Yes, Annabelle, what is it?"

"One of my coworkers at Agriculture is tapped into a lot of inside gossip in this city. He thinks Dickie Shuster has more scandal up his sleeve for next week's article."

"Obviously."

"Scandal about Luke. Horace's wife is a secretary at the War Department, and she swears she handled some paperwork that awarded Luke a diploma from the Naval Academy last year."

Gray's eyes widened, but there was no other change in his expression. "Luke doesn't have a diploma. Not from the Naval Academy or anywhere else. He would have been shouting it from the mountaintops if he did."

"Are you sure about that?" He stiffened, and she rushed to continue. "What I mean is that Luke was pretty good about keeping secrets. Horace's wife said that a lot of important military people showed up and signed off on Luke's diploma, so he's obviously well-connected within the department. Horace thinks Luke might have been acting on orders from higher up in the War Department. That there are more spies to be sniffed out."

Gray's eyes narrowed in confusion as he

425

slowly shook his head. "I don't believe it. Tell me where you heard this again?"

She did her best to recount everything Horace said, and how her co-worker's voracious hunger for gossip was infamous. The corners of Gray's mouth turned down, and his face hardened.

"I don't buy any of it," he said bluntly. "Rumors and gossip fly around Washington like plagues of locusts, and most of it is a pack of lies."

"Horace also said that Dickie took a bribe from the Magruders to tell the story. A pair of expensive bay horses."

Gray stifled a bitter laugh. "Possible."

"Maybe you could use that to stop the next story. If the editor at *The Washington Post* knew Dickie took a bribe, it would cast doubt on his story."

Gray rubbed the skin between his eyes. "Annabelle, you're in over your head. Most of this is just standard Washington rumors and innuendo. Don't be so naïve."

She bristled. "I may be naïve, but I'm not stupid." Gray looked immediately contrite, and the air went out of her in a rush. "I'm sorry," she said. "I think we're both tense and under a lot of pressure."

"What pressure have you been under?" The concern in his gaze was genuine, and it got to her. It had been easier to be strong when he was snippy.

"My sister is getting married." *And my mother hates him. My heart has been broken, and it still hurts every time I see you. I feel adrift.*

"I suppose weddings are always stressful," Gray said. "Who is she marrying?"

"Walter Talbot. He owns a grocery store in a fancy part of town."

Before she could say more, the door to the distillery banged open, and Mrs. Riley strode forward. "There's no tea inside," she said bluntly.

Annabelle withdrew a step, although maybe that made her seem guilty. She and Gray hadn't been doing anything wrong. Nevertheless, Mrs. Riley seemed to have noticed their close proximity and gave her a cat's smile.

"Now I remember where I've heard your name," Mrs. Riley said. "The 'thoroughly modern couple' of *Good Housekeeping* fame. Somehow I expected you to look very different." Her gaze flicked to Annabelle's plain dress. She didn't need to add another word; her mocking expression said it all.

"I'd better get back to work," Annabelle said, sliding toward the door, which Mrs. Riley still effectively blocked.

"What are you, a secretary?" Mrs. Riley asked.

"Lab assistant."

The stylish woman's smile could not be any more fake if she'd purchased it in a store. "Of course, of course," she said. "Washington does abound in these clerical positions to keep feeding grist into the grist mill."

Gray stepped to Annabelle's side. "Miss Larkin is many things, but she's never been grist," he said shortly. "Please excuse us for a moment."

His hand was warm around Annabelle's arm as he led her outside the distillery. At least he had stood up for her against that horrible woman, but it couldn't change the facts. Gray had moved on with a beautiful and sophisticated woman who would probably fit into his world with ease. Annabelle drew her cloak closer against a chilly gust of October wind.

Gray turned to her, his face serious. "Thank you for coming today, but I'd prefer it if you forgot whatever you heard about Luke. I don't believe it's true, and whatever Dickie has up his sleeve, I'll handle it." He paused for a moment, then gave her a hint of a smile. "The information about his new bay horses will be helpful. Thank you."

Annabelle stood only a few inches from him. She didn't want to walk away, because he was looking at her with kindness and gratitude.

He touched her arm for the briefest moment. "Thanks again," he said before turning to head back inside the vanilla distillery.

Gray asked Caroline to meet him on the *Pelican.* If anyone knew about the possibility of Luke having somehow acquired a Naval Academy diploma, it would be Caroline. Meeting her at the White House was out of the question, and besides, he wanted Otis and Captain Haig in on this discussion. All of them knew Luke well, and they would get to the bottom of the nagging suspicion Annabelle had raised.

He hadn't been able to stop thinking about her. He'd been stunned when she walked into the distillery earlier today, even though she'd looked like she was facing a public execution. Was he that intimidating to her?

Activity on the *Pelican* was in full swing as crewmembers sanded the decks and laid down a fresh coat of marine spar. Next week Captain Haig and Otis would set sail, first for Bermuda, then Lisbon, then on to Madagascar. The scent of harbor air and

429

varnish surrounded him as he walked down the passageway to the bridge.

Caroline was already there, pacing the tight confines of the bridge while Otis and Captain Haig both nursed cups of coffee at the compact table.

"Why are we all here?" she asked as soon as Gray entered and secured the door behind him.

"Because your friends at the White House weren't so welcoming the last time I was there to talk about Luke."

She sucked in a quick breath. "What about Luke?"

"Rumor has it he was awarded a diploma from the Naval Academy last year. Do you know anything about that?"

He locked eyes with Caroline, who seemed baffled. "That's nonsense. He would have told me."

"Are you certain?" he pressed.

"Gray!" she said in exasperation. "We all know how you berated him for the past eight years over getting kicked out of school. He hated it. He would have done anything to make you proud of him, and if he somehow managed to finagle forgiveness and a diploma out of the Naval Academy, he would have run it up a flagpole for all to see."

He clenched his fists, wishing he could take back every harsh word he'd ever said to Luke about getting kicked out of school. His brother was sweltering in a prison cell and probably would be for the rest of his life. This odd bit of gossip from Annabelle was the only sliver of hope that there might be more to the story than Gray assumed, and Caroline's wholesale dismissal of it hurt.

He turned his attention to the others. "Otis? Did you ever notice Luke meeting with people from the navy? Or hitting the books for no apparent reason?"

Otis shook his head. "He hit the taverns and bars of Washington, but I never noticed any studying."

Captain Haig was a little less certain. "Getting kicked out of the Naval Academy was always a bur under his saddle. He acted like he didn't care, but that was typical Luke. That boy always hid whatever bothered him the most. Covered it over and made jokes about it."

It was true. Gray once brought a parrot back from French Polynesia as a pet for Luke, who doted on the bird. He trained the parrot to say a few words and let it ride on his shoulder as he walked around town. When Luke was twelve, the parrot died, and he tried to pretend he didn't care. He joked throughout the makeshift funeral he'd arranged in their backyard, but that evening Gray heard Luke bawling in his bedroom. If Luke was hurting, he'd make a joke before admitting it.

"What about Philip Ransom?" Otis asked. "Does he have an opinion on this?"

Of anyone, Luke's old college roommate might know enough about the Naval Academy's internal workings to shed insight.

"I haven't talked to him," Gray said. "I came straight to the three of you first."

Caroline plopped onto a stool, the fight draining out of her. "I'd give anything to believe it might be true, even though it doesn't sound like Luke. I'll track down Philip Ransom. If he knows anything, I'll wring it out of him."

Gray nodded, grateful for her help but equally skeptical that Philip would have useful insight. The only thing he knew for sure was that Luke was far more adept at covering his tracks than any of them had given him credit for.

"Where did you hear about this?" Caroline asked.

"It doesn't matter."

"Of course it matters," she said. "If I can pin this rumor on a reliable source, Philip is less likely to wriggle off the hook if there's any truth to it."

Gray shifted uncomfortably. Annabelle was the last person he wanted to bring into this conversation, but the daisy chain of connections that ultimately led to the War Department was a detail that might help.

"A secretary at the War Department saw the diploma and was charged with getting it delivered to Luke."

"The secretary's name?" Caroline queried.

There was no avoiding it. He confessed he didn't know and that the secretary was the wife of Annabelle's coworker at the Department of Agriculture. "Annabelle tracked me down at the vanilla distillery to pass it on," he admitted.

Caroline bristled, but the other two men looked amused.

"And how is the other half of our 'thoroughly modern couple'?" Captain Haig asked, holding back his laughter.

"Still sharpening her knives to stab more people in the back?" Caroline asked tightly.

Gray ignored the comment. "She's fine. Still working at Ag. She heard the rumor and thought I needed to know." He skewered Caroline with a pointed glare. "That's all. I don't want you nagging me over this."

There was little else to be said. He and

Caroline left the *Pelican* and headed toward the dock. Twilight was beginning to fall. Artists called this time "the blue hour," that transcendent time of evening just after the sun slipped below the horizon but night hadn't quite arrived. It had always been Gray's favorite time of day. He paused beside the rope line to admire the harbor. Most of the ships in port were steamships, but an old-fashioned, two-masted schooner was heading toward port, its white sail gently billowing in the wind.

"What a pretty ship," Caroline said as it drew closer.

Gray leaned forward, squinting for a better look, and could just make out the elegant lettering on the side of the ship. "It's the *Eastern Wind,*" he said quietly.

"The what?"

Caroline couldn't be expected to know. They'd lost everything during the war, but Gray remembered every one of their ships. His earliest memory was of riding on his father's shoulders as they strode on the deck of the *Eastern Wind.* As a boy, Gray had been dazzled by how loud it sounded as the canvas sails snapped and billowed in the breeze. The *Eastern Wind* was one of their four merchant vessels confiscated by the government during the war. None of them had ever been returned. They were a forfeiture of war.

"It was one of Dad's ships," he said, determined not to let it get under his skin. The loss of their ships was the past. They'd rebuilt their fortune. It was time to move forward and quit obsessing over —

He recoiled as a horrific possibility smacked him in the face. The government could confiscate property intended to aid or abet a rebellion against the United States. It was the excuse they had used to seize the *Eastern Wind*.

"The *Pelican*," he choked out. "Luke is part owner of the *Pelican*. That means the government can seize it."

Caroline's face went white. He didn't need to explain further. They both ran back toward the *Pelican* and shouted until someone lowered the gangway so they could board. Gray was out of breath by the time he raced to the bridge and grabbed Captain Haig.

"I want this ship loaded and out of American waters within twenty-four hours," he ordered.

An article announcing Luke's treachery had just been splashed across the pages of *The Washington Post*, and it could plant ideas in some bureaucrat's mind about a

435

quick way to enrich the government coffers. The *Pelican* represented most of his fortune. It was insured for full value, but insurance wouldn't pay if a ship was seized in a legal manner by the government.

And if that happened, Gray would be broke once again.

THIRTY-SIX

Try as she might, it was proving impossible for Annabelle to shed the memory of Gray with that woman. The tangible proof that he was moving forward with his life had been encased in a form-fitting sheath of lavender silk and wrapped in smugness.

But it was time to put Gray Delacroix out of her mind and concentrate on ensuring Elaine's wedding day was perfect. Their mother had brought her own wedding dress for Elaine to wear, and Annabelle smiled with relief when it fit almost perfectly. The hem would need to be let out at the bottom, but she and her mother could do that this evening. She beamed with pride while fastening the last of the dozens of buttons on the high-necked wedding gown.

"You look gorgeous," she told Elaine. Their mother didn't seem to share the opinion, but nothing pleased Maude Larkin these days.

"Do I?" Elaine asked.

The gown was pretty, but best of all was Elaine's face, radiant with quiet joy. Annabelle did her best to describe how lovely her older sister looked.

"The lace collar frames your face, but it's the puffed sleeves that make it so special. You look very regal. Feminine but regal. Like a princess. Walter is going to be over the moon when he sees you heading down the aisle toward him."

Maude rolled her eyes. Elaine couldn't see the gesture, but for days Maude had been making perfectly audible comments that subtly belittled Walter. Their father, always in the background in their family, kept his nose buried in the newspaper.

Elaine's fingers trembled as she smoothed the satin at her hips. "I just hope I don't spill anything on it. That would be just like me to drop a big lump of custard on my lap."

"You don't need to worry," Annabelle said, for she'd already discussed the wedding menu with Walter and Martha. As the father and wife of a blind soldier, they both understood the challenges of eating while blind. "Everything is going to be bite-sized finger food with no sloppy sauces."

Maude huffed. "I guess we won't be

treated to any of that fancy mustard Walter sells."

Annabelle ignored the comment. "There are going to be crab cakes, and Martha will make miniature cheese quiches, and then of course wedding cake. Walter has arranged for the best baker in town to supply the cake."

"Sounds good," her father said. How different Roy Larkin was from almost everyone else in Washington. His canvas trousers and plaid shirt never looked out of place on the farm, but it was more than his clothes that made him stand out here. With deep grooves on his face and thickly calloused hands, he was a man who worked in the sun and battled frigid winter wind. Her father was salt of the earth, and she loved him for it.

He stepped outside while Elaine changed back into her regular dress and Annabelle hung the wedding gown carefully. If she ever got married, it would be nice to wear this dress too. It was the finest garment in their family.

But it paled in comparison to the fancy lavender dress Gray's companion had worn.

She sighed. It was only because Elaine was getting married that Annabelle felt so abandoned and alone. And useless. Once it had been her job to escort Elaine to and from the library each day, but now Walter arrived at their apartment and drove Elaine to the grocery, where she was learning to prepare the delicacies they sold in the shop.

"Shall we go out for dinner?" Elaine asked once she was properly dressed again and their father had rejoined them. "It will be better than anything Annabelle and I can prepare."

"Let's!" Annabelle said. "There's a German deli on the corner that has wonderful sausages and the largest pretzels you've ever seen."

"Do they serve overpriced mustard with the pretzels?" Maude asked.

Elaine's jaw stiffened, but she said nothing as she tied the ribbons on her bonnet. Her father also ignored the jibe as he rolled down his sleeves and buttoned his cuffs. Her mother must have taken the silence as consent to continue.

"I only ask because I know a place that has all sorts of fancy sauces no ordinary deli is likely to have. Although spending hard-earned money on imported mustard seems a ridiculous —"

"Would you please shut up!" Elaine screeched as she ripped off her bonnet and threw it on the floor. "I found a wonderful man, and all you can do is prattle on about his awful mustard. Mustard! You're trying to make me disapprove of a man of character and compassion because of mustard!"

Maude lifted her chin. "Trust me, it's not the mustard I object to."

"Then don't ever mention it again," her father said firmly.

Annabelle caught her breath. Maude normally led the family while her father was the mild, quiet man in the background. Not today, and she prayed her mother would listen.

Nobody said anything for a long moment, and Elaine managed to regain control of her temper.

"For a long time I wished I had died after I became blind," she said in a ragged voice. "I felt useless, with no purpose and nothing to offer the world. I didn't know why God had left me alive to be a miserable burden for everyone around me, but I've finally figured it out. Yes, Walter is a lot older than me, but he is the rock on which his entire family depends. He is strength and optimism and fortitude. He employs a dozen people in his store. Someday he will be too old to lead the family anymore, but that's where I will come in. By then I will be able to run the store. I will care for Walter as he ages and needs someone to lean on. I want to be a pillar for that family when Walter is no longer able, and he wants that for me too. I never wanted to be blind, but if it's the price I must pay to have found Walter Talbot . . . then I'm glad it happened."

Her parents stood in stunned silence, but Annabelle had never been prouder, for Elaine had finally found her purpose.

Annabelle went for a walk with her father after returning from the deli. There had been no more backbiting after Elaine's outburst, but things were still tense, and Annabelle's battered spirit needed a reprieve.

"Thank you for reining Mother in," she said as soon as they were out of earshot of the open window of the apartment.

"Probably should have done it earlier," Roy replied. "She's just feeling sore and sorry, knowing that Elaine will never come home."

Annabelle said nothing as they continued their walk. The last streetcar of the evening rolled toward them, and her father paused to watch it pass, admiration on his face. Ever since arriving in the city, he had been fascinated by the streetcars, the elevators, and the water system. With his farmer's curiosity and knack for fixing things, he always scrutinized every facet of the moving parts.

"That sure is a mighty fine piece of equipment," he said as he admired the streetcar's brass fittings gleaming beneath the streetlamp. "It's hard to look at something like that and not dream of all the possibilities." He continued talking after the streetcar rolled past. "I imagine there's all sorts of jobs people can do in a city like this. I never had much choice in life. My dad was a farmer in Kansas. My grandfather was a farmer in Ireland. I pretty much always knew what life had in store for me."

He said it simply and without complaint. Her father never complained. No matter how dire their circumstances, he simply rolled up his sleeves and got the job done.

"I wanted my girls to have choices," Roy continued. "That's why I fought hard for you to go to college. Maude thought it was a waste, but I always knew I would do whatever was necessary to make sure the whole wide world was open to my girls."

A lump grew in her throat. If she lived to be a hundred, she'd never be able to thank her father for the sacrifices he'd made. At times like these, she grew homesick for Kansas. She missed the fields of wheat and their sunflower harvest. After Elaine was married and gone, Annabelle would be even more alone in this big, anonymous city. Once she had seen it as a place bursting with hope, but things hadn't turned out so well. Would she ever be at peace with the decision she'd made to work for those two horrible generals?

"After Elaine gets married, I think I should come home," she said.

Her father stopped and turned to gape at her. "I thought you loved it here."

She did, she just didn't feel useful anymore. Her parents needed her more than Elaine did. The farm was failing, and maybe what Annabelle had learned here in Washington could be put to good use in turning the farm's fortunes around. Mr. Bryant would probably even give her some durum wheat to take home with her.

"I've learned a lot about wheat that can survive dry conditions," she said. "It might be the answer. You can't afford another failed harvest if the drought comes back next year."

Mention of the drought sparked a shadow of fear in Roy's gaze. "It's a risk," he said. "I don't know the first thing about this new-fangled wheat."

"I do. And I can help."

He glanced away as a series of emotions came over him. Then his face crumpled up, and two fat tears rolled down his face, but he covered his eyes with a large, work-roughened palm to swipe them away. She cringed at the sight. She hadn't expected this. Things had been bad for years, but she hadn't expected this.

Just as quickly as Roy had lost his composure, he got it back. "That would be more than fine, Annabelle," he said on a ragged breath. "More than fine."

Her adventure in Washington was something she would always remember, but staying here would be selfish. Their farm teetered on the edge of ruin, and through the grace of God, she'd been given insight that might save it.

It was time to go home.

THIRTY-SEVEN

Gray had never seen the harbor illuminated at night, but Captain Haig had arranged for a pair of carbon arc lamps to be set up outside the *Pelican* while a crew of longshoremen were paid double wages to load the ship through the night. The carbon arc lamps lit the dockside with an eerily white glow, making the cranes look like hulking black silhouettes as they loaded cargo.

Gray worked too. At first, he and Otis worked side by side to lug crates of flaxseed down into the hold. Once that was done, they stooped over to roll barrels of tar, turpentine, and pitch. His spine ached and blisters formed on his palms. A longshoreman laughingly called him a lightweight and tossed him a pair of gloves. Gray pulled them on and got back to work. Maybe he was paranoid, but from the moment he'd realized the *Pelican* could be seized, he'd not had a moment's rest, and there were still four hours to go before sunrise.

At six o'clock the last hold was secured and locked. The ship still had room for more cargo, but Gray wanted it out of port and into international waters before the government got any ideas. The *Pelican* wouldn't pull into an American port until the case against Luke had been decided.

Gray stood on the pier and watched the *Pelican* sail on the morning tide. It had taken a herculean effort to get it off so quickly, and he was proud of their work. He was also proud that the ship sailed with twelve empty vials for the collection of rice in Madagascar. Otis would collect the rice and hand it over to Annabelle when he returned.

Gray could no longer see the *Pelican* once it had traveled a couple of miles, but international waters began at twelve nautical miles from shore. He headed to the nearest telegraph station. Otis had promised to wire him the moment they entered international water.

It felt like there was grit beneath his eyelids as he staggered into the telegraph station. A slack-jawed boy slept behind the counter, and Gray envied him. Every joint ached as he lowered himself into a chair to wait for the message.

447

It wasn't long coming. The wire buzzed with an incoming communication, and the boy jerked awake. Gray stood at the counter, wishing he could make sense of the cascade of rattling clicks. The boy scribbled the message on a card.

"Are you Gray Delacroix?" the boy asked.

Gray nodded, and the boy handed over the card.

20 nautical miles east. Next stop Bermuda.

Gray sagged in relief, feeling every one of the last thirty-six hours. Too many emotions swirled inside for him to make sense of them. Fatigue, relief, exhilaration. He wished he had someone to share this moment with.

Once home, he drew the curtains in his bedroom, collapsed onto the mattress, and stared at the ceiling. The house was so quiet. Lonely. He wanted to sleep for a solid week but didn't have that luxury.

He needed to go to Cuba and get the truth out of Luke.

It took three days to reach Cuba. Gray went well-armed with cash and two pistols. Rebuilding projects were underway all over the island, but years of warfare couldn't be patched over in a few months. Agricultural fields had been devastated, bridges destroyed, and people were hungry.

It was part of the reason Gray didn't mind paying bribes, for the money would go to feed the guards' families. He would have preferred to meet Luke out in the prison yard like the last time he was here, but shortly after Gray arrived, the sky opened, releasing sheets of rain. Holding his coat over his head, he darted around rapidly forming puddles in the prison yard as he made his way through the gates.

Once in the foyer, he shook water from his coat and dried off as best he could with his handkerchief, but everything still felt damp. It smelled like wet brick in here. The officer in charge of the jail remembered him from his last visit, and after accepting the perfunctory bribe, the officer noticed a bag of food Gray intended to give to Luke. It required yet another bribe, but soon the guard led him down the hallway to Luke's cell. While the guard rattled through the keys, Gray braced himself for what he would see on the other side of this door. It had been four months since Luke's arrest. The heat and deprivation were bound to be getting to him.

Luke was asleep on the cot, his mouth slack and an open book splayed on his chest. His skin was pasty white, making the bruise darkening one eye and a cut on his lip look even worse. A fight with the guards? Other prisoners? Either way it was sickening, and Gray lowered his head to pray.

Dear Lord, what am I supposed to do? This can't be your will.

No answers came. The cut on Luke's lip was healing and the bruise looked old, so this couldn't be a daily thing, but it still made Gray ill. He struggled to compose himself, then gently kicked the foot of the cot to wake his brother. It took a few nudges before Luke blearily awakened. A smile cracked across his face, but he made no effort to rise.

"Gray?"

Gray stepped forward into the cell. "Just off the boat."

Luke braced a hand on the thin cot to push himself up. Sitting made him look even thinner, his shirt hanging open to expose a bony ribcage. Gray tossed a sack of beef jerky, chocolate, and almonds on the cot. He'd had to pay a fortune to get it past the guard, but the expression on Luke's face was worth it as he tore into a chocolate bar, taking a small bite from the end. He extended it to Gray.

"Want some?"

Even starving, Luke instinctively offered him a bite of chocolate. Gray shook his head and asked the questions that were impossible to hold back.

"Fight with the guards?" He gestured to Luke's eye.

Luke shrugged. "I'm not the most popular guy in here."

That certainly had to be true. The soldiers staffing the jail were working in conjunction with the Americans, and anyone suspected of siding with the insurgency and potentially setting back the island's reconstruction was in for a rough time.

"Is there anything I can do?" Gray asked, knowing it was probably a pointless question.

Luke batted his concern away. "Don't worry about it. I'll be fine. There are a couple of guards who sometimes pull weekend duty who really don't like me, but they hardly ever get assigned to this ward."

"What are their names?"

"Forget it. Trying to interfere will only make it worse."

Gray's stomach clenched, because it was probably true.

Luke eagerly absorbed all the news from

home, leaning forward with delight on his face as Gray spoke of Caroline's work at the White House and of how Otis had just set off on his first voyage with Captain Haig.

Luke only ate half the chocolate bar, carefully wrapping the foil around the rest. He stood to put the entire parcel of food into a rope sack dangling above his cot. "Mice," he explained with a reluctant smile. "Nothing gets left on the floor unless I want to share it with them."

Gray nodded, looking around the miserable cell, noting that it wasn't quite so barren as the last time he was here. A jug of water rested on a crate that doubled as a table. Luke had writing implements and a few books. The book that had been lying on his chest when Gray entered still rested on the cot. He tilted it to see the spine and raised a curious brow.

"A Bible?"

Luke shrugged. "I'm working on saving my soul. Heaven knows I've got the time. I've read it three times since I've been in here. Go on — open it to any page and test me."

Gray hadn't come all this way to discuss the Bible with Luke. He needed answers, and their hour was getting short. He wished the light in the cell were better. He needed to scrutinize Luke's reaction carefully. "An odd rumor found its way to me. Something about you getting a diploma from the Naval Academy a while back."

Luke froze, but there was no change of expression on his face. "Where did you hear that?"

"Around."

"Philip?"

Gray shook his head. "Philip denied it. Caroline stormed his office and gave him the third degree. She probably terrified him out of his skin — you know how she can be when she's on the warpath — but he claimed not to know anything about it."

"What about Caroline?"

"She thinks it's just a stupid rumor. She's convinced you would never keep a secret like that from her."

"You should listen to Caroline."

Luke still hadn't denied it. The rain had stopped, and it was getting hot again. Gray hadn't traveled more than a thousand miles to let Luke dance around the issue.

"I want the truth," he said earnestly. "None of this has smelled right from the day I learned you were arrested."

"Gray, thanks for coming down here, but don't push this, okay? I know what I'm doing."

453

"Then tell me."

"No. And get Caroline to back off as well. Tell her to leave Philip alone. He doesn't know anything. I *don't* have a degree from the Naval Academy or anywhere else. Even if I did, what does it matter? I was caught spying, and I'm guilty."

A gnat swirled in the air, and Gray batted it away but didn't break eye contact with Luke. "What does the Bible have to say about lying?"

The sentence hung in the air for a moment before Luke looked away and flopped back onto the cot, the fight draining out of him as he stared at the ceiling. It looked like he was struggling to find the right words, and Gray waited, counting the beats of his heart and praying against all evidence that Luke had some logical explanation for all this. He would do anything humanly possible to get his brother out of this cesspit, but he couldn't do it without Luke's cooperation.

"It hasn't been easy," Luke finally said. "Every day I'm stuck in here to swelter and count my regrets, and they are endless. I've squandered so much in life. I've gone down dead ends and broken the rules just for the challenge of it, but every now and then I stumble into doing something *right,* and I've got to protect that. I don't have much in my life to be proud of, but . . ."

It looked like he wanted to say more, but he abruptly closed his mouth, crossed his arms, and kept staring at the ceiling. Could Luke be somehow proud of this imprisonment? That was what it had sounded like he was about to say.

"Tell me how I can help, and I'll do it," Gray said earnestly.

Luke pushed himself upright and shook off his momentary gloom. "Get Caroline to stand down and quit worrying about me. Tell her I'm going to be fine."

With a bruised face, sunken chest, and pasty skin, Luke didn't look fine.

"Can I tell her you were awarded a degree from the Naval Academy?"

A devilish smile briefly appeared on Luke's face. "I'd prefer that you didn't."

It was as close to an answer as Gray was going to get. If anything, Luke had delivered a rather forceful denial, but Gray could usually tell when Luke was lying. Even as a child, if Luke got caught with his hand in the cookie jar, he'd scratch behind his ear while forcefully denying it. And Luke had scratched behind his ear a lot this afternoon.

As he boarded the ship home, Gray knew

in the marrow of his bones that Luke was hiding a much larger story.

THIRTY-EIGHT

Good weather meant that Gray arrived back from Cuba a full day earlier than expected. A gust of chilly wind pushed a swirl of autumn leaves down the cobblestone street. Normally he loved October. He was rarely in Alexandria as the leaves curled and dropped, releasing that peaty scent and a glorious riot of color before the town braced for winter.

As he dismounted at the public stable, he was surprised to see Caroline's horse in one of the stalls. It was Sunday, the only day she could escape the White House, but she usually spent it in the city with her friends.

"My sister is here?" he asked the stable owner.

"Came by about an hour ago with an older gent," the stable owner said. "Never seen him before."

That was odd. Caroline wasn't expecting Gray to return until tomorrow, so he had no idea why she was at the townhouse with "an older gent." He quickened his steps as he headed home. The four-block walk gave his mind plenty of time to come up with all sorts of distasteful possibilities. Caroline was a beautiful woman yet had no regular suitor, but maybe she was meeting someone on the sly.

He vaulted up the front steps and wiggled the doorknob. It was locked, and it took him a moment of fumbling with his key to open it. Voices from down the hall stopped the moment he stepped inside.

"Gray?" Caroline looked ill at ease as she scurried from the kitchen. She quickly masked it with a pleasant expression. "Welcome home! I thought you were coming back tomorrow."

He said nothing as he strode down the hallway, determined to see the older gent before an escape out the back door was possible. But the man sitting at the kitchen table made no attempt to escape, merely rotated a cup of tea with a smug expression on his face.

Gray blanched in revulsion. "Do you know who this man is?" he demanded of Caroline.

"Everyone in Washington knows Dickie Shuster."

"Yes, Gray, everyone in Washington knows me," Dickie tittered.

"Get out of my house," Gray said bluntly.

"Gray," Caroline said in a warning tone, "Dickie is my guest, and this house is mine as well as yours."

Papers lay spread out before Dickie, but he gathered them into a stack while sending Caroline a smarmy grin. "I'd hate to stir discord in the family. Perhaps we should simply scuttle the deal."

Caroline clenched her fists, but her face remained calm. "That wouldn't be in either of our best interests, would it?"

Dickie slid the papers into his satchel, a mournful look on his face. "My time is valuable. . . ."

"I'll make it worth your while. Perhaps I can persuade the first lady to have tea with us after all."

A delighted expression came over Dickie's face. "Excellent! I shall look forward to the invitation with delight. Good day to you both."

The way Dickie swaggered toward the front door made Gray's teeth ache. Caroline followed, making pleasantries with Dickie on the front stoop for a few minutes before closing the door after him.

Gray leaned against the wall of the

kitchen. A week of travel was catching up with him, and to be confronted with that man in his home was his limit. Dickie's abandoned teacup still rested on the table. Gray didn't even want to touch it, but he picked it up and dumped it in the trash. Then he braced himself for a battle with Caroline as she returned to the kitchen.

"What was that all about?" he asked.

She looked triumphant. "Dickie has been neutralized," she proudly announced. "The editor at *The Washington Post* got wind of his two new horses and threatened to fire him. Dickie is terrified. If he loses his job, his ability to be the biggest gadfly in Washington will be ruined, but the *Post* is worried about those horses. They've issued a complete and total retraction about the article he wrote, and he won't be printing any more stories at the behest of the Magruders."

"How did the editor find out about the horses?"

Caroline slanted him a glance as though he was a simpleton. "I told him, of course, but Dickie doesn't know that. He's merely grateful for my help salvaging his reputation with his editor by facilitating an exclusive interview about the president's marriage."

"Why on earth would anyone want to read

460

such a thing?"

"People are wildly curious about it," Caroline defended. "Ida McKinley is the least popular first lady in history, and it's becoming a problem for the reelection. One of those vile political cartoons depicted the first lady as a harpy with the president curled up like a poodle in her lap. It's true that he brings her flowers every day. It's true that even during the darkest days of the war, he left cabinet meetings to say bedtime prayers with her before returning downstairs for business. People want to know what he sees in her."

In all honesty, Gray had wondered as well. While he didn't approve of the president, William McKinley's steadfast devotion to his wife was a credit to him.

Caroline continued. "My goal is to bolster her image — not for her sake, but because it will show the president in a good light. I've got one month before the election to do everything possible to see McKinley win a second term."

The desperation in her tone hinted at something beyond politics. "Why is that so important to you?"

"How else can I get a presidential pardon for Luke?"

It took a moment for the stunning pronouncement to sink in. "That's your goal?"

"That's always been my goal," she asserted. "I'm not a lawyer who can defend Luke in court or a warrior who could break him out of prison, but I've got access to powerful people, and I intend to use it to save my brother."

He understood. Since the minute he learned of Luke's arrest, he'd been preoccupied with the awful finality of a life sentence. Their family would never be whole while Luke was stuck in a six-by-ten-foot jail cell, his fate in limbo.

Exhaustion set in as he leaned his head against the back wall, gazing at Caroline fondly. "All right," he murmured. "I understand."

She sobered. "Now, tell me how Luke is doing."

The last thing he wanted to talk about were the cuts and bruises on Luke's face, the weight loss, the fetid jail cell. Instead he relayed the only piece of truth he could.

"He's still in good spirits. He categorically denied having a degree from the Naval Academy. He looked me straight in the eye as he said it."

"Do you believe him?"

"I don't know what to believe anymore," he said truthfully. He relayed the rest of the conversation to her, growing more exhausted with each passing moment.

Caroline noticed. "Don't look so glum. I'll work on getting a presidential pardon for Luke, and then I intend to solve all your problems, too. Maybe Samantha Riley isn't the perfect woman for you, but I know dozens of other eligible ladies. Just you wait! I'll find a wife for you yet."

He snorted. "Please don't bother."

"Why not? For pity's sake, you're *forty*, Gray. We don't have the luxury of time! In the next few months there will be dozens of election parties. I'll arrange for you to escort a different lady to each one. Trust me. I can have you engaged before the new year."

He tried not to shudder. It had been difficult enough trying to court Samantha Riley when his heart was still firmly lodged with Annabelle, and that part still hadn't mended. "I'd rather you didn't."

"Now, Gray," she said in her best schoolmarm's voice, "don't tell me you are still obsessing over that woman."

He said nothing. The last time he had seen Annabelle was the morning she came to the vanilla distillery to tell him the rumors about Luke. She had walked in on a difficult conversation as he attempted to disentangle himself from the overly eager clutches of Samantha Riley, who couldn't be more different from Annabelle. He infinitely preferred Annabelle's wholesome curiosity to Samantha's coy sophistication.

Caroline bristled. "You and I both know she is an unacceptable choice."

"Do we?" he finally asked after a long hesitation.

Apparently those were fighting words, for Caroline shot to her feet and began pacing in the narrow kitchen. "Yes, we do. Don't even *think* about reconciling with her."

The scorn in her voice rubbed him the wrong way. "This isn't any of your business, Caroline."

"Don't forget who she is," his sister warned. "She's already stabbed us in the back once, and Dickie says she's now working with the committee at Agriculture, investigating how to pass food purity laws. Picture it: armies of government bureaucrats tromping through your factory, looking over your shoulder, nosing into your business."

He instinctively recoiled from the prospect. Once the government got their foot in the door, they wouldn't stop with inspections. They'd have the power to seize goods, shut down operations, and drive companies out of business.

Then again, if someone had been watching, perhaps the Magruders would never have gotten away with selling tainted coffee.

"Maybe she was right," he said quietly.

"Bite your tongue!"

"I'm not talking about Luke. I'm talking about adulterated coffee and fake applesauce. About using chemicals to flavor food in ways we can't even begin to imagine. Maybe the price of freedom in this industry is simply too high." He flexed his hands, mulling through his options. "Did you ever get your hands on a copy of the contract the Magruders are about to sign with the military?"

She nodded and quickly described the nature of the multiyear contract to supply tons of canned food to military outposts all over the world. Thanks to an avalanche of government regulations, large-scale contracts such as these required public meetings before they could be finalized. It gave journalists the opportunity to observe government spending and competitors a chance to throw their hat into the ring.

"I think I can use the public meeting to force the Magruders to clean up their operations."

Caroline looked intrigued. "I'd love to score one over the Magruders."

The only problem was his name. It would

be better for the charge to come from someone whose last name wasn't Delacroix. Ideally, it should come from a government agency that was already on the march, and there was only one.

"Annabelle has connections in the Department of Agriculture. We should get her on board."

The comment set off a bomb in Caroline.

"Forget about her," she said. "I have all the connections you need."

Maybe. But he still wanted Annabelle. "It will look like a personal vendetta if I take the lead on this. I've worked with Annabelle before, and she's up to the task."

Caroline narrowed her eyes. "Let me be blindingly clear. That woman is poison. She isn't worthy of you. She's as bad as Benedict Arnold or Judas Iscariot."

Her discernment was seriously hampered if she thought Annabelle belonged alongside those two, for Annabelle was a thoroughly good person who'd been forced into a lousy corner. Time had given him that perspective, and a piece of him still desperately longed for her, despite everything that had happened. He might someday be able to rebuild a relationship with Annabelle, and he wouldn't let his little sister dictate to him on this.

"Don't make me choose between you and Annabelle," he said quietly.

The wind left Caroline in a rush. He could see the wheels calculating in her mind as she processed what he had said. She clenched her fists and worked her jaw as though biting back a torrent of words. But she swallowed them all back.

"Let's get to work," she said stiffly.

THIRTY-NINE

As the maid of honor, it was Annabelle's job to ensure Elaine had the best wedding day possible. At first that meant helping Elaine get dressed and arrange her hair, then leading her to an antechamber at the back of the church as the last guests settled in the pews. Their father looked stiff in his best suit as the three of them waited for the ceremony to begin.

Elaine pressed Roy to describe what was happening inside, but it soon became clear that he didn't know how to report the important things, like what the ladies wore and who was sitting beside who.

"Let me take over," Annabelle said, sliding up beside Elaine to describe the exact details of Martha's new bonnet and how Walter looked as he stepped into place before the altar. "He's wearing a dove gray three-piece suit, very distinguished-looking," she whispered. "His collar is starched, and I've never seen him look so formal. He only looks a little nervous. Oh! He just stepped over to shake the hand of a man who's got the largest handlebar mustache I've ever seen."

Elaine clasped Annabelle's hands so hard it almost hurt. "That must be Bruce Ellsworth. Does his wife have twins?"

Annabelle craned her neck to see. "Yes! There are two boys following them. They look ten or twelve years old. Identical!"

Annabelle kept supplying the essential details while urging Elaine not to move toward the opening. "Back, back!" she urged. "Walter keeps peering down the aisle, trying to get a glimpse of you. Don't let him see you until the last moment."

Elaine grinned as she flattened herself against the back wall of the vestibule.

At last it was time, and a church attendant closed the doors to the main church so that Elaine could move into position in the center of the aisle. Roy stood beside her, and they prepared for the grand opening of the doors. As soon as the music started, Annabelle would lead the procession as the only bridal attendant.

At least, that was the plan.

"Annabelle!" Elaine whispered. "Will you walk on my other side? I wouldn't have got-

469

ten this far without you. Besides, I want someone to report every detail as I walk down the aisle."

Annabelle glanced at Roy, hoping he wasn't offended, but he merely shrugged. "It's fine with me. I've already told her that everything looks very nice."

She took a step back to stand on Elaine's other side. "I've got it covered," she whispered.

The organ music began, and the church attendant opened the doors. A joyous melody from Bach filled the church, and it was hard to breathe as the three of them began the stately walk down the aisle. The church looked lovely, but Annabelle knew exactly what Elaine wanted to hear.

"Walter is at the front of the aisle, looking like he's about to burst with pride. He's rocking back and forth on his heels, and his smile is so wide. Now he's laughing! He's beaming at you like it's the best day of his life."

Everyone in the church swiveled to watch as they progressed down the aisle. Annabelle didn't care if they looked odd as she leaned in to whisper everything into her sister's ear. This was Elaine's moment, and she deserved the full experience.

"Okay, he quit laughing, and he's just

470

smiling now," she continued. "Dad's eyes are getting watery. The priest looks scary, but don't worry. Walter's got everything under control."

"No doubt about that," Roy murmured, and it was true. Elaine was going to be in good hands.

Annabelle took a step back as they reached the altar. Roy greeted Walter, then stood aside while the groom took Elaine's hand in his own. It was the proudest moment of Annabelle's life. She had helped Elaine get this far, and now her sister was embarking on a new and wonderful life with the blessing of God and the community. After today, Annabelle's work here was done.

Gray's insatiable, churning desire to stop the Magruders in their tracks had consumed him, partly because he suspected them of playing a role in Luke's downfall, partly because it was simply the right thing to do. Aside from a little egg on their face, the Magruders had suffered no lasting damage from the *Good Housekeeping* article. More work needed to be done.

The plan he had worked out with Caroline could impede the Magruders' ability to foist cheap, adulterated food on the market, and he wanted Annabelle to be a part of it.

He strode through the front doors of the Department of Agriculture and vaulted up to the third floor, all the while dragging his hands through his hair and straightening his collar. Annabelle deserved his respect, and he didn't want to look like a slovenly lout who'd raced across town. He needed her. He couldn't explain precisely why and didn't have the time to examine his motives too closely, but he needed to mend this rift with Annabelle.

He strode through the door of the laboratory where she worked but only saw her two coworkers. What they said made no sense. They tried to tell him that Annabelle had resigned, but he couldn't believe it.

"What do you mean she's resigned?" he demanded.

"She's quit," the younger man said with relish. "Said she needed to go back to Kansas to save the family farm, took a sack of durum wheat kernels with her, and set off for the wild west. I was appalled. Do they even have electricity in Kansas?"

The other man was more sober. "Miss Larkin turned in her resignation last week, which I accepted with regret. I have no idea if she's still in Washington."

This couldn't stand. Gray wasn't certain he could ever repair the chasm between them, but he didn't want her in Kansas. The thought was intolerable.

He raced outside and toward the nearest streetcar stop. During the twenty-minute ride across town, he clenched the overhead strap, willing the streetcar to go faster. How could she leave without saying good-bye? Maybe they weren't on the best of terms, but she owed him at least that much.

His anxiety ratcheted higher. He wouldn't know how to reach her if she'd already gone back to Kansas. It was a huge state, and she could be anywhere. He'd be forever stuck with this gnawing sense of regret and dreams of what might have been.

He hopped off the streetcar in her working-class neighborhood, then barreled down the street, anger alternating with fear at each passing block. What if he was too late? How could he track her down in Kansas? He finally reached her apartment, vaulted up the stairs and down the dimly lit hallway, and pounded on the door.

"Annabelle?" he called out. He wiggled the doorknob, but it was locked. "Annabelle? Answer this door." He struggled to contain his breathing.

He heard footsteps, but the door remained firmly closed. A voice called out from the other side, "Gray, is that you?"

Relief crashed through him. "It's me. Please open the door."

She did, gaping at him in bewilderment. Behind her, the apartment was littered with traveling bags, and fear roared back to life. She really *was* leaving!

"What are you doing?" he demanded. "The people at your lab said you quit and are returning to Kansas."

"Yes, I am," she said in that same bewildered tone, and from the look of things, her departure was imminent.

"Just like that?" he asked, snapping his fingers. "You can't."

She snapped her fingers right back in his face. "Watch me."

He was being foolish, but it was a struggle to tamp down this roiling combination of panic, hurt, and regret. All he knew was that he couldn't let her go. Not yet. He stepped inside the apartment and shut the door. They had unfinished business. Mostly personal, but business-business too. It was a lot easier to deal with the business aspect.

"I need your help getting the upper hand on the Magruders," he said. "It's important. You can help."

And just like that, the bright smile lit up her face. She'd always, *always* been able to capture him with that smile.

He leaned down to grasp her forearms. "It's a long shot. That's why I need your help."

"I'd prefer that you don't touch my daughter," a stern woman's voice commanded.

Gray dropped his hands. Two people had just stepped out of the bedroom. Annabelle's parents? The man looked like a farmer, with a flannel shirt and a craggy face that had seen a lot of sun. The woman looked like she was sucking on a pickle.

Gray stepped away from Annabelle, offering the older man his hand. "Gray Delacroix," he said. "Annabelle and I have . . ." How to say it? Fallen madly and gloriously in love before it all imploded? Sailed to Boston, where they conquered the publishing world?

"I know who you are," her father said. A man of few words, apparently.

Gray turned his attention to the mother and nodded. She nodded back. This was awkward. He glanced at the luggage stacked in the middle of the room.

"Where's Elaine?"

"Married and gone," Annabelle said. "There's no more reason for me to stay in Washington."

"Yes, there is. I need your help."

"How much will you pay her?"

"Mother!" Annabelle burst out, but the older woman stepped farther into the room, looking gaunt, hard, and tough.

"We have three tickets back to Kansas on this evening's train," the older woman said. "They weren't cheap, and if they get canceled, it doesn't come free."

Now he knew where Annabelle got her thrifty good sense, although the source of her smile remained a mystery. Both parents looked at him with poker faces.

"I shall naturally cover the costs of any additional expense. I'll pay for Annabelle's time as well."

"What do you need?" Curiosity mingled with a nascent sense of adventure lurked in Annabelle's hesitant smile.

"I'm ready to cooperate with the government," he said, never believing he would utter those words, but it was time. "I'm ready to recommend that anyone who sells processed food in this country be required to list the ingredients on the label. If Magruder had been doing that all along, maybe those people in Philadelphia wouldn't have died."

"And how can I help with that?" she asked.

He breathed a little easier as she gestured him toward the table. When she tried to take the seat next to him, her mother yanked her

476

back and took it instead. Annabelle and her father sat on the bench opposite him, and he began outlining the plan.

On their way to meet with Caroline, Gray warned that his sister was "still pretty bitter" about what happened to Luke, but Annabelle was too busy gaping at the White House looming before her to be worried about a protective sibling. They followed a brick path to the side entrance reserved for people who had official business in the residence. These columns were so huge! They didn't look this big from a distance, but up close she had to crane her neck to see all the way up.

Gray jerked her elbow. "Careful. You were about to walk into the planter."

She'd worn her nicest dress but still felt overwhelmed as they entered a foyer blanketed with a scarlet carpet and decked in gilt chandeliers. A life-sized portrait of Abraham Lincoln hung on the wall straight ahead of her, and she started choking up. She was walking in a house where *Abraham Lincoln* once lived. He'd surely stood in this exact room. Lincoln came from humble roots too. He carried the world on his shoulders for four years during the Civil War. He wouldn't have been anxious about having to work with Caroline Delacroix, and the thought made her stand a little taller.

"Ready?" Gray asked.

"Ready."

They were to meet with Gray's sister in a conference room on the second floor. After walking the length of a gilded hallway, the butler finally delivered them to the correct meeting room and showed them inside.

Gray stepped forward to greet his sister with a kiss on her cheek, so it was a moment before Annabelle got the full effect of Caroline's ensemble. Her royal blue jacket had a nipped-in waist, a high-stand collar, brass buttons, and gold epaulettes at her shoulders. All she needed was a colonial-style musket, and she'd be ready to fall into line behind General Washington at Yorktown.

"Annabelle," Caroline said in a frosty tone.

Annabelle nodded in reply. "I'm happy to be here and help however I can."

"Then let's get started," Gray said. "Our goal is to force the Magruders to list every ingredient on their labels. We'll use the government contracts to start the process."

He held out a chair and helped Annabelle sit at a table with a glossy finish and inlaid wood. It looked too fancy to touch. Neither

Caroline nor Gray had such qualms as they spread out paperwork, including an issue of *Good Housekeeping.*

"I've already sent a copy of this article to the officer in charge of finalizing the military contract," Gray said. "Our job at the public meeting is to dangle the threat of bad publicity if the army buys adulterated food to feed the troops."

Caroline shook her head. "Philip Ransom told me the army struck applesauce from the contract just yesterday."

Annabelle smiled. "So that means the *Good Housekeeping* article is already working, right?"

"Hardly," Caroline said. "It embarrassed them into taking applesauce from the contract, but they've still got maple syrup and condensed milk made with artificial thickeners in the deal. The army is interested in the bottom line, so they'll buy it unless journalists raise enough of a stink that the army pressures the Magruders into printing an accurate ingredient list on every product they sell."

"Oh." Annabelle felt like a country bumpkin for getting so excited, but Caroline continued strategizing.

"If the army buys the Magruders' cheap food, the navy will follow. The navy has

479

always been the poor stepchild in Washington and will follow the army's lead. Unless we scuttle this entire contract, the Magruders will grow fat on this military deal."

Until Annabelle came to Washington, she'd never seen an army officer. Even here in Washington, most people worked in an office, a school, or a shop. For every man in uniform, this country had a thousand who wore civilian clothes. Why were they only concentrating on the military?

"I don't think you're aiming high enough," she said, drawing an arched brow from Caroline. "I'm sure the military contract is important, but it's small potatoes when compared to the millions of ordinary people in this country. If something looks and tastes like maple syrup but is less expensive than the real thing, plenty of people will gladly buy it. My mother certainly would."

"What do you recommend?" Gray asked.

Annabelle paused and called up her mother's image. Maude Larkin was so thrifty that after frying bacon, she rinsed the pan with a cup of water and saved it to make gravy. She tossed egg shells to the hogs so the residue inside the shells wouldn't go to waste. Frankly, Maude wouldn't care if coffee was cut with chicory or if applesauce was fake. If it was cheaper, Maude Larkin would buy it, and so would most of the hardworking families she knew.

Thrifty people weren't ignorant or uncaring. Nobody knew the value of a dollar better than people who had to sweat for every penny, so what would make Maude Larkin and the millions of people like her turn their back on artificial maple syrup if it tasted good?

The answer came to her quickly.

"Nobody likes a cheater," she said. "If the Magruders want to sell corn syrup that's been flavored to taste like maple syrup, let them say so. My mother will still buy it. But if she thought they were *cheating*? Tricking ordinary people out of their hard-earned money? She'll go to war to stop them in their tracks."

Caroline crossed her arms in frustration. "You've already tried to reach those people through magazines and newspapers. It barely made a dent." She held up the issue of *Good Housekeeping*. "This magazine has a quarter of a million subscribers, which sounds impressive until you realize there are seventy-six million people in the United States. How can we possibly reach them all?"

Annabelle mulled over the problem. It wasn't in her nature to give up. Her parents

481

had both read the *Good Housekeeping* article and been proud of her contribution to the magazine, but were not appalled by what the Magruders did. Food was food, and her mother cared more about the coins in her purse than the ingredients printed on the label.

Unless someone made her care.

She looked at Gray. "How much do you suppose it costs the Magruders to make a bottle of the cheap vanilla flavoring?"

"Four cents," he said immediately. "I had Otis figure it out."

"And how much do they sell it for?"

"A dollar."

"And do you know how many bottles they sell?"

Gray shook his head. "I know they cook it up by the tanker, but I don't know how much they sell. A lot, I'm sure."

And plenty of those bottles would have been sold in Kansas. For each adulterated product, the Magruders pocketed plenty of money, and that meant they were tricking farmers in Kansas, factory workers in Boston, and meat packers in Chicago. All over America, there were people who stood on their feet while laboring hard for every penny, and they had a right to know what they were buying.

"I know the meeting is only going to deal with the military contracts," Annabelle said, "but why not hold the Magruders' feet to the fire for every jar of food they sell anywhere in the country?"

"The army isn't going to entertain discussion about the general food supply," Gray said.

"Wait a minute." Caroline straightened as a look of fierce concentration came over her face. "What if they don't *know* our real aim? Perhaps we focus on a demand to list ingredients on food supplied to the military, get the Magruders to agree, then hit them with a second punch. Demand they treat the general market with the same respect as the military. I can be sure the press is there so they can report on every word. If we play our cards right, we can paint them into a corner."

It would take a mountain of data to prove the Magruders had been systematically cheating their customers, but Annabelle knew how to start looking.

FORTY

Over the next three days, Annabelle worked alongside Gray in the glorious reading room of the Library of Congress, plowing through census records to create a demographic profile of the country. They used commercial reports to figure out how much food was produced and sold within each state. The Bureau of Labor Statistics told them how much the average farmer, factory worker, and store clerk earned. The Magruders' meeting with the army was fast approaching, so they worked through lunch and dinner to compile their mountain of statistics.

Annabelle loved working with Gray, which was a problem. In four days she would return to Kansas to begin the formidable task of reversing the fortunes of their family farm, but her renewed feelings for Gray were spiraling out of control. Even now, as she watched him at the reference desk, his tall, serious figure was irresistibly attractive to her. He listened intently as the librarian passed him another set of records. His footsteps echoed off the towering marble walls of the chamber as he wended his way through the work tables and back to her. The corners of his mouth tilted in the barest hint of a smile as he set the records on the table before her.

"Two decades of baked bean sales and exports," he whispered.

"Excellent!"

His face warmed, and he touched her shoulder. "We won't know until we plow through the numbers."

"Ahem!" her mother said as she glared at Gray's hand, and he immediately withdrew it. Maude had been a constant presence for the entire three days. While her father pounced on the extra time in Washington to explore the city, Maude refused to waste money on streetcar fare and insisted on sticking close to Annabelle.

Which was a blessing in disguise. Maude had an encyclopedic memory for the price of every item sold in grocery stores in the entire county of Pottawatomie, Kansas. She knew the price of a bushel of cucumbers, a gallon of vinegar, and a pint of salt, and could therefore estimate how much the

Magruders spent to manufacture a jar of pickles.

"Can you cost out the ingredients for a batch of Boston baked beans?" Gray whispered.

"Naturally," Maude said. Her mother might look grim, but Maude was in her element. All of them were. Working toward a cause wasn't a chore, it was fun. Yes, her mother could be terse and opinionated, but the moment Annabelle asked for help, Maude was fully committed to bringing honest and affordable food to the working people of America.

In his own way Gray was every bit as patriotic. Their work today wasn't about advancing Gray's spice company. Indeed, if they were successful, it would cause additional burdens and regulatory hoops for his business, but his sense of fair play drove him on this mission, and she was proud to work toward this goal with him.

But in four days she would go home. Roy tried to hide it, but he was sweating bullets, being away from the farm this long, and a huge part of Maude's insane need to pinch pennies was rooted in the farm's dire straits. If Annabelle could deliver on this one last crusade, she would feel good about returning to Kansas.

At least, that was what she told herself.

Gray strode toward the War Department building, doing his best to show no emotion despite the tension roiling inside him. He needed to surrender most of this mission to the Larkins, and they'd have to play this hand of cards perfectly to succeed in painting the Magruders into a corner. Constantly at the back of his mind was the crushing thought that today might be the last time he ever saw Annabelle. She and her parents were leaving on tomorrow's train, and she'd take a piece of his heart he'd never get back.

Like all government buildings in this part of Washington, the War Department was built to impress, with acres of gray stone gleaming in the sunlight. Inside it was just as impressive, but in a completely different manner. The columns, pilasters, and beams were constructed of wrought iron, and the woodwork was Honduran mahogany. Alcoves lined with iron provided benches for small gatherings.

Annabelle and her parents had already arrived. So had the Magruders. Father and son stood near the staircase, their heads bent in quiet discussion, but they'd noticed Gray's arrival. Given the astonishment on Clyde's face, he had no idea Gray would be here today. Gray nodded to the Magruders but headed straight toward the Larkins, all of whom looked out of place as they stood in one of the iron-lined alcoves. Maude had asked if they should wear the formal attire they'd brought for Elaine's wedding, but he'd advised them to come in their everyday clothes. Roy wore a plain flannel shirt and brown pants held up by suspenders. Maude's calico dress was well made but faded from many washings. They were the embodiment of hardworking Americans and would help make the case today.

Gray shook Roy's hand and nodded to Maude. "Thank you for coming." He couldn't even bear to look at Annabelle, but he sensed her presence. Radiant, fresh, and wholesome.

Clyde Magruder was heading their way, an overly broad smile on his face as he held out a hand. "These people are with you?" he asked Gray.

"Miss Larkin is a friend," he said, offering a perfunctory handshake. "Mr. and Mrs. Larkin are her parents."

For a fraction of a second, Clyde stiffened, but he recovered quickly. "So you're Annabelle Larkin of *Good Housekeeping* fame. You don't look at all like I expected." He didn't bother to mask an amused snort of laughter.

They still had ten minutes until the meeting convened, and Clyde put that time to good use, prodding for insight into their unexpected presence. When he discovered the Larkins were farmers, he asked polite questions about the nature of their farm, but all the while he kept glancing nervously at Gray.

"Are you here for the military contract hearing?" he asked Gray. "It's going to be a triumph. Our biggest ever. Of course, you'll probably be disappointed. It's mostly baked beans and chipped beef. They contain no hidden ingredients or chemicals you can pretend are dangerous, so there's no follow-up story in it for *Good Housekeeping* in a lame attempt to tarnish our reputation."

"I'm actually relieved to hear it," Gray responded. His goal wasn't to ruin the Magruders, it was make them print an accurate list of ingredients on every can of food they sold.

"I'll just bet you are," Clyde drawled. "By the way, how's your brother doing in prison? Any news?"

Gray flushed but said nothing. Thinking about Luke during this meeting had the potential to throw his concentration, and he couldn't afford it.

489

Clyde leaped into the uncomfortable silence as he turned to the Larkins. "You heard about his brother, right? Spy for the Cubans? Due to stand trial for treason next year? All very shocking."

Given the way Maude and Roy shifted in discomfort, this was the first they'd heard of it. Roy nervously glanced at Annabelle, who gave the tiniest nod to confirm the story.

"That's a real shame," Roy said uncomfortably. "A real shame."

The Washington Post had printed a retraction of Dickie Shuster's original story, claiming Luke Delacroix was in Cuba to trade in cigars and no charges for treasonous activities had been filed against him, which was all true. Those charges were surely coming, but for now the retraction would protect Caroline's job at the White House.

"So what brings you to a military contract negotiation?" Clyde asked Roy, his gaze flitting to the older man's suspenders and work boots. "The deal is for eight hundred tons of baked beans and six hundred tons of chipped beef. Not exactly something of interest to a man with a hundred-acre wheat farm."

Roy kept rotating his hat in his hands.

"Oh . . . I'm very interested," he stammered.

Clyde laughed and clapped Roy on the shoulder. "I like your initiative." He grinned. "Hold on to that positive attitude, and you might go far."

Annabelle looked ready to combust, and Gray put his hand on her shoulder to calm her. It was time to leave for the meeting, and letting Clyde feel like he had the upper hand was fine. He'd learn otherwise soon enough.

A conference table dominated the center of the meeting room, while rows of additional seating circled the room. Gray led the Larkins to the first row of seats that had been reserved for the public. Annabelle looked nervous, Maude sour, and Roy craned his neck in every direction to gape at the gilded decorations on the coffered ceiling.

Soon journalists and other members of the public filled in the rest of the seats, while government officials took their places at the table. Lawyers, accountants, secretaries, an auditor, a stenographer, and representatives from both the army and the navy added up to twenty people. This was precisely the sort of government bloat Gray resented.

Clyde and old Jedediah Magruder took a

491

seat at the end of the table. Clyde carried only a slim folder, and they hadn't brought a lawyer. They were obviously confident of their position.

Finally, the officer in charge of army procurement arrived to start the meeting. Major Gilligan had a scowl on his face and a brusque demeanor as he took a seat at the head of the table and flipped open his file.

"Let's get started, gentlemen. What are we buying today? Let's see, baked beans and Magruder chipped beef." His face was instantly transformed. "I *love* Magruder's creamed chipped beef! To this day, one of my favorite meals. When I was growing up in a dirt-poor mill town, Magruder's creamed chipped beef was the best thing I'd ever tasted. We only got it on Friday as a special treat. Well done, sir!"

Jedidiah Magruder pushed himself to his feet and took a little bow. Clyde looked at Gray and smirked.

"To continue," Major Gilligan said, settling back into business, "a draft of the contract for the beef and canned beans has already been distributed. Prices agreed on. Why are we even here?"

"The public has a right to be informed and respond with any concerns," one of the lawyers said. Paper copies of the contract were distributed by a junior officer, and Gray snatched two, handing one to Roy and skimming the other quickly.

"Gentlemen?" Major Gilligan asked after a few minutes. "Any comments for the good of the nation and mankind?"

"We've reviewed the contract and had it approved by the accountants," the lawyer for the army said. "We are prepared to proceed."

"Anyone else?" the major asked. Silence lengthened as no one around the table had anything to add.

This was it, his chance to insist on a list of ingredients. Gray raised his hand, and the major acknowledged him and gestured him forward. Gray introduced himself, and the government stenographer captured every word.

"I'd like for the contract to require that all canned foods purchased by the army contain a complete list of ingredients on the label."

Instead of outrage from the Magruders, Clyde appeared to be enjoying himself. "Already done. Paragraph two, line three of the addendum."

Gray flipped to the appropriate page. It was the same draft Caroline had supplied to him five days ago, but he still pretended surprise. He assumed a properly abashed stance and gave a brief nod. "Excellent."

He sat, and Maude Larkin stood.

"I've got something to say," she announced.

Major Gilligan looked at her in surprise. "Ma'am?" He gestured her forward. "Please step up to the table so the stenographer can hear."

Maude came forward with a copy of the contract and determination in her eyes. She pointed to the line in the contract where the Margruders agreed to print the ingredients on every can of food sold to the military. "I'd like to know why food sold to ordinary people won't have the ingredients on the label. You charge a lot for baked beans, and we're entitled to know what's inside. Are you using bacon or not?"

"Of course," old Jedidiah said. "Plenty of bacon."

Maude nodded. "Good. I think you should print the ingredients on the label for everybody, not just the military. Because if there's no bacon, I'm not buying."

Major Gilligan looked at the Magruders. "Is there any reason you don't print ingredients on the cans sold to the public?"

"Because it's pointless," Clyde said.

"Everyone knows what baked beans taste like."

Major Gilligan looked amused. "You have to admit, the lack of bacon can break a deal."

The clicking of the stenograph machine continued, capturing every word, but hopefully Clyde had forgotten he was on the record. He leaned over to confer with his father, speaking behind cupped hands. After a moment, Clyde addressed the crowd.

"Too much administrative hassle," he said simply.

"If there's nothing wrong with it, why not just print the ingredients on the label?" Major Gilligan asked, appearing genuinely curious.

Jedidiah's brows lowered in annoyance. "Our baked beans are one hundred percent pure. Real beans, real brown sugar, real bacon. We've already met with a pair of your government lawyers after that magazine story slandered our products. There are no fillers or substitutes in our baked beans."

"Then I'd like to see the ingredients on the label," Maude said. "I want to know if there's real bacon in the can or just pork fat. Because real bacon —"

"It's real bacon," Jedidiah groused.

"Then put it on the label so everyone can

495

see," Maude said. "Not just for the military, but for everyone."

"Fine!" Jedidiah said. "Fine. Clyde, make the changes."

Clyde opened and closed his mouth, uncertain how to overrule his father, for it would look bad if he backtracked now.

"While we're on the topic, I'd like to discuss your maple syrup," Maude said.

Major Gilligan pinched the bridge of his nose. "No disrespect, ma'am, but we are veering far off topic."

Gray stood. "Not at all. The army is also contracting for condensed milk, pancake mix, and maple syrup. It fell below the threshold for public consideration, but the American people have a right to know if the government has been overpaying."

"You certainly have been," Maude said. "The Magruders use flavored corn syrup and pass it off as maple. Corn syrup costs ten cents a tin, while maple syrup is ninety cents more. Now mind you, I bought a tin of that fake maple syrup, and it tasted fine. But I had a right to know that it wasn't the real thing. Frankly, I overpaid, and I'd like my ninety cents back."

Clyde opened his wallet, peeled out a dollar bill, and handed it to the orderly. "Please give this to the good lady on the far side of the room. Tell her she can keep the change."

The young man held the bill, uncertain what to do.

Maude raised her hand. "I'll take it."

Muffled laughter rippled through the crowd as the orderly carried her the bill. Maude rolled it neatly and pushed it into her coin purse. Now she was ready to bring out the big guns.

"Based on my calculations of how much syrup the Magruders sold last year, the people in Kansas overpaid $240,000 on artificially flavored corn syrup. Thank you for my dollar, but I think you owe almost a quarter of a million dollars to the rest of Kansas. I've got the numbers for what people overpaid in Oklahoma Territory, Nebraska, Missouri, and both Dakotas too. I'll let the east coast come after you on their own."

Major Gillian looked baffled. "Is there a point to any of this, ma'am?"

Gray had to bite his tongue. Everything in him wanted to stand up and drive the point home, but it would sound better coming from Maude.

"The point is that by tricking people about what they're selling, the Magruders have cheated us out of our hard-earned money. And that's just maple syrup." She held aloft a piece of paper. "I've also got numbers for their pancake mix, applesauce, condensed milk —"

Jedidiah smacked the flat of his hand on the conference table, causing the water glasses to jump. "That's enough, woman," he growled. "Our products are pure. Our products are excellent."

Maude wasn't intimidated. She raised her chin and met old Magruder's gaze without flinching. "Not your maple syrup. I was cheated, and your son just admitted it."

"I know all about genuine maple syrup," Jedidiah said, his voice trembling with anger. He stood and jerked his suit jacket off, then began rolling up his sleeves. Clyde tried to coax his father down, but Jedidiah shrugged him off. "I was harvesting and boiling maple sap when I was eight years old. You see these scars?" he demanded, holding up his forearms. "That's what comes from getting scalded on a sap boiler. I'm proud of these scars. I'm proud of every product coming out of a Magruder factory. Of course our maple syrup is pure. I have no problem listing exactly what is in every tin of Magruder syrup."

Clyde stood and tried to force the old man to sit down, but Jedidiah was having none of it, continuing to rant that all Magruder products were pure. The journalists scribbled to keep up with the stream of angry promises, but most important was the government stenographer, whose rattling machine captured every word. Jedidiah's ranting carried no legal weight, but he was still painting his company into a corner.

Maude held up a paper summarizing their research from the Library of Congress. "I'd also like the company to address their fraudulent applesauce, vanilla flavoring, coffee —"

"That will do," Major Gilligan interrupted. "This is irrelevant to the military, but you can send those papers over to the Department of Agriculture. They'd probably care; they love that sort of thing."

"Actually, we're here," someone said at the back of the room. Four men in plain suits stood, introducing themselves as members of the committee for food standards. "We are overjoyed the Magruders have agreed to list ingredients on their products for all the American people. Well done, sir!"

Jedidiah finally realized his every word was being recorded, and plopped back into his chair, breathing heavily, while Clyde remained standing and took over for his father.

"That's not going to happen," Clyde said. "I know that government bureaucrats may lack an understanding of the complexities of labeling processed food —"

"I don't," Gray said. "It's actually quite easy to get new labels printed up. I can show you how."

Clyde's eyes narrowed, no doubt remembering the laughing mice on the label Luke had designed. "Nothing said here today is legally binding," he bit out. "The only thing that matters are the words written on that contract, and it's for baked beans and chipped —"

A commotion in the doorway caused Clyde to pause. Two bull-necked men entered the room, followed by Caroline pushing a dour-looking woman in a wheelchair. The first lady? The middle-aged woman wore a high-necked gown, and her steel-gray hair was braided around her head like a crown. Caroline met Gray's gaze across the crowded conference room and winked. In front of her, Ida McKinley sat in the wheelchair like it was a throne, wearing a fierce expression as she banged her cane on the floor with considerable vigor.

"Why did this meeting start without me?" the first lady demanded, her voice ringing through the chamber. Even Maude Larkin

500

dropped into her seat, stunned into dazed silence.

Major Gilligan rose, looking distinctly uncomfortable as he adjusted the collar of his uniform. "We were unaware you planned on attending, ma'am."

"I take an avid interest in the health of our troops. Everyone knows that."

Major Gilligan gestured to a young orderly to make space at the table. "Please join us, ma'am. We certainly welcome your insight on supporting our troops."

Ida McKinley was as welcome as a wasp at a picnic. She was notorious for her surly disposition and gauche personal attacks, which was why she rarely made public appearances. Caroline looked serenely smug as she positioned Mrs. McKinley's wheelchair at the conference table, then glided into the neighboring chair like a princess. With a smile at Clyde, she set a copy of *Good Housekeeping* on the table before Mrs. McKinley.

Clyde looked ready to choke. His eyes narrowed and his hands fisted, but Mrs. McKinley was sermonizing about the health of the troops, and he could hardly interrupt the first lady.

"The canned food served to our troops during the recent war was an abomination,"

Mrs. McKinley pronounced. "What did those newspapers call it?" she asked, turning to Caroline.

"Embalmed beef, ma'am," Caroline supplied.

Mrs. McKinley smacked the table before her. "Embalmed beef!" she said in a scornful tone and turned to Major Gilligan. "To send our young men overseas and feed them slop? I'm ashamed of our conduct. Ashamed! I certainly hope there is no embalmed beef on that contract before you."

"No indeed, ma'am," Major Gilligan said. "Magruder's chipped beef is the only canned meat in the contract, and I can attest it is a recipe I myself enjoy. Our troops will, as well."

Mrs. McKinley swiveled her steely gaze to Clyde. "You are Mr. Magruder?"

Clyde gave a stiff nod.

"Aiming to be Congressman Magruder, if the rumors are true," Mrs. McKinley said.

"They are," Clyde said. "I aspire to represent the great city of Baltimore."

"It is indeed a great city," Mrs. McKinley said. "Baltimore is the home of Fort McHenry and birthplace of 'The Star-Spangled Banner.' Next month the crown princess of Greece will be visiting, and her itinerary will take her through Baltimore. I can only hope there will be no counterfeit applesauce on the menu?"

"Of course not," Clyde said, flustered by this unexpected turn in the meeting.

"Good, because some of the shoddy food I've seen in Washington never fails to amaze me. You should have seen the stale tea cakes I was served by the Ladies Temperance Union. You would think those women would have —"

Caroline placed a hand on the first lady's wrist, and she immediately stopped talking as Caroline whispered in her ear, gesturing to the military contract on the table. Mrs. McKinley nodded and straightened, focusing her attention back on Clyde.

"Well, we aren't here to revisit that luncheon, no matter how substandard the tea cakes. I need to be assured that the leading food manufacturer in this nation, led by a man who hopes to grace the halls of Congress, will not foist counterfeit applesauce on the crown princess of Greece."

Clyde flushed and got to his feet. "If I am honored to meet with the crown princess, all will be prepared by the finest chefs —"

"Because the princess has very discriminating tastes. I would take it as a personal embarrassment if she's fed embalmed beef."

"Of course, ma'am. And may I state that my company had no part in the embalmed beef controversy during the late war."

Mrs. McKinley sent him a withering stare. "That's a low bar, Mr. Magruder."

Gray could almost feel sorry for Clyde Magruder. He didn't deserve the attacks coming from Mrs. McKinley, but the journalists were catching every word, and tomorrow's newspapers would laud the first lady for valiantly standing up for American troops while castigating Magruder Food.

Clyde Magruder's congressional hopes had just been dealt a body blow.

After the meeting, Annabelle stood beside her parents, watching the aftermath continue in the lobby. Her parents gaped at Mrs. McKinley as she was wheeled out of the conference room, reporters surrounding her to take advantage of her rare public appearance. Caroline dutifully stood beside her, keeping the journalists at a distance but gamely helping Mrs. McKinley field their questions.

The meeting had surpassed Annabelle's expectations, exposing the Magruders in a fashion that would delight Luke's mischievous sense of humor. Thanks to Maude, the food company's practice of cheating people a few pennies at a time had been laid bare. Ida McKinley's distaste for cheap Magruder imitations had been icing on the cake. While Mrs. McKinley's tirade appeared impulsive, Annabelle had noticed the subtle interplay between Caroline and the first lady and suspected both women knew exactly what they were doing. Even now Caroline and the first lady seemed to be enjoying themselves while the reporters scrambled for attention.

Not so the Magruders, who made a beeline for the exit, avoiding questions and looking as dark as thunderclouds. They had gotten their military contract, but not without a pummeling to their reputation. Although the fight for legislation for pure food would be waged for years to come, the drumbeat of change had begun. She and Gray had played only a small part in it, but no matter how long she lived, Annabelle would be forever proud of what they'd accomplished.

She gazed at Gray across the crowded lobby as he stood beside Caroline. What a proud, magnificent man he was. She drank in the sight of him, trying to imprint it in her memory, for by this time tomorrow she would be on a train back to Kansas.

"Time to leave if we're going to meet

Elaine for dinner," her father said, cutting through her thoughts.

"I know."

Even as she spoke, she met Gray's eyes across the lobby, and he began angling through the throng of people toward her. She braced herself, not sure how to say good-bye. He seemed ill at ease too.

"The two of you are good soldiers to have in a fight," he said to her parents, offering both of them a handshake. "Well done, Maude. Roy."

Roy nodded but Maude beamed. Then Gray turned his attention to Annabelle, and it felt like her heart was in her throat.

"So you're leaving for Kansas tomorrow?" he asked.

Her gaze locked with his, and the first cracks in her heart began to split. She wanted to rush into his arms and lay her head on his shoulder, turn back the clock, and run away with him.

Instead she managed a smile. "My boss gave me a sack of durum wheat. We'll be the first farm in Kansas to test it. Maybe it will be the answer for us."

Gray's eyes warmed in affection and a hint of regret. "I hope so," he said and extended his hand. "Best of luck, Annabelle."

Was she really going to bid farewell to the

506

only man she'd ever loved by shaking his hand? But she did, and he touched the side of her face before turning away to follow his sister out of the building.

After the thrill of the day's events, Gray found the loneliness in his townhouse unbearable, for there was no one with whom to share his triumph. Annabelle was leaving for Kansas, Caroline now lived at the White House, and Luke . . . well, Luke was probably gone forever.

Like the irresistible urge to wiggle a sore tooth, Gray felt the need to torment himself by heading upstairs into the cold loneliness of his younger brother's bedroom. Everything was exactly as Luke had left it four months earlier. A half-used bar of shaving soap lay on a dish alongside a canister of tooth powder. Some books from the local library were stacked on the corner of the dresser. It was past time to return the books and dispose of the toiletries, but Gray had been delaying the inevitable. He just didn't want to face the fact that Luke wasn't coming back.

He sighed and paced the room, turmoil and loneliness clawing at him. The only sound in the empty house was his footsteps echoing in the empty room. *Thud, thud,*

thud, thunk . . .

That was odd. He stepped on the hollow-sounding spot again. *Thunk.*

The floor was covered by an oriental rug Luke had bought a few years ago. Gray remembered being surprised by it, for although Luke had always been a sharp dresser, he'd never spent anything on furnishing the house. So why the pricey rug?

Gray knelt to peel back the carpet and saw that a square about two feet wide had been cut into the floorboards. His heart accelerated and his palms began to sweat. Whatever was hidden here, Luke had gone to a lot of trouble to hide it.

A notch on one of the boards was barely large enough to wiggle a finger into and lift up the board. Dust swirled and Gray's nose twitched as he lifted the other boards free. The cache was filled with books and papers. He dreaded what he was about to see, for the top documents were in Spanish.

Nausea filled his stomach. If this was related to Luke's treasonous activities, did he have the fortitude to surrender it to the government? If it could save lives, it would be the right thing to do. It was still a vile thought. Was this how Annabelle felt when she'd been confronted with the exact same situation?

He lifted out the first book, staring at the title. He couldn't read Spanish, but the language was enough like French that he could tell it was a book about the banking system of Spain. *Banking?* The pages were filled with mathematical charts and monetary tables. The other books in Spanish looked equally harmless, merely books on the history and economy of Cuba.

He quickly rifled through the other documents, and relief trickled through him. There was nothing relating to the military or troop positions, but Luke had gone to a great deal of trouble to hide these papers, and Gray desperately wanted to know why.

He kept digging into the cache, but the other books were entirely different. There was a well-thumbed copy of Saint Augustine's *Confessions* and a fat book of commentary on the New Testament. Works by Thomas Aquinas and Martin Luther and copies of the Bible in Greek, Latin, and Aramaic. Tiny notes in the margin were all in Luke's handwriting.

There was an accounting ledger going back several years, also in Luke's hand. Far from proving his brother incompetent with money, this ledger reflected sophisticated bookkeeping. Gray carried it across the room, sitting on the bed to scan the entries carefully, and his heart sank. At long last, he knew where Luke had been spending his fortune all these years.

An orphanage in Baltimore; a tuberculosis clinic in Bethesda; a leper colony in Hawaii; and three families in Philadelphia. No wonder Luke never had any money. He was giving it all away.

Oh, Luke . . . why are you still torturing yourself?

Gray dropped the accounting ledger and buried his face in his hands to pray and give thanks. Luke wasn't a bad man. The proof of it was all in this cache. Although Luke had stumbled and become ensnared in some kind of treasonous scheme, it looked as though he was a man desperately seeking redemption.

And that was good, for Jesus promised there was no sin that could not be forgiven. Luke was struggling to find a way through the darkness and into a world of blazing hope and salvation. It was impossible to know what fate had in store for him, but his soul was on its way to being saved, and Gray couldn't ask for more than that.

He knelt beside the hiding place to return the books. Almost everything here was proof of Luke's decency and compassion, and what an irony that he worked so hard to

510

hide it from the world. Luke was going to be all right. Maybe not in this life, but his restless struggle toward salvation had to count for something. God didn't expect them to be perfect, only a valiant effort to try, and Luke had been trying.

Gray sat on the bed, staring at the open cache at his feet, shame washing over him. He hadn't understood the real Luke for years. All he saw was the carefree bon vivant Luke wanted the world to see, not the tormented soul seeking redemption. Gray had entirely missed that.

Ever since his arrest, Luke had been sending the same message over and over, and Gray had ignored those messages too. Luke pleaded to be left alone. He told them not to worry. He said not to blame Annabelle. He had fired the attorneys Gray tried to hire, and refused to speak to American authorities. He hindered, stonewalled, and resisted all efforts of help. The only thing he didn't do was try to earn his freedom. Was he in the middle of some sort of plan? Or was it a form of misguided penance for his sins?

Gray could never stop worrying about Luke or trying to win his freedom. The one thing he could do was take Luke's wishes to heart and stop blaming Annabelle.

FORTY-ONE

The journey back to Kansas would take three days, and they were beginning with an argument. Annabelle stood on the train station platform, trying to keep out of it as her parents argued about whether to exchange the tickets Gray had bought them for a cheaper version.

"We don't need a private compartment," Maude said. "We can save forty dollars by exchanging them for third-class tickets. Forty dollars!"

Roy didn't look happy. "I've never ridden in a first-class compartment in my life, and unless we use these tickets, I never will."

The bickering continued, but Annabelle couldn't listen. Her gaze drifted to the skyline behind the depot, trying to memorize the details of the city. In a few days she would be back on the farm, and that would be a good thing, for there was no beauty in the world quite like Kansas. The sunflowers. The nights. The crickets. And the *sky*. The most awe-inspiring sight she'd ever see was the wide expanse of sky sheltering a million acres of golden wheat. She could be happy in Kansas. She *could*.

And it wasn't as if she would never see Washington again. They would come back someday to see Elaine.

But she would never see Gray again. He would forever linger in her memory as her biggest regret. He was a man of courage, innovation, and dry, understated humor. She loved him and probably always would, but it was time to move on.

Roy scored a rare victory in the battle to keep their first-class tickets. When it was time to board, Annabelle entered the first-class car and followed the porter down the narrow, carpet-lined aisle to their compartment.

"Holy moly," Roy said in admiration as they stepped inside. The compartment was lined in maple paneling. Two padded benches faced each other with a small table in between. They had a picture window all to themselves.

A menu for lunch was on the table, and Roy let out a low whistle as he scanned the options. There were no prices listed, but the porter assured them the meals came with their tickets. He took their orders and told them their meals would arrive about an hour into the journey.

Annabelle drew a steadying breath, wishing the train was already underway. She'd feel better once the option to stay was behind her. The time must be getting near, for the stationmaster strode along the platform, making final call. Then came the doors slamming closed, the clicking wheels, the hiss of steam, and the train jerked into motion. She drew a ragged breath as the depot slid into the distance, and she bid a silent farewell to the city that had changed her life.

Leaving hurt, but she must hold on to the thought of how much she'd learned during this time in Washington, for it had challenged her in ways she'd never imagined. It was her choice to go back to her old world, and she would make it a good one.

Within ten minutes the city was behind them. How quickly the stone buildings and telephone wires gave way to open fields and white farmhouses. The train sped past cabbage fields, and then a pair of young men rolling hay into bales. Would the Department of Agriculture's new seeds ever reach this farm? Or their bulletins about crop rotation and soil amendments? She hoped so. How desperately she wanted good things for every farmer in America. For a few short months, she had gotten to be part of the wonderful crusade to make that happen.

She'd even helped change Gray's mind about things. Someday when she was old and wrinkled, that bit of effort in recruiting Gray to the department's mission might prove to be the biggest contribution of her life. It had been fun too. It was hard, challenging, and sometimes painful, but oh, how she had loved working alongside him.

She balled her fists and blinked faster.

"Don't cry," Maude said, not unkindly.

Annabelle dared not turn her gaze from the cabbage fields outside the window or the tears would spill over. "I won't," she said quietly. Maybe someday remembering wouldn't hurt so much.

There was a knock on their door, and Roy opened it for the porter, who brought a teapot and four cups. "A gentleman asked to join you," the porter said.

Annabelle sucked in a quick breath, for Gray stood behind the porter, looking nervous and ill at ease.

Roy stood. "I didn't realize you were on board."

Gray locked gazes with her. "I've got a seat a few cars down. My ticket only goes

515

to Stanton, but your compartment has room for six, if I'm welcome to go on to Kansas with you."

"Why would you want to go to Kansas?" Annabelle asked, not quite believing this moment was happening.

Gray ducked his head to step inside the compartment and sat on the bench beside her. The porter slid the door closed, and all of them sat in exquisite discomfort.

"I've been to China and India and Africa," Gray finally said. "Last year I traveled from Siberia to Ceylon, but I've never been to Kansas. The main thing I've learned from traveling all over the world is that it isn't the place that matters, it's the people. It's *you,* Annabelle. I want to go to Kansas because it is a huge and important part of you."

He turned to her parents, who still looked astonished at his sudden arrival in the middle of a Virginia cabbage field. "I've never met anyone like the two of you. Maude, you walked into a room of cynical military officers and knocked them for a loop. And, Roy, I know what you sacrificed to send Annabelle to college. Your two daughters may be short in stature, but when it comes to courage, they are both giants. And I would very much like to visit the place where Annabelle and Elaine were raised."

Her parents both gaped at Gray, uncertain what to say. They looked at each other, and Roy found his voice first. "You're welcome to visit the farm." He stood and gestured for Maude to stand as well. "I think my wife and I would like to go explore this fine train we're riding on. I heard there's a lounge car up ahead."

Gray's laugh was nervous, but his voice was grateful. "Two cars ahead."

"All right, then." Maude shot Annabelle a beaming look of encouragement on her way out the door.

Gray stepped back inside after her parents left the car. He rubbed his palms on his pant legs as he took the bench opposite her.

"Why are you really going to Kansas?" Annabelle asked.

For the first time, a hint of amusement lightened his face. "Do you really need to ask that?"

Yesterday she had stood in a government lobby with her heart in her throat as he shook hands with her to say good-bye forever, so it wasn't an unreasonable question. "I'm asking."

He sobered and reached for the pot of tea.

His hands trembled as he poured them both a cup.

"I've always viewed myself as a protector," he said after setting the teapot down with a gentle click. "It was my duty to provide for and protect my family. Building our company sent me all over the world, and I lost sight of some things. I thought that by providing for my family, everything else would fall into place like vines growing on a trellis. Things didn't turn out that way. By the time I got home, Caroline and Luke had both chosen their own paths in life. They didn't want or need my protection."

She looked away. Luke and Caroline were her two least favorite subjects on the planet. One she had betrayed, and the other was the only enemy she had in the world.

Gray reached out to cover her hand with his. "Annabelle, I let you down," he said urgently. "When you were pigeonholed into an impossible position, instead of being your protector, I abandoned you. That was wrong, and I'm sorry."

She met his gaze and immediately felt the weight on her chest ease. She hadn't even realized it was there.

He continued talking. "I know what your love for this country cost you. There were no easy choices, but your instincts were always right. Your compass needle pointed true north, and you never wavered. I want us to find a way forward. I can run my company from Kansas if that's where you want to be. I don't care if we live in Kansas or Washington or on the *Pelican.* I'll never make the spice company the center of my world again, because in doing so, I lost track of my family." He swallowed hard. "It's time for me to rebuild it, and I want to begin with you."

She feared broaching the most dangerous topic, but this conversation was pointless until they did. "What about Luke? Have you forgiven me?"

To her surprise, the corners of his mouth tilted in a gentle smile. "There's nothing to forgive. You didn't put him in that jail cell. He got there all on his own." He pushed the teacups aside and clasped both her hands in his. Warmth and strength radiated from him, but best of all were his eyes burning with gentle appeal.

"Annabelle, I love you. I love your idealism and patriotism. I love that durum wheat discoveries keep you enthralled. Annabelle . . . will you marry me?"

It was hard to believe this was really happening. It was so fast, and there were still so many obstacles ahead.

"Your sister hates me."

"But I love you. And you'll be marrying me, not Caroline."

She stood and navigated around the table to join him on the opposite bench. Then she was in his arms, her vision watery with tears as she looked over his shoulder at the cabbage fields flying past. They lived in a huge and expansive country, filled with choices and opportunities. Not all of them were easy, but she had found a man of character who would step into that world with her, and nothing had ever felt so right.

"I'll gladly marry you, Gray."

FORTY-TWO

Three weeks later
November 6, 1900

It was almost midnight, but Gray was too anxious to feel tired. Hundreds of people packed Anderson Hall on the Kansas State Agricultural College campus, awaiting the results of the presidential election. Never had an election been so personally important, for a presidential pardon was Luke's only real hope for freedom. Even with a McKinley victory, winning a pardon would be a long shot, but all of Gray's hope rested on the outcome of this election. He hadn't been able to swallow a bite of food all day.

Most of the crowd gathered tonight were farmers, but students and people who worked at the college were here as well. The grounds were blanketed with election posters, banners, and patriotic bunting. Buttons supporting William Jennings Bryan had been handed out to the few people who didn't already have one pinned to their suit coats. Bryan, who hailed from the neighboring state of Nebraska, was a stalwart champion of the American farmer and had overwhelming support from the crowd here tonight.

"I think we're the only ones here rooting for McKinley," Gray whispered to Annabelle.

"Shh," she urged. "We're *definitely* the only ones, and it's best people don't know about it. I don't want to be tarred and feathered before we head home."

Hearing Annabelle refer to Washington as "home" warmed his heart. They would return to Washington next week, where they would soon marry, and Annabelle would return to the Department of Agriculture. Surprisingly, Maude and Roy would be moving to Washington as well. They wanted to be closer to their daughters, and Roy was getting too old to manage the farm on his own much longer. While Gray and the Larkin women had gathered data at the Library of Congress, Roy had been riding the streetcars, marveling at the technology and talking to the drivers, dreaming of what might have been. Now he planned to sell the farm so he could explore the world of possibilities the city held for him.

A gust of chilly air came through the open door as the dean of the college entered the main hall. "Ten more minutes until the midnight fireworks," he announced. "Last call for hot chocolate and coffee before the show begins."

The fireworks would be set off at midnight whether the election results were in or not. It could be dawn before the election was decided, and Gray didn't know how he'd endure much more of this gnawing anxiety. He was rubbing at the tension gathering in the back of his neck when Maude angled through the crowd, handing Gray and Annabelle each a mug.

"Free hot chocolate!" Maude said. "Drink it down fast, then I'll go get more."

The thought of a sugary beverage made Gray's stomach turn. "No, thanks," he said, trying to refuse the mug, but Maude wouldn't take it.

"Never pass up free food," she said. "Although it's not really free, since our tax dollars went to buy it, so drink it down." She headed back to the concession tables.

"Sorry about that," Annabelle muttered as she took his mug and set it on a table. "Mother will always be something of an embarrassment."

Gray laid a finger across her lips. "Your

523

mother is a fighter," he said. "Now I know where you get it from. Your kindness comes from your father, but your grit and gumption is all Maude Larkin. Be grateful for her."

Annabelle's eyes sparkled as she gazed up at him. "I know. Sometimes I forget, but I know."

A door banged open down the hall, and a harried man rushed forward, carrying a card toward the dean of the college. The two men put their heads together and conferred, their faces grim.

Gray held his breath and reached for Annabelle's hand. "I think the results just came in," he whispered with a nod toward the two men, who furtively studied the card.

Others had noticed, and voices began tapering off as the dean stepped up to the podium. It only took a few taps of the gavel for the crowd to settle down. Expectation hung in the air.

"My friends, it has just come across the wire that President McKinley has been re-elected."

The breath left Gray in a rush, and he curled over. The crowd booed and sent up howls of protest, but all Gray could do was concentrate on dragging in breaths of air as relief crashed through him.

Annabelle squatted beside him. "Are you all right?" she asked, her voice trembling with excitement.

"I'm all right," he managed to gasp.

They were surrounded by groans of disappointment as the champion of the American heartland went down in defeat. The dean continued reading the telegram, reporting a landslide victory for President McKinley, even though most of the crowd had stopped listening. Someone tore down a swath of patriotic bunting behind the podium. Another threw a cup of coffee at an election poster of McKinley.

Roy Larkin stepped up to the podium, his face just as doleful as the rest of the crowd. "Settle down, folks," he called out.

"Why should we?" someone bellowed. "That scoundrel stole the election!"

"No one stole anything," Roy said. "This is a loss and it hits us hard, but we gave it our best shot."

People shook their heads and commiserated. The dean of the college spoke a few words about how the electoral process worked, but no one cared, and Roy could sense that. The weathered farmer nudged the dean aside and took the podium again.

"In four years we'll try again," Roy said. "And in four minutes we're all going to go outside and enjoy the best fireworks anywhere in the state. And tomorrow morning the college professors in this hall will teach their classes, and our young people will sit in their seats and learn. I'll pack up my load of sunflower seeds for market. Doc Gilmore will treat his patients, Mr. Bellefonte will open the general store, and Mrs. Mays will accept a new shipment of books at the library. Life is going to go on. We're going to be okay, folks."

People still weren't happy, but every word Roy spoke was true.

Gray pulled Annabelle into an embrace and lifted her feet off the ground, burying his face in her neck so the others wouldn't see the elation on his face. He rejoiced partly for Luke, but mostly because he was about to marry into a family unlike any he'd ever known. This country had been built on a foundation laid down by farmers and stalwart farmer's wives. It was made great by college professors, inventors, gamblers, industrialists, and dreamers. The politicians at the helm would change every four years, but the heartbeat of America would stay strong.

And outside, the fireworks had begun.

HISTORICAL NOTE

In 1897 the U.S. Department of Agriculture created a program to search the world for seeds that could diversify the nation's food supply. Led by plant explorer David Fairchild, the program introduced many of the fruits and vegetables we now take for granted, such as avocados, soybeans, tangerines, mangos, and kale. Perhaps the department's most successful import was durum wheat from central Russia. This hardy strain is now one of the most commonly grown types of wheat in America.

The problem of adulterated food reached mammoth proportions in the early twentieth century, when a shockingly high percentage of all canned food was either mixed with fillers, mislabeled, or infused with untested preservatives. There was no law against such practices, prompting the Department of Agriculture to begin clinical tests on the safety of chemical flavorings and preservatives. Their work culminated in the passage of the Pure Food and Drug Act in 1906, which required labels to accurately describe a product's contents.

Concerned by the adulteration of commonly sold food and drink, the magazine *Good Housekeeping* created its legendary consumer product testing facility in 1900 and immediately began alerting their readers to the problems of "dishonest food." They also highlighted products that lived up to their claims. Beginning in 1909, those products were awarded with the Good Housekeeping Seal of Approval, which is still in operation today.

After saffron, vanilla is the most labor-intensive crop in the world and continues to command shockingly high prices. Although chemical substitutes for vanilla were once pale imitations of the real thing, improvements in artificial vanilla extract have made it almost indistinguishable from genuine vanilla.

As of this writing, the progenitor of the vanilla orchid alluded to in the beginning of the novel remains in hiding, but plant explorers are still looking.

QUESTIONS FOR DISCUSSION

1) Did Annabelle make the right choice to spy? Did she have any other options?

2) If you were in Gray's shoes, would you be able to come to terms with what she did?

3) Most of the preservatives used in American food today have been deemed safe. Do you believe it? How would you feel about eating processed food that has no preservatives?

4) Luke shows all signs of being guilty of a terrible crime, and yet his family stands beside him. How do you feel about that? Are there limits on the support a family member owes a loved one who has gone astray?

5) Annabelle briefly contemplated keeping

her spying a secret from Gray. Had she tried, what effect do you think it would have had on her in later years?

6) Gray attempts to court another woman while clearly still mourning Annabelle. Is this fair? Can it help a person heal from heartbreak, or is it simply dishonest?

7) Annabelle, Elaine, and Maude Larkin are all strong women but in different ways. Who do you think is the strongest? Who do you identify with the most?

8) Roy tells Annabelle he was determined that both his daughters would have "the whole wide world open to them" because he never had much choice in his life. Throughout the book, Annabelle is plagued by the stress of difficult choices. How important is it to have choices? Can life actually be easier if you don't have choices?

9) Late in the book we learn that part of Elaine's motivation for leaving Kansas was to escape Maude's smothering attentiveness. Knowing how badly Maude fears for Elaine, can you find more sympathy for her? How would you respond if you be-

lieved a fragile loved one was on the verge
of making a dangerous, possibly irrevers-
ible choice?

ABOUT THE AUTHOR

Elizabeth Camden is best known for her historical novels set in Gilded-Age America, featuring clever heroines and richly layered storylines. Before she was a writer, she was an academic librarian at some of the largest and smallest libraries in America, but her favorite is the continually growing library in her own home. Her novels have won the RITA and Christy Award, and she lives in Florida with her husband, who graciously tolerates her intimidating stockpile of books. Learn more at www.elizabethcamden.com.

The employees of Thorndike Press hope you have enjoyed this Large Print book. All our Thorndike, Wheeler, and Kennebec Large Print titles are designed for easy reading, and all our books are made to last. Other Thorndike Press Large Print books are available at your library, through selected bookstores, or directly from us.

For information about titles, please call:
  (800) 223-1244

or visit our website at:
  gale.com/thorndike

To share your comments, please write:
  Publisher
  Thorndike Press
  10 Water St., Suite 310
  Waterville, ME 04901